SHE'D HAD IT FOR YEARS – BUT SHE DIDN'T KNOW WHAT TO CALL IT ...

'I've lost control of my emotions completely,' Alicia said. 'One minute I feel like laughing for no reason at all, and the next, I could weep. I've never felt more alive. If that isn't love, I'd better see a doctor, because something is certainly wrong with me.'

Reina blinked in surprise. She had endured the same emotions herself. And not just for a day, but for the past three years. Since Ulysses had come home from law school, to be exact!

'Is something wrong, Reina?' Alicia asked. 'You're pale as a ghost.'

'Wrong?' Everything was wrong. Why hadn't she realized it before? She was in love with Ulysses Pride – a man who thought less of her than the dirt beneath his feet.

Now she understood why she'd clung to her virtue with such fierce determination, why she'd shunned all masculine attention. She had been saving herself for Ulysses!

How Ulysses would laugh if he knew. His teasing and tormenting would be endless.

'You know, some people say and do the exact opposite of what they think and feel,' Alicia continued. 'A writer has to observe people to understand their motives. Ulysses doesn't take his eyes off of you when you're together.'

Reina quickly squelched the ember of hope Alicia's words ignited. 'With an imagination like that, you're bound to be a success as an author!'

Also by Alexandra Thorne

Creative Urges
Past Forgetting
Sophisticated Savages
The Ultimate Sin
To Speak of Triumph

About the author

Alexandra Thorne has spent her life in the arts. She majored in music at the University of Pennsylvania, went on to a career as an acclaimed sculptor, and wrote her first book in 1987. She is the author of five previous novels published by Hodder and Stoughton: *Creative Urges, Past Forgetting, Sophisticated Savages* ('good raunchy stuff' – *Publishing News*), *The Ultimate Sin* and *To Speak of Triumph*. She lives on a lake outside Houston, Texas, with her husband and two Weimeraner dogs.

Copyright © 1995 by Alexandra Thorne

The right of Alexandra Thorne to be identified as the Author of the Work has been asserted by her in accordance with the Copyright, Designs and Patents Act 1988.

First published in paperback in 1995
by Hodder and Stoughton
A division of Hodder Headline PLC

A Coronet Paperback

10 9 8 7 6 5 4 3 2 1

All rights reserved. No part of this publication may be reproduced, stored in a retrieval system, or transmitted, in any form or by any means, without the prior written permission of the publisher, nor be otherwise circulated in any form of binding or cover other than that in which it is published and without a similar condition being imposed on the subsequent purchaser.

All characters in this publication are fictitious and any resemblance to real persons, living or dead, is purely coincidental.

British Library Cataloguing in Publication Data

Thorne, Alexandra
Indecent Lady
I. Title
813.54 [F]

ISBN 0 340 66032 5

Typeset by Hewer Text Composition Services, Edinburgh
Printed and bound in Great Britain by
Cox and Wyman Ltd, Reading, Berkshire

Hodder and Stoughton
A division of Hodder Headline PLC
338 Euston Road
London NW1 3BH

An Indecent Lady

Alexandra Thorne

CORONET BOOKS
Hodder and Stoughton

To Nancy and Tracy Thorleifson,
the fearless ladies who married my sons.

641555

MORAY COUNCIL
Department of Technical
& Leisure Services

Author's Note

When I began writing *Sophisticated Savages*, the first of the Pride books, I had no idea I would spend the next twelve months writing two more. However, I just had to get to know the Pride family better. *The Ultimate Sin* and *An Indecent Lady* are the result of that desire.

One of the pleasures of writing the trilogy was having the opportunity to learn a great deal about my adopted state of Texas. For historical buffs, the Driskill Hotel opened six months later than it does in the book. The Great Die-off of Longhorn cattle – due to summer droughts and record winter storms – lasted from 1884 to 1887. The city of Indianola was battered by a series of hurricanes that left it uninhabitable. I used the 1875 hurricane as my model.

I am indebted to the Austin Historical Society for help in my research, to the staff of the Driskill Hotel, the staff of the governor's mansion, and to the numerous historians whose works served me so well.

I am especially grateful to Shirley Estes, a fellow artist and indefatigable traveling companion, who made trips into the hinterlands of Texas a true joy.

I would also like to thank Denise Little and Rob Cohen for believing in this project.

Courage is a kind of salvation.
    – Plato, *The Republic*

Prologue

TEXAS – 1869

Once a month, as regular as clockwork, Ulysses Pride went to heaven. His best friend, Reina DeVargas, always went with him.

The sickly, asthmatic eight-year-old boy never thought the five-year-old girl was an unsuitable companion. He liked Reina for her devil-take-the-hindmost attitude to life; he liked her because she never made fun of his scrawny body and bookish ways; he liked her because she so obviously liked him.

Heaven was the Dietz Bakery in Fredericksburg, Texas, a bakery his mother had owned before she married his father. Heaven was the sweet agony of having to choose a single pastry from a cornucopia of delicious treats. Heaven was being left alone with Reina, feeling like a man among men and master of his own destiny.

'Take good care of my little girl,' Reina's mother said as Ulysses and Reina settled at one of the bake shop's tables one brisk October day.

'I will, ma'am,' Ulysses replied solemnly. Mrs DeVargas said the same thing every month, and each time he gave her the same reply.

'Don't eat too fast,' his own mother admonished

him. 'You don't want a stomachache on the way home.'

Ulysses loved his mother but he hated it when she fussed over him. He wished she and Mrs DeVargas would go do their shopping.

The aroma of apple strudel and steaming hot chocolate was almost irresistible. However, he had to resist it a little longer. 'I'll be sure to chew nice and slow.'

Leaning down to kiss him, his mother said, 'Have fun.'

Seeing a couple of older boys at a nearby table, he jerked away. 'Aw, Ma, not in public.'

She settled for a pat on the head. 'We'll be back in half an hour, same as always.'

Ulysses waited until his mother and Mrs DeVargas disappeared through the bakery's front door before turning back to Reina.

'I bet I can finish my strudel faster than you,' he said.

Her eyes danced with mischief as she began cramming pastry in her mouth.

'That wasn't a fair contest. You got a head start,' he protested when she won, her strudel gone but for tiny flakes of dough on either side of her smile.

'It was too fair. I'm littler so I get to start before you do,' Reina declared with irrefutable female logic.

Ulysses hadn't been aware that the older boys were watching until they sauntered over. 'You gonna let a snot-nosed girl make a fool of you?' one of them asked.

'Ain't you that whore's daughter?' the other said to Reina. 'My Daddy told me he used to stick his whanger inside your mother all the time. He called her the queen of whores.'

Ulysses shrank away from the cruelty of their

words. Instinct brought him to his feet – not to fight but to run. Then, remembering his promise to take care of Reina, he subsided into his chair. Surely nothing bad could happen to them in a bakery full of customers.

'We aren't bothering you. Just leave us alone,' he whispered, hating the thin sound of his voice and the fear that trembled through him.

The two older boys looked at each other and snickered. 'I should have known you'd stick up for her, you being a bastard and all,' the larger one said.

Ulysses felt his face heat up. He'd heard the word and knew what it meant. He'd get his mouth washed out if he ever used it. Certainly, no one had ever applied it to him before.

'You stink you – stink like horse shit,' Reina sputtered, her pastry-daubed face twisted with fury. 'Don't you talk to my friend like that.'

To Ulysses' horror, she erupted from her chair like an avenging angel and kicked the smaller boy in the shin. He howled and grabbed his injured leg.

The second boy shoved Reina so hard that she fell on the floor. She clamped onto his ankle and bit him while Ulysses watched in frozen horror. It all happened so fast that he couldn't seem to make his muscles work.

Mr Dietz came out from behind the bakery's counter, his white apron flapping as he hurried to their table and parted the struggling children.

'You boys go fight with someone your own size,' he said, keeping a firm grip on Reina as he shoved the boys toward the door.

The two of them marched off in lock-step, then turned to fire a parting salvo. 'You're a damn sissy, letting a girl fight for you,' the bigger one said, glaring at Ulysses.

'Yeah,' the other boy chimed in. 'Him and that girl are two of a kind. A sissy and a scaredy-cat, a bastard and a whore.'

After they were gone, Ulysses couldn't bring himself to look at Reina or Mr Dietz. The words, bastard and whore, thundered through his mind. His stomach churned and for a terrible moment, he thought he was going to spew apple strudel and hot chocolate all over the table.

His well-ordered existence had tumbled around him like a house of cards. Was Reina really a whore's daughter? Could Mrs DeVargas have done that?

His fevered brain conjured up a series of barnyard images, substituting Mrs DeVargas and a faceless man for a mare and a stallion. He groaned out loud. Had his parents done it too? Was he a bastard? And what did that make his mother and father?

'It's all right, Ulysses. Don't take on like that. I'm not hurt.' Reina's voice put an end to the sickening vision. But not to the horror it aroused.

He felt as if a vise had tightened around his chest. 'It's not all right,' he wheezed, struggling for breath. 'It's never going to be all right again.'

Time proved him right.

That night, in answer to his questions, his parents told him about his birth and their subsequent marriage, and about a woman named Charlotte Hawthorne, his father's first wife. They talked about how much they loved him, but he barely heard the words.

For months afterwards, he hated his gentle mother and his brave father. He hated Reina too, for witnessing his cowardice, for being there and hearing the truth. Most of all, he hated himself.

A few months later, he called her *Queenie* for the first time.

'I don't like that name,' she objected, her little face screwed up in an expression of repugnance.

'I don't see why. *Reina* means queen in Spanish.'

'You're just being mean. Those boys at the bakery called my mother the queen of whores. That's why you're calling me Queenie. I hate that name and I hate you.'

They had been alone in the Prides' parlor, playing dominoes while their mothers visited in the kitchen. Reina launched herself at him, punching and kicking. Their mothers ran into the room and it took both of them to pull her off him.

The next time he saw her, Reina retaliated by calling him *Useless*. Unlike Ulysses, she didn't make excuses for her childish spite. She knew just why she felt the way she did.

He was *Useless* in her eyes from that day on.

One

The Pride Ranch – 1885

Reina DeVargas understood horses better than men. She knew all the cowboys who lined the corral by name – had known some of them all her life – but she had no idea what made them tick.

She had no difficulty understanding the horse they were watching, though. Fear made Starfire arch his neck and shake his head as he fought her father's grip on the bridle. The white stallion's hoofs drummed a thundering tattoo. His nostrils flared. His rolling eyes revealed bloodshot rims.

He looked dangerous.

He was dangerous.

Fear made all animals dangerous.

'Anyone else want to try their luck?' her father, Rio, challenged the onlookers.

'I do,' Reina called out, unable to resist the opportunity to show the men up.

She gazed at the enormous dog by her side, said 'Stay, Useful,' then jumped from her perch on the top rail of the corral. She landed with feline grace, her boot-shod feet kicking up puffs of dust.

'You ain't gonna let your little girl get up on that devil, are you, Rio?' one of the new hands called out.

'You offering to take her place?' Rio's lifted brow lent a saturnine aspect to his weather-beaten visage.

'I'd just as soon stay in one piece – if it's all the same to you.'

Rio's grin flashed white against his dark skin. 'Ulysses Pride wants this horse broke and it looks like my Reina is the only one with the grit to get the job done.'

'It's her funeral,' another hand grumbled, rubbing the shoulder he had landed on when Starfire unseated him.

Reina ignored the dire prediction as she studied Starfire. His sweat-soaked hide glistened in the September sunshine. His deep chest and straight back spoke of a Spanish/Arabian lineage that could be traced to the days of the Conquistadors.

He was the most magnificent male animal she had ever seen. God, what she wouldn't give to own him.

Like her, Starfire had been born to the Texas Hill Country. He had run free all his life and wouldn't willingly surrender to any man. She knew her femininity would be her greatest asset in the coming contest of their wills.

At her approach, the stallion tossed his head and blew a shrill challenge through his nostrils. Rio gripped the bridle tighter, the whitening of his knuckles betraying the strain of holding the horse.

He was a wiry man in his mid-sixties. All muscle and bone, he didn't have an ounce of spare flesh. His Comanche ancestry showed in the hawk-like jut of his nose and the oblique curve of his cheek bones. Reina had inherited her ebony hair, skin that tanned to coppery perfection, and finely carved features from him. Her horse sense, too.

She owed her jade eyes and her curves to her mother.

She approached the stallion with a self-confident stride, blissfully unaware of the effect those curves – displayed in form-fitting Levi's – were having on the bystanders. More than one cowboy found himself adjusting his trousers at the crotch.

'Easy, Starfire, I'm not going to hurt you,' she said, her voice surprisingly deep and mellow for so small a woman.

'Don't hurry him,' Rio advised. 'You can't break a horse like this one. You've got to win him over.'

'I know, Daddy.' Her hands gentled the stallion, her husky tone soothed him. She reached in her pocket for a sugar cube and held it out.

Starfire sniffed at the treat, then took it, his lips wet, warm, and surprisingly dainty on her palm. She continued to hold her hand outstretched and he snuffled at it again, taking in her scent.

She waited until her father gave her a little nod, then gathered the reins in one hand, continuing to caress the stallion. His muscles rippled, then settled under her touch. With practised ease, she shortened the stirrups, talking to the horse all the while.

'Don't spur him like those other damn fools did,' Rio said, as she reached for the pommel.

She vaulted up onto the horse's back in one flowing movement. Her feet found the stirrups, and she settled in the saddle.

'He's all yours,' Rio called out, letting go the bridle.

For a second, Starfire stood still, assessing the weight on his back and the tension on the reins. The previous riders had felt as heavy as boulders, and they had cut his mouth cruelly with the bit. This new rider sat so lightly that he barely felt any weight. The bit didn't cut into his mouth either. Still, he wanted to be rid of her. He tensed, then reared up, his flashing hooves reaching for the sky.

The load on his back lessened as the rider leaned forward along his neck. Puzzled, he dropped back to the ground with a jarring thud, then kicked out his hind legs. The load lifted again, seeming to float along his haunches. Bewildered, he stood still, trembling with distress as the rider leaned forward and patted his neck.

'We're going to be great friends,' Reina said. She clucked her tongue against the roof of her mouth and gently nudged the stallion's sides with her heels.

Starfire took a tentative step forward, then another. The weight was still there. He gathered his muscles to rid himself of it, leaping and twisting like a demented creature.

Reina was determined to keep her seat. She sensed the horse's heart wasn't really in his gymnastic gyrations. Although the mutually bruising battle finally came to an end, Starfire continued to dance in agitation.

'Open the gate,' she told her father. 'I'm going to let him run.'

Starfire saw the barrier swing wide. His ears pricked forward, his mighty heart thundered in his chest. He couldn't throw the weight off. Perhaps he could outrun it. He leapt forward, going from a standstill to a gallop in a few ferocious strides. The wind ruffled his mane and his tail streamed behind him as he raced for freedom.

Reina's thighs tightened around Starfire as she leaned over his neck and gave him his head. She thrilled to the raw power of him, the wild speed. Few men would dare to make such a ride.

Her father had taught her that some horses

couldn't be broken in a corral, surrounded by a fence. The bravest and best of them had to be allowed to run. The trick was to maintain control.

She held the reins loosely but firmly, letting the stallion choose his own pace. Slowly, ever so gently, she taught him to follow the command of the leather in her hands.

By the time they reached the massive limestone gates that marked the entrance to the Pride ranch, Starfire was tired enough to surrender to her will completely. She reined him to a walk, rode up to the mail box, leaned over and retrieved the contents.

The huge dog came bounding up. Although his widespread mouth and lolling tongue revealed lethal-looking canines, he seemed to be smiling.

'Hi, Useful,' Reina called out. 'That was some gallop. I'm surprised you kept up. I don't think I've ever ridden a faster horse.'

The dog woofed a couple of times in apparent agreement, then trotted at her heels as she turned Starfire back up the two-mile drive that ended at the Pride mansion.

Ulysses Pride stood in the shade of the expansive front porch, heedless of the glorious pastoral view of jutting hills and sparkling river, as he gazed at a vision only he could see.

A tall man, impeccably groomed in a three-piece suit tailored to his measurements, nothing visible remained of the sickly, ineffectual boy he had been. The broad spread of his shoulders strained at his grey tweed jacket. Perfectly cut trousers emphasized his long limbs. A crisp white shirt and a school tie in Harvard's colors added to his aura of unassailable dignity.

He had created the aura with infinite attention

to detail, and it had served him well in last year's election.

Distracted, he finger-combed his thick blond hair, his strategy running through his mind. There was no more cruel or contentious an arena than Texas politics. He had hoped to run a clean campaign, to concentrate on the issues rather than indulging in personal invective. His opponent didn't see politics that way. He had raked up the old Pride scandal.

Ulysses firmly believed that the circumstances of his birth weren't half as important as the things he could accomplish in the legislature. Fortunately, the voters had agreed. But it had been too damn close for comfort.

Texas had been in a decline since the Civil War. Bereft of outside investment and economic opportunity, its citizens eked out a living in agricultural pursuits while northerners grew rich from new industries. He wanted those riches for his state, and for the rawhide-tough people who lived there.

Eastern-owned railroads had been raping Texas for years. He was determined to end their pillage of public lands and public trust. The condition of schools for black and white alike needed to be improved. And that took money. He intended to attract new businesses that would add to the tax rolls.

He closed his eyes, thinking of the good he could do, a good that went beyond the boundaries of Pride's Passion to encompass the entire state. He could do it all if repeated stories of his bastard birth didn't cripple his effectiveness.

It was one hell of a big *if*.

The sound of Reina DeVargas's voice interrupted his introspection. 'Hi, Useless. Have you managed to throw any widows and orphans off their land lately?' she called out with typical impudence.

'I've been too busy in the legislature, Queenie,' he drawled.

Reina's sally had been carefully calculated to annoy Ulysses. He sat on the board of a bank that had repossessed several small ranches over the last few years. Logic told her it hadn't been his fault. But she'd never been able to think logically about Ulysses Pride.

'I wouldn't waste my time if I were you. You probably won't be re-elected,' she said with mock concern.

Ulysses' smile displayed his white, even teeth. It was a politician's smile, as empty of meaning as a blank page. 'I appreciate your interest.'

Her answering smile was as cold as a blue norther. 'I'm just trying to look out for your best interests. I know how easily you get hurt.'

His blue eyes darkened. It reminded her of the way the sky seemed to shade to a deeper color before storm clouds obscured the sun. He had the most incredible eyes. Intelligent and often somber, they could go icy one minute and flash with heat the next. It was all she could do to tear her gaze away from them.

He moved out of the shadows into the sunlight. It spangled his hair with gold. 'I appreciate your concern for my well-being. Does that mean I can count on your support?'

With his broad shoulders, slim hips, and perfectly tailored apparel, he looked like the answer to every girl's prayers. But clothes don't make the man, she reminded herself, doing her level best to ignore his potent appeal. He might look like a golden god but she know how unreliable and self-centered, how judgmental he was.

Yet – heaven help her – she wanted him. Wanted and hated and loved and loathed, all at the same time.

Why did he have to grow up to be the handsomest man in Kerr County? Make that all Texas. She would have given anything to wipe that grin off his face. The trouble was, she didn't know whether it would be more satisfying to do it with a kiss – or a roundhouse punch.

She'd been mistaken, thinking Starfire was the most magnificent male animal she had ever seen. That honor belonged to Ulysses. Did he know the effect he had on women? Did he use it to lure innocent girls to his bed? Did he parade public virtue while indulging in private vice?

'I'm much too busy working on the ranch to squander time on politics. The only dirt on my hands is the honest kind.'

Reina's voice was as heavy and sweet as honey straight from the hive. A deceptive sweetness, Ulysses mused. The girl was as prickly as barbed wire. The man who got ensnared by her charms was bound to regret it.

His sardonic grin carved matching crescents on either side of his mouth. 'You've already helped me more than you can possibly know.'

Surprise widened her eyes. 'What do you mean?'

He laughed heartily, knowing it would rile her and thinking how devilishly pretty she looked with an angry flush on her cheeks. 'Sparring with you all these years has been the best possible training for politics.'

Reina held his gaze a moment, then pretended to be intensely interested in adjusting the reins.

Starfire. Damn her. She was riding Starfire. 'Who gave you permission to ride that stallion?'

'My father. The horse needs breaking. I volunteered. Do you have any objections?'

He did. But he couldn't voice them. Not to her. In addition to being her father, Rio DeVargas was the foreman of Pride's Passion — and his father's best friend.

'I have no interest in who you ride.' At least not in the damn horses, he thought. 'What do you think of Starfire?'

Reina's expression warmed. 'He's quite an animal. Smart, too. He'd make a wonderful cutting horse.'

The bleak years of their estrangement dropped away as they shared a moment of pleasure in the magnificent stallion. Then Ulysses remembered how he'd planned to take Starfire to Austin with him.

However, he'd feel like a damn fool, riding a horse that had been broken by a girl. Especially a girl like Reina DeVargas.

A whore's daughter. The ugly words filtered into his consciousness, and with them came even uglier memories.

Every time he saw Reina he was reminded of that day in the bakery, and how it had changed his view of himself and his parents. He'd been so damn vulnerable, so unable to deal with the sudden knowledge of his parents' sexuality.

Things haven't changed that much, he thought grimly as he looked at Reina. Now he was having trouble dealing with his own.

'I brought your mail,' Reina said, sliding from the saddle.

Her breasts bobbled when she hit the ground. Damn her. She didn't have the sense to corset her body the way decent women did. But then, there was nothing decent about Reina DeVargas.

She rode astride, her thighs spread like a man's. Her Levi's emphasized her every curve, from a waist he could span with his hands, to hips he longed to straddle.

A female had no damn business wearing trousers that fit like a second skin – trousers that made a man think about the naked flesh underneath.

Ignoring the rush of blood to his groin, he took the porch steps two at a time. He swallowed hard, concentrating on the mail she held out rather than on the seductive sway of her bottom as she walked up to him.

She was so small, she could have stood under his chin with room to spare. Her scent – a blend of soap, sweet grass, and female musk – wafted in his nostrils, heightening his desire.

He loathed himself for reacting so strongly to a woman who was the antithesis of everything he esteemed in her sex. He'd be damned if he'd permit himself to be led around by the organ between his legs rather than the one in his head. He'd set goals for himself, goals that would help his state and all the people in it. A woman like Reina would only get in his way.

'Is something wrong, Useless?' she asked.

'I didn't know you cared.'

'I don't. You look so bilious, I thought you might be coming down with something. And believe me, I don't want anything you've got.'

As if to reinforce her warning, her dog growled, displaying inch-long canines.

'Don't worry. I have no desire to give you anything, Queenie.'

Her lips thinned. She shoved the mail into his

hands and swung back up into the saddle, affording him a tantalizingly brief look at her buttocks. Her pants were so tight that the cleft between each globe was clearly visible. For a moment, he allowed himself to imagine what those globes would feel like in his hands. Hot silk, he decided.

'Maybe you have time to stand around jawing, but the rest of us have work to do,' she said, then kicked Starfire to a canter.

With her jet hair flying in the wind, she reminded him of a goddess in Greek mythology. Not Diana, though.

Medusa was more like it.

Reina felt edgy as she rode back to the corral. Her encounters with Ulysses always left her feeling as if her skin had been flayed, exposing the raw nerves beneath.

Starfire seemed to pick up on her emotions. He skittered and sidestepped, his ears twitching, his tail flicking restlessly.

'Easy, boy,' she crooned, leaning forward to pat his neck.

Her own mare, a buckskin, was waiting at the corral. Rio was nowhere in sight. Most likely, he'd gone home for lunch.

The noonday calm had settled over Pride's Passion.

Reina dismounted and took Starfire into the big stone barn. After giving him a rubdown, she left him in his stall, then headed for her parents' ranch.

The initial one hundred acres had been a gift from Patrick Pride on the occasion of her parents' marriage. They had added to it over the years, using money from the sale of her mother's business. Now the DeVargas spread encompassed a thousand acres.

AN INDECENT LADY

Reina was proud of her parents. They had built a loving relationship and a comfortable home at an age when other people might not have had the courage to start over. But she worried about them, too.

Velvet had never been able to live down her past. Except for Elke Pride's friendship, she lived in virtual seclusion. And Rio was getting on. A sixty-seven-year-old man had no business putting in eighteen-hour days running his own spread, and acting as Patrick Pride's right hand, too.

Ulysses ought to have shouldered his share of the load by now, she thought angrily. At twenty-six, he should have been ready to settle down. But he didn't give two hoots about the ranch – or anyone else for that matter. Since going off to Harvard, then opening a law practice in Kerrville, and finally winning a legislative seat, he hardly spent any time at home.

It wasn't right, she thought, frowning fiercely. If she stood to inherit a place like Pride's Passion, she'd spend every waking hour getting to know its 100,000 acres and all the animals on it.

Ulysses. Why did every thought seem to lead her straight back to him?

Here she was, twenty-three and well on her way to spinsterhood because she'd never been able to see another man past the shadow Ulysses had cast over her life.

Two

Elke and Patrick Pride were already seated when Ulysses walked into the dining room. 'Was that Reina I heard outside?' Elke asked, giving him a smile.

'She brought the mail.'

'How thoughtful of her.'

'Thoughtful isn't a word I'd use to describe Reina,' he replied, handing the mail to his father before taking his own seat.

'Now, Ulysses, you don't mean that. She's a lovely girl,' Elke chided.

'And a hell of a horsewoman,' Patrick added. 'Rio is a lucky man.'

'How so?' Ulysses couldn't help asking.

'A man doesn't need a son when he's got a daughter like that. She knows almost as much about running a ranch as her father does.'

Anger hardened Ulysses' features. He was tired of hearing his father hold Reina DeVargas up as a paragon – tired of the less than subtle comparisons where he always came off second best.

'There are more important things than a good seat in a saddle,' Ulysses said, struggling to maintain his composure.

Patrick had a gimlet look in his eyes. 'You may be right when it comes to city folk. But we're ranchers. At least your mother and I are ranchers. I reckon

AN INDECENT LADY

horses and cattle don't mean much to a lawyer like you.'

'That's enough, you two,' Elke said, before Ulysses could come up with a retort. 'Can't we have one meal without a disagreement?'

Patrick gazed at Elke with such naked adoration that Ulysses felt like a voyeur. 'Of course we can. I just wish—'

'Never mind what you wish. You and I have had all our wishes come true. It's Ulysses' turn now.' Elke's strong words were spoken so lovingly that Patrick couldn't take issue with them.

No one else could handle his father the way his mother did. Sometimes, seeing them together made Ulysses feel a million years old. His parents acted younger and more carefree – with their teasing, their laughter, their tender words and glances – than he had ever felt.

In the dining room's soft light, Elke looked far more youthful than her fifty-four years. Strands of silver threaded her blonde hair, and faint lines etched her brow and the corners of her eyes. But her skin still had a youthful freshness and her figure was almost girlishly slim.

She's lost weight, Ulysses suddenly realized. His anger at his father faded as he studied his mother. She looked a little pale. Tired too, as if she hadn't been sleeping well. He was about to ask about her health when Patrick passed out the mail.

As usual, most of it was for Elke. She had made countless friends over the years – from the abolitionists she had known before the Civil War, to the tutors Ulysses had had because poor health prevented him from riding five miles to school in Kerrville, to acquaintances she had made on her rare trips away from the ranch.

She sorted through the envelopes, her face lighting up as she recognized familiar names. 'Oh look, here's a letter from Charlotte,' she exclaimed happily. She opened the envelope, being careful to save the stamp intact for Patrick's collection. 'It's been months since I've heard from her.'

Ulysses' innards felt as if they had been tied in knots. He had never understood his mother's long friendship with the scheming bitch who had been his father's first wife – the woman who had been responsible for his bastard birth.

Elke was so kind and trusting that she would manage to find some virtue in the devil.

In Ulysses' estimation, Charlotte Hawthorne, the Countess of Glenhaven, ran the devil a close second.

'Would you like me to read it out loud, darling?' Elke asked Patrick.

'Your food will get cold. Why don't you wait until after lunch?'

Saved by the bell, Ulysses thought. He doubted he'd have any appetite after listening to another of Charlotte's puerile missives. She spent more time writing about clothes, about the places she had been and the important people she had met than a correspondent for *Godey's Ladies Book*. For the life of him, he couldn't imagine what his mother – a serious, thoughtful woman – had in common with the countess, other than having been married to the same man, a fact Ulysses would have preferrred to forget.

He pushed his uneasy thoughts aside and concentrated on the meal. Elke – a superb cook in her own right – had trained her kitchen help well. The roast chicken, browned potatoes and creamed peas were delicious.

However, Ulysses couldn't help noticing how little Elke ate. No wonder she looked so thin. Surely, if something were really wrong with her, his father would have noticed. Perhaps she was just worrying about her figure.

'Charlotte usually writes every couple of months. However, I haven't heard from her in a long time. I wonder why?' Elke mused.

'She's probably been too busy spending Nigel's money,' Ulysses replied.

Elke seemed to deliberately misconstrue Ulysses. 'She certainly is generous to a fault. When I think of the gifts she has sent us over the years—'

Ulysses clenched his jaws to keep from making an even more acid remark. The countess's gifts had been notable for two things. Their cost – and their utter uselessness. There had been a lavish Worth ballgown that his mother had no place to wear; a Sheffield silver tea service that intimidated the local ladies so much that Elke never used it; to say nothing of the Irish Wolfhound that the countess had sent on his twenty-first birthday in complete disregard of the fact that he had no place to keep the animal at Harvard. Reina had gotten the dog by default, and had added insult to injury by naming him Useful.

'That was excellent,' Patrick said, pushing his empty plate aside and gazing at his wife. 'Remember when you first came to the ranch and all Conchita knew how to cook were beans and side meat?'

Elke's blue eyes sparkled with amusement. 'Poor Charlotte was desperate for a decent meal by the time I got here.'

'Poor Charlotte was born desperate,' Patrick replied. 'I've never known a needier woman.'

'But she was such fun. And brave too, in her own way.' Elke rang for the maid, waited until the table had been cleared, then picked up the letter again. 'Shall I read it now?' she asked.

Patrick nodded and rocked back in his chair.

'*Dear Elke and Patrick,*' Elke began, '*I'm sorry not to have written before this. So much has happened that I haven't had time to take pen and paper in hand. I have the saddest news. My beloved Nigel passed away in his sleep six months ago. My one consolation is knowing he didn't suffer, and that he is with the angels.*' Elke stopped reading. Tears sheened her eyes.

'I believe that's two consolations,' Ulysses said drily.

'How can you be so unfeeling when the poor woman is telling us she's lost her husband?' Elke burst out in a rare show of temper.

Poor woman, my ass, Ulysses thought. The Countess of Glenhaven had undoubtedly inherited a fortune. As long as she had her fancy clothes, her jewels, her London townhouse and her baronial country home, he doubted she'd miss her husband all that much.

'I don't think I can finish,' Elke said with a catch in her voice. 'Would you read the rest for me, dear?'

Patrick got to his feet at once. He came around the table to Elke's side and kissed her brow, laying a comforting hand on her shoulder. Then he took the letter and squinted at it.

'I'm sorry, my love. These old eyes of mine need a little more light.' Regret at leaving Elke's side was evident in the way his hand lingered on her shoulder until the last possible moment, and in his heavy tread as he walked over to the window.

'*As you can imagine, settling Nigel's estate has been a heavy burden and a constant reminder of loss. I couldn't have gotten through it without my daughter. Alicia has been an anchor in a turbulent sea.*

AN INDECENT LADY

'Now that Nigel's affairs are well in hand, I owe my dear girl a change of scene. By the time this reaches you, we will be on our way to Natchez to visit my family. I shall, of course, visit Patrick's brothers and sisters while I'm there. I plan to bring him news of them in person.

'I couldn't cross the Atlantic without coming to see you, too. Dearest Elke, I never needed your kindess, your understanding, your strength, as much as I do now.

'Please don't think you have to go out of your way to entertain us. Seeing you and Patrick again after all these years will be joy enough. If it's not inconvenient, we will arrive on your doorstep some time in December. I shall count the days.

'Until then, as always, your devoted friend, Charlotte.'

Elke sighed. 'I shall write to her at once, telling her she's more than welcome.'

Patrick walked back to Elke and put the letter on the table. 'It's hard to imagine that Nigel is gone. As I recall he was a few years younger than I am, and so vital — so full of life.'

'Charlotte loved him so much. She must be lost without him. A month or two on the ranch will do her a world of good. I'm so glad she's coming,' Elke enthused.

'Well, I'm not,' Ulysses said forcefully. 'Of all the unmitigated gall. I can't believe that woman would presume on our hospitality after the heartbreak she's caused this family.'

'*That woman* is one of my dearest friends,' Elke replied.

'For heaven's sake, Mother, try to look at her visit from my point of view. I won a seat in the state legislature last year. During the campaign, my opponent dredged up things about our family that are best forgotten. No matter what the Countess wrote about not wanting to be entertained, I doubt she will tiptoe into town. She probably travels with an entourage complete with maids, footmen, and God alone knows what else. Her presence here is bound to cause a stir. People are going to talk and I don't think we'll like what they say.'

'Who are you worried about?' Patrick's voice had a harsh edge. 'Yourself or your mother?'

'I can't believe you'd ask me a question like that, Father. I'm worried about our family's good name. Mother has spent her whole life in charitable pursuits, trying to live down the past.'

Patrick shook his head in fierce denial. 'If you think that's why your mother helps people, you don't know her at all. She cares about *them* – not what they think about us. There is no more respected or loved a lady in the Hill Country. Your mother is a saint.'

'A saint would have waited until she wore a wedding band before conceiving a child,' Ulysses muttered under his breath.

The instant the words left his lips, he would have gladly bartered his soul not to have said them. He didn't realize his parents had heard them, though, until he saw Patrick's face turn white, then red.

Minutes earlier, his father had been complaining about his ageing eyes. Now, as he reared out of his chair and glared at Ulysses, he looked formidable enough to lick his weight in wildcats.

'How dare you say something like that, you insolent bastard.'

The cruel epithet swept the room, leaving destruction in its wake. Ulysses bolted to his feet so quickly that his water glass tumbled over. The muscles in his arms ached with the strain of not striking back at Patrick.

'If I am a bastard, Father, it was you who made me one.'

'Stop it this minute,' Elke's voice cracked through

the air like a whip. Her posture was so rigid that she looked as though she had been carved in stone. 'I can't believe the two men I love most would think – let alone say such awful things in our home. We're a family. It's time the both of you acted like one.'

Patrick's choler faded in the face of Elke's anger. He looked as shamefaced as an errant schoolboy – a feeling Ulysses shared. At least they had that much in common.

Elke pressed her hand against her heart as though they had wounded her so deeply that her lifeblood might spill out at any moment. 'Son, you owe me an apology,' she said, 'and Patrick, you owe one to our son.'

Remorse welled up Ulysses' throat, tainting the delicious meal with bitter gall. He owed Elke so much more than an apology. She had always been the bulwark between his father's expectations and his own aspirations. More than anyone else, she had shaped his life.

She had read to him constantly during his sickly boyhood, filling his empty hours with her love of books. She had tutored him when he wasn't well enough to go to school. She had been his first friend – and his inspiration. She had interested him in politics – in the need to do something for his fellow man.

She had insisted he be allowed to attend Harvard when Patrick wanted him to stay at home and take his place as the heir to Pride's Passion. No parent had cheered louder than Elke when he graduated from Harvard magna cum laude with a doctorate in law.

How could he have wronged the woman who had been his champion as well as his mother?

If Patrick hadn't loomed between them like a vengeful god, Ulysses would have fallen on his knees in front of her. 'I'm sorrier than I can possibly say,

Mother. I'd sooner cut out my tongue than use it the way I just did.'

Elke managed a wan smile. 'I can't imagine a politician without a tongue.' She turned to Patrick. 'It's your turn, dear.'

Patrick's mouth opened and closed a couple of times before he got any words out. When he finally did, his voice had a metallic rasp. 'I'm sorry, too. It's just a word men use when they're angry.'

It might be just a word to Patrick, but that word had branded Ulysses. Patrick had never understood the way Ulysses felt about the circumstances of his birth – or so many other things.

He loved his father – admired and respected him despite their differences. But it hadn't been easy, coming of age in his house. The last few years, they had drifted so far apart that they seemed to speak a different language.

'I just have one more thing to say,' Patrick continued. 'This is our home, your mother's and mine. We'll damn well have any guest we want under our roof. If you can't handle that—'

'Please, Patrick,' Elke interrupted, 'don't say another word. I'd like to forget this conversation ever happened.' She reached for his father's hand. 'I'm feeling a little tired. Would you help me upstairs?'

A look of concern replaced Patrick's glower. 'Are you all right, dear?'

She smiled up at him. 'I'm always all right when you're with me.'

Patrick helped Elke to her feet. Arm in arm, gazing into each other's eyes, they left the room in such perfect harmony that the argument might never have taken place. Ulysses subsided into his chair, listening to them go. They were so completely in tune that their footsteps sounded in unison as they mounted the stairs.

When he was little, he used to feel that he existed on the fringe of their singular love. Now that feeling swept over him again.

He'd been a lonely child – and had grown up to be an even lonelier man. Would he ever love someone the way his parents loved each other? Could he summon the courage to surrender himself to another's tender mercies?

He repressed the urge to return to Kerrville and the impersonal solitude of his suite in the Nimitz Hotel. He had promised his mother that he would stay all weekend and stay he must. He couldn't hurt her more than he already had.

The DeVargases were finishing lunch when Reina walked into the kitchen.

'You're late,' Velvet said, getting up to fill a plate from the pot of stew simmering on the stove. 'Did Starfire give you any trouble?'

'Fat chance,' Rio answered for his daughter. 'There isn't a horse in all Texas that our girl can't ride.'

Velvet smiled at the pride in Rio's voice. Reina had been born in her father's forty-fourth year. Rio had never gotten over the wonder of becoming a father so late in life.

'Starfire is a dream to ride,' Reina replied, her husky voice brimming with enthusiasm. 'I'm late because I stopped by the Prides to drop off their mail.'

'Did you see Elke?' Velvet asked anxiously.

'I gave the mail to Useless.'

'What's he doing home? Is Elke ill?'

Reina shrugged. 'Why all the questions, Mother?

Useless didn't say. I didn't ask. His comings and goings are of no interest to me.'

'I'll never know how a loving couple like the Prides could raise a cold fish like Ulysses. Lawyers!' Rio spat the word out. 'They're a plague on the rest of us. So are politicians. Wouldn't you know that boy would choose to be both. He's a real disappointment to his father.'

'I couldn't agree more,' Reina was quick to agree.

Velvet's heart spasmed as she heard the false note in her daughter's voice. Reina had never once discussed her true feelings for Ulysses. However, Velvet hadn't spent years in the oldest profession without learning a thing or two about men and women. Her daughter was crazy in love with Ulysses – although she didn't know it.

Velvet breathed a silent prayer that she never would. Velvet had long since grown accustomed to the fact that Ulysses had no use for her. But she'd skin him alive if he hurt Reina. If Rio didn't do it first.

'Dad, do you know what Patrick is planning to do with Starfire?' Reina asked.

'Ulysses has his eye on that stallion. He said something about taking Starfire to Austin.'

'I don't suppose either of them would consider selling him.'

'Where would a bitty little girl like you get her hands on that sort of money?' Rio teased.

'I've been saving,' Reina said stoutly.

'Honey, I thought you were going to use your money to have some dresses made,' Velvet said.

'You and Daddy buy me all the clothes I need. Besides, what would I do with a bunch of fancy dresses?'

What indeed? Velvet mused, guilt weighing on her

so heavily that her breath seemed to be trapped in her chest. Reina had never been invited to parties like other girls. Despite her beauty, there hadn't been a single suitor for her hand. She hadn't been a bridesmaid and it looked as though she would never be a bride. Thanks to Velvet's unsavoury past, Reina seemed destined for a lonely spinsterhood.

Elke Pride couldn't ever remember feeling so tired – not even after birthing Ulysses. The last few weeks, exhaustion had embedded itself in her bones. Getting up each morning demanded a triumph of mind over body.

As she prepared for bed, she could hardly wait to lie down between the clean cool sheets and close her eyes. But she was determined to talk to Patrick about their son first. God alone knew how much time she had left for such a conversation.

She heard Patrick coming up the stairs and squared her shoulders. He mustn't see her sagging like wet linen on a laundry line.

The bedroom door opened and she saw him in the mirror over her dressing table. How handsome he looked, how strong and vital. His fifty-eight years sat so easily on his broad shoulders. But for the strands of grey frosting his thick brown hair, he didn't look much older than Ulysses.

The thought of leaving them both ached through her. Should she have told them the truth? Had she done the right thing by keeping her deadly secret?

'Did I ever tell you I married the most beautiful woman in the world?' Patrick said, coming up behind her.

'About a thousand times. But I love hearing it.'

He pulled her to her feet, turned her around and wrapped her in his arms. After all these years, his touch still had the power to set her aflame.

She had loved him the very first time she saw him when she was only seventeen. And she loved him still – only deeper and more fully now than she had ever imagined it was possible to love another person.

She pressed against him, yielding herself up to his strength. His embrace had always been both heaven and home.

'Are you feeling better?' he asked, leaning back to study her face.

Concern clouded his grey eyes. God. Did he know? She couldn't bear that. 'What do you mean?'

'You were so upset at lunch. If Ulysses were younger, I'd take him out behind the barn and tan his hide for upsetting you like that.'

She took Patrick's hand, led him to the bed, and motioned for him to sit down beside her. 'You never tanned his hide when he was little. Now that he's a strapping six-foot-three, it's a little too late to start.'

Patrick scowled. 'Maybe that's where I made my mistake. Our son is too headstrong for his own good. And that tongue of his must have been dipped in acid.'

Elke put her arm around Patrick's waist and rested her cheek against the broad, muscled expanse of his chest. 'I imagine your father used to say the same thing about you.'

'I don't think that's a valid comparison.'

'Of course it is, dearest. Your father wanted you to read law and join him in his practice, and you wanted Ulysses to take over the ranch. I suppose it's only natural for a man to want his son to follow in his footsteps.'

'My father had three sons,' Patrick said. 'I only have one.'

AN INDECENT LADY

Elke tilted her head and kissed his cheek. His stubble prickled her lips. 'That's all the more reason for you to love and understand Ulysses. If you push him away, you don't have another son to take his place the way your father did.'

'Don't you think I know that?'

She would have given anything to heal the hurt she heard in his voice. 'Forget the ranch for a moment. It's more important to have a son you can be proud of – and you do, dearest. Ulysses is intelligent and caring. He didn't run for office because he craves being in the limelight. He did it because he wants to do something for the citizens of this state. You ought to support him.'

'I try. I really do. It's just that we seem to rub each other the wrong way.'

'Promise me that you'll always be there for him, no matter what happens.'

'He doesn't need me as long as he has you.'

She almost weakened and told him then and there. Her chest felt tight. A deep, throbbing pain ran along her arm. 'Promise me, Patrick.'

Instead of answering, he gave her a long, sweet kiss. Tomorrow, she thought, ignoring her pain as she kissed him back, she would make Patrick promise tomorrow.

Three

Ulysses crossed his arms behind his head and stared up at the ceiling. He'd spent a restless night. The scene at the lunch table had played over and over in his mind like an elusive melody that, once remembered, refuses to go away. He kept on seeing his mother's stricken face, and wishing to God he'd managed to hold his tongue.

Elke had forgiven him far more easily than he was managing to forgive himself. His apology had done little to expiate his guilt. When he returned to town, he'd have flowers sent to the ranch, he decided, and a gift.

Other women might prefer jewelry, perfume, or some such feminine gewgaw. Nothing pleased his mother more than a new book. With any luck his copy of the latest best-seller, *The Rise of Silas Lapham*, would have come in. Instead of reading it himself, he'd have it delivered with the flowers.

Pushing the covers aside, he went to the window and looked out. Dawn had just begun to wrap the eastern sky with a veil of gold. A rooster crowed in the distance, and birds called out from their roosting places.

The cheerful sounds failed to lift his spirits. He wished he were back at his law office, concentrating on the consequences of other people's miscreant behaviour rather than his own.

Although it wasn't cold, he shivered and gooseflesh pebbled his skin. Conchita would undoubtedly say that someone had just walked over his grave – or some such superstitious nonsense. Still, logic couldn't banish the dread vibrating through him.

Patrick rolled over in bed and gazed at his wife. The drawn drapes cast the room in shadows. He could just make out her profile. She was sleeping so soundly that he couldn't see her breathing. Good, he thought. She needed her rest.

He had begun every day of the last twenty-seven years by giving her a kiss and telling her how much he loved her. Smiling, he pressed his lips to her cheek. Lord, she felt cold. He got out of bed and pulled an extra cover over her, half expecting her to stir.

Barefoot, he padded across the floor, opened the drapes, then returned to Elke's side. Why was she so still? 'Elke,' he said, his tone tentative. 'Elke, are you all right?'

Her golden hair lay across the pillow like a shimmering halo. She looked so peaceful and calm that he considered not waking her. But he just had to be sure she was all right.

'Elke,' he said, louder this time.

Again, there was no response.

He bent over her, listening. His own heart pounded with such apprehension that he couldn't hear hers.

'Elke, please wake up, dearest.'

He stared down at her, willing her to say something, anything – and thinking he would die if she didn't.

A premonition of loss keened through him but he

pushed it away, grabbing her shoulders to give her a gentle shake. Her head lolled from the stem of her neck like a broken flower.

'Elke,' he wailed, 'don't leave me.'

Even as he cried her name, he knew she had gone far beyond the sound of his voice. It wasn't supposed to happen this way. He was five years older. He should have gone first. A sob tore from his throat and then another as he clutched her to him.

'I can't live without you,' he cried out. 'For the love of God, Elke, come back to me.'

Ulysses had almost finished dressing when he heard the sound – the sort of anguished howl a mortally injured animal might make.

'What the hell is that?' he muttered under his breath, shoving his stockinged feet into a pair of boots.

He reached for the door knob and the sound hit him again – a moan so full of pain that listening to it made his chest feel tight.

He stepped into the hall and looked around, half expecting some spectral vision to greet him. This time, when the sound came, he could distinguish the words.

'Elke, don't leave me,' his father cried out.

What in the world was going on? His mother was as likely to leave his father as it was to snow in July.

Indecision froze Ulysses in place. He'd never felt free to march into his parents' bedroom when he was little, and God knew, after yesterday he was even less inclined to take such a liberty.

The hair on his nape lifted, as the sounds became more intense. Merciful heaven. Could those sounds actually be coming from his father's throat? Throwing caution to the winds, Ulysses raced down the hall and flung the door wide.

AN INDECENT LADY 35

Patrick was on his knees, by the bed, cradling Elke in his arms.

'Is something wrong with Mother?' Ulysses asked.

Ulysses barely recognized the face his father turned towards him. Patrick seemed to have aged ten years. His eyes had sunk into their sockets and deep lines grooved both side of his mouth.

'Your mother is dead.'

Ulysses stumbled back. 'Are you sure? Should I send for the doctor?' he asked, grasping at anything that would put off the moment when he had to accept the truth.

'The doctor can't help her. No one can. She's so cold. Do you think I should cover her with another blanket?' Patrick sounded as helpless as a lost child. He continued to rock Elke, his every movement a silent paean to grief.

Ulysses crossed the floor and gazed down at his mother, fighting the tears that threatened to spill from his eyes. He had to see that she was beyond help for himself, he thought, reaching down to touch her hair.

He didn't know what he expected, certainly not the alive feel of it as it slipped through his fingers. Could his father be wrong? A tiny spark of hope ignited in his brain. Perhaps she'd had a stroke. Bad as that would be, it was preferable to death.

He lay a hand on her cheek.

The tiny spark flared out. Her skin was cold – ice cold. She was gone.

Patrick shoved Ulysses' hand away. The light of madness burned in Patrick's eyes. 'Don't touch her. Don't you dare touch her. You broke your mother's heart yesterday. You killed her. And if you don't get out, I may just kill you.'

'You don't mean that. You can't.' He had just lost

his mother. Had he lost his father too? Had Elke's death unhinged Patrick's mind?

'Get out,' Patrick hissed. 'Get out while you still can.'

Ulysses took one step back and then another, his gaze never leaving his father's face. Patrick had turned back to Elke. Tears coursed down his cheeks. The sounds he made would have melted a heart of stone.

Ulysses longed to comfort him. He wanted to tell his father he loved him, and that he wasn't alone. He wanted to hold his father and share his grief. He wanted to do all the things a caring son should do for his father. But, damn it to hell, he didn't dare.

Rio DeVargas always got up at the first crowing of a cock. During the ten years he had lived in the Pride bunkhouse, he'd risen before dawn to get a jump on the young hands who were always challenging him one way or another.

After his marriage, much as he hated to leave the warm bed he and Velvet shared, he'd continued the habit because he liked to have coffee perking on the cast iron stove when Velvet got up.

Being a rancher's wife wasn't easy. He couldn't give Velvet much help with the household chores. But he could sure see to it that she got her day off to a good start.

He was alone in the kitchen, waiting for the fire to get hot enough to brew the coffee, when he heard a loud knock at the door. They sure as hell weren't expecting company at this hour of the morning. The knock spelled trouble.

Although most city men had stopped carrying guns, he'd as soon go without chaps on a cattle drive. He buckled his holster on his hips every morning, right after he put on his boots. He checked the load in the pistol, then walked to the door with a fluid grace that belied his age.

'Who's there?'

'It's Ulysses. I need your help.'

The boy sure sounded strange, as if something sharp had stuck in his throat. What sort of help would he need at this hour of the morning – or at any hour for that matter? Considering the way he treated Velvet and Reina, why should Rio give it to him?

'It's my father,' Ulysses called out.

Patrick was another matter altogether, Rio thought, slipping the latch and opening the door.

'Thank God you're up,' Ulysses said. He looked as white and drawn as a fresh-killed pig. 'My father's in a bad way.'

Rio's heart kicked like a bee-stung mule. 'Is he sick?'

Ulysses chewed on his lower lip as if he planned to have it for breakfast. 'No, it's Mother. She died sometime during the night and Dad is half out of his mind. He needs you and Velvet.'

'I'll get my wife,' Rio replied.

'I'm already here,' Velvet said from behind him.

Rio turned to see Velvet's face wet with tears. He'd have given a lot to have been able to break the news to her easy-like. Not that it would have changed her reaction. Crossing the floor, he pulled her into his arms. 'It's all right, sweetheart. Cry it out.'

Velvet made a strangled hiccupping sound and then freed herself from his embrace. 'I've already cried a bucket of tears over Elke and I expect I'll cry a bucket more. But Patrick needs us now. The poor man didn't know what was coming. He didn't have any warning.'

Know what was coming? What in the world was Velvet talking about? Rio gazed at her quizzically. She was fully dressed, as if she'd known she'd need to leave the house first thing.

'Rio, go hitch up the buggy,' she said. 'I'll be with you as soon as I tell Reina what happened.' Despite the watery tracks tears had left on her face, Velvet's tone was firm. She was plain amazing, Rio thought as he headed out the door to do her bidding.

Ulysses' heart was still pounding like a hammer on an anvil, and his breath came in ragged gasps. He felt as if he'd raced the two miles to the DeVargas ranch on foot instead of on horseback. His mother's sudden death seemed like a bad dream. He stood rooted in place – unaware that Velvet had left the room to wake Reina, as he was unaware of Velvet's return.

'You'd better get back to your father,' Velvet said. 'We'll be there directly.'

'I can't go back. He doesn't want me there.' Although Ulysses had held Velvet at arm's length for years, he had an almost uncontrollable urge to seek the solace of her embrace.

'Don't talk nonsense. Now that Elke's gone, Patrick's going to need you more than ever.'

'You don't understand. He blames me for Mother's death.'

'Good Lord. Of all the ridiculous—'

'It isn't ridiculous,' Ulysses interrupted. 'Mother and I had a terrible quarrel yesterday – about Charlotte Hawthorne. I said some unforgivable things.'

Velvet wrapped a shawl around her shoulders and headed for the door. 'People don't die from a quarrel. I'll set your father straight on that account. In the meantime, you're welcome to stay here as long as you need.' She cut a glance toward the stove. 'That coffee should be ready in a minute.

Help yourself. And there's whisky in the cupboard to go with it.'

There was nothing more distressing than the sight of a strong man with a broken heart, Velvet thought, opening the door to the Prides' bedroom. Patrick was on his knees, making a thin, keening sound as he cradled Elke's body against his chest.

Velvet put her own grief aside as she crossed the floor. She needed to be strong now, for Patrick's sake.

'I'm here,' she said, laying a hand on Patrick's shoulder. 'I'll take care of Elke. Go on downstairs with Rio and let me do what needs to be done.'

Patrick gazed up at her, but she couldn't be sure he had heard her. He continued to clutch Elke. Velvet had to loosen his fingers one at a time. But he offered no resistance as she tugged him to his feet.

She took Patrick's robe from the bedpost, draped it around his shoulders, then motioned for Rio to join them. 'Take him downstairs and give him a drink – and I don't mean tea. I'll be down as soon as I can.'

Rio took hold of Patrick's arm and led him away, half supporting him. Although her husband had always been a man of few words, he managed to keep up a comforting litany.

'I know you're going through hell right now, old horse. Don't you worry, though. My Velvet will take good care of Elke just like she's always done.'

Rio continued talking as he guided Patrick out of the room. Velvet waited until she heard them going down the stairs before turning to the task at hand. Only then did she give in to the luxury of a good cry.

When she joined Patrick and Rio in the library half

an hour later, the two men were sitting on the sofa with a half empty bottle of whisky in front of them. A little color had seeped back into Patrick's face. Seeing Velvet, he got to his feet, swaying a little.

'Is Elke all right?'

'I laid her out nice and proper,' Velvet replied. 'She looks like an angel.'

'She was an angel.' Patrick's voice broke. 'Oh God, I don't know how I'm going to live without her.'

Velvet crossed the floor, gave Patrick a fierce hug, then pushed him back down onto the sofa. 'I could use some of that whisky,' she told Rio.

Rio rose and went to the sideboard to get another glass. Velvet took his place beside Patrick. 'I can't tell you how sorry I am. I can't believe she's gone.'

Patrick wrapped his arms around himself and rocked back and forth. 'It's Ulysses' fault. He killed his mother.'

'I know how much you're hurting. I feel the same way. But you can't blame your son.'

Patrick continued to rock. 'He broke his mother's heart yesterday. And it killed my Elke.'

'He told me they had words, and I'm sure he regrets them more than we'll ever know. But he isn't responsible for Elke's death. She had a bad heart for years.'

Patrick was finally still. 'She was never sick a day in her life!'

'You're wrong. She was sick every day of the last two years.'

Patrick grabbed Velvet's shoulders so hard that she almost cried out. 'How do you know?'

'A couple of years ago, she told me she'd been having a little chest pain. At first, she thought it was heartburn. When it persisted, she asked me if I would go to the doctor with her. Remember the time we went up to Llano to see the doctor who saved your life after the gunfight with the Detweilers?'

'I thought it was just a friendly visit.'

'Elke trusted him to figure out what ailed her, and even more, to tell her the truth. He said her heart was giving out, and that there wasn't anything to be done. He gave her a prescription for when it got real bad, and told her she ought to take to her bed.'

'Why in God's name didn't she tell me? I'd have taken her back East to the best specialists.'

'That's just why she didn't tell you. Elke didn't want to spend the rest of her life going from doctor to doctor in a vain search for a cure – let alone back here in bed like an invalid. She wanted to live the time she had left to the hilt. She made me swear to keep her secret. So you see, her passing didn't have anything to do with Ulysses. It was just a matter of time.'

Patrick lifted his wounded gaze to Rio. 'Did you know?'

'This is the first I heard of it. Oh hell, Patrick, I ain't much good with words but I know Elke went the way she would have wanted.'

Reina dressed hurriedly after her mother left, knowing Velvet would need her at the Prides' house. Once word of Elke's death got out, folks would stop by in droves to express their condolences.

They would have to be fed. There'd be pots of coffee to brew, sandwiches to be made – and cakes to bake if there was time. Nothing seemed to stir folks' appetites like a death. Perhaps it was just their way of reaching out to life, Reina mused.

In Elke's honor, she got into one of her few dresses, then quickly brushed out her hair. She couldn't resist putting boots on instead of high button shoes that would only hurt her feet.

She doubted she'd have much time to sit down today. In any case, her long skirt would hide her boots. If it didn't, people would talk about her some more – not that she cared. She'd never set too much importance on what other people thought of her. She couldn't afford to.

She hurried into the kitchen, thinking she would have a quick cup of coffee before heading on over to the Prides'. A man stood in the middle of the floor with his back to her. His shoulders were shaking, as though he had the ague. Good heavens, it's Ulysses, she thought. She had assumed that he'd gone back to Pride's Passion with her parents.

He was crying – but he didn't seem to have the hang of it. He wasn't making a sound.

'Oh, Ulysses, I'm so very sorry about your mother,' she said, circling around to face him.

'Is that you, Reina?' He knuckled at his tears the way he used to when he was little. 'I thought I was alone.'

'There's no need to apologize for what you're feeling.'

Acting on raw instinct, she reached for him.

He grabbed her and held her close, his body trembling with the force of his grief. She stood on tiptoe and pulled his head down to her shoulder.

Ulysses didn't care that it was Reina's body he felt pressed against his own. His need was so great that he sheltered in her warmth, taking comfort from the gentle hands that caressed his back and stroked his hair, while painful *should haves* carouseled through his mind.

He should have realized his mother was ill.

AN INDECENT LADY

He should have asked why she'd lost so much weight.

He should have insisted she see a doctor.

He should never have quarreled with her.

He held onto Reina for dear life, needing her as he had never needed a woman before. She offered a safe harbor in the storm of his loss, and he took grateful anchor in it. He felt her tears through his shirt, felt her body shake as his did. She had loved his mother, too – she was suffering, too.

At first, as he ran his hands down Reina's back, he only meant to comfort her as she was comforting him. She felt as delicate as a child, and yet there was no denying she had a woman's body.

'It's going to be all right,' she said, her breath warm on his chest, her husky voice soft in his ears.

Brave little Reina. She always thought everything was going to be all right.

Her hands roamed his back, leaving a trail of heat in their wake. He'd been so cold – so very, very cold that he thought nothing could ever warm him again.

Reina only meant to help Ulysses endure his pain. She would have done as much for anyone. But when his mouth covered hers, she couldn't stop herself from kissing him back. His lips felt as soft as silk, yet they mets hers with heart-stopping hunger.

Velvet had long ago told her what happened between a man and a woman – had explained the mechanics of love in such a matter-of-fact way that Reina thought there would be no surprise when it finally happened to her.

Nothing her mother had said prepared her for the fire of longing a man could ignite. She let go a little gasp of surprise. Ulysses' breath mingled with hers, his tongue slid past her parted lips.

She had always wondered what it would feel like to kiss a man.

Now she knew, and lord – it was a powerful thing.

A current of desire swept through her and her knees went weak. His arms were so strong, his chest so broad, his scent so manly, and his need so great that it carried her away. She returned his growing passion with a wildness that seemed to come from a part of her that she hadn't even known existed.

Her hands reached up with a will of their own to press him closer to her yearning flesh. Her nipples felt even harder than they did when she got out of bed on an icy morning.

It was Ulysses who warmed her now, filling her belly with an all-consuming heat. She forgot all about their unhappy past – and the present tragedy that had brought him to her arms. Their differences melted away as her body melded with his. Time itself seemed to stand still.

And then, an urgent scratching at the door broke the spell that bound them. Reina froze. Of all the times for Useful to demand to be let in, she thought as time resumed its orderly progression.

Ulysses thrust her away with a force that sent her stumbling backward. 'How could you let me do that?' he demanded angrily.

Ulysses was appalled by what he'd done. How could he have permitted himself to come so close to ravishing a woman when his mother's body . . . He couldn't bring himself to finish the thought. The image of Elke – dead in her bed – quieted the last hot whispers of desire.

'Let you? How could I have stopped you?' Reina demanded.

'For God's sake, Reina, my mother just died.'

AN INDECENT LADY 45

'I know. I wouldn't have touched you with a ten-foot pole otherwise. I was just trying to express my sympathy.'

'You have a damn peculiar way of doing it. But then, you are your mother's daughter.' Ulysses turned away from the stricken look on Reina's face.

She was at fault, he reassured himself as he yanked the kitchen door wide. A decent woman would never have let him take such liberties.

The huge Wolfhound came bounding in, took one look at Ulysses and bared his teeth, putting his own body between his mistress and the man who had so recently held her in his arms.

It would serve Ulysses right if Useful bit him, Reina thought, giving free, if silent rein to her anger and hurt. How dare Useless cast aspersions on her mother? If the circumstances had been different, Reina would have taken considerable pleasure in giving him a piece of her mind.

His grief had seemed so sincere that it had fooled her into thinking a human being hid behind the perfectly groomed facade he showed the world. He had taken advantage of her sympathy, her lack of experience. He was to blame for what had happened – not her.

Elke, Reina thought, with a swift dart of pain. How could she be thinking about herself when Elke had just died?

Reina's anger fled. The hurt remained. She wanted to weep – for Elke, for her mother, for herself, for all the women whose lives were controlled by some man. But she'd be damned if she would cry in front of Ulysses.

'I am my mother's daughter,' she said, standing straight and proud, 'and I won't apologize for it.'

Ulysses gave her a piercing look and turned on his heels, walking out the door and slamming it so hard that it shook the room.

Good riddance, she thought. Hell could freeze over and cows would fly before she ever let Ulysses Pride touch her again. And then, unable to control the turbulent emotions that roiled through her like a river in flood, she lowered her head and wept.

Velvet downed her whisky in one greedy gulp, then waited a moment for it to warm her before turning back to Patrick. 'I know you haven't had time to think about it yet, but Elke told me her last wishes.'

He gazed at her blankly. 'What wishes?'

'She had her own ideas about her funeral.'

Patrick shrank away as if she'd struck him. 'Do we have to discuss this now?'

Velvet braced herself for what she had to say. 'I'm sorry, but we do. Elke didn't want an undertaker to touch her body. That means we don't have much time.' Velvet could only hope Patrick would understand she was trying to tell him, as gently as possible, that Elke's body had already started to decay.

Patrick's posture straightened. He seemed to have dug deep inside himself for the courage he needed. 'Go on.'

'She wanted a simple funeral – a few friends, a coffin made here on the ranch, Ulysses giving her eulogy with Rio singing "Amazing Grace" afterward. She asked to be buried down by the Guadalupe River alongside Otto and the baby she lost.'

Patrick almost cried out at the thought of Elke going to her rest by her first husband. But then he realized how utterly unworthy of his beloved Elke the

AN INDECENT LADY

thought was. She would need a guide on her journey. He couldn't think of a better one than Otto.

'Is that all?'

'Not quite. She wanted me to get her ready, and she asked to be buried in that dress Charlotte sent. Elke said it was probably the only use she'd ever have for it.' Velvet smiled at the memory. Elke had been so brave in the face of death.

'When do you think we should do it?' Patrick's voice was so low that she had to lean close to hear him.

'Day after tomorrow at the latest.'

Patrick groaned deep in his chest. 'I don't know if I can let her go so soon.'

'You don't have a choice, old horse,' Rio said, refilling their whisky glasses. 'I'd consider it an honor if you let me make the coffin. I thought the world of Miss Elke. You can count on me to do a good job.'

Patrick lifted his gaze to Rio's face, then quickly looked away from the sympathy and concern he saw there. He couldn't break down again in front of Rio and Velvet. If he did, he might never stop crying. Elke would want him to be strong. She would want him to make it up with Ulysses, too. Somehow, he would have to find the courage to do both.

Word of Elke's death spread quickly through the Hill Country. Patrick was so besieged by friends and neighbors offering condolences that he never found time alone with his son.

Now, as he looked around the crowd gathered by Elke's grave, he was surprised to see so many people had shown up despite the fact that there hadn't been time for the Kerrville paper to print an obituary.

The flowers the mourners brought covered the raw wound in the earth with brilliant splashes of color. If only something could shield him from the wound in his heart. Although Rio and Velvet stood on either side, and Ulysses was behind him, Patrick had never felt more alone.

He would gladly have quit life and laid down on the ground beside Elke. But he couldn't take the coward's way out. Although he quailed at the thought of a future without her, he would have to find some way to endure it.

He hadn't paid attention to the minister's words, hadn't realized that Ulysses had moved to the head of the grave until he heard his voice.

Ulysses had dreaded eulogizing his mother. He had written half a dozen speeches and discarded them all. Now, he doubted his ability to talk past the huge lump in his throat. In his sorrow, he couldn't summon up any of the speeches he had written. He had to trust his heart to tell him what to say.

'Friends, neighbors, and family, my mother would be surprised to see so many of you here – and worried, too. She'd be wondering how to feed so many people on such short notice. But knowing her, she'd have found a way.

'My mother was a truly remarkable woman. She spent a large part of her life in the service of others. The world will be a poorer place without her.

'She came to Texas in 1847 with the Adelsverein Society. On the way, she lost both her parents to typhoid. I never understood how lost she must have felt, how alone. I do now.

'She told me that she almost gave up and returned to Germany. But she had remarkable courage. She decided to stay.

'This was a wild and dangerous land in those days. She helped to tame it – not with bravery alone but with gentleness. She believed in

AN INDECENT LADY 49

decency, in honor, in having compassion for her fellow man.

'As all of you leave her grave today, I pray that you will carry those things away with you. For that is the legacy she left us. If we live according to those precepts, it will be a fitting testament to her life.'

Ulysses was unaware of the nods of approval, the muffled sobs, the squaring of shoulders and straightening of spines that his words elicited. He stepped away and Rio DeVargas took his place.

'I ain't handy with words, like Ulysses here,' Rio said, 'but Miss Elke asked me to sing her to her last rest. I'll do my best.' He took off his Stetson and held it across his chest; when he opened his mouth the words to 'Amazing Grace' floated in the air like a benison.

When, overcome by emotion, Rio's voice faltered, another even sweeter voice picked up the refrain. Reina's contralto swooped and soared, lifting Rio's voice with it – lifting the soul of every person who heard their sweet harmony.

After the last notes faded away, Patrick stepped forward. His hands trembled as he dropped the first clod of dirt on the stout coffin Rio had built. 'Sleep well, my love,' he murmured.

Then he stepped back to let Ulysses take his turn. Ulysses took a single clod of Texas earth and let it fall. It landed on the coffin with a hollow thud. The finality of the moment almost unmanned him, and he swayed on his feet.

To his surprise, the hand that reached to steady him belonged to Reina. 'I shall miss your mother,' she said.

He pushed a 'Thank you,' past frozen lips.

They stared at one another in silence. He tried to read her eyes, but they were as carefully shuttered as an empty house. Then, with the smallest smile, she rejoined her parents.

One by one, the other mourners took part in the solemn ritual of filling the grave. When it ended, Patrick and Ulysses led the way back up the hill to the crepe-draped house.

It seemed an eternity before the last of their neighbors drove away. For them, Elke's burial had been a sad interlude. For Patrick and Ulysses, it marked the beginning of a new and lonelier life – a life neither of them relished or wanted.

'I haven't had a chance to tell you yet,' Patrick said when they were finally alone in the parlor, 'but I'm sorry for what I said the morning when—' His voice drifted off as if he couldn't bring himself to finish the thought. 'Velvet told me the truth.'

'It's all right, Father. She told me, too.'

'What are your plans now?'

'It's time I returned to Austin. I have a great deal of work to do before the legislature goes into session.'

Ulysses gazed at Patrick, waiting for his response. If Patrick had made one gesture of affection or need, Ulysses would have changed his plans on the spot.

'I suppose that's for the best,' Patrick said.

Without another word, he turned and left Ulysses in the achingly empty room, taking with him the last vestiges of Ulysses' youth.

Four

Ulysses left a household deep in mourning. He returned from Austin in mid-December to a lifeless tomb.

Although he had written his father several times, Patrick hadn't responded. He hadn't seen Patrick since the funeral, and wondered if his father would be pleased to have him home – or indifferent. Would the rancor between them be forgotten, or would it worsen without Elke to act as their referee?

He was startled to see the crepe-draped funeral wreath still hanging on the door. Didn't anyone remember it was Christmas? Elke loved the Christmas holiday and put her own stamp on it. She used to spend hours decorating the house, fashioning garlands from the evergreens, holly and yaupon that grew on the ranch.

She took more care choosing a Christmas tree than she ever did picking a dress. Last year at this time, a wreath had adorned the door and candles glowed in every window. To ignore the season seemed tantamount to forgetting what it had meant to Elke.

Ulysses climbed the steps to the porch and let himself in. Shadows cloaked the entry hall. He saw no light in the parlor, no fire burning on the hearth.

'Is anyone home?' he called out, waiting for one of

the maids to come take his coat and carry his saddle bags up to his room.

No one appeared.

His mother had run the house so effortlessly that Ulysses had taken the comforts of home for granted. Patrick must be working late, and the help was taking advantage of his absence to neglect their duties. He would have to give the staff a stern talking to in the morning.

He headed down the hall to the kitchen, opened the door, and memory struck another blow.

Last year, the kitchen had been filled with the aroma of spices. The scent of fruit cake, plum pudding, and *Pfeffernussen* were as much a part of his holiday recollections as the opening of presents.

Now, the room smelled of stale air and mildew. A single kerosene lamp burned overhead, revealing Conchita bent over the stove, stirring something in a small pot. She looked more like one of Macbeth's witches than an old family retainer.

Her daughter, Maria, had taken over the cooking years ago. Where was Maria? Ulysses wondered, walking up behind Conchita and touching her shoulder.

'*Dios Mio*,' she cried out, turning to face him as quickly as her bent, arthritic body permitted. 'You gave me a fright, *Senor* Ulysses.'

'I wrote Father I'd be home today. Didn't he tell you?'

Conchita shook her head. 'He doesn't read his mail – he doesn't leave the house. He just sits up in his bedroom staring at your mother's picture. Thank God you're home. Perhaps you can cheer *Senor* Patrick up.'

'I'll try,' Ulysses said, although he doubted he'd have much success. 'Where is everybody?'

'Your father dismissed the other servants weeks ago. He wanted me to go, too, but I couldn't leave him.'

'What about the ranch? Surely he hasn't lost interest in it?'

'Rio tried to get him back to work. The last time, *Senor* Patrick cursed at him.' Conchita made the sign of the cross with a liver-spotted hand. 'This has become a house of ghosts. Sometimes I think I hear your mother walking the halls at night.'

Ulysses shrugged at Conchita's superstitious fantasy. 'I assure you, there are no ghosts in the house — just a hell of a lot of dust.'

Conchita lowered her obsidian gaze. 'Wait until you see your father. He's little more than a spirit himself.'

Conchita was exaggerating. His father was the strongest, bravest man he knew — and not the sort to become a recluse.

A decorated war hero, Patrick had turned a wilderness land grant into a successful ranch. He had been so obsessed with the land that neighbors had dubbed the ranch Pride's Passion.

Ulysses couldn't believe that anything — not even his mother's death — would keep Patrick from looking after his vast holdings.

'If it's all the same to you, I'll have supper before I see my father.'

'Supper?' Conchita looked as though she'd never heard the word before.

'Whatever you're cooking there will be fine.'

A flush stained Conchita's withered cheeks. 'It's only porridge. Your father can't be bothered eating most of the time. I can usually get him to swallow some grits.'

Perhaps Conchita wasn't exaggerating after all. 'Never mind about supper. I had better go see Dad.'

In the three months he'd been gone, the household had come apart at the seams, Ulysses mused. The kerosene lamp that lighted his way up the stairs revealed the house's sorry state. Dust balls retreated at his approach. Cobwebs caught at his face and arms.

He left his saddle bags in his room, then knocked on his father's door.

'I'm not hungry, Conchita,' came the thin sound of Patrick's voice.

Not waiting to be invited in, Ulysses opened the door.

The state of the house had shocked him. But Patrick's condition was worse than shocking. His clothes hung on his newly gaunt frame. His skin had lost its habitual tan. An unkempt beard added to the impression of malaise.

'Is that you, Ulysses?' Patrick said, not even bothering to get up.

'I'm home for the holidays,' Ulysses replied with forced *bonhomie*.

Patrick didn't stir. 'If you want Christmas with all the trimmings, you had better go back to Austin. There isn't going to be any holiday here.'

The road from Kerrville to Pride's Passion followed the winding course of the Gaudalupe River. The river's jade waters traveled their bed with a throaty tumult. The sound echoed off the bordering limestone cliffs and rollings hills.

Charlotte Hawthorne kept the livery stable buggy moving at a brisk pace as every turn revealed another familiar vista. But for the ugly barbed wire fences, the countryside appeared unchanged since she last made this drive, twenty-seven years ago.

'The more things change, the more they stay the same,' she muttered.

Her daughter, Alicia, looked askance at her. 'What do you mean?'

Although trepidation ruled Charlotte's thoughts, she tried to give her daughter a reassuring smile. 'My life couldn't be more different. However, this place looks the same.'

'It's nothing like home,' Alicia smiled back, 'but it's very beautiful. I think I'm going to like it here. I can't believe I'm really in Texas.'

When they reached the limestone-pillared entrance to Pride's Passion with the distinctive P/P brand burned into an overhead cross beam, Charlotte reined the buggy to a stop.

Alicia reached across the front seat and touched her mother's arm. 'Is something wrong?'

'I need a moment to collect myself.'

'Is it much further?'

'The house is still two miles away.'

'Does Mr Pride own all this land?' Alicia asked with a sweeping gesture.

'All that and more. Pride's Passion is the biggest ranch in the Hill Country. I can hardly wait to see Elke. You're going to love her.'

'You don't feel at all awkward about the circumstances?'

'Should I?'

'You will admit it's a little strange, paying your first husband and his wife a visit.'

'You won't think so once you meet them. Besides, I did them both a favor by running off with your father. Elke and Patrick were madly in love.'

'I know, Mother.' Alicia gave her a fond smile. 'Just the way you were with Father.'

Charlotte didn't comment. She flicked the whip over the horse's back and the buggy moved off up the drive. She had told her daughter so much about the past – and nothing of the present.

She *had* fallen wildly in love with Nigel when he first showed up at the ranch, so badly injured that no one knew if he would walk again.

To her infinite regret, that love hadn't lasted. Nigel had killed it with casual cruelty, just as he had killed all those animals he had hunted before his injury made hunting impossible.

The years had metamorphosed the dashing young blueblood into a bored, embittered man who spent his life and his fortune in the restless pursuit of amusement. In the process, he had destroyed Charlotte's romantic illusions one by one.

She couldn't destroy Alicia's. She'd sooner die than tell her daughter the truth about Nigel – or the desperate straits he had left them in.

At the top of the rise, she finally saw the house she had come to as a bride. The late afternoon sun touched the creamy limestone walls with gold. The veranda that embraced the facade seemed to promise a safe haven.

God, how she needed that, Charlotte thought, urging the horse to a faster gait.

Alicia cut a glance at Charlotte, wondering what her mother was feeling. She looked so very determined, as if she were going into battle rather than having a reunion with old and dear friends.

Alicia had heard a great deal about the Prides, but she had never expected to meet them in person – and certainly not during the year-long mourning period that was *de rigueur* in their circle.

Charlotte had been in the strangest mental state since Nigel's death. Alicia had expected and could have handled tears. However Charlotte had been dry-eyed when she told Alicia that Nigel had died in the middle of the night. If Charlotte ever wept, she did so in privacy.

After the funeral – an affair of incredible pomp and circumstance – Charlotte had become increasingly secretive and withdrawn. She spent so much time running from one solicitor to another that they barely had any time together. Then, out of the blue, she had announced the trip to America.

Was her mother running away from something – or towards something?

'You told me the Prides had a lovely home,' Alicia said. 'You didn't tell me it was a mansion.'

'It wasn't the last time I saw it,' Charlotte replied. 'Elke wrote me that they added a new wing.'

The house had always been handsome. Now, it looked imposing. Over the years, Elke had occasionally written about how well they were doing. Seeing visible evidence of it gave Charlotte a profound feeling of relief. She hadn't traveled thousands of miles in vain.

She looked up at the veranda, remembering when she met Elke for the first time. It had been twenty-seven years ago – almost to the day. She had been sitting on the porch, surrounded by holly branches, making a mess of her attempt to turn them into decorations for the party she had planned. Elke had come to her rescue then – just as she hoped Elke, or rather Elke's son, would come to her rescue now.

Charlotte gazed toward the front door, wishing her old friend would come rushing out to greet them. What she saw instead made her gasp.

'Oh, no,' she exclaimed, clapping a daintily gloved

hand to her mouth. 'There's a black wreath on the door.'

There had been similar wreaths on the London townhouse and Glenhaven Hall when Nigel died. Seeing this one filled Charlotte with dread. She couldn't endure more bad news. If she'd had anyplace else to go, she would have turned the buggy around and driven away. Instead, she brought it to a stop.

Alicia got out, then helped Charlotte down. 'I'm sure we would have heard if something had happened to the Prides,' she said. 'It's only a matter of weeks since we saw Mr Pride's brothers and sisters in Natchez. Perhaps an old retainer passed on.'

Charlotte let go her pent-up breath. Her heart returned to its normal rate. 'You're such a sensible girl,' she said, reaching up to touch her daughter's cheek. 'I don't know what I'd do without you.'

Charlotte gathered her skirts, headed for the porch, and climbed the steps as memories chased each other through the hallways of her mind. Nigel had courted her on this very porch.

No, she silently amended, to be truthful she had courted him. What a wild, impetuous creature she had been in those days – always working on some scheme. And here she was, about to launch on yet another one – not for her own sake this time, but for her daughter's. She would do anything to secure Alicia's future. Well, almost anything.

Thank heavens, Alica was nothing like her. She couldn't have asked for a more dutiful daughter.

'It's awfully quiet,' Alicia said, gazing around.

'We're in the country, darling. Patrick spends the day in the saddle. If I know Elke, she's undoubtedly in the kitchen preparing a fabulous supper. She's the most marvelous cook.'

AN INDECENT LADY

Stifling her foreboding, Charlotte knocked on the door. When no one answered, she knocked again, louder this time.

Ulysses was in the library, making notes on a bill he hoped to propose when the legislative session began in Austin in the spring. A loud knock interrupted his train of thought.

'Who the hell can that be?' he muttered.

Conchita had told him that Patrick turned away everyone who came calling in the weeks after Elke's death.

He waited for Conchita to go to the door, then cursed under his breath when she didn't. She was so deaf she probably hadn't heard the knock.

Getting up, he went to answer the imperious summons. His footsteps echoed hollowly down the long hall. The house felt empty and abandoned. What was it Conchita had said about ghosts?

That morning, after opening the drapes and shutters to see things were even worse than they had appeared, he told Conchita to send for Maria and the other servants. But it would be a day or two until they arrived and gave the place a proper cleaning. In the meantime, whoever wanted admittance would have to take them as they were.

He opened the door to reveal two of the loveliest, most fashionably dressed ladies he had ever seen. The younger one was breathtaking. Her pale gray traveling attire revealed a tiny waist and well-rounded bosom. Of medium height, her blonde hair, blue eyes, and refined features indicated a patrician breeding that was rare in these parts.

The older woman was petite, dark of hair, not more than thirty-five, he decided. She was dressed in somber black from head to toe. On another woman, such an outfit would have been depressing. She carried it off with eye-catching panache.

She looked up at him with the most incredible amber eyes and said, 'You must be Ulysses. Forgive me for presuming to use your first name without being properly introduced, but your mother has written so much about you that I feel I know you.'

Her voice was even more memorable than her appearance. It sounded breathy and childlike, laced with a honeyed drawl.

He prided himself on never forgetting a face or a name. It stood him in good stead in politics. But he had no idea who the callers might be – let alone how one of them knew him by name.

'You have the advantage of me, madame,' he said, uncomfortably aware of his own dishabille. With his sleeves rolled up and his shirt half unbuttoned, he must look like a loafer. Damn it all, he hadn't expected company – let alone such lovely visitors.

'Dear boy, surely your mother mentioned we were coming.'

Dear boy. Who the hell was she? And then it hit him. She had to be none other than the detestable Countess of Glenhaven. Although the countess hardly looked old enough to have a grown child, the other woman must be her daughter Alicia.

He had forgotten all about their proposed visit. 'I'm afraid you've arrived at the most inopportune time.' He gestured at the crepe-festooned wreath. 'We're in mourning and not prepared to receive visitors.'

'I understand perfectly,' Charlotte said, sweeping past him into the entry. With an eloquent shrug, she gestured at her dress. 'As you can see, my daughter and I are in mourning, too. However, your mother and I are very dear friends. I feel

AN INDECENT LADY 61

certain she would want to see me. Please let her know I'm here.'

Her authoritarian manner did nothing to endear her to him. He wasn't some damn servant to be dismissed at her whim.

Had he taken time to compose himself, he would have found a gentler way to break the news. But the countess had already walked into the parlor as if she owned the place.

He followed her. 'My mother is dead.'

'What?' The countess whirled around. Her dusky complexion went chalk white. Her lower lip trembled. 'What did you say?'

'My mother died three months ago.'

The countess's eyes rolled up in their sockets and she swooned. He just managed to catch her before she hit the oak planks.

'Conchita,' he shouted. 'Get in here.'

'Mother,' Alicia wailed, dropping to her knees and chafing the countess's hands.

'Conchita,' Ulysses shouted even more urgently. 'Get the smelling salts.'

'I carry some in my purse – for emergencies.' Alicia opened her reticule, took out a blue glass vial, opened it and held it under her mother's nose.

The scent of ammonia filled the air. The countess sputtered, coughed, and pushed the vial away.

'I'm all right,' she said, although she looked far from it.

Not taking her at her word. Ulysses carried her to the nearest chair and deposited her in it.

'Is it really true?' Charlotte asked, her extraordinary eyes shimmering with tears.

'I'm afraid so.'

'I must see Patrick.' Without further warning, Charlotte filled the room with great, gut-wrenching waves of sound that moved up and down the scale like the howls of a demented coyote.

Either she really had cared about his mother, Ulysses concluded, or she was a better actress than Lily Langtry.

From his bedroom at the front of the house, Patrick had heard the buggy come up the drive. He'd been too dispirited to get up and find out who was there, though. The unexpected arrival was quickly followed by a loud knocking on the door.

He had given Conchita standing instructions to send everyone away. He hoped Ulysses would have the good sense to do likewise.

Patrick had spent the last three months shut off from the world. He couldn't endure the thought of seeing people going about their business as though nothing had happened. He couldn't pretend to care about anything when the only thing he cared about was gone. Elke had been his true passion. Without her—

He never finished the thought. A terrible noise jarred him from his reverie. It was the sound of a woman crying – and as recognizable to anyone who had heard it before as a photograph. He had only known one woman who made such a production of her tears.

Bewildered, bemused – not even sure what year it was let alone what day – Patrick got to his feet. He followed the sound to its source at the bottom of the stairs. A woman approached him – and time spun backward.

'Is that you, Charlotte?'

His heart hammered. His spit dried. His breathing stopped. Good God. It was Charlotte and she didn't look a day older than she had the last time he saw her.

Had all the years between been a dream? Was Elke alive and well in Fredericksburg?

'Patrick?' Charlotte said in the breathy voice he remembered so well.

She ran across the floor, and threw herself into his arms. She even smelled the same, he thought as, shuddering and shaking, she soaked his shirt with her tears.

'Oh Patrick, my dear, I just can't bear it. I'm so sorry about Elke.'

Charlotte's declaration broke the spell. It wasn't twenty-seven years ago after all.

Alicia couldn't have been more astounded by her mother's behaviour if Charlotte had held up her skirts and started doing a cancan.

Alicia had never seen Charlotte fall apart like that, not even when her father died. That she would do so in front of strangers added to Alicia's discomfort. She had heard that the rules of society weren't quite so stringent in America. However, her exposure to her mother's family in Natchez hadn't borne that out. It shocked her to see her mother acting as if there weren't any rules at all.

'Perhaps we had better leave them alone,' she said to Ulysses.

'I think you're right,' he replied, looking equally abashed.

He led the way to a far corner of the parlor where neither of them could see their parents. He was, she decided, a most unconscionably handsome specimen of manhood – but definitely not her type. Perfect features, blond hair and blue eyes didn't set her pulse racing. She preferred a man with a few years on him, one with an interesting story.

'I suppose we had better introduce ourselves,' he said. 'I'm Ulysses Pride. But then, I imagine you knew that.'

'And I'm Alicia Hawthorne. I imagine you knew that, too.' Overwhelmed by the situation, she let go a little giggle.

She had never walked up to a man and introduced herself before, let alone one who — but for a quirk of fate — might have been her brother. 'I am so sorry for intruding like this. We didn't know about your loss. Mother and I saw your aunts and uncles in Natchez a couple of weeks ago and they didn't mention your mother's passing.'

'I imagine my father neglected to let them know. He's been taking it very hard.'

'My mother took my father's death hard, too. She really hasn't been the same.'

Alicia blushed at having such an intimate discussion with a total stranger. Having exhausted the only subject they had in common, she didn't know what else to say. Thank heaven, the sounds her mother had been making seemed to have diminished.

'We'll be on our way as soon as my mother is up to it,' she said.

Ulysses Pride gave her a bleak smile. 'I'm forgetting my manners. Won't you sit down?'

'I'd rather stand, thank you. It was rather a long ride from Fredericksburg.'

She turned to see her mother walk into the parlor, supported by Patrick Pride. 'Are you all right, Mother?' she said, hurrying to join them.

Just then, an elderly woman burst into the room,

took one look at Charlotte and let out a piercing scream. 'Aiyeee, I knew this house was haunted,' the crone said to Charlotte, 'but I didn't know it was haunted by you.'

Five

'I'm no ghost. I'm flesh and blood,' Charlotte said, taking Conchita's icy hand in hers.

'Then you must be a *bruja*,' the housekeeper sputtered, 'because you don't look a day older.'

'What a – a – an interesting thing to say.' Either Conchita had learned how to turn a weird sort of compliment – or her eyesight was failing. Charlotte suspected the latter.

Having an inane discussion with Conchita – the queen of beans, of all people – was the last thing Charlotte wanted to do while the news of Elke's death ached through her heart. Still, the housekeeper's intrusion did supply a little comic relief.

Conchita's suspicious gaze never left Charlotte's face. 'No one told me to expect company.'

'I'm afraid that's my fault,' Patrick said.

Keeping a firm grip on his arm, Charlotte graciously absolved him of responsibility. 'You had other things on your mind.'

So far, the conversation had limped along like a poorly played game of cards, Charlotte mused. She kept on dealing – but no one played the first hand. The star player had left the game and there was no one to take her place.

Alicia and Ulysses remained mute, as if the situation had rendered them incapable of speech.

AN INDECENT LADY

Patrick was monosyllabic — and Conchita continued to look as though she'd seen a ghost.

Charlotte had hoped to be alone in the parlor with Elke, having an intimate *tête-à-tête* by now. It would have been such a relief to unburden herself, to borrow a little of Elke's strength and optimism. The world was a darker, drearier place without her.

Charlotte leaned on Patrick even more as a sense of futility swept over her. He responded by tightening his grip on her waist. Despite his gaunt, disheveled appearance, his body felt as hard and strong as she remembered.

She had thought about him a lot in the years since she left this house — and often those thoughts had been tinged with bitter regret.

'Are you all right?' he asked.

'Not yet, but I will be,' she replied with renewed resolve. Perhaps things could still work out.

Decades spent in aristocratic and exotic milieux had prepared Charlotte to handle the most awkward situations. And God knew, they didn't get much more awkward than this.

'I don't know how the rest of you are feeling, but I could use a cup of tea,' she said, easing all of them past the discomfort of the moment.

'I'd prefer something a little stronger,' Patrick replied. His voice had a peculiar rasp, as if he hadn't used it much lately.

She gave his arm a sympathetic squeeze. The poor man looked as if he was in bad need of some tender, loving care — the kind Elke had supplied with unstinting abundance.

'I would love a cup of tea — if it isn't too much trouble,' Alica said.

'I'm afraid we're not in any condition to entertain guests. Conchita is our only servant,' Ulysses declared.

Clearly, he wasn't pleased to have them there. And yet she couldn't help thinking what a handsome couple he and Alicia made as they stood side by side.

Charlotte smiled up at him, in total disregard for his lack of hospitality. There were ways to melt the most unfriendly man. It shouldn't be too difficult to thaw this one. Especially when she had such a beautiful daughter for an unwitting accomplice.

Letting go of Patrick, Charlotte squared her shoulders like a general about to review the troops. Then she gave Ulysses her most dazzling smile. 'I hope you don't look on us as company. I'll be glad to help Conchita fix a tea tray.'

Not giving Ulysses the opportunity to voice another objection, she grabbed Conchita's arm and propelled her from the room. As she led the way to the kitchen, her glance took in a new piece of furniture here, an old and familiar one there.

All of them showed signs of neglect, though. The house was in as bad need of a woman's touch as its owner.

After Charlotte left, Ulysses went to the hearth and busied himself making a fire. He needed time to regain control of his emotions. Anger, dismay, and most of all, surprise, rioted through him.

Charlotte Hawthorne wasn't at all what he had expected. He had imagined her to be a frivolous creature who never had anything more on her mind than the latest fashion. However, after she recovered from her swoon and her tears, he had discerned a certain steel in her gaze and a quick mind behind her actions.

He didn't trust her. Had she really traveled thousands of miles to see an old friend? Would she make a graceful exit now that she knew of Elke's death?

Somehow, he doubted it.

The thought made him acutely uncomfortable. He cut an anxious glance at his father. Patrick would be such easy prey for a clever woman like Charlotte Hawthorne.

Ulysses waited until the logs caught fire, then joined his father and Alicia. They were seated side by side on the sofa. He settled in a nearby wing chair.

The girl was looking at Patrick with what appeared to be genuine concern. 'As I told your son, I fear we've come at the most inopportune time,' she said.

To Ulysses' amazement, Patrick replied, 'Nonsense. I'm very happy to have you here.'

Patrick did look better, Ulysses noted. He had a little color in his cheeks and his eyes had lost that dead glaze.

'I was so sorry to hear about your father.' Patrick gave Alicia the sort of fond glance he often bestowed on Reina. 'He was a remarkable man, and a brave one too.'

'You're very kind to say so.'

Kind didn't do justice to Patrick's remark, Ulysses thought with sour amusement. Considering the circumstances, his father's tolerance and generosity were nothing short of miraculous.

He'd supposed Patrick tolerated Elke's friendship with Charlotte. Now, Ulysses realized Patrick had played a willing part in the strange tangle of their relationships.

'My wife and I often talked of crossing the ocean to visit your parents,' Patrick said.

Ulysses grimaced. If they had, it was news to him.

'Speaking of trips, Alicia has had a long journey,' he said, wondering how she managed to look as fresh and dewy as an English rose at the end of what must have been a difficult day. 'Would you like to freshen up?'

She nodded. 'I do feel a bit travel-worn. But my things are all in the buggy.'

Good heavens, he'd forgotten all about the poor damn horse. 'Let me get them for you. I'll have one of the hands grain and water your horse, too.'

Color flared on Alicia's cheeks. She really was a beauty, he thought. 'I'm afraid you wouldn't be able to find what I need. You see, mother and I packed for an extended visit. The buggy is crammed with valises and trunks.'

'Why don't you come outside and show me what you want,' he said, getting to his feet and offering her his hand. He wouldn't mind having a little time alone with her to ask a few discreet questions.

'That's an excellent idea,' Patrick quickly agreed. 'I could use a few minutes to freshen up myself.'

News of Ulysses' return had reached the DeVargas household within hours of his arrival. That night, it was the chief topic of conversation at the dinner table.

'It's high time Ulysses gave some thought to his father instead of to his damn politicking,' Rio said.

'I hope he'll be able to draw Patrick out,' Velvet replied.

'He doesn't care about his father or he would never have left him alone,' Reina declared, venting her anger. She hadn't been able to forget what had happened in this very room three months ago.

AN INDECENT LADY 71

The memory of Ulysses' kiss ruined her appetite. Unable to eat, she fed Useful from her plate when her parents weren't looking.

The conversation drifted to other topics, but Reina continued to think about Ulysses. As the dinner hour ended with bedtime, she kept on coming up with new reasons to hate him.

He was a cad – a bounder – a self-righteous prig who sat in judgement on the rest of the world.

He had no more feelings than a tree stump.

The milk of human kindness had turned to vinegar in his veins.

He was self-interested, selfish, and cruel.

Time and again, she told herself she never wanted to see him again. By morning though, she had rationalized a reason for doing just that.

She spent the day doing a few of the thousand and one chores a working ranch demanded. She finished at four and returned home to change her weary mount for a fresh horse. She thought about changing her clothes, too, but she didn't want Ulysses to think she had gussied up on his account. So she settled for a brisk wash at a watering trough, then mounted up and whistled Useful to her side.

The short winter day was drawing to a close as Pride's Passion came into view. It was a lovely house, far grander than the one her father had built. She couldn't imagine why Ulysses spent so much time away from it. If she ever owned a spread like Pride's Passion, wild horses couldn't get her to leave.

As she rode up the drive, she saw a strange buggy parked in front of the house. From the sorry look of the horse and rig, it had to be a livery stable rental. She had heard that Patrick wasn't seeing anyone. Had the visitor come to see Ulysses?

Her question was answered as she saw him walk

out of the front door with a woman – a beautiful woman – on his arm. She took in every detail of the stranger's appearance.

The woman had that rare color of ash blonde hair that nature only bestows on the most fortunate females. Her strawberry and cream complexion had obviously never been exposed to the sun. Her slender body was as well put together as a thoroughbred filly's.

Although Reina never gave any thought to clothes, she knew quality when she saw it. The ladies in Kerrville would die to own such a fashionable traveling suit. The high collar hugged the woman's swan-like neck. The curve of the lapels emphasized her high bosom.

Either she was wearing a murderously tight corset, or she'd been blessed with an impossibly tiny waist. Who was she and what was she doing with Ulysses?

Reina's chest ached the way it had the day she'd been kicked by a mule. She had known he would choose a bride someday. Could this be that woman? She choked on the question.

Instinct urged her to leave. Before her body could obey, Ulysses looked up and saw her. 'Good afternoon, Queenie. What can I do for you?'

Not a damn thing, she thought angrily. 'I have some business with your father.'

'As you can see, we have guests. Perhaps you could drop by tomorrow.'

'Ulysses, aren't you going to introduce me?' the woman said. She had the darnedest accent. It made what she said sound fancier and more important than it should.

'Certainly. Lady Hawthorne, this is our foreman's daughter, Reina DeVargas.'

'Pleased to meet you, ma'am,' Reina said, feeling miserably aware of her mud-stained pants and worn-out jacket. She looked like hell – and felt even worse. Her stomach had a knot in it the size of a fist.

Without bothering to say goodbye, she reined her mare around and gave her a solid kick in the ribs. Unaccustomed to such rough treatment, the mare jumped like a startled rabbit.

The name Hawthorne stayed in Reina's mind all the way home – along with the vision of its elegant owner. Reina thought she had heard that name before – but she couldn't quite place where and how.

'What an extraordinary girl,' Alicia commented, as Reina rode off.

Ulysses tore his gaze from Reina. 'Extraordinarily rude, you mean.'

'Perhaps her manners leave something to be desired. But that's not what I meant. I've never seen a woman riding astride before, let alone wearing trousers while doing so.'

He took Alicia's arm and helped her down the porch steps. 'I assure you, it's not a sight you're likely to see again unless you happen to run into Reina.'

'You sound as though you don't approve. But it seems terribly sensible to me. Every time I've ridden to the hounds on a side-saddle, and fallen behind men who aren't half as good a rider as I am, I've thought about riding astride.' She had been holding her skirts up as she descended the stairs. Now she dropped them. 'Skirts can be such a nuisance. They're forever picking up dirt. The hems tear. And if you're not very careful, you trip over them.'

'You sound very liberated.'

Alicia looked up at him, and laughed. The sound

reminded him of a bubbling brook. 'My mother wouldn't be happy to hear you say that. I can't help being envious of a free spirit like – what did you say her name was? You called her Queenie but then you introduced her as Reina De – De Something.'

'DeVargas. Reina is her given name. It means queen in Spanish.'

'It suits her.'

'Suits her? You must be joking.'

'I thought she sat her horse like a pagan queen. With her dark complexion and black hair, she looked like one, too.'

A pagan queen, my foot, Ulysses thought, Reina DeVargas was a hoyden who cared nothing for the customs and habits of polite society.

'Her dog was remarkable, too. I never expected to see a quality Irish Wolfhound in Texas.'

So she didn't know the dog had been a gift to him from her mother. With any luck, she would never find out.

'I told you we packed for a long stay,' she said, gesturing at the heavily loaded buggy.

He gave her his practiced politician's smile. 'When your mother wrote that you were coming, I imagined you arriving with a retinue – footman, outriders, and a gaggle of maids.'

'We're nowhere near that pretentious. My mother let most of our servants go months back.'

He lifted an eyebrow. That hardly sounded like the Countess of Glenhaven he knew from her letters. 'I find that a bit surprising.'

'My mother is a very practical person. She said it was foolish to keep such a large staff since entertaining was out of the question after my father's death. I imagine she'll hire a new staff when we return to London.' She pointed at a valise. 'That's the one.'

AN INDECENT LADY

Ulysses took the valise in one hand, and offered Alicia the other. 'How long were you planning to stay with us? Before you learned about my mother, that is.'

'I don't know exactly. Mother said something about needing to be back in London by the summer.'

As Patrick washed his hands, he barely recognized the face he saw in the mirror over the sink. His nose and cheek bones stood out from his gaunt face. His eyes had a haunted look. He didn't smell all that good, either. When had he bathed last? He couldn't recall.

He hadn't given any thought to his appearance since Elke died, and hadn't realized how much he had deteriorated. He'd been so caught up in self-pity that he hadn't given a thought to much of anything.

Now, a deep feeling of shame swept through him. Charlotte had found the courage to go on without Nigel. Surely he could do the same.

He wished he had time to shave and bathe. But he didn't want to keep Charlotte waiting and it wouldn't take long to ready a tea tray. The thought made him smile.

Charlotte in the kitchen?

During their brief marriage, she had thrown a fit when he suggested she teach Conchita how to prepare something other than beans.

He combed his hair and his beard, and washed his hands, then hurried to his room to put on a clean shirt.

Ten minutes later, he returned to the parlor to find Alicia and Ulysses chatting amiably. The sound of their voices lifted his spirits.

Charlotte returned from the kitchen carrying the magnificent silver tea service she had sent Elke. 'You were right about not being prepared to receive guests,' she said with a rueful smile. 'I couldn't find anything to go with the tea except for some tinned biscuits.'

She put the tray down on the table in front of the sofa. 'Ulysses, does your father still keep the whisky in the library?'

'You have a good memory.'

'Would you fetch a bottle for your father? And take Alicia with you. I know she'd like to see more of the house.'

After they were gone, Charlotte turned her attention back to Patrick. Concern filled her eyes. 'You mustn't go on neglecting yourself. Elke would be so upset with you.'

Patrick drew a deep breath. 'I haven't figured out how to go on without her.'

She took his hand. 'I know. I felt the same way when Nigel passed away. But we have to get on with our lives for the sake of our children.'

'How have you managed?' Patrick asked.

'One day at a time. I wouldn't have managed at all if I didn't have Alicia to think of.'

'It's different with a son. Ulysses is his own man. He doesn't need me.'

'Perhaps not. But the ranch does. You must get back to it, my dear.'

'I've told myself that a hundred times. The thought of working all day and coming home to an empty house . . .' His voice trailed off. The sympathy in Charlotte's eyes told him she understood.

'I know, my dear, I know. I grew to hate Glenhaven Hall. Every time I turned a corner, I expected to see Nigel. It was more than I could bear. So I left.' Charlotte's expression brightened. 'You know, I may have the perfect solution to our mutual problems. I have no desire to return home just yet – and this house clearly needs a woman to bring it back to life. If I stayed, we could help each other through a very difficult time.'

Patrick let go a sigh. Although their marriage had been a colossal disaster, they had parted on good terms. But he wasn't sure he wanted anyone doing the things Elke had done.

'Please, don't think I'm trying to take Elke's place. Nothing could be further from my mind. However, we both know I did you a grave injustice years ago. I'd welcome the chance to make up for it.'

'You're very frank.'

'I'm too old and too tired to say one thing and mean another.'

She wasn't the woman he remembered. The old Charlotte had played verbal games. She never would have been able to organize tea, either. The old Charlotte didn't know how to boil water. The old Charlotte never would have made so unselfish an offer.

'I appreciate your kindness, but I can't take advantage of it.'

'You'd be doing me a great favour – and Alicia, too. She was so excited about seeing something of the American West. I would hate to have to disappoint her.'

'Can this be Charlotte Devereux, the belle of Natchez, talking? I thought you hated housework.'

Her smile deepened, revealing the entrancing dimples he had all but forgotten. 'I don't plan on doing any polishing and scrubbing myself. However, I do know how to run a large establishment. Glenhaven Hall had over one hundred rooms.' She took his hand and gave it a squeeze. 'Please, Patrick. I need to do something to keep busy.'

For a fleeting moment, he remembered how easily she had manipulated him years ago. But he put the thought aside as being unworthy of the woman she had become. 'I'd be happy to have you stay.'

'What's this about staying?' Alicia asked, preceding Ulysses into the parlor.

'Your mother just agreed to stay on and whip this house back into shape.' Patrick ignored the quick flare of displeasure on Ulysses' face. 'I was about to accept – that is, if you have no objections.'

Alicia clapped her hands in delight. 'I'd love it. To tell you the truth, Mr Pride, your ranch has truly entranced me. I'm anxious to get to know it, and you, better.'

Velvet was setting the table when Reina walked into the kitchen. 'Mother,' she said, 'does the name Hawthorne mean anything to you?'

Velvet was so startled that she almost dropped a plate. 'Did you say Hawthorne?'

'Then you have heard the name before?'

'Did the name belong to a beautiful lady?'

Reina shrugged. 'I suppose you could say so – if you like the type.'

'And did she have a handsome blond gentleman with her?'

'Not that I could see. Useless was with her.'

Velvet couldn't ignore the hurt in her daughter's eyes. 'Did he say something ugly to you?'

'No. He just introduced me to Alicia Hawthorne.'

'Alicia? The lady I knew was named Charlotte.'

'This one was called Alicia. I can't say she impressed me much. She had the strangest accent, and she was wearing the fanciest rig I've ever seen.'

AN INDECENT LADY 79

Strange accent? Fancy clothes? Velvet mused. She had heard that Charlotte and Nigel had a daughter. 'She must be Charlotte Hawthorne's daughter. What is she doing at Pride's Passion?'

'You mean aside from making eyes at Useless?'

Velvet ignored Reina's remark. 'The countess must be paying the Prides a visit. If that doesn't beat all. She always did have more nerve than—'

'What countess?'

'It's a long unhappy story, sugar.'

'You sound like you don't like her.'

'Actually, I liked her a lot. I'd be happy to see her again. But she did live by her own rules.'

Reina looked at Velvet with open curiosity. 'You never told me you knew a countess.'

Velvet pressed her lips together. There were lots of things she had never told Reina.

'Why would Countess What's-her-name visit the Prides? Were they friends?'

'Not exactly.' Velvet gestured at a chair, then took one herself. 'I guess it's time I told you about the Prides' past. Do you remember that day in the bakery when those boys said those awful things to you?'

'What does that have to do with the countess?'

'Everything. She's the reason Ulysses is a bastard.'

Reina's eyes widened in surprise. 'I know Ulysses' parents weren't married when he was born. But I don't see what that has to do with some high-falutin' English lady.'

'She was Patrick's first wife.'

'What?' Reina jumped to her feet so abruptly that her chair fell over backward. Hands on her hips, color flaring on her cheeks, she glowered down at her mother. 'I've never forgotten a thing about that day. I came home and asked you what the words *whore* and *bastard* meant. You told me a whore was a woman who sold her love to make lonely men happy – and a bastard was someone whose parents weren't married. You even told me you had been a whore, but that you had stopped being one long before you married Daddy. If you could tell me that, why didn't you tell me the rest?'

Velvet needed a moment to gather her thoughts. She set the chair back on its legs, then looked her daughter straight in the eyes. 'To be perfectly blunt, a whore gets in the habit of keeping secrets. I certainly did. I could have blown Fredericksburg wide open if I had told the so-called *good women* what I knew about their husbands and sons. If I could do that for strangers, I could certainly do it for the people I loved.'

'Is this Alicia Patrick's daughter?'

Velvet steeled her heart against the hopeful gleam in her daughter's eyes. 'No, honey. Her father is Nigel Hawthorne, the Earl of Glenhaven.'

'So she really is a lady. I thought Useless just called her that to make me feel bad, seeing as how he thinks I'm anything but.' Reina stopped pacing and sat back down. 'Did you know the earl, too?'

'Yes. So did your father. Rio used to call him Earl, as if it was his name instead of his title. They were quite fond of each other. Your father saved Nigel's life. The earl had come to Texas to hunt. He was on the trail of a cougar when he had an accident and broke his leg real bad. Your daddy set it better than most doctors could have. Then Patrick brought him to Pride's Passion for Elke to nurse.'

'I'm not following you. If Elke and Patrick were married, how did this Charlotte get into the picture?'

'Elke and Patrick weren't married. Charlotte and Patrick were. Elke was their housekeeper.'

AN INDECENT LADY 81

'Elke used to tell me how she fell in love with Patrick when she was just a girl. Why didn't they get married then?'

'You know Elke was orphaned right after she came to Texas. Otto Sonnschein took her in and gave her a job in his bakery. He married her when she was seventeen. She met Patrick afterward and, heaven help them, it was love at first sight.'

'But Otto died. He's buried here on Pride's land. Why didn't Patrick marry Elke then?'

'He didn't know about Otto's death. He'd gone home to Natchez to visit his folks. That's where he met Charlotte. The poor man wanted a wife and a family, and she was the prettiest thing in the world back then. When he brought her back to Pride's Passion, he found out Elke had been widowed.' Remembrance shuddered through Velvet. 'Those poor people were in such a mess. When Charlotte fell in love with the earl and ran off to England with him, it was a blessing all the way around.'

'Tell that to Ulysses,' Reina said bitterly.

Velvet sighed. 'I know. He was two years old by the time Charlotte and Patrick were divorced. He probably doesn't remember, but he was there when Elke and Patrick got married. It was a terrible scandal. My standing up with them didn't help matters.'

'When did Ulysses find out about his parents?'

'They told him after what happened in the bakery. I don't think he ever quite forgave them.'

'You should have told me,' Reina said, looking as though she wouldn't forgive Velvet either.

'By the time you were old enough to tell, the scandal had died down. I thought it best to let sleeping dogs lie.'

'But it could have made a difference with Ulysses and me,' Reina cried out.

Velvet longed to take Reina in her arms and soothe away the hurt in her eyes. However, she had always been a practical woman. The sooner Reina faced the truth about Ulysses, the better off she'd be.

'Ulysses will always associate you with his most painful memories. I said he forgave his parents. But I don't think he understood them. He never will unless he falls in love with someone the way they did with each other. Considering how he's closed himself off from his feelings, I don't suppose that will ever happen. Men like Ulysses don't marry for love. They marry because it's good for their careers or their bank accounts or their social standing.'

They don't marry whores' daughters, Velvet silently added.

Six

Time seemed to spin backward as Charlotte gazed around the familiar bedroom, taking in the four-poster bed, the marble-topped dresser, the large armoire. Nigel had recovered from his shattered leg within these walls. They had made love in this very bed, she thought, sagging onto the quilted cover.

'Nigel,' she whispered, as if by uttering his name, she could magically conjure him up.

She didn't miss the man he had become – but dear God, how she missed the man he had been before his infirmity twisted his nature as surely as broken bones had twisted his leg. She longed to curl up under the covers and hide her head the way she used to when she was the spoiled darling of the Devereux family.

There was no hiding from her past. Patrick had asked her how she managed to get on with her life. The truth was, she didn't have any choice. Nigel had been on the brink of bankruptcy when he died, leaving her to cope with the wreckage he left behind – a mountain of debt, a heavily entailed estate, and bitter memories.

When Nigel took her to England twenty-seven years ago, his fortune had been so vast that she'd never imagined anyone could spend it all. Nigel had encouraged her to indulge her passion for fashionable clothes and lavish parties. For three enchanted years, they'd been the most sought after couple in England.

He'd showered her with costly gifts – a gilded coach that rivaled the queen's, racing horses and thoroughbred dogs, fabulous furs and jewels. Even now, she couldn't help grinning at the memory of the diamond he'd bought for her navel during a trip to India – and the erotic uses he'd found for it. But her grin evaporated as she recalled the use she'd had for that diamond a few months ago. It had paid for their first class passage to America.

Dear God, where had all the money gone?

She had wearied of their frenetic social life years ago – the frantic jaunts to the four corners of the earth, the restless search for new thrills. After Alicia's birth, she had begged Nigel to settle down at Glenhaven Hall and raise a family.

'We're too young to spend our lives in the country,' he had said with a sardonic grin – and then proved his point in bed.

When a second pregnancy ended in miscarriage on a trip to Russia, she had blamed him. Over time their small disputes had escalated into all-out warfare. Her hands fisted as she recalled the night a so-called friend had told her that Nigel had taken a mistress.

'It's your fault,' he said when she confronted him. 'If you weren't so determined to bury yourself at Glenhaven instead of staying in the city with me, I wouldn't have turned to another woman for comfort.'

When he began gambling heavily, he blamed her for that, too. 'I'm bored,' he had said. '*You* bore me with your constant complaints. I need excitement in my life. You knew that when you married me.

For God's sake, it's not as though I can't afford to gamble.'

'I'm not worried about the money, Nigel, I'm worried about Alicia. She needs a father. She needs you.'

How wrong she'd been. She should have worried about the money. Alicia had turned out wonderfully despite Nigel's absences.

A shudder rippled down her spine as she thought about her last meeting with Nigel's solicitor. 'Unless you come up with a new source of capital to pay off your husband's creditors, you're going to lose everything,' he had told her.

'Everything?' she had gasped in surprise.

'Everything, my lady. Your London home, Glenhaven Hall and all the land that goes with it – to say nothing of the Hawthornes' good name.'

There was no sympathy in the man's eyes. He seemed to take particular pleasure in the prospect of her imminent ruin, as if what had happened was her fault and hers alone. But then, he'd never approved of Nigel marrying an American divorcée.

'You know I don't have money of my own.'

The disdain in his eyes chilled her to the bone. 'Your family does.'

She'd be damned if she'd tell him that her family's fortune hadn't survived the Civil War, and that they had been reduced to genteel poverty. She knew only one man who had the sort of fortune she needed. And that man had a very eligible son who would inherit all of his father's holdings.

As she left the solicitor's office, a plan had sprung to life in her brain. Other noble English families had saved their estates by marrying their titled sons to American heiresses. If it had worked for them, surely it would work for her.

What man could resist a beautiful girl like Alicia, especially with a clever mother manipulating the match behind the scenes?

Charlotte squeezed her eyelids tight, as if to close out the ugly memories clamoring for her attention. She had come to Texas for her daughter's sake. Surely there could be no guilt in that?

Elke's recent letters had mentioned her longing for grandchildren, and her growing concern that no woman would ever meet Ulysses' exacting standards. If Elke had been alive, she might have applauded Charlotte's scheme.

Charlotte let go a sigh and, with a shrug, got up to walk over to the formidable pile of luggage that Ulysses had dumped in the middle of the floor. As far as she was concerned, *if* and *should have* were the sorriest words in the English language. She had taken the only action left open to her. The rest was in the lap of the gods.

As she opened the first trunk she heard Alicia call through the door.

'May I come in, Mother?'

'Of course, darling.'

Alicia swept in, still wearing her smart gray traveling suit. Despite the grueling day, she looked as dewy fresh as an English garden.

'I thought you'd be unpacked by now,' she said.

'I laid down for a while.'

Alicia cut a worried glance at Charlotte. 'Are you sure it's wise for us to stay here under the circumstances?'

'I could hardly walk out on poor dear Patrick after promising to help him.'

'I just don't want you to take on too much. I'm worried about you. I have the feeling you've been keeping something from me.' Alicia opened a trunk, took out a dress and hung it in the armoire. 'Won't you tell me what's troubling you, Mother? I'm not a little girl. I'm twenty-two years old.'

'I haven't kept anything from you, darling. If I haven't seemed myself, it's because I've been through a very difficult time. But I have a feeling that Pride's Passion will be good for both of us. You'll see, my sweet. Everything is going to work out. Now, why don't you go to bed and let me take care of my things.'

She gave Alicia a peck on the cheek, propelled her to the door, and stood watching until Alicia disappeared inside her own room. She'd have to be more careful around Alicia in the future. She must never suspect why Charlotte had brought her mother to Pride's Passion.

Alicia undressed quickly, took her diary from the bedside table, turned up the kerosene lamp, and sat down on the edge of the bed. She could hear her moving around in the adjacent room.

What had her mother meant about things working out? The thought of Charlotte grappling with an unknown dilemma filled Alicia with a sense of helplessness. How could she pursue her own dreams if troubles dogged her mother?

Putting her worries aside, Alicia took a leather-bound book from the night table and chewed on the end of her pen while the events of the day ran through her mind. Then she began writing in her fluid, Spencerian hand.

Mother and I arrived at the Pride ranch late in the afternoon. Ulysses Pride admitted us to the house, and told us that Elke Pride was dead. Mother was visibly upset by the news.

Biting her lip, Alicia read what she had written. God, it was terrible! she thought as she tore out the offending page and crumpled it up. How could she ever hope to become a writer if she couldn't convey feelings along with actions?

Inspired by the writings of the Brontë sisters and Mary Shelley, she had begun keeping a daily journal five years ago. Her life had been incredibly dull in those days – her writing even duller. But she had kept on scribbling with dogged determination until now there were times when she was almost satisfied with her efforts.

Opening the diary, she began again.

> *Our hearts brimmed with happy expectation when Mother and I arrived at Pride's Passion this afternoon. In the waning daylight, the limestone mansion gleamed like gold – fool's gold as events soon proved.*
>
> *The empty windows gazed at us as if they resented our intrusion. The wind plucked at our skirts and whistled eerily as we alighted from our carriage. A raven soared over our heads like a harbinger of doom.*

She crossed out the word *raven* – Edgar Allen Poe had already written the quintessential raven – substituted *crow* and studied the sentence. *Crow* didn't work either, she decided with a swift shake of her head. It added nothing to the mood she was trying to create. She crossed it out, too, and wrote *vulture* instead. That's more like it, she thought, continuing with the story.

> *'Where is everybody?' I felt compelled to whisper, although no one was in sight.*
>
> *'I don't know,' my mother replied.*

AN INDECENT LADY 89

> *Seeing a black-draped wreath on the front door, she clutched my arm. 'What terrible tragedy has befallen this house?'*
>
> *As if in response to Mother's question, a handsome man with flaxen hair and cruel blue eyes opened the door. 'You've come at a terrible time,' he declared in a sepulchral voice. 'My mother is dead.'*
>
> *Hearing those dread words, my own mother wailed like a soul who has had a vision of Hades. 'What are we to do?'*
>
> *'Fear not,' I cried out, gathering my heavy skirt in my hands and racing to her side. 'I'll take care of you.'*

As her pen skimmed across the page, Alicia's lips were in constant motion. She liked to try out the sound of the dialogue before committing it to paper. She smiled, frowned, lifted one brow and then another, grimaced, tilted her head and shrugged with silent eloquence, unconsciously acting out each scene. Had anyone been in the room, they might have surmised what she wrote by the play of expressions on her mobile features.

She filled two pages, then paused a moment. The words she had crossed out seemed to rebuke her. One of these days, she was going to have to buy one of Mr Remington's marvelous typing machines so she could easily repair her mistakes.

But first, she'd have to come up with a plausible reason for needing one. She didn't want her mother to know what she was doing until she had a book contract in her hand.

Pursing her lips, she searched for a really dramatic way to conclude the entry, then grinned when it came to her.

> *There are mysteries locked away in the tenebrous shadows of this brooding house — secrets knit up in*

the hearts and minds of the two men who reside here. I will not rest until I have unraveled them all.

She stopped writing and closed the book with a flourish. Of course, there hadn't been any wind, and it was Ulysses who had rushed to her mother's aid – but it made so much better reading the way she wrote it. Besides, an author was entitled to take a little artistic license.

Still smiling, she turned off the light and crawled under the covers. Despite her worries about her mother, she felt better.

She had been afraid that her circumscribed life would never give her the sort of experiences she needed to become an author. Although she missed her father, his death had liberated her. Here she was in the wilds of the American West.

Since arriving in Texas, she had seen her first Indian, to say nothing of real cowboys, longhorn cattle, coyotes, and even cactus. She just knew she'd find an exciting plot here.

Closing her eyes, she began telling herself a story, the way she had every night of her life for as long as she could remember. Of course, she was always the heroine while the hero was a mature man with laughter – and a soupçon of world weariness – written on his face.

Patrick slept through the night for the first time since Elke's death. He woke to the delicious aroma of brewing coffee and the sound of women's voices drifting up from the ground floor. For a moment, he allowed himself to luxuriate in the peaceful feeling a man gets when he has a woman to see to his needs.

Then, remembering that the woman was Charlotte,

his euphoria faded. Should he have asked her to stay on? God knew, they had nothing in common when they were married.

Now though, grief bound them together more surely than their marriage vows ever had. Misery did love company, he thought as he swung his legs over the side of the bed.

In a week or two, Charlotte would grow weary of the ranch's isolation. By the new year, she was bound to long for the bright lights of a big city. In the meantime, he'd put up a good front and make her feel welcome.

He dressed quickly, then went to the water closet to relieve his bladder and wash up. He shaved off his beard, and decided to shave off his mustache, too.

Like most men, he'd worn facial hair since he was old enough to cultivate it. Feeling naked, he rubbed his jaw to accustom himself to bare skin where he had recently sported a luxuriant growth. Then he slicked his hair back with brilliantine, splashed on a liberal sprinkling of Florida Water, and looked at himself in the mirror.

Good God, what did he think he was doing, getting all dandied up? Would Charlotte think he had done it for her?

He'd soon set her straight if she did. It had nothing to do with her, he told himself as he opened the bathroom door.

Ulysses spent a restless night. He woke before dawn and got up to pace the floor while his facile mind wrestled with the problems presented by Charlotte Hawthorne's presence.

Patrick was in no condition to have company, let alone beautiful female company. He was far too vulnerable to be subjected to Charlotte's charms. She had damn near ruined his life once.

While Ulysses paced, he made up his mind to save Patrick from himself – and from the countess. He had to outwit the woman. Given her sex, that wouldn't be too hard.

The sound of a bedroom door opening and closing interrupted his train of thought. It had come from the countess's room. Her footsteps pattered down the hall. The light of her lamp flickered under his door.

What the hell was she doing up at this hour? He had expected her to sleep until noon.

Did she really intend to run the house?

He finished dressing, his lawyer's mind grappling with questions. Why was Charlotte here? He refused to take the reason she had given for her visit at face value. She must have an ulterior motive, and a compelling one, to leave a life of luxury behind. But he'd be damned if he could figure it out.

She had just inherited a fortune. She had an important place in society, and a beautiful daughter who was perilously close to spinsterhood if she wasn't soon married off. The two of them had every reason to stay in London.

Answers eluded him as the newly risen sun cast a roseate glow over the sky. He heard Patrick step into the hall, and opened his own door.

His eyes widened as he saw that the grizzled hermit with the haunted eyes had been replaced by a man who looked ten – no, make that fifteen – years younger than he had yesterday. The transformation couldn't have been more surprising – or compelling.

'Good morning, Father,' he said lamely. 'I'd like a minute of your time, sir.'

How sad, that they had drifted so far apart that they were reduced to talking like polite strangers. He wished he could take his father in his arms, give him a bear hug, and tell him how good it was to see him up and about.

He wished his arrival had been the cause. That Charlotte Hawthorne had wrought the miracle added to his sense of estrangement.

'Don't just stand there staring at me, son. If you have something on your mind, spit it out.'

Ulysses hadn't realized his gaze had been riveted on Patrick's face. 'I didn't mean to stare. It's just that you look so much better than you did last night.'

Patrick looked as uncomfortable about getting the compliment as Ulysses felt giving it.

Just then, Charlotte called from the foot of the stairs. 'Patrick, breakfast's ready.'

'She won't take it kindly if we keep her waiting,' Patrick said with an almost sheepish grin.

The way Charlotte had waltzed into the house and taken his mother's place galled Ulysses. However, he made up his mind to keep his thoughts and feelings to himself for the time being. He couldn't deny Patrick a respite from sorrow.

Marriage to Nigel had taught Charlotte to live in the moment. Things could be worse, she thought as she helped Conchita make a hearty breakfast that included eggs, some of Elke's homemade sausage, and biscuits – as well as Conchita's ever-present beans.

When the dishes were prepared, she put them in serving bowls and platters, carried them to the dining room, and put them on the buffet. In the absence of servants, they could wait on themselves.

'Something smells wonderful,' Patrick said, walking into the dining room with his son at his heels. 'Don't tell me you've learned to cook.'

Her heart fluttered at the sight of his freshly shaved face and she had a sudden – and totally inappropriate – memory of kissing him years ago.

'I have a rather limited cuisine. But I can prepare shirred eggs if the circumstances are desperate – and believe me, they are. It was either my cooking, or beans and side meat. I'll be glad when the rest of your help gets back. It's going to take a lot of work to have the house ready for the holidays.'

'Holidays?'

'It will be Christmas soon,' she said, filling his plate.

His eyes sobered. 'I wasn't planning on celebrating this year.'

She was about to object when she saw a look of satisfaction in Ulysses' eyes. He'd love to see her take a wrong step, she realized. What did he have against her?

'I'm sorry, Patrick. I was so happy to be here that – for a moment – I forgot we are both in mourning.'

Alicia couldn't have chosen a more opportune time to join them. Her cheerful presence diffused the tension in the room.

'Oh, Mama, you've made your famous eggs,' she said.

The tightness in Charlotte's chest relaxed. 'The only thing they're famous for,' she said, giving Patrick a grin, 'is their rarity.'

'Then I count myself doubly fortunate,' Patrick replied with his old charm, as he got up and helped Alicia into a chair.

'I can't tell you how happy I am to be here, sir,'

she said. 'I've read everything about the West, but it doesn't compare to seeing it in person.'

'Oh?' Ulysses lifted his brow, as if to say he could hardly credit Alicia with a taste for books. 'What have you read?'

'All the articles I could find. Fiction, too. I'm particularly fond of Bret Harte's *The Luck of Roaring Camp* and *The Outcasts of Poker Flat*. And I adored Mark Twain's *Roughing It*,' Alicia replied.

To Charlotte's delight, Ulysses' expression warmed. He looked so much more accessible when he smiled. 'Those are some of my favorites, too.'

After that, Ulysses and Alicia chatted amiably about books they had read. *Good for you, darling*, Charlotte silently cheered from the sidelines.

Patrick seemed content to enjoy his meal and leave the conversation to the young folks. It gave Charlotte a chance to study him. He had a formidable presence, an aura of accomplishment, that shone through his grief.

He finished his breakfast, then pushed his chair away from the table and got to his feet. 'It's high time I went back to work.'

Alicia and Ulysses got to their feet, too. 'Ulysses has offered to show me a little of the ranch. Do you mind, Mother?'

Charlotte repressed the urge to dance a little jig. Mind? She was ecstatic. 'I have lots to do. You two go off and have a good time,' she said, shooing them from her presence.

Patrick lingered a moment after they were gone. 'You might drop in and see Velvet DeVargas, if you have a chance.'

In the crush of events, Charlotte had forgotten that Velvet lived nearby. They had been friends once. Suddenly, she could hardly wait to see her.

'I'll make the time. And thank you for the reminder.'

'I'm the one who should be thanking you.' To her amazement, he gave her a quick hug. Then, seemingly embarrassed by the spontaneous gesture, he hurried from the room.

The warmth of his embrace lingered long after he'd gone.

Seven

Charlotte spent the morning taking stock of the Prides' larder. The spacious pantry bulged with Elke's delicious homemade jams, jellies, preserved vegetables and fruits. Bins contained dried apples and peaches from their orchard, and raisins from their grape arbor. Bacons, hams, and sausages hung from the rafters along with a couple of smoked turkeys.

The root cellar held an abundant supply of potatoes, squashes, carrots, turnips, rutabagas and other vegetables that would last the winter. Sacks of flour, cornmeal, sugar, and other baking necessities filled the supply room. The overall impact was one of wealth and care lavishly given. It was almost as if Elke had anticipated her own death and prepared for it, Charlotte thought as she finished her inventory.

Conchita's daughter, Maria, returned to the ranch at noon. She had been a seventeen-year-old when Charlotte last saw her, with a seventeen-year-old's uncertainties. Now in her mid-forties, she had matured into a self-confident woman.

Maria discussed a variety of cuisines – her own native Mexican foods, German dishes, a smattering of Cajun and French recipes – with the casual aplomb of an experienced chef. A half hour of conversation assured Charlotte that she need have no further worries about the quality of their meals.

'Elke taught me well. I miss her,' Maria concluded with heartfelt simplicity, her brimming eyes more eloquent than any words.

'I miss her, too,' Charlotte replied. 'I know I can never take her place, but I hope we will be friends.'

'I hope so, too, *senora*.'

Charlotte had never offered her friendship to a servant before. She had never been in such dire straits before, either. It would be good to have an ally in the house.

But for the changing of a line on a map, Maria's family might have owned a place like Pride's Passion. But for a war, Charlotte's parents would still own a large plantation instead of living amidst its wrecked splendor. She couldn't let Alicia suffer a similar fate.

Renewing her vow to safeguard her daughter's future no matter the cost, Charlotte returned to the matter at hand. After deciding the week's menus with Maria's help, Charlotte spent a couple of hours going through the rest of the house, making careful lists of all the things that needed to be done.

The new wing piqued her interest. Its fifteen rooms included a game room, a conservatory, and a music room on the ground floor, a magnificent master suite and several spacious guest chambers on the second story. All of them were beautifully finished with fine moldings, satiny plastered walls, gleaming oak floors – and all of them were empty.

Why had Patrick erected the wing if he and Elke never intended to furnish it? Had they built it with a daughter-in-law and grandchildren in mind? Did Ulysses already have a fiancée? Perish the thought.

At three that afternoon, Charlotte had completed her lists. Unable to act on them until the staff

AN INDECENT LADY

arrived, she changed into her second-best riding habit and headed for the barn. One of the hands saddled a gentle mare and gave her directions to the DeVargas ranch.

A thirty-minute canter brought her to a low one-story structure of the traditional Hill Country limestone. Although the house was nowhere near as grand as the Prides' mansion, it had a piquant charm. She expected no less of Velvet DeVargas's home. In her day, Velvet had been as fashionable and glamorous as an actress.

Charlotte dismounted and tied the reins to a hitching post. As she crossed the flagstone walk to the front door and knocked, her heart thudded with nervous anticipation.

A thick-waisted woman opened the door a crack and peered out myopically. 'Can I help you, ma'am? Are you lost?'

'Don't you recognize me?' Charlotte burst out.

The woman opened the door all the way. 'Is that really you, Charlotte, or am I dreaming?'

'I hope you don't think you're having a nightmare,' Charlotte teased, 'because it really is me.'

Velvet reached in her apron pocket and put on her glasses. Vanity kept her from wearing them most of the time, but she wanted to see more of Charlotte than a blurred image. 'Oh my God, you haven't changed a bit,' she exclaimed, repressing a twinge of envy as she thought about her own matronly appearance.

'Neither have you,' Charlotte replied.

'Oh, hell. We've got too many miles on us not to be honest with each other. The only thing you're likely to recognize on me is the red hair. And that comes from henna.'

'You look wonderful just the same,' Charlotte said

in that butter-wouldn't-melt-in-her-mouth voice that Velvet had never forgotten.

'Shame on me, keeping you out here on the stoop. Come on in and visit a spell. We've got a lot of catching up to do.' Velvet glanced at the lone horse tied to the hitching post. 'Did Nigel make the trip with you?'

'Nigel made a long trip nine months ago,' Charlotte replied cryptically.

Hearing the distress in Charlotte's voice, Velvet took a closer look at her old friend. Despite the countess's slender figure and youthful face, she looked a little worn around the edges, like a velvet gown that has gone to too many parties.

'Do you still enjoy a glass of sherry?' Velvet asked, leading the way into the seldom used parlor.

'I prefer brandy, if you have any.'

'Of course I do. I haven't changed *that* much,' Velvet replied, letting go a robust laugh.

Despite their different social status, she'd always felt a kinship with Charlotte. She'd never forgotten how Charlotte had welcomed her to Pride's Passion with open arms all those years ago, when other so-called decent women had crossed the street to avoid having to say 'good day.'

'There's nothing like a fine French brandy to ease you past the hard places in the road,' Velvet said on a sigh, 'and lately, sugar, there've been a lot of them.'

'You mean Elke?'

Velvet nodded. 'I knew she was sick, so her passing didn't come as a shock. It took poor Patrick by surprise, though. He's been taking it real hard. We've all tried to help him – only he seems bound and determined to shut his friends out.'

Velvet took a decanter from the sideboard and

poured two generous measures, then carried the glasses back to Charlotte.

'Don't stand on company, sugar. Take a load off,' she said, gesturing at the overstuffed sofa that had come all the way from Saint Louis five years ago and, thanks to their few visitors, still looked good as new. 'My daughter, Reina, met your daughter yesterday, so I figured you were here. Frankly, I'm surprised Patrick didn't send you packing the way he has everyone else.'

'Perhaps it's because Patrick and I have something in common,' Charlotte said in a shaky voice.

'Because you used to be married?'

'I suspect Patrick would just as soon forget that.'

'Nonsense. He and Elke were real fond of you.'

To Velvet's dismay, Charlotte burst into tears.

'I didn't mean to upset you. I guess you're not used to the idea that she's gone.' Velvet took Charlotte's hand to give it a reassuring pat.

Charlotte grabbed hold like a suckling pig clinging to a tit. 'I know it sounds selfish – but I'm almost angry at Elke for dying. I really needed to talk to her.'

Velvet couldn't help responding to the pain in Charlotte's voice. 'We weren't close like you and Elke – but you can talk to me. I'm pretty good at keeping other folks' secrets. What's this about you and Patrick having something else in common?'

Charlotte let go of Velvet's hand, picked up her glass, and drank the contents in a shuddering gulp. 'We're both in mourning. Nigel is dead.'

It took a moment for Velvet to digest the news. Nigel had been as full of life as any man she knew. In her mind's eye, she still thought of him as a handsome twenty-nine-year-old man, fussing and fidgeting because his shattered leg kept him confined to bed. 'I sure am sorry to hear that. You must miss him terribly.'

Charlotte let go a strangled laugh. She seemed oblivious to the tears coursing down her face. 'Miss him? If he were still alive, I'd kill him myself. He died in another woman's arms.'

'Were you and your father close?' Ulysses asked Alicia as they waited for one of the hands to saddle their horses.

Common courtesy demanded he make an effort to entertain the girl. That she was exceptionally pretty made the task less odious. However, he planned to use the time alone with her to learn more about her mother's plans.

'Not very,' she replied, with a wistful smile. 'Mother and I spent most of our time at Glenhaven Hall and Father preferred London. It wasn't unusual in our circle – or any circle for that matter.'

'What do you mean?'

'While men go about their business – adventures in business, politics and war – women and children have traditionally kept the home fires burning.'

'Does that bother you?'

'I'd be a fool to find fault with the natural order of things, wouldn't I?'

Her reply startled him. She sounded as though she'd read Darwin. 'I don't think you're foolish at all. It is the natural order of things, and you're very wise to realize it.' Unlike Reina, who thought she could do most things better than a man, he silently added.

The arrival of the horses interrupted the conversation.

He couldn't help admiring the handsome picture she made in her sidesaddle, with her fashionable riding habit draped decorously over her limbs.

He'd wager she would never dream of riding astride and flaunting her body in men's trousers the way Reina did.

No matter what he thought about the countess, there could be no arguing that Alicia was a lady through and through.

Starfire danced eagerly as he vaulted into the saddle.

'What a magnificent horse,' Alicia enthused. 'What's his breeding?'

'Your guess is as good as mine. He ran wild up until a few months back.'

'Did he run off from some farm?'

'In Texas, a man can get strung up for helping himself to another man's horse.' He smiled at her inexperience. 'Pride's Passion used to be full of wild herds. We call them mustangs. Starfire was the last of the breed on Pride's Passion. It took years to capture him.'

He set the stallion to an easy trot that would permit Alicia to keep up.

'Mother tells me you own over a hundred thousand acres,' she said.

So Charlotte had been talking about the size of the ranch. Why should she be interested? *Interesting – very interesting*, he mused, filing the information away. 'Your mother was mistaken. I don't own anything. My father does.'

'But the ranch will be yours someday. I can't imagine owning a place that's larger than some European countries – let alone running it.'

Neither could he. 'What else has your mother told you about the ranch?'

'Not enough, I assure you. I'm anxious to know more.'

Either Alicia was more devious than she looked

with those guileless blue eyes, or she was just what she appeared to be – an artless young woman with a lively curiosity.

'I would have loved growing up in a place like this,' she enthused. 'My father traveled constantly. But, except for a couple short trips to the Continent, Mother and I were a couple of stay-at-homes.'

She was pretty enough to make him wish he had something to talk about, rather than a sickly, housebound childhood. 'Living on a cattle ranch can be interesting – even dangerous at times,' he said, although he had never experienced those dangers himself.

'I just knew it!' she said triumphantly. 'I imagine you have had some fascinating experiences. When was the last time you fought the Indians?'

He reined to a stop and stared at her. All those books had filled her head with a lot of nonsense. 'I hate to disillusion you, but the Indians were on reservations before I grew up.'

She colored prettily. 'Oh, dear, then you haven't killed anyone?'

He grinned. 'I had a reputation for being quite blood-thirsty when I was in court. I'm a lawyer.'

'Do you try cases?'

'I did, before running for public office.'

'Have you ever tried any murder cases?'

'I handle property disputes, wills, partnerships – things like that. Still do when I have the time, although my partner does most of the work these days.' Seeing her eyes glaze over, he felt a brief twinge at having disappointed her. A pure male need to show off in front of an attractive female prompted him to add, 'I'm a state senator now.'

'How fascinating,' she said, although the look

on her face made it clear she thought nothing of the sort.

He'd never known a girl to be so interested in blood, gore, and mayhem. Could that have something to do with whatever had brought her and her mother to America? Were they in some sort of trouble? Could it be that the earl hadn't died of natural causes? Had the countess hurried him to his last good night to get her hands on his estate?

'You must think I'm perfectly mad, asking such questions,' she said, dimpling so prettily that she almost succeeded in distracting him.

'Not at all. Would you mind if I asked one of my own?'

'Turnabout is fair play.'

'How did your father die?'

Talk about treating her like a witness, he thought, seeing her complexion pale. 'I know it's a painful subject, but I don't want to say the wrong thing to your mother.'

'I see.' She bit her lip. 'My father was in London when he passed on. He died in his sleep. You'll understand if I prefer to change the subject.' Ulysses Pride had to be the strangest man she'd ever met. One minute he seemed like the ideal companion for a leisurely cross-country ride, and the next he acted like the perfect cad.

Surely a well-bred man should have the sense not to bring up a painful subject. Of all the cheek! She was tempted to ask for the gory details of his mother's death.

Instead, she cracked her whip across the mare's flanks and the horse leapt forward, gathering speed with every stride and leaving Ulysses in her dust. That ought to show him a thing or two about the natural order of things, she mused, enjoying the thought of his discomfiture.

By the time he caught up, she had managed to outrun her outrage. 'What are those ugly cows with the huge horns?' she asked, pointing at a group of cattle in the distance.

'They're Longhorns.'

'They don't look a bit like English cattle,' she said, taking in the dangerous sweep of their horns, and thanking heaven a barbed wire fence separated them. 'How many Longhorns do you own?'

'It's been a long time since anyone counted them.'

She frowned. Did he think she was a complete idiot? 'We raised champion Herefords at Glenhaven. I can't imagine not knowing how many we owned.'

'The Longhorns were here when my father claimed the land – just like the horses. All a man had to do if he wanted to start a cattle ranch was round them up and brand them.'

So he had been telling the truth. She gave him an encouraging smile. She wanted to hear all about life on a working cattle ranch. 'Where did the cattle come from originally?'

'The Spanish conquistadors brought them by ship three hundred years ago. A few got away and they've been multiplying ever since.' He looked askance at her. 'Are you sure I'm not boring you?'

'Not at all. Do ranchers still help themselves to cattle?'

'Rustling is a hanging offence in Texas. You don't need a judge or a jury – or a lawyer either – if you catch someone in the act.'

A frisson of pure excitement raced down her spine. 'Have you ever hung a rustler?'

'I'm in the other end of the law business. But we

AN INDECENT LADY

have fewer problems with rustlers than most big spreads. One of our former hands is a famous Texas ranger. Terrell Meeks still keeps an eye out for the ranch. Rustlers don't want to cross his path, so they stay away. I guess you could call Terrell a legend in his own time.'

Alicia shivered with delight. She'd never heard a man called a legend before. 'Does he visit often?'

'He just got transferred back to Kerrville a couple of months ago. If you'd like to meet him, I'll ask him to come out to the ranch the next time I'm in town.'

'How thoughtful of you. When might that be?' Alicia struggled to mask her excitement. A man who was a legend in his own time might be the very man to base her first book on. She could hardly wait to hear Terrell Meeks relate some of his exploits.

Although Ulysses continued speaking, she no longer heard him. Her imagination was talking much louder.

Terrell Meeks would be young – but not too young. Muscular – but not musclebound. A man's man – who knew how to treat a woman. He'd ride like the wind – and kiss like the devil.

They'd meet in Kerrville by accident. One look at her and he'd be instantly smitten. The street would be puddled from a recent rain. He'd throw his coat down to keep her feet from getting wet.

'You don't need to do that,' she'd say with a maidenly blush.

He'd stare so deep into her eyes that she'd feel him reaching out to her soul. 'I do need to do that. I couldn't let a lovely lady ruin her shoes.'

No, she thought – she could damn well come up with something more original. Sir Walter Raleigh had long ago done the quintessential coat-in-the-mud trick.

'I think we could both use another drink,' Velvet said, getting to her feet and refilling their glasses.

Charlotte's confession had shaken her. It was shocking to hear of Nigel's infidelities. But who the hell had been cruel enough to tell her the truth?

Velvet carried the refilled glasses back to the sofa and handed one to the countess. 'Are you sure you know what you're talking about? I don't have to tell you how people love to gossip.'

'Nigel's mistress was so afraid she'd be blamed for his death that she sent a messenger to fetch me. For Alicia's sake – to spare her from knowing the truth – I brought Nigel's body back to our London townhouse and put him in his own bed before I called the doctor.'

'You poor thing. You've been through hell.'

'That isn't the half of it.' Charlotte hadn't started out to tell Velvet the truth. Now, the secrets she had kept locked in her heart all these months demanded to be let out. 'He left me with more debts that I can possibly pay. I'm broke, Velvet.'

It was Velvet's turn to finish her brandy in one long gulp. 'You and I have had such different lives that your definition of broke may not be the same as mine. Do you mean you're going to have to sell a piece of property, or let a few servants go?'

Charlotte grimaced at Velvet's naiveté. 'I can't sell any property because it's all entailed, and I let the servants go months back. The creditors were all but knocking at the door when Alicia and I left London. I sewed my jewels into my clothes or I might not have been able to take them with me. If I don't come up with some money soon, we'll lose everything.'

'I don't know what to say.'

'You don't have to say anything. I feel better just getting it off my chest.'

'Does Alicia know any of what you've told me?'

Charlotte felt the blood drain from her face. 'God, no. I want you to swear you'll never tell her. I came here to shield her from the truth.'

'She'll find out eventually.'

'No, she won't – at least not for the foreseeable future if she gets married and stays here.'

'Is that why you brought her to America – to look for a suitable husband?'

'Yes, and I'm not ashamed of it, either,' Charlotte said, holding her head high. 'I'd do anything for my daughter.'

'You don't have to explain. I'm a mother, too. And I've got my own problems where Reina is concerned. But why didn't you stay in London so she could marry an English blueblood like her father?'

'I'd sooner die than have her marry someone like Nigel. He made my life hell. Besides, no one in our circle would have her under the circumstances. It will take a small fortune to pay Nigel's debts.'

'Your Alicia isn't likely to find a rich husband in Kerrville.'

'You couldn't be more wrong. I've already found one for her,' Charlotte said quietly.

Understanding dawned on Velvet's face. 'My God, you mean Ulysses.'

'Don't you dare judge me, Velvet. You'd do the same in my shoes.'

'But you don't know him.'

'I know his parents. That's good enough. The acorn never falls far from the tree.' Thinking she might have revealed too much, Charlotte quickly changed the subject. 'Why are you worried about Reina?'

'For the same reason you're worried about your girl. I want her to marry and settle down.'

'Do you have someone in mind?'

'I sure do. You might remember Terrell Meeks. He's a Texas ranger now, and as fine a man as you could meet.'

'So what's the problem?'

'They like each other well enough. However they don't seem to have any romantic inclinations.'

Charlotte choked on a giggle. Velvet ought to be an expert when it came to romantic inclinations. In the old days, Velvet's boudoir would have given a eunuch sexual ideas.

'With some careful planning, any woman can arouse a man's interest. Given propinquity, nature should take care of the rest.'

'Propinquity? Is that an English word for good old-fashioned lust?'

'You could say that. Propinquity is a powerful weapon in any woman's armory.' Charlotte leaned closer, and lowered her voice. 'I think I have the perfect solution to both our problems.'

Velvet jumped to her feet. 'I turned over a new leaf when I married my Rio. I won't do anything immoral, dishonest, or illegal. And I sure as hell won't do anything that might hurt my girl.'

Charlotte gave Velvet a reassuring smile, took both her hands and tugged her back down onto the sofa. 'You won't have to. I promise, your Reina will have the time of her life.'

Eight

'I will not get all gussied up.' Reina stamped a boot shod foot for emphasis.

'Don't you want to make a good impression?' Velvet replied with infuriating serenity. She had been rummaging through Reina's wardrobe, clucking like a flustered hen at the preponderance of male clothes.

'I don't care what the countess and her inspid blonde daughter think of me. And I sure don't want to waste an afternoon drinking tea when there's work to be done.' Furthermore, although Reina dared not say it, she wasn't ready to see Ulysses again.

Since hearing the true circumstances surrounding his birth, she'd been thinking about him a lot – rationalizing his faults in the light of her new knowledge, and wondering if she hadn't judged him too harshly in the past.

She had assumed he was one of the many children who had been born on the wrong side of a wedding ceremony during the turbulent war years. No one thought any the less of those children – certainly not her.

Now she knew that Ulysses' circumstances were scandalously different. He had idolized his parents more than most kids – looked up to his father and worshiped his mother. How horrified he must have been when he learned the truth about them – and himself.

She felt so sorry for him that she had been trying to work up the nerve to see him in private, to attempt to forge some sort of truce between them. But she wasn't sorry enough to sit by and watch him making eyes at Alicia Hawthorne. The thought of it churned in her stomach like spoiled meat.

With a despairing shake of her head, Velvet finally took Reina's second best frock off its hanger and lay it down on the bed. 'If the countess was kind enough to invite you, the least you can do is put on a dress.'

'Oh please, Mother, not that one.' Reina had reluctantly agreed to buy the dress a couple of years ago. But wearing it required a corset, to say nothing of a bustle that made sitting in a chair an act of torture. She snatched it off the coverlet and hung it back up.

She couldn't imagine why her mother was so set on the visit. She'd seen the way other women treated Velvet – the cool disdain, the behind-the-back whispering – and she had no desire to see her mother endure more of the same. It was bound to be a miserable afternoon for them both.

Velvet checked the watch pinned to her apron. 'We're going to be late if you keep this up.'

'I'll go – as I am.'

'Suit yourself. I guarantee you'll be sorry.' Velvet eyed Reina from head to toe with obvious displeasure. 'Just let me brush your hair out.'

Not giving Reina a chance to object, she tugged her over to her dressing table, quickly undid the thick plait that hung down Reina's back, and applied the brush vigorously until Reina's hair rippled around her shoulders in a cascade of waves.

'At least, with your hair down, no one will mistake

you for a boy,' Velvet said grimly, then gentled her words with a smile. 'You have such beautiful hair, you ought to wear it down all the time.'

'Sure. And the next time I chase a steer into a mesquite thicket, I'll leave half my hair behind.'

'Then leave chasing them to the hands,' Velvet snapped.

Reina swallowed an angry retort. She rarely had words with her mother. It made her intensely uneasy, as though the floor had shifted under her feet – and she blamed the countess. The woman had interrupted the even tenor of their lives.

Since her visit, it had been 'the countess' this and 'the countess' that. Reina had heard enough about Charlotte Hawthorne to last a lifetime. By the time she hitched up the buggy and drove it to the front of the house, she'd made up her mind that she'd sooner chew nails than drink tea with the countess and her daughter.

Velvet was waiting on the front stoop. She had changed into a green velvet jacket that complemented her plaid wool skirt. A feathered bonnet perched on the top of her head like a prairie chicken on its roost. Only her work-reddened hands betrayed the fact that she didn't make a practice of going to tea – and she quickly covered them with fine leather gloves.

'I don't know why you're being so disagreeable,' she said after she was settled in the front seat beside Reina. 'I thought you'd be happy to have someone your age living nearby.'

Reina gave Velvet her most winning smile. 'I don't need friends. I've got you and Dad and the ranch. Besides, I don't have anything in common with a girl like that.'

'Don't you want to have fun?'

'I have all the fun I can handle, working with critters. I love what I do.'

'You know what they say about all work and no play. It's time you had some good times, honey. And you're dead wrong about not having anything in common with Alicia. *Neither one of you is married.*'

Where in the world did that come from? Reina wondered, cutting a glance at her mother. She couldn't recall ever seeing Velvet in that outfit, either. This afternoon, her mother looked and acted like a fashionable stranger.

'I don't understand why you're so set on being sociable all of a sudden.'

'I'd have been a lot more sociable if anyone had ever given me the chance – besides Elke,' Velvet replied grimly.

Reina felt her chest tighten. Velvet rarely discussed her lack of a social life. But for the damn countess, she wouldn't do it now.

'Have you considered the possibility that you might actually enjoy yourself this afternoon?' Velvet asked.

'I'm not counting on it,' Reina muttered.

'Promise you'll at least try. And don't forget your manners.'

Reina grimaced. 'Don't worry. I won't slurp my tea from the saucer or chew with my mouth open.'

Thinking she had covered every possible contingency, Reina pulled a Pendelton blanket over their laps to ward off the chill. The air had a real nip. It was the sort of winter day when sensible folks stayed home by their fires. The sky looked threatening, as though a blizzard were in the offing. Strange, she mused, because it seldom snowed in the Hill Country. At least it would give them an excuse to leave early.

AN INDECENT LADY 115

She set the horse to a smart trot and concentrated on her driving. A half hour's ride brought them to the Pride mansion. She reined the buggy to a stop, jumped to the ground and hurried to help her mother down, hoping her solicitude would smooth over the awkwardness between them.

Velvet gestured at the door. 'Look, the mourning wreath is gone.'

Reina's gaze followed where Velvet had pointed. Just then, the door burst open and Alicia Hawthorne came charging out as though her drawers were on fire. 'I'm so glad you're here, Reina,' she called out gaily. 'I've been hoping we'd get to spend some time together.'

Her fashionable dress whipped in the breeze, revealing her slender figure. The wind caught at her hair, tugging ash blonde tendrils from the chignon at her nape. With a sinking feeling, Reina realized that Alicia was even prettier than she remembered.

'You must be Velvet DeVargas,' Alicia said, offering her hand to Velvet. 'My mother has told me so much about you.'

I'll just bet, Reina thought, refusing to be taken in by Alicia's slick manners. Miss La-di-dah Hawthorne reminded her of one of those traveling salesmen who stopped by the ranch occasionally – all oily charm and about as trustworthy as a snake in the grass.

'It's a pleasure to meet you too, Alicia,' Velvet said, with an almost beatific smile.

Alicia took Velvet's arm. 'Mother is waiting for us in the parlor.'

Reina reluctantly trailed behind them as they made their way inside the house. She hadn't paid a visit since the funeral but Velvet had told her how neglected the place had gotten. There was no sign of that neglect now, though.

As they entered the parlor, a woman rose from the sofa – a breathtakingly beautiful woman who was as exquisitely put together as one of those new-fangled mannequins in Schreiner's Mercantile. The woman gave Velvet a smile of such melting warmth that it almost overcame Reina's antipathy.

'Velvet, I'm so happy you could come,' she said. 'I've been looking forward to our little get-together all week.'

Reina listened for a false note in the countess's voice – and failed to find one.

'And this must be your daughter.' The countess looked Reina over from head to toe, then took Reina's calloused hands in her own. Reina half expected the countess to say something derogatory about her calluses and broken nails. To her infinite surprise, the countess exclaimed, 'You're even lovelier than I had imagined. In fact – although you have your father's coloring – you look very much the way your mother did when we first met.'

The compliment breached Reina's carefully marshalled defenses. Her misgivings faded in the face of the countess's considerable charm.

'And you don't look old enough to be her mother,' Reina blurted, indicating Alicia with a jerk of her head.

The countess let go a throaty chuckle. 'What a lovely thing to say. I could listen to you say things like that all day. Please, come sit by me.'

Reina found herself following the woman to the sofa as docilely as a shoat being led to the slaughter.

Ulysses was at his mother's desk in the library, working on the ranch's books, when he heard the front door open. Although he knew Velvet and Reina were coming to tea, he continued making entries.

His mother used to keep the books and no one had touched them since her death. Ulysses had volunteered to bring them up to date. He sat back, going over what his recent labors had revealed. He hadn't realized the full extent of his father's wealth.

Ranching had boomed after the war. His father had gotten top dollar for every steer he drove to market. Profits had increased when the coming of the railroads eliminated the need for long and risky cattle drives. The price of cattle had risen with the ever-increasing demand.

His father was a millionaire several times over. Could that be the reason for the countess's visit?

Don't go borrowing trouble, Ulysses told himself. Countess Glenhaven had her own fortune. She didn't need Patrick's. And she certainly had lived up to the bargain she had made with Patrick.

The oak floors gleamed with fresh wax, the furniture had been polished to a mirror sheen, the bedding no longer smelled musty, and the scent of wood fires burning on every hearth mingled with savory aromas coming from the kitchen.

The house looked every bit as cared for as it had during his mother's life – better to be honest. Elke had been too busy – or too ill the last few years – to bother with feminine touches like keeping vases filled with flowers grown in the conservatory.

Charlotte Hawthorne seemed too good to be true. Yet his observations hadn't produced a single reason for him to suspect her of anything, other than loneliness and the desire to be needed.

As a lawyer, success often depended on his ability to judge character. He wasn't accustomed to being wrong. But he couldn't deny the evidence. He had misjudged the countess.

A week ago, taking tea with her would have been unthinkable. Now, he found himself looking forward to feminine company – even though that company included Reina.

He finger-combed his hair, straightened his tie, put on the jacket he'd left hanging over the back of his chair, then followed the lilting sound of female voices to the parlor. The double doors were open wide. He paused in the entry, his gaze travelling from woman to woman.

Charlotte was dressed in black *peau de soie*. She had alleviated the somber color by draping a paisley scarf around her shoulders. Alicia wore a soft woolen dress in a delicate shade of pink that exactly matched the bloom on her cheeks. Velvet had on a flamboyant outfit that pushed good taste to its outer limits – but miraculously didn't go one step beyond.

Ulysses' approving smile faded as his gaze came to rest on Reina. In her boots, denim pants and drab work shirt, she looked like a weed intruding on a colorful garden. She needed a stern talking-to about proper decorum. Sadly, her mother didn't seem to realize it.

If the sight of Reina hadn't made him so damn angry, he might even have felt sorry for her. His anger mushroomed as he thought about the way he got all hot and bothered every time he looked at her – and he blamed her for it. God knew, the sight of a decent woman never made him feel that way.

Hell and damnation. No one else had ever made him think – and feel – and imagine – the things Reina did.

Seeing the way her hair spread across her shoulders like a cloud of black silk, he couldn't help picturing the way it would look spread across his pillow.

Seeing how her trousers molded her thighs, he could almost feel those thighs wrapped around his hips.

Seeing her full breasts straining against her blouse, he had a vivid vision of their silken weight in his hands.

It wasn't right – it wasn't honorable – it wasn't seemly to feel that way. Damn Reina. *Damn her to hell,* he thought as he struggled to subdue the heat flooding his loins.

He had sown his share of wild oats in college. There had been enough shop girls – girls whose reputations preceded them and who relished the prestige of going out with a Harvard man – to satisfy a satyr's lust.

Since coming home three years ago and setting up his law practice, his behavior had been – by necessity – far more circumspect. But no one expected him to be a saint.

Before his mother's death, he had taken his pleasure at sporting houses in Austin and San Antonio. Since then, he'd lived like a eunuch.

He hated himself for using a woman, even a whore, to satisfy his lust. He wouldn't succumb to such temptation again, he told himself sternly. Whores offered only temporary relief. He needed a wife, someone he'd be proud to have on his arm – someone like Alicia, he realized with a start.

Just then, Charlotte saw him in the doorway and brought his musing to an end. 'Please join us,' she said, gesturing to the seat alongside Reina.

'Queenie, you didn't have to dress up on my account,' he drawled as he crossed the floor.

Reina felt her face heat up. She would have given

a great deal to be able to plant one of her boots on an unmentionable part of Ulysses' anatomy.

Goaded by his caustic comment, she turned to the countess and said the first thing that came to mind. 'I would have changed, but I worked with the cattle until the last minute, and Mother was afraid we'd be late.'

'Don't give it another thought, dear. We're just glad you're here,' Charlotte replied before turning to Ulysses. 'Is your father with you?'

'He's upstairs, *changing*,' Ulysses said with heavy emphasis, as if to insure that Reina took his point.

She was sick of the way he sharpened his tongue on her. How could she have been foolish enough to imagine a truce between them? He was as odious, as priggish, as cold and unfeeling as ever.

'Do you really work with the Longhorns?' Alicia asked. 'I thought they were dangerous.'

Reina let go a little laugh. 'What – or rather *who* – gave you that impression?' she said, although she felt damn sure she knew the answer.

'Ulysses told me a ranch can be a dangerous place. I just assumed it had to do with the cattle. They certainly look formidable.'

Reina cut what she hoped was a scathing glance at Ulysses. 'They aren't at all dangerous – that is, if you know what you're doing.'

Alicia leaned forward, an eager expression lighting her eyes. 'What exactly *do* you do with them?'

'Everything a man can do – only I do it better. I help with the dipping in the summer, pull calves in the fall, give them extra feed in the winter, brand and castrate in the spring . . .'

Her voice trailed off as she became aware of the silence that met her mention of castration.

'You sure have a way with words, Queenie,'

Ulysses said, a broad smile making him look even more handsome, 'but some of them aren't used in polite company.'

Reina didn't give a damn what Ulysses thought of her — seeing as how he always thought the worst — but the disappointment in her mother's eyes cut all the way to the bone.

Maybe Ulysses was right about her after all. She didn't belong in polite company. God knew, she didn't know how to dress or to act — or what to say. She'd rather rope an angry bull than face another sociable afternoon like this one.

'I'm sorry. I didn't mean to upset you all,' she muttered, lowering her gaze to the floor and wishing it would open up and swallow her before she had a chance to make an even bigger fool of herself.

Charlotte let go a breathy chuckle. 'There's no need to apologize. I find your candor quite refreshing. Ulysses is probably unaware of the fact that we raise champion Herefords at Glenhaven. I'm proud to say they are the best in all Great Britain. There isn't a term Alicia and I haven't heard when it comes to cattle. However, I am surprised to learn that your calves are born in the fall.'

Latching on to Charlotte's verbal lifeline, Reina lifted her gaze. 'Spring-born calves can die from an infestation of flies and their larva,' she explained, her aching heart and hurt feelings taking shelter in the warmth of the countess's amber eyes.

'Don't you run the risk of losing calves if you have a hard winter?' the countess countered.

'There's always some risk when you're raising cattle. We weigh one against the other.'

'You must have made the right choices. Elke wrote me about how well you all have been doing.'

'We have,' Reina answered with unbridled enthusiasm. At last, someone wanted to talk about something she knew. 'We can't keep up with the demand for beef. My father says it's because immigrants have been pouring into the country, taking jobs in all those new factories back East. He says a man needs meat in his stomach if he's going to work hard all day.'

'Fascinating, just fascinating,' the countess murmured as though she really meant it.

'My Reina can tell you anything you want to know about ranching,' Velvet boasted, her pride in Reina seemingly restored. 'She had a good teacher in Rio.'

'I'd love to hear more of your experiences,' Alicia interjected. 'Perhaps we could go riding together tomorrow.'

The appearance of a maid pushing a tea cart prevented Reina from answering. Charlotte pointed to the area in front of Alicia's chair. 'Just put the cart there, Lupe.'

In addition to an elegant silver tea service, the cart held plates of dainty sandwiches with the crusts cut off, fancy pastries all iced and decorated, an assortment of cookies, and some sort of funny-looking biscuits chock full of brown specks that looked like bugs from a distance, but were most likely currants, considering this wasn't a cattle drive.

'Are you expecting anyone else?' Reina asked.

She was about to add that it looked like enough food to feed the entire bunkhouse when the countess answered, 'Just Mr Pride.'

Reina snapped her mouth closed and vowed not to say another word for fear of making yet another mistake. Velvet had warned her to mind her manners – and she'd been trying. However,

AN INDECENT LADY

her past experiences hadn't prepared her for this tea.

'Will that be all, ma'am?' Lupe asked, dropping a cursty as though Charlotte was the queen of England.

Elke's help had always been courteous, but they'd never made such a fine display of it. That curtsy intimidated Reina even more. She couldn't help wondering if she should have done the same when she met the countess.

'Yes, and please tell Maria the tea looks heavenly,' Charlotte said. After the maid had gone, she turned to her daughter. 'Would you pour, dear?'

Reina expected Alicia to pick up the teapot and start filling cups. However, there proved to be a great deal more to *pouring* than that. Alicia warmed each cup with hot water first, poured the water off into another container, then asked how everyone took their tea.

'Hot and sweet,' Reina replied when it was her turn.

'Two lumps or three?'

'I – I don't like lumps in my tea.'

'Perhaps you'd prefer honey?'

Reina felt her face flame as she realized Alicia had been referring to sugar. 'That would be fine.'

Alicia's casual display of etiquette, and the perfection of her appearance, made Reina feel horribly inadequate. She had been right about not having anything in common with Alicia – and yet she found herself wishing they could be friends despite the fact that Ulysses hadn't taken his eyes off of Alicia.

He'd been gazing at her, all squinty-like, and blinking a lot. However, she hadn't paid him any undue attention. In fact, she seemed more interested in talking to Reina.

'I see you're wearing trousers again,' Alicia said, handing Reina a cup of tea liberally laced with honey. 'I'd love to get a pair myself. Who makes them for you?'

'The Levi Brothers,' Ulysses responded with a sardonic lift of his brow.

'I've never heard of them. Are they tailors – or couturiers?'

'I don't know what you'd call them.' Reina wished she knew what a koot-whatchamacallit was. Talking to Alicia gave her a glimpse of a wider world. 'You can buy Levi's trousers at Schreiner's Mercantile in Kerrville. You can buy most anything you want there.'

Ulysses chuckled. 'Levi's are Reina's idea of fashion.'

'Now you stop teasing Reina,' Alicia said with a flutter of her lashes. 'If I worked on a ranch, I'd wear pants, too. Mark my words, the day will come when women will wear trousers for comfort and convenience, just like you men.'

It was all Reina could do not to jump up and give Alicia a hug. The girl had some spunk after all. 'I'd be happy to ride with you tomorrow,' Reina declared. 'If you like, we can even go into town and stop at Schreiner's.'

'That sounds wonderful,' Alicia enthused. 'I still have some Christmas shopping to do.'

Hearing the invitation, Velvet breathed a sigh of relief. The afternoon had begun so poorly that she had feared Charlotte was doomed to failure.

'Is it safe for the girls to go off by themselves?' Charlotte asked.

'I have business in town. I'll be happy to go with them,' Ulysses offered. 'I'd be delighted to take Alicia to lunch – and Reina, too, of course.'

'Oh, Ulysses,' Alicia gushed, 'you're so thoughtful.'

Velvet steeled herself against the pain in Reina's eyes. If – *no*, she silently amended – once Ulysses and Alicia were engaged, Reina would have to get over him. And, if everything went according to plan, Terrell Meeks would be there to console her.

Patrick's appearance interrupted her musing. 'It's good to see you, Velvet,' he said, crossing the floor to kiss her cheek. 'I've missed you.'

'I've missed you too.' He looked so much better than he had the last time she saw him. Charlotte's arrival had done him a world of good.

There wasn't a man born who knew how to take proper care of himself. Oh, they made a brave show of being independent. But when it came right down to it, bachelors and widowers were a sorry lot. Perhaps that was why the good Lord had arranged it so that men didn't live as long as women.

Patrick had grieved so hard that Velvet had been afraid he might lose his mind. Now, though Elke's loss had etched new lines on his face and streaked his hair with grey, he seemed to be in full possession of his faculties again.

He greeted the others, then pulled a chair up by Reina. 'Your father told me you did double duty, working your ranch and mine, while I was under the weather. I'll never be able to thank you enough. I have some money for you in my office.'

Reina flushed with pleasure. 'You don't need to thank me – or pay me. I'm just glad I was able to help. There is something I'd like to ask you though.' She paused, and ducked her head the way she always did when she was nervous. 'It's about Starfire, sir.'

'Is something wrong with him?'

'He was fine when I rode him yesterday,' Ulysses interjected.

'He's a magnificent animal,' Alicia added.

Reina clasped her hands together in an unconscious gesture of supplication. 'I've been wondering – that is, I've been thinking about training Starfire to be a cutting horse, and I was hoping you would consider selling him to me.'

Patrick gave Reina a kindly smile. 'I would – but the horse isn't mine. Starfire belongs to Ulysses. What do you say, son? Will you sell him to our Reina?'

Velvet held her breath as she waited for Ulysses to answer. Please, Lord, make him refuse. No way did she want Ulysses to look, sound, or act like a decent human being where her daughter was concerned.

'I'll have to think about it,' Ulysses replied.

'What is that supposed to mean?' Reina burst out.

'Just what I said, Queenie. I'll think about it.'

Reina subsided in her chair, her bruised feelings and dashed hopes so plainly written on her face that it was all Velvet could do not to take her in her arms. Better a few hurt feelings now than a lifetime of unhappiness. It was time for Reina to look beyond Ulysses Pride and give another man a chance.

Seeing Charlotte give a little nod, Velvet turned to Patrick. The first part of their plan had succeeded. The meeting between their daughters had been an unqualified success. It was up to her to put the second part in motion. 'Charlotte has told me you don't have any plans for the holidays. Rio and I would sure like it if you and your guests joined us for Christmas dinner.'

She waited, half expecting him to refuse.

AN INDECENT LADY

'Oh please, Patrick, could we?' Charlotte asked in her breathless little girl voice.

'I don't see any reason why not,' he replied, looking from one woman to the other, 'as long as it's a quiet family supper.'

'Oh, it will be,' Velvet replied. 'The only other person I'm asking is Terrell Meeks.'

Nine

Ulysses bade Charlotte and Alicia good night at ten o'clock on Christmas Eve. He watched their graceful sway as, skirts in hand, they ascended the stairs. Alicia paused at the top and, with an impish grin, blew him a kiss.

'May all your Christmas wishes come true,' she said before disappearing into the darkness of the upper hall.

Christmas wishes? He didn't have any, except perhaps to finally find the inner harmony that had always eluded him. He had been at war with his past far too long.

He stayed at the bottom of the risers, listening to the muted murmur of felicitous female voices as Alicia and Charlotte said their own good nights. How he envied their mutual devotion, and wished he and his father had half as warm a relationship.

Feeling very alone, missing Elke more than ever at this time of the year, his shoulders sagged as he went down the hall to the storage closet where he'd left his gifts. He carried them into the parlor and put them under the tree. Last year, presents had spread beneath it like far-flung roots. This year, his few gifts looked lonely.

Patrick had retired early, pleading exhaustion, leaving Ulysses to accompany Charlotte and Alicia to the candle-light service in Kerrville. Ulysses suspected his father couldn't bring himself to face his first Christmas without Elke in front of so many well-meaning friends.

The church had been crowded when they arrived. He'd been surprised by the number of people who remembered Charlotte – and more surprised at the warmth of their greetings.

Charlotte seemed equally delighted at seeing so many familiar faces. The mayor and his wife had even talked of holding an official reception in her honor after the holidays.

No one seemed to remember – let alone care about – the scandal that had plagued Ulysses' youth. Perhaps they were simply overwhelmed by Charlotte's charm. God knew, she had won him over with ease.

Although his weary body commanded him to the comforts of his bed, he knew he wouldn't sleep. Despite the chilly rigors of the drive to and from town, he felt restive. He walked over to the fireplace and stirred the glowing embers to new life, nagged by the feeling that he had left some important task undone.

It bothered him. A lot.

He prided himself on having a well-ordered mind – and on the behavior that flowed from it. As a lawyer, his cases were always well researched and carefully organized. No one needed to remind him to use due diligence. The habit had been engraved in his bones. He liked to think his personal behavior was equally punctilious. What could he have forgotten?

He'd had boots custom made to Patrick's last, months ago. When he'd accompanied Alicia and Reina on their trip to Kerrville, he had taken time off from his office to choose gifts for Alicia and Charlotte.

Nothing too ostentatious, mind you. He abhorred vulgar displays. Nevertheless, a token of the growing esteem in which he held the women had definitely been in order. He'd been fortunate enough to find a delicate French lace shawl for Charlotte, and a cameo brooch with matching earrings for Alicia.

He had purchased smaller gifts for the household help and his office staff weeks ago – had talked to his father about giving bonuses to all the hands in accordance with their years of service. Tomorrow they would enjoy a bountiful meal followed by all the Kentucky bourbon they could drink.

Knowing his father wasn't up to any Christmas shopping, he'd even bought a leather vest for Rio and a pair of delicate kid gloves for Velvet. Who had he left out?

Reina's name burst into his mind with dismaying force.

He shook his head, as if to deny her presence there.

They hadn't exchanged gifts since they were children. Besides, she had no interest in feminine fripperies. In any case, it was too late to get her anything – even if he'd had the inclination. Still, he couldn't banish her from his mind.

Her piquant features seemed to rise up from the flames. No one had worked harder at Pride's Passion during the months Patrick had withdrawn from the world. Common courtesy demanded some recognition, some recompense for her efforts – and he knew Patrick hadn't been to town to get anything.

Ulysses left the fireplace and wandered around the room, his eyes darting here and there as if the perfect token gift was duty-bound to present itself.

AN INDECENT LADY 131

Damn the girl for finding a new way to torment him, he thought, coming to a stop in front of a window.

He could see lights on in the bunkhouse. A faint glow came from the barn. The hand assigned to the night watch must be inside, keeping warm.

For the second time, a name burst into Ulysses' brain. *Starfire*. He had a vivid memory of Reina's face when she asked to buy the stallion. Her wide-set brown eyes had been as hopeful as a child's and as quick to show pain when he told her he'd think about it.

He hadn't kept his word, though. He had ridden Starfire every day without once considering Reina's request. Although he didn't get attached to animals the way she did, he liked Starfire more than any horse he had ridden in the past. Dear God, was he really contemplating parting with the magnificent stallion?

Of course not. Starfire was more than a token — much more. Starfire was the sort of gift a man gave a woman when he had marriage in mind.

And yet, having thought of it, he couldn't let the idea go. Reina had broken the horse. That afternoon, when she brought the mail, she had looked magnificent on Starfire's back. He had never seen two untamed creatures in such perfect harmony. Besides, what did one more horse matter when he could afford to buy any horse he wanted?

He pressed the palm of his hand against his forehead to test for heat. No, he wasn't feverish. So why was he giving serious thought to the patently absurd idea of parting with Starfire?

As was his habit when faced with a complex problem or a difficult decision, he took a deep, calming breath, then began a silent enumeration of the pros and cons, certain the scales of justice would weight heavily against so munificent a gesture.

He would be giving up a fine piece of horseflesh — but a man of property had an obligation to put that property to its highest and best use, and Starfire *would* make a marvelous cutting horse.

He had hoped to use the stallion at stud — but Reina loved horses too much too object if he asked to breed him to the best of the Pride mares.

Reina might misconstrue his reason for the gift, might think that something more than practicality had influenced his decision — when nothing could be further from the truth. No way did he want her to imagine any personal motivation on his part.

On the other hand, Alicia was bound to be impressed by his generosity — and he certainly wanted to impress *her*. She had chided him for the way he treated Reina — and hadn't believed him when he told her Reina didn't mind a bit of teasing. The two women had developed an unlikely friendship. It wouldn't hurt his cause if Reina had reason to say something nice about him.

He shook his head, as if doing so would banish his confusion. To his amazement, the pros didn't outweigh the cons. In fact, the scale of justice seemed to be in perfect balance — but for one thing. Deep down, for reasons he didn't dare hold up to the clear light of day, he truly wanted to give Reina the horse.

God, how he'd like to be there when she found Starlight in her father's barn. Considering how poorly she concealed her emotions, her surprise and pleasure would be something to behold!

Oh hell, he thought, walking into the entry, and taking a warm jacket from the hall tree. Who the hell did he think he was fooling? There had

AN INDECENT LADY 133

never been any question about what he wanted to do.

'Merry Christmas, Queenie,' he murmured as he headed out the door.

Hearing Ulysses leave the house, Charlotte opened her bedroom door and tiptoed into the hall. No light came from under Alicia's or Patrick's doors. But for the soulful soughing of the wind as it curled around the eaves, the house was quiet.

She returned to her room, cinched the belt of her velvet robe tighter, then bent to pull a pile of wrapped gifts from under her bed. Although her presents weren't as lavish as those she had given in previous years, she felt immensely pleased with all her choices – and even happier at the prospect of spending Christmas Day with people she really cared about.

The last decade of her marriage to Nigel, the holidays had been a bitter charade – a one-act play put on for Alicia's benefit.

Nigel had always arrived from London on Christmas Eve and departed before evening the next day. She had pretended to be ecstatically happy at having him home – had carried on over the expensive baubles he gave her when, all the while, she knew his latest mistress had probably received something even grander. She had watched him act the loving father and quelled her own jealousy at Alicia's ardent response, determined not to destroy her daughter's illusions the way her own had been.

But she mustn't let bitter memories intrude on the present. Her plan couldn't be going better, she thought as, lamp in hand, she made her way down the hall.

Alicia and Ulysses had been spending a great deal

of time together. Getting Patrick to agree to let them put up a Christmas tree — and then sending the two of them out alone to cut one — had been a stroke of genius, she mused with a flush of self-congratulatory pleasure.

Alicia had been so bright-eyed when they returned and Ulysses had been so attentive. Had he stolen a kiss while they were away? God, she hoped so.

Patrick, for all his heartbreak, had managed to catch a little holiday spirit. He'd looked so funny, stringing cranberry garlands with those big hands of his, that she'd been hard put not to throw her arms around him. She hoped he liked his present — and that it brought him joy rather than intensifying his grief.

The picture of Elke had been taken twenty-seven years ago when an itinerant photographer had begged a night's lodging at the ranch. She had insisted that he take photographs of her and Elke, and had gone to considerable pains over her own appearance, trying on gown after gown until she was sure she had chosen exactly the right one.

Elke, on the other hand, had insisted on sitting as she was, in a work dress and apron. She had stared into the camera fiercely, her indomitable will shining in her eyes, while Charlotte had pasted a simpering smile on her face when she posed.

The pictures hadn't arrived for weeks, and then the package had been addressed to Charlotte. She'd been so appalled to see Elke looking so beautiful that she had never even shown her the photograph. But she'd never been able to throw it out either. It had traveled all the way to England with her, tucked away in a trunk, and had been hidden away in a dresser at Glenhaven all these years.

She'd brought it with her, intending to give it to

AN INDECENT LADY

Elke. Now, resplendent in an ornate silver frame and wrapped in shiny paper and red ribbons, it joined the other gifts under the tree.

In this house of mourning, those gifts surprised her. She paused to read the attached cards and saw they were from Ulysses. How thoughtful of him. He must have left the presents before going on whatever errand could draw a young man out on a cold winter's night.

Charlotte placed her gifts next to his. The one she had chosen for Alicia was quite special, even though it hadn't cost her a penny. Charlotte no longer had any use for the ruby and diamond necklace, earrings, and bracelet that Nigel had given her on their first trip to India.

They had still loved one another then. The magnificent parure had been a token of that love – just as it was a symbol of the feelings she had for her daughter today.

How splendid the jewels would look on Alicia. Who knew? If Ulysses fulfilled his political ambitions, Alicia might wear them in the White House someday.

Last, Charlotte put a box under the tree for Ulysses. She had thought long and hard over what to give him, and decided on a rather subdued set of jet studs that Nigel had worn and liked until his taste became more ostentatious. She planned to make a pretty speech when Ulysses opened the present, saying she thought of him as a son.

If he was half as smart as he seemed to be, he would get the hint.

Her errand finished, she straightened up and gazed straight ahead, seeing memories rather than the Christmas tree. She had spent her first Christmas away from home in this house, had held a Twelfth

Night party and danced with the redoubtable Sam Houston in this very room. What a splendid rogue he had been – but not half as splendid as Patrick. Patrick outshone every man that day.

With a sad smile, Charlotte gathered her skirts and made her way back upstairs. How could she ever have fled this house? she wondered as she tiptoed to her room. How could she have walked out on Patrick? What a misguided, foolish creature she had been.

On this most sacred night, she felt especially blessed to be here.

The pungent aroma of brewing coffee eased Reina from sleep. She smiled, then stretched luxuriously as she thought about the coming day. She knew there would be fresh baked stollen, chock full of candied fruit, to go along with the coffee.

She and her parents wouldn't open presents until they had eaten their fill of the yeasty treat. Then they would troop into the parlor where gifts waited under the tree. One year, her parents had given her a marvelous doll with bluer than blue eyes that opened and closed – another year, a sled and skating blades. She still used the custom-made saddle they had given her when she was sixteen. But it wasn't the memory of the presents she most cherished. It was the love they embodied.

Althoug she was far too mature to approach this Christmas with a child's unbridled glee, she hastened from her bed and into her clothes.

'You're sure up early, honey,' Rio said as she walked into the kitchen. 'I reckon you couldn't wait to open your presents.'

'I couldn't wait to have some of your good coffee,'

she replied, rumpling his hair as she passed him on her way to the stove. 'Is Mom awake?'

'Are you serious? She was up half the night fussing and fretting over today's dinner. I expect she'll be back from the outhouse any minute.'

Reina gave him a rueful grin. 'I had better get out there myself before I have that coffee.'

'Mind you dress warm. And speaking of presents, take a look in the barn while you're outside.'

'Whatever for?' A frisson of excitement raised goose flesh on her skin. 'Oh, Daddy, what have you done?'

'I ain't done nothing, honey. But someone else sure did. Go on now. Put your coat on and take a look.'

Rio gave her a fatherly swat as she headed out the door.

'It's days like this,' Velvet called out as she came down the path from the outhouse, 'that I wish we had indoor plumbing.' Her cheeks glowed scarlet from the frosty air. Reina giggled, imagining that her mother's other cheeks were probably equally red.

'Don't be long,' Velvet said. 'I think Santa Claus left something special for you under the tree this year.'

'I hear he left something special in the barn, too. You wouldn't happen to know anything about it, would you?'

The blank look Velvet gave in reply told Reina her mother wasn't in on the secret. 'See you in a minute, sugar,' Velvet called over her shoulder as she hurried back to the house.

Reina ran, slipping and sliding on a thick carpet of frost, to take care of nature's call, then headed to the barn. Night still held the day in abeyance but a full moon shone through the hay loft, turning the prosaic barn into a silvery domicile more fit for fairies than four-footed animals.

For a moment, Reina allowed herself to be caught up in the magic. Had a handsome prince left a jeweled treasure to woo her maidenly heart?

Fat chance, she thought, returning to reality. She reached for the kerosene lamp that always hung by the door, lit it and looked around. The fairy's domicile had metamorphosed back into a barn. The pungent aroma of urine, manure, and hay cut from sweet grass filled her nostrils.

One of the barn cats curled around her ankles, meowing for attention. She picked it up and rubbed her cheek against its silken fur.

'Where's my surprise?' she whispered in the cat's ear as she made her way along the stalls.

The milch cow mooed a plaintive greeting. Her favorite mare, Sandy, whickered softy as she passed by. Reina stopped long enough to pet each animal before proceeding down the wide passage. Foot by foot, the flickering lamplight conquered the gloom. She had almost reached the last stall when she saw a white back rising above the cross bars at the furthest reach of the light.

Her heart beat faster, her hand started to shake. She put the cat down. Holding the lamp higher, she hurried forward – then stopped in mid-stride. It couldn't be – but it was.

'Starfire, oh, Starfire, is it really you?'

The stallion flared his nostrils to take in her scent, then let go a shrill whinny as if to confirm his presence. Hanging the lamp on a hook, she opened the gate to his stall, stepped inside, and reached in her jeans' pocket for the sugar cubes she always carried. Starfire took them from her palm as daintily as a king dining from fine china.

AN INDECENT LADY

She waited until he was accustomed to her presence in his realm, then threw her arms around his neck. 'I can't believe it — I can't believe you're here. Are you mine, boy?'

She couldn't think of any other reason for the stallion to have spent the night in their barn. He had to be a gift. Who had been the giver?

The question accelerated her already rapid pulse until her heart seemed to leap into her throat. She could have stayed with Starfire much longer, but she had to solve this mystery. Giving Starfire a final caress, she left him to the barn's pungent comforts.

'Daddy,' she called out, bursting into the kitchen on a blast of icy air, 'did you buy Starfire for me?'

'I wish I could say I did, but I don't know anymore about it than you do.'

'Then — he must be a gift from Ulysses.' A feeling of euphoria swept over Reina. She felt as if her feet had floated off the floor. 'I can't believe I misjudged him so badly. There isn't anything anyone could have given me that would mean as much as Starfire.'

Reina was too caught up in her own emotions to see the quick flare of anger on her mother's face. 'You haven't misjudged Ulysses. He's too mean-spirited and self-centered to give you anything, and you know it. Why, he's barely civil to you. I reckon Patrick played Santa last night. He knew how much you wanted that horse.'

Velvet's reasoning punctuated Reina's exhilaration like a needle bursting a balloon. She sagged into the nearest chair. 'Of course, you must be right. I'll thank Patrick as soon as he gets here.'

Terrell Meeks never used two words when one would do. Rather than indulging in diatribes and polemics, he let his actions speak for themselves.

Although the holiday season filled him with a melancholy awareness that he had somehow gotten out of step with the rest of the world – and his room in Mrs Messner's boarding house was a sorry place to wake on Christmas Day – and he stubbed a toe on a bed post as he straightened the rumpled covers, all he said was, 'Darn.'

He knew lawmen whose language was as colorful as their occupation, who laced their every pronouncement with expletives. But Terrell had no use for swearing. Despite having killed six men in the performance of his duty, wounding a dozen others, and bringing countless miscreants to the bar of justice in shackles and chains, he was a gentle man at heart.

He peered into the clouded mirror over the dresser as he struggled to tame his hair, plastering the red blond curls close to his head with a liberal application of pomade. As a youth, he'd kept watch over the Prides' herds. As an adult, he'd tracked and captured some of the West's most notorious desperadoes. And all of it, the good and the bad, was clearly written on his face.

The freckles splashed across his nose and cheeks lent an aura of youth to his features. But there was nothing innocent about his deep-set blue eyes. They had a world-weary look that came from gazing deep into men's souls, and not liking what he saw there.

He stripped yesterday's long johns from his lean body, shivering in the cold air as he searched his dresser for clean underwear. His skin goose-bumped, his testicles shriveled. Not that he had much use for them. A forty-one-year-old ranger with blood on his hands and no money in the bank wasn't likely to attract female attention.

He dressed quickly, putting on his best suit, the one

he wore to funerals, hangings and church, then went downstairs to join the other boarders for breakfast. How hollow their Christmas greetings sounded, how false their good cheer.

Like him, they were society's flotsman and jetsam – the losers who had never managed to establish a home and family of their own.

He took his place at the table, hid behind the newspaper to avoid making small talk, and breakfasted on coffee and dry toast. He'd long since learned that a man who might take a bullet in the gut before the end of the day should take a few simple precautions – including controlling his appetite until he was ready to retire for the night.

Finishing his abstemious meal, he folded the newspaper into a precise square, mumbled 'Good day,' and left the other boarders to their eggs, grits, and biscuits. The grandfather clock in the hall chimed eight times. He had five hours to kill before heading for the DeVargas ranch.

He had a limited choice of activities. The churches offered services at various times, depending on the whims of the clergy – but he had never been a church-going man. The saloons would be open – but he wasn't a drinking man either. And the local emporiums had closed yesterday so their owners could spend the holiday at home.

Terrell decided to stop by the sheriff's office to see if any new *Wanted* posters had come in. He settled a Stetson on his head, compressing his curls, then shrugged his broad shoulders into a sheep-skin lined jacket.

The cold had a real bite as he went outside. He couldn't remember a chillier December and winter had barely begun.

A two-block walk along Water Street brought him

to the center of town. Kerrville had sure changed since his youth. Then, it had been a hang-out for two-footed, pistol-packing vermin. Today, thanks to the booming market for sheep and cattle, it had a rosy future.

Schreiner's Mercantile had grown so much over the years that it took up one whole corner at Water and Earl Garrett. A couple of hotels, several restaurants, a post office, churches, a pharmacy with a soda fountain, even an opera house, reminded him that the frontier was dead and gone.

Why, there was even talk of installing trolley tracks and gas lamps if the town fathers could find the money.

He had devoted his life to taming this wild land, and by doing so had outlived his usefulness, he mused as he reached his destination. Civilization had marched on down the road – and left him behind.

Ten

Terrell Meeks headed for the livery stable at noon. He spent a few minutes examining his horse's hooves for any sign of problems. It had been his experience that a cast shoe or an injured hoof had brought more man-hunts to a halt than the Mexican border.

Having done everything he could think of to while away the morning, he saddled the gelding, mounted up and headed out of town even though he knew he'd get to the DeVargas ranch early.

Thank heaven Rio and Velvet weren't the sort of folks to stand on ceremony. Early or not, they'd greet him with open arms. And little Reina too, although, come to think of it, she wasn't that little any more. She had to be a full grown woman by now.

The road to the ranch followed the course of the Guadalupe, passing several small homesteads along the way. They looked so warm and cozy, with their lights glowing against the wintry gloom, that they intensified his melancholy. If Velvet hadn't invited him to supper, he'd have eaten his Christmas meal alone.

How long had it been since he dropped in on the DeVargases? A year. And even then, he only stopped by long enough to ask if Rio had seen any sign of a couple of rustlers he'd been trailing. It had been even longer — maybe five years — since he'd laid eyes on Reina.

Rangering wasn't conducive to long-lasting friendships — or any friendships for that matter. He had made a point of not forming close attachments. He never wanted to worry about who he was leaving behind every time he walked out the door. He didn't want a shootist with a grudge, wreaking vengeance on those he held near and dear.

During his twenty-three years of service, he'd been stationed in a half dozen different towns, always living in boarding houses or hotels. Considering all that moving around, he felt as if he'd met half of Texas.

He had lots of acquaintances — but very few friends. Holidays like this, he really felt the lack. Perhaps he ought to give serious thought to settling down. But where and with whom? If he left the rangers, how would he make a living for himself and a wife?

Rangering had sure changed since he joined up. But for Geronimo and his bunch, the hostiles had all been pushed onto reservations. Stage coach robbers had disappeared along with stage coaches.

Now, he faced a mountain of paperwork every time he made an arrest. It chapped him to think how criminals were molly-coddled by the courts. If ever a man should be looking to make a change, he was that man.

It was the nature of the change he couldn't get a handle on. He still had restless feet — still wanted to see what was on the other side of the horizon.

Rio sure had been lucky, finding a terrific lady like Velvet so late in life, Terrell mused as the DeVargas homestead came into view.

Rio had chosen the site well, tucking the house

in a small valley surrounded by sheltering trees that would keep the place cooler in summer and protect it from the winter's cold winds. Smoke curled from the kitchen stovepipe, carrying the scent of cooking on the icy breeze. *Roast goose*, he thought, salivating like a hungry hound.

Rio emerged from the barn as Terrell rode up. 'I've got an empty stall for your horse,' he called out.

'I reckon I'm early,' Terrell replied, sliding a leg over the saddle and jumping to the ground as easily as a man half his age.

'Hell, boy, the way I look at it, you're about a year too late. I figured we'd see more of you when you got transferred to Kerrville. But you sure as hell have been keeping yourself scarce. Velvet has been after me to ask you on over.'

Rio had been Terrell's first boss in the days when Terrell was as green as spring grass. He was the only man in the world who could get away with calling Terrell *boy*. Everything Terrell had learned about horses and cattle – and most of what he'd learned about men – he'd learned from Rio.

'I've been meaning to come by but rangering has kept me on the go.'

'You don't need to apologize. I remember how it was, being footloose and fancy free. I'm just glad you could make it today. Velvet will skin my hide if we don't go straight on over to the house,' Rio said, after stabling Terrell's horse. 'I reckon you won't mind if we go in through the kitchen.'

'Suits me fine,' Terrell replied with an easy grin. 'I'm sort of anxious to get closer to the food I smelled when I rode up.'

'If you aren't a sight for sore eyes! Reina, honey,

come see who's here,' Velvet exclaimed as they walked in the kitchen door.

She had been stirring something in a bowl. Wiping her hands on her apron, she crossed the floor and enveloped Terrell in an embrace.

He hugged her back, his earlier gloom banished by the warmth of her greeting. 'You're as pretty as ever, Miss Velvet.'

'Sure I am, if your taste runs to fat and wrinkles,' Velvet replied with a hearty guffaw, then pushed him away. 'What's that lump on your chest? Did someone shoot you again?'

He reached inside his jacket and, with a flourish, drew forth a bottle. 'Do you still have a taste for a fine brandy wine?'

'I sure do, sugar.'

'This one came all the way from France. Look, it says Cognac on the label.' He put the bottle in Velvet's hand.

At that moment, another woman entered the kitchen. She had Reina's face, all right. But there was nothing childlike about her figure.

'God almighty, Reina, you sure turned out to be a beauty,' he said, whipping off his hat.

The toddler who used to chase him around the corral and beg to get up on his horse – the eight-year-old girl he'd taught to rope and the teenager who proved to be almost as good a shot as he was – had blossomed into something pretty damn special.

She was going to warm a lucky man's bed one of these days. Warm it? That was an understatement. A woman with a body like Reina's could set a bed on fire. A part of him wished he could be that lucky man. But it would be like sleeping with his younger sister, he thought with a wry grimace.

'Where have you been keeping yourself?' Reina demanded, coming forward and standing on tiptoe to give him a kiss.

The softness of her lips and the sweet taste of her mouth made him feel a little less brotherly. He pulled away and took a much longer look at her. He had been thinking about settling down. A man could do a lot worse than Reina DeVargas.

'If I'd known what I was missing, I'd have gotten here a lot sooner,' he said huskily.

'You're a year late – and an hour early,' Velvet said, beaming at him. 'I've still got some cooking to do.'

'I'd be happy to help.'

Rio burst out laughing. 'When did you learn to cook?'

'I didn't. But I'm the best taster God ever made.'

Ulysses helped Charlotte and Alicia into the buggy's back seat, then pulled a thick buffalo robe over their laps. 'Are you ladies warm enough?' he asked before climbing into the front seat beside Patrick.

'We're fine,' they replied in unison.

Ulysses took up the reins, then turned to his father. 'Ready, Dad?'

'I guess so.' Since he opened Charlotte's gift, Patrick had had a faraway look, as though he were listening to a distant voice rather than the people around him.

Ulysses had been surprised to receive a gift, too – and even more surprised that Charlotte would part with something that obviously had so much sentimental value attached to it. He'd been quite moved by her little speech about how she thought of him as a son.

But for an accident of fate, she might have been his

mother. God knew, she'd been doing her level best to stand in for Elke during the holidays. Christmas would have been unendurable without Charlotte and Alicia.

As if Charlotte were privy to his innermost thoughts, she said, 'Could we stop by Elke's grave on our way to the DeVargases? I'd like to be with her for a while today.' She lay a gloved hand on Patrick's shoulder. 'Or would it be too painful for you?'

Emotion roughened Patrick's voice. 'I'd like that very much. I've been thinking of Elke ever since you gave me that photograph.'

'I hope it didn't upset you.'

'That picture brought back a lot of happy memories. Sometimes, when I get to missing Elke, I forget all the good times we had.'

When they reached the small family graveyard overlooking the Guadalupe, Ulysses realized what Charlotte intended to do with the brightly berried spray of holly, yaupon and evergreens she clutched in her gloved hands.

'This is for you, dearest,' she said, bending to put the spray by Elke's tombstone, 'a reminder of the season. I imagine you're up in heaven showing the angels how to make garlands. They're probably learning faster than I did all those years ago.' Charlotte's breathy voice deepened. 'We're all here – Patrick, Ulysses, Alicia, and I – thinking of you and missing you. The four of us are on our way to supper with the DeVargases.' She continued talking, having a one-sided conversation with her old friend.

Although Ulysses stopped paying attention to what she said, the murmur of her voice soothed him as he looked down on his mother's final resting place.

He had been so very wrong to argue with Elke about Charlotte's visit. How he wished he could take back all the cruel things he'd said that day. Now, the only way to atone for them was to treat Charlotte the way his mother would have wanted.

The graveside visit proved more healing than he had expected. By the time the four of them had settled in the buggy again, Patrick's eyes had lost that faraway look. He even managed to join in the conversation during the remainder of the drive.

The Wolfhound was in the DeVargases' yard when Ulysses reined the buggy to a stop. The huge dog stalked over to the carriage, hauteur visible in his rigid posture, menace audible in his low growl.

'What a magnificent animal,' Charlotte exclaimed without a sign of fear. 'He looks very like the dogs we used to breed at Glenhaven.'

Ulysses tore his gaze from his four-footed nemesis and managed a sickly grin. 'He ought to. That's the dog you sent me. I've been a little leery of telling you that I didn't keep him. You see, I was away at Harvard at the time – and Reina wanted him desperately. I hope you don't mind.'

Charlotte made a *moue*. 'The only thing I mind is that I sent you a gift you couldn't use. It was very thoughtless of me.'

Although Ulysses had certainly thought so at the time, he replied, 'Nonsense. It's the gesture that counted.'

To his horror, Charlotte didn't wait to be helped down from the carriage. She jumped from the front seat and held her hand out to Useful. The dog's canines gleamed like ivory sabres as he drew closer.

Ulysses didn't dare cry out a warning for fear of arousing the beast. He held his breath, thinking the dog would take Charlotte's hand – her arm, and whatever else he had a taste for.

'You magnificent baby,' Charlotte cooed, letting Useful get her scent.

To Ulysses' amazement, the Wolfhound's tail began a rhythmic beat.

'Oh, Patrick,' Charlotte exclaimed, 'I think he remembers me. I wonder if Reina would like me to send a mate for him.'

Ulysses repressed a groan at the thought of a dozen little Usefuls roaming the DeVargas ranch.

'Is something wrong, Ulysses?' Alicia asked from the buggy's high seat.

'Not at all,' he replied, keeping an eye on the dog as he got down and then helped Alicia to the ground. Fortunately Useful was too preoccupied with Charlotte and Patrick to pay him any attention as they made their way to the house.

Although Ulysses continued to keep a wary eye on Useful while holding Alicia's elbow so she wouldn't slip on the icy path, his mind skittered in a new direction. He couldn't wait to see Reina's reaction to his gift.

She was going to have to eat a little crow along with her Christmas dinner. He relished the thought of her being duty-bound to say something pleasant to him for a change.

He smiled to himself in anticipation of her thank you. Perhaps she would even have the wit and grace to offer an apology for calling him Useless all these years.

Would she blurt out her appreciation the minute she saw him – or would she wait for a more seemly moment? Knowing Reina, he suspected she would enjoy keeping him waiting. But she damn well better not make him wait too long, he thought, knocking on the front door.

Reina answered his summons, flinging the door

AN INDECENT LADY

wide and wishing them all a merry Christmas. She hugged Charlotte, Alicia and Patrick in turn, then acknowledged Ulysses with a cool nod. It wasn't the greeting he expected.

She wasn't the Reina he expected, either.

The jean-clad hellion had metamorphosed into a carefully coiffed female in a russet-colored dress that matched the highlights in her eyes. She must have laced herself into a corset because her waist looked small enough to span with his hands.

Instead of taming her breasts, however, the corset made them ride higher so that they trembled like aspic with her every breath. The gown's high neckline and ruffled bodice seemed to draw attention to those twin mounds – at least his attention, he thought, lifting his gaze back to her face.

Reina would never appear ladylike the way Alicia did. Her dark coloring was too exotic, her figure too full, her gaze too frank, for that. But today, Reina looked every inch a woman – and a damn desirable one at that.

'Come on in before you all catch your death,' she said. 'Mother's still fussing over supper, but Dad and Terrell are waiting for you in the parlor.'

Thank heaven, she seemed unaware of his discomfiture. By the time she mentioned Starfire, he intended to have his emotions well in hand. He decided he would accept her thanks with casual disinterest, as if his magnificent gift hadn't weighed so heavily on his mind that he had barely slept.

There was a flurry of activity as everyone took off their coats. Ulysses handed his over to Reina – and waited for her to say something as she hung the garment on the hall tree. She turned her back to him, though, and led the way to the parlor.

The room smelled like Christmas – a melange of

wood burning on the hearth, sap oozing from the Christmas tree, and good food. There had been a time when he felt as at home within these four walls as he had in his parents' house – and an unexpected longing for that time swept over him.

He was so distracted that he forgot all about making the introductions. Fortunately, they weren't needed. Terrell took one look at Charlotte and broke into a grin. 'As I live and breathe, is that you, Miss Charlotte? I heard you were back, but Rio didn't tell me you were coming to supper, too.'

'You were so young when I left, I'm flattered you remember me,' Charlotte said, taking both of the ranger's hands in her own, looking him up and down as though she liked what she saw.

'A man isn't likely to forget a lady like you,' Terrell responded with surprising gallantry.

'You Texans certainly know how to make a visitor feel welcome. And speaking of ladies – ' Charlotte beckoned Alicia to join her. ' – I'd like you to meet my daughter. Alicia, darling, this is Terrell Meeks.'

Alicia couldn't have looked more impressed if she'd just been introduced to a member of England's royal family. Although, come to think of it, she probably knew them. 'It's an honor, sir, I've heard so much about you from Ulysses. I'd love to have the opportunity to talk to you about your exploits – at your convenience, of course.'

'I'd be happy to talk to you, Miss Alicia. But I haven't done anything that special.'

'Please let me be the judge of that.' Alicia stared at poor Terrell so hard that the redoubtable ranger blushed.

Just then, Velvet came into the room, carrying a tray laden with steaming mugs. A hubbub of greetings met her appearance. 'I thought you all could use a hot toddy after your ride,' she said after the second round of greetings subsided.

'To old friends and happier times,' Velvet said, offering up a toast after passing the drinks.

'And new friends, too,' Alicia amended, her blue-eyed gaze fixed on Meeks.

For a while, everyone seemed to talk at once, reminiscing, laughing and enjoying themselves. It was some time before Ulysses thought about Starfire again. He was trying to think of a roundabout way to mention the stallion when he overheard Reina say to Patrick, 'I don't know how to thank you for your present.'

When the hell had Patrick gotten her a present?

Patrick looked bewildered. 'I don't know what you mean.'

'I found Starfire in the barn this morning – and I couldn't be more thrilled.' Reina stood on tiptoe and gave Patrick a kiss.

Damn, that should have been my kiss, Ulysses thought, struggling to master his bruised feelings.

'You're the kindest, most wonderful man I've ever known – except for my father,' Reina continued. 'I promise, you won't be sorry you gave Starfire to me. I'll take very good care of him. Daddy said he'll help me train him. He's going to be the best cutting horse in the Hill Country.'

'Whoa. Slow down there, Reina,' Patrick said. 'I would gladly have given you the horse – if he'd been mine to give. But he belongs to Ulysses.'

Reina's eyes widened. 'You didn't buy him back?'

'It never even occurred to me.'

'Then what was he doing in our barn this morning?'

'You'll have to ask my son,' Patrick replied, a bemused expression on his face.

'Oooooh.' Reina's brow knit in a frown. Her lips continued to form an O long after she stopped making a sound.

She turned to Ulysses. 'I'm sorry. I just thought—'

He fought down the urge to throttle her. He should have known she would find some way to make him regret his generosity. 'I know what you thought,' he said, being careful to keep his voice low so that the others couldn't hear him. 'When you found Starfire, I imagine you told yourself I was too mean to do something as generous as giving you the horse.'

Seeing her blush deepen, he knew he was on the right track. 'I can hear you now. "Useless wouldn't ever give me anything so valuable. Useless is a low-down-mean snake in the grass who only thinks about himself." Does that about sum it up, Queenie?'

Reina struggled to control her emotions. She had made a terrible mistake – one Ulysses wasn't likely to forgive or forget. He glared at her as if she were something he wanted to scrape off his boots.

Damn him! Why couldn't he be fair for once? Considering how he had treated her in the past, what had he expected her to think – that he had played Santa Claus and left Starfire in the stable when Patrick was the only logical candidate for the role?

Her reaction had been utterly logical. Even Velvet had said so. No, Reina mused angrily. She wasn't to blame. Ulysses should have left a note if he wanted her to thank him. Thank him – hell. He acted as though he had expected her to kiss his feet.

Her eyes sheened – but her tone was defiant. 'You left a few things out, Useless. Would you like me to repeat them now?'

AN INDECENT LADY 155

Velvet looked her way and said, 'What are you two talking about?'

'It's nothing, Mother,' Reina muttered.

'It's less than nothing,' Ulysses growled in agreement.

'Good. Then you won't mind if I send Reina to the kitchen to make some more toddy.'

'Not at all,' Ulysses replied with the best smile he could summon up.

At that moment, with his shattered expectations lodging in his chest like splinters, he wouldn't mind if Reina DeVargas went straight to hell.

Eleven

Alicia was unaware of Ulysses' problems with Reina. She hadn't heard one word of their exchange. And although Charlotte and Velvet were deep in conversation, she hadn't heard one word they said, either.

She had been in a state of suspended animation since being introduced to Terrell Meeks, so overcome that she forgot to breathe until her oxygen-starved lungs begged for air.

The French had an expression – *le coup de foudre* – that described what had happened to her. Literally translated, it meant the blow of . . . of . . . of what? She wished she had taken her French lessons more seriously.

Foudre sounded a lot like *poudre*, which meant powder. Surely *le coup de foudre* didn't mean the blow of powder. She giggled at the thought, and her mother gave her a peculiar look.

She would have to be more careful around Charlotte. She didn't want to have to explain her tumultuous new feelings until she had dealt with them herself.

She didn't have to translate *le coupe de foudre* literally to know what it meant. Her body was giving her a lesson in its exact import.

Her mouth felt dry. Her cheeks burned. A flock

of birds seemed to have taken wing in her stomach. She wanted to jump for joy – and weep at the sheer thrill of being alive. The man she had conjured up in a thousand girlish daydreams, the man she had waited for all her life, stood a few feet away – close enough to touch if she dared.

His sculptured features adorned a marvelously weather-beaten face that looked as if he'd endured – and triumphed over – all life's vicissitudes. A warm yet wary expression, that seemed to say he'd seen the best and the worst in mankind and lived to tell about it, simmered in his gaze.

The freckles splashed over his cheekbones and the reddish gold hair that fell to his collar softened the lines of age on his face. He could be thirty, or forty, or any place in between. His suit, poorly cut though it was, revealed broad shoulders and a toreador's waist. He had a lean and hungry look . . .

No, she silently edited herself. Shakespeare had already used that particular confluence of words. Surely at a time like this, she could be more original. Make it lean and lonely – or lean and lithe – or just plain heart-stopping. She cut a quick glance at Reina to see if the ranger had the same effect on her, only to find that Reina had left the room.

Alicia turned her gaze back to Terrell Meeks. He had the most mesmerizing eyes, as blue as sapphires. *The things he must have seen with those eyes.*

His hands merited attention, too. Fine-boned and slender, they belonged on a pianist rather than a gunsel. *The things he must have done with those hands.* A frisson trembled down her spine as she imagined him touching her.

Would he be gentle or rough, shy or bold? Would he ever touch her at all?

Mercifully, Terrell Meeks was unaware of her

unladylike preoccupation. She leaned closer to hear what Terrell was saying to Rio. She couldn't have been more fascinated if she had been listening to Aristotle discoursing at the foot of the Parthenon.

'I don't like the look of the weather these last few days, Rio. If I were you, I'd bring my herd closer to home.'

'Patrick and I are way ahead of you,' Rio replied. 'We've spent the last few weeks moving the stock closer to the homeplace. And we've got enough hay stored up to get them through a rough winter.'

'Do you expect some sort of trouble?' Alicia directed her question at Terrell.

'Not the kind I deal with,' he replied. 'But I've got a couple of old wounds that always ache when the weather is about to take a turn for the worse. And they've been giving me fits.'

Alicia's knees almost gave way when he looked at her. She couldn't care less about the weather. However, she did want to hear more about Terrell's injuries. Had he been hurt badly? she wondered, her heart constricting at the thought.

Although she knew she shouldn't be so bold, she couldn't help asking, 'What sort of wounds?'

'I got in the way of a bullet a time or two, Miss Alicia. It's not a topic that's fit to discuss with a lady such as yourself.'

How bravely he dismissed his suffering. 'I don't embarrass easily,' she answered in a firm voice that seemed to come from someone else. 'I've never met a lawman before. I can't imagine a more romantic profession.'

He gave her a bemused grin – or was it a grimace? 'I don't think I'd call it romantic, Miss Alicia. Just the opposite. I spend most of my time waiting for something to happen and when it does it's never pleasant.'

'I wasn't talking about that sort of romance,' she declared. 'Did you know that the word, *romance*, is derived from a Latin root? It means a story told in verse. I just meant you must have some of the most wonderful stories.'

'I don't tell stories, ma'am. Folks have got to be able to rely on a lawman's word.'

Again he had misunderstood her. It only strengthened her resolve to make her meaning crystal clear. 'I can tell, just looking at you, that you must be a very truthful person. I've never seen such resolve – such character – on a man's face before. I meant what I said about wanting to hear your adventures.'

Terrell's eyes widened. A scarlet flush suffused his skin. His freckles faded into it.

'Alicia is a bit of a Western buff,' Ulysses said, coming to Terrell's rescue. 'Don't let her questions upset you. Her interest isn't personal. Learning about Texas is sort of a hobby with her.'

Ulysses couldn't have been more wrong. Her interest was personal – *very, very personal*. She wished Ulysses would go away so that she could have Terrell all to herself.

'Indeed, I am a Western buff, Mr Meeks. I find Texas absolutely fascinating. The vistas, the big sky, the rugged terrain – there's nothing like it in my country. It's intimidating – yet welcoming, beautiful – yet rugged, brooding – yet boisterous. It's . . .' She finally ran out of adjectives and spluttered to a halt. 'I want to know all about it before I go home,' she concluded lamely.

'When might that be, miss?' Terrell asked with polite interest, although she wouldn't blame him if he thought she was one of those misguided women who suffered from a runaway tongue and a lack of brains.

Her brain was in fine shape. She couldn't say as much for her heart. It leapt in her chest like one of those pronghorn antelopes Ulysses had pointed out the last time they went riding.

'I'm not sure. It depends on a great number of things,' she answered cryptically.

Terrell nodded as if what she'd said made perfect sense. Only his eyes betrayed his befuddlement. Perhaps his confusion could work to her advantage. Men were supposed to like a woman of mystery – at least they did in the books she had read – and she definitely wanted Terrell Meeks to like her. She could hardly wait to write about him in her diary tonight.

'I hope it won't be soon,' Ulysses said, reclaiming her attention. 'Having you and your mother with us has been very good for my father – and for me too, I might add.'

Oh, dear. Staid, stolid Ulysses sounded almost flirtatious. They'd spent hours together and he'd never said anything remotely personal to her before. Did he see a rival for her affections in Terrell? Or did Ulysses have another motive for suddenly paying her court?

If only she knew more about men.

Velvet need not have stayed up half the night worrying about the menu. Her guests devoured the meal as if they hadn't eaten in weeks. The apple-garnished roast goose and the rice and broccoli casserole had been particularly good, if she did say so herself. And the desserts – mincemeat pie with fresh whipped cream and plum pudding with brandy sauce – had been the perfect finishing touch.

Now she stood at the sink, her hands deep in soap suds, washing dishes while Reina dried.

'I think supper was a success, don't you?' she said, giving tongue to her thoughts.

'Everyone seemed to have a good time,' Reina agreed. 'And heaven knows, they ate enough.'

Velvet nodded. 'Especially Terrell. I reckon he's starved for home cooking. It sure was nice to see him again, wasn't it?'

'It sure was,' Reina agreed.

'I notice you spent a lot of time talking to him.'

'How could I help it, since you sat the two of us side by side at supper?'

'But you do like him, don't you?'

'Of course. He's been a wonderful friend, putting up with me the way he did when I was little.'

Velvet took out her frustration on the pan she was scrubbing. She had hoped for a more enthusiastic answer. 'You're not a child anymore. Terrell knows it, if you don't.'

'For heaven's sake, Mother, what a thing to say.'

'I saw the way he looked at you when you walked into the kitchen. It's plain to me that Terrell Meeks has a soft spot in his heart just for you.'

From the way Reina clattered the dishes as she put them away, the conversation was making her uncomfortable. Still, Velvet pressed on. 'Terrell sure jumped at the chance to see you again when I asked him to dinner next week.'

'You said it yourself – he's starved for home cooking. Did you have to ask Alicia and Ulysses, too?'

'I thought you liked Alicia.'

'I do. I've never had so good a friend. It's Ulysses I can't abide.'

Velvet turned away from the sink to see if the expression on Reina's face matched the anger in her voice. 'Ulysses wasn't very gracious about you thinking Patrick gave you Starfire. It's just like

Ulysses to make a grand gesture and then expect folks to fall all over him, don't you agree? For the life of me, I don't know what a sweet girl like Alicia sees in him.'

'What makes you think she sees anything in him?'

Velvet forced herself to chuckle although she felt like weeping over Reina's misplaced affection. 'Why sugar, it's perfectly obvious that the two of them are courting.'

Charlotte changed into a dressing gown, then went down the hall and knocked at Alicia's bedroom door. 'It's Mother,' she called out.

'Come in,' Alicia replied.

She was sitting in a wing chair by the window, her legs drawn up under her, a pensive look on her face. Most likely she was thinking about Ulysses, Charlotte mused.

'Did you have a nice Christmas?' she asked, settling in the chair opposite Alicia's.

'Very nice. But Mother, you shouldn't have given me those jewels. It was far too extravagant of you.'

'Nonsense. In any case, they'll all be yours someday.'

Charlotte prayed Alicia never found out that the ruby and diamond parure should have gone to their creditors to pay off Nigel's debts. The last letter from Nigel's solicitor had warned her that the situation grew more desperate with every passing week. He had all but ordered her back to England.

She pushed his ultimatum from her mind. She wasn't going to let anything spoil what little remained of the day. 'It seems this was your Christmas to get jewelry.'

'How so?'

'Surely you haven't forgotten the lovely cameo and matching earrings that Ulysses gave you. He has such refined taste.'

'I suppose.' Alicia looked and sounded a thousand miles away – but then, infatuated young ladies tended to be a little dreamy.

'In the short time we've been here, I think Ulysses has become very fond of you – perhaps more than fond. He looked positively pale when Terrell asked when we were going home.'

Alicia finally seemed to be paying attention. She sat up straighter. 'When are we going home, Mother?'

'I hadn't given it much thought. But I wouldn't dream of making an ocean crossing in the winter. Do you miss Glenhaven Hall?'

'Not a bit,' Alicia declared emphatically. 'I wouldn't mind staying in Texas forever.'

Now that's more like it, Charlotte thought. Alicia was far too virginal, too naive to admit it yet – even to herself – but Ulysses had to be the reason she had fallen in love with the ranch.

'I'm just glad we were able to help Patrick through a difficult time. And Ulysses, too, of course. It's obvious he was devoted to his mother. I like that quality in a man, don't you?'

'I suppose it is rather admirable.'

'Ulysses *is* a most admirable man. He couldn't be more different from the men we knew in London. He's intelligent, hard-working, loyal, and generous to a fault. Who would have imagined he'd give Reina that magnificent horse?'

Alicia's expression brightened. 'I'm so glad he did. I've talked to him about the way he treats Reina.'

The gift had worried Charlotte – until now. 'Aaah. I see.'

'You see what, Mother?'

'A woman can be the most wonderful influence on a man – bring out the best in him. I doubt Ulysses would have given Reina so valuable an animal if you hadn't talked to him.'

'I don't think I had much to do with it.'

'Don't be silly, darling. You had everything to do with it. He thinks the world of you and I'm sure he hoped to make a favorable impression on you.'

'If you say so.'

'Now, darling, it's not what I say. It's what I know. You're much too young and inexperienced to understand men the way I do. I assure you, Ulysses is very smitten. He has all the signs.'

'What signs?'

'Men become quite distracted when they fall in love. They can't keep their minds on business. And even you must have noticed that Ulysses wasn't himself today. Have you thought what you'll say if – no – make that *when* he asks for your hand?'

Alicia gasped. 'Oh my, do you really think he will?'

Charlotte almost said, *I pray he will*, before she thought better of it. She could only push Alicia so far. 'He's going to make some lucky woman a marvelous husband. I'd be so happy if it were you. That way, you could live in Texas forever,' Charlotte explained with a smug grin. 'And now, my darling girl, it's time I got to bed. It's been a long day – but a wonderful one.'

She rose to kiss Alicia's forehead, and swept from the room with a sibilant swish of her taffeta dressing gown.

Alicia waited until she heard her mother's bedroom door close before she took her diary from its hiding place. So much had happened since her last entry twenty-four hours ago that she barely knew where to begin.

Patrick had never gotten accustomed to sleeping alone. He piled pillows on Elke's side of the bed so he would feel something against his body during the night. But pillows were a poor substitute for the woman he loved.

Rolling onto his side, he gazed at the picture of Elke that Charlotte had given him. He had put it on the nightstand so it would be the last thing he saw before going to sleep, and the first thing he saw when he woke up in the morning.

Although he tried to concentrate on Elke's image, Charlotte kept intruding on his thoughts. How like her it had been to hide the picture years ago. She must have been green with envy when she saw Elke looking so beautiful. In fact, he wouldn't have been surprised if she had torn the picture to pieces instead of keeping it all these years.

But then, he had never understood the bond between Charlotte and Elke. The only thing they had in common was him.

Elke had always been inordinately fond of Charlotte – and time had proven her to be a better judge of character than him. Charlotte had been little more than a child during the brief months of their marriage – a child spoiled by two rich and doting parents, a child who had never been given any reason not to think the sun rose and set on her needs and desires.

But that spoiled child had matured into a thoughtful, kind, and competent woman. What could have happened to change her so? Had it been Nigel's death?

She had made the holiday season bearable. Was

he being selfish, leaning on her strength? How long could he expect her to stay when the whole wide world was hers to command?

Terrell Meeks made his way back to town in the gathering gloom. Overhead, thousands of blackbirds were flying to their roost, creating swirling black plumes of motion against the darkening sky. The setting sun tinged the western horizon to the soft rose of a woman's cheeks.

He huddled in his heavy jacket, reaching a gloved hand up to settle his hat more firmly as his mind returned to the cozy home he had so recently left. He couldn't remember the last time he'd enjoyed Christmas the way he had this one. Spending it with two breathtakingly beautiful women had certainly made *his* day.

Although he usually felt intimidated in a beautiful woman's company, Reina had put him completely at ease at supper with her talk of cattle, horses, and the merits of various types of barbed wire.

Conversing with her was pretty much like talking to a man – until you looked at her. A girl that pretty should have young ones at her knee by now. God knew, she'd need a man to help her run the ranch after Rio was gone. And, although it pained him to think about it, at seventy Rio had already outlived most of his peers.

Terrell spurred his horse as the sun slipped beneath the horizon. Lord, it was cold this winter, he mused before his mind returned to Reina.

He'd been thinking about setting his feet on a new path, settling down in one place, and he couldn't imagine a better place to do it than the DeVargas ranch. He and Reina would be better suited than lots of couples he knew. And

AN INDECENT LADY

he'd be delighted to have Rio and Velvet as in-laws.

Marrying up with Reina made perfect sense. So why couldn't he stop thinking about Alicia Hawthorne? He must be out of his mind. Lady Glenhaven was completely beyond the reach of a man like him.

Besides, she was damn peculiar when he got right down to it. He'd never known a woman to ask so many silly questions. She talked too damn much — but he sure liked the sound of her voice. She had a way of stringing words together so that they came out like poetry.

Poetry! Now he knew he'd lost his mind. What the hell did he know about poetry? For that matter, what the hell did he know about Alicia Hawthorne? Except that her hair reminded him of sunlight shining through clouds, and her eyes, of rain-washed sky.

Twelve

The morning after Christmas, Alicia sat at the table pushing eggs and bacon around her plate. She had spent a miserable, sleepless night. She was feeling things she had never felt before, thinking thoughts that were utterly foreign to her experience.

Inchoate longings swept through her, sparking physical responses that made her feel as if her body belonged to someone else. Her life had been turned upside down by a chance encounter with a man wearing a badge on his chest. And what a glorious chest it was.

Two days ago, she hadn't known Terrell Meeks at all. This morning, her very existence seemed to depend on getting to know him better.

'You've hardly touched your breakfast,' Charlotte said.

'I guess I ate too much yesterday. I'm not at all hungry.'

Charlotte frowned. 'You do look a little green around the gills, darling. Perhaps you need a restorative, something to cleanse your blood. I could ask Conchita to brew one of her herbal teas, something with emetic properties.'

Alicia gagged at the thought. She wouldn't put it past Conchita to add snails, toads, and puppy dog tails to her noxious brews. No way would Alicia ever submit to drinking one.

Mercifully, the most marvelous idea popped into Alicia's mind like a perfect paragraph that needs no editing. She could kill two birds with one stone – escape her mother's scrutiny and find out more about Terrell Meeks in one fell swoop.

'Perhaps all I need is a little fresh air. Reina mentioned something about exercising Starfire first thing today. If you don't need me, I'd like to join her.'

'Should I see if Ulysses is free to escort you to the DeVargases'? I believe he's in the library, working on a brief.'

'For heaven's sake, Mother, will you please stop treating me like a child? I'm perfectly capable of riding over to Reina's without getting lost.'

Charlotte blinked several times, her face a study in confusion, as if she didn't know how to handle Alicia's rare show of temper. 'Of course you are, darling. It's just that I can't help worrying about you. You're all I have left. One day when you're married and have children of your own, you'll understand. And I hope that day won't be too long coming.'

How bourgeois her mother sounded, as if marriage and children were the only goals a woman could aspire to. Rebellion hid beneath Alicia's placid exterior like lava beneath the earth's crust, threatening to break through at any moment.

Charlotte would never understand, let alone accept, that she longed for a different sort of future than the one Charlotte envisioned for her. If she ever married, it would be to someone as bold, dashing, daring, and courageous as her father had been – someone like Terrell Meeks, she mused, feeling a flush heat her cheeks, rather than someone as prim, proper and staid as Ulysses.

The thought of Charlotte's inevitable disappointment ached through Alicia. However, the thought of complying with Charlotte's wishes hurt even more. If only she could prove herself and her talent by selling a book.

First, however, she had to write one. She just knew she had found the perfect inspiration in Terrell Meeks. He looked like a man who had lived long and fully enough to fill hundreds of pages. All she had to do was get him to tell her about his experiences.

Ulysses had done her an unwitting favor, paving the way for her queries by describing her as a devotee of all things Western. Now, Alicia could only hope that Reina would agree to an even bigger favor.

Alicia suddenly realized her mother had been talking to her. 'I'm sorry, Mother. I'm afraid I was doing a little wool gathering. What were you saying?'

'I was saying that I don't need you here. Considering how you're acting, though, I'm not at all certain I ought to let you go riding off without an escort.'

Inspiration winged into Alicia's brain like a homing pigeon seeking its roost. She knew just how to calm her mother's fears. 'I was thinking about the things we discussed last night,' she murmured, lowering her gaze and fluttered her lashes in a fine show of maidenly chagrin. 'Mostly about Ulysses. That's why I seem so absentminded.'

Charlotte reacted as Alicia had hoped. 'You should have told me. It's nothing to be ashamed of. All young women react that way when they're infatuated for the first time. A good brisk ride will be just what you need to sort out your feelings.'

Reina was in the corral, preparing to mount Starfire, when Alicia showed up. 'What a pleasant

AN INDECENT LADY 171

surprise. I'm glad I didn't miss you. I was going to exercise Starfire.'

'I'm in the mood for a ride myself.'

Reina led Starfire through the corral gate, shut it behind her, then leapt into the saddle with no more apparent effort than it took a butterfly to land on a leaf.

'For the life of me, I can't imagine how you do that,' Alicia exclaimed, her eyes bright with admiration. 'I can't get into a saddle without using a mounting block.'

'You could if you didn't wear a skirt,' Reina replied. 'You really must buy some Levi's the next time we go to town.'

'I asked my mother if I could buy them the last time we went to Kerrville, but she refused. It really isn't like her to be stingy.'

'Where would you like to go?' Reina asked, changing the subject.

'It doesn't matter as long as we can talk. I have a problem – a serious problem – and I need your advice.'

'I doubt I'll be much help, unless your problem has something to do with livestock. I'm not an expert on anything else.'

'You know more than you think. I want to talk to you about Terrell Meeks.'

'What about him?' Reina asked, holding Starfire to a walk. She cut a glance at Alicia. Her friend had the strangest look on her face, as though something was hurting her bad – and she was enjoying it.

Alicia sighed. 'He's the most fascinating man I've ever met. I wan't to know everything about him.'

Reina let go a startled giggle. 'I'm not sure I'm the person you ought to talk to.'

'Why not? Are you sweet on him?'

'On Terrell? No, of course not. When I think of him at all, it's as an older brother. He almost was a brother to me years ago. But I haven't seen all that much of him lately.' Reina took a moment to study Alicia's face, taking note of her pallor and the glitter in her eyes that made her look feverish.

Intuition prompted Reina's question. 'Am I reading you wrong, Alicia, or are you sweet on Terrell yourself?'

Alicia guided her mount closer with the ease of an experienced horsewoman. 'How did you know? You must tell me so that I don't give myself away when I'm with my mother. She thinks I'm infatuated with Ulysses. If she knew I wasn't, I don't think we'd stay at Pride's Passion much longer.' She paused, then said in a low voice. 'What I have to say has to remain between the two of us.'

Intrigued by Alicia's revelations, Reina nodded her agreement.

'When we left England, I thought Mother needed a change of scene to help her get over my father's death. But I don't think that anymore.' Alicia's brow furrowed. 'She never talks about my father. It's almost as if she wanted to forget he ever existed. I think she came here to play matchmaker between me and Ulysses. For all I know, Elke was in on the plan, too.'

Reina swallowed hard, in a futile attempt at ridding herself of the lump that suddenly filled her throat. 'Useless does seem very taken with you.'

Alicia shook her head in vehement denial. 'Nothing could be further from the truth! He's polite at best most of the time.'

Reina felt the lump recede. 'To hear my mother tell it, you and Ulysses are headed for the altar. She's trying to push me in that direction with Terrell.'

AN INDECENT LADY

Alicia's eyes widened. 'You don't want to go, do you?'

The conversation was becoming too convoluted for Reina. She had grown up with parents who spoke their minds – and she believed in speaking hers. 'I'm very fond of Terrell, but I'm not romantically inclined toward him – no matter how much my mother wishes I was. I'm sure he feels the same way about me.'

'Thank heaven for that.' A tremulous smile made Alicia look about ten years old. 'I wouldn't want anything to interfere with our friendship.'

'Neither would I,' Reina replied fervently, 'especially not a man. They're not worth it.'

'I'm freezing,' Alicia said. 'Is there somewhere we could go to talk?'

'The Prides have a line shack a mile ahead.'

'What are we waiting for?' Alicia spurred her mount to a gallop.

Reina quickly caught up and the race was on. They reached the shack in a dead heat, dismounted, tied their horses in the adjacent lean-to, and hurried inside, their girlish laughter leaving a trail of frosty breath in the air.

The shack was sparsely furnished with a couple of chairs, a table, and a cot built into one wall. Splits of wood had been left by the hearth in anticipation of some cowboy needing warmth and shelter.

Reina piled some of them in the fireplace, reminding herself to tell her father that someone would need to replenish the supply. While she lit the fire, Alicia dragged the two chairs close to the hearth.

She collapsed into one of them and held her hands out to the sputtering blaze. What she said next took Reina by surprise.

'Do you believe in love at first sight?'

'I'm not sure I believe in love at all.'

'What about your parents? They certainly seem to love each other.'

'They're supposed to love each other. It's different at our age. How do you know when you've met someone you want to spend the rest of your life with? How can you tell if they feel the same way? It's all so complicated.'

'Not all married people love each other,' Alicia said solemnly.

'Didn't your parents?'

'I used to think they did.' Biting her lower lip, she confided, 'I'm not sure anymore. But I don't want to talk about them. I want to talk about Terrell.'

'Don't tell me you think you're in love with him. You don't even know him.'

'It doesn't matter. I know me. When I saw him in your parlor yesterday, I felt as though the breath had been knocked out of me. I'd heard about Terrell and I had been looking forward to meeting him, but I never expected to react so strongly. I've lost control of my emotions completely. One minute I feel like laughing for no reason at all, and the next, I could weep. Colors seem brighter, scents seem stronger, sounds seem sweeter. I've never felt more alive. If that isn't love, I had better see a doctor because something is certainly wrong with me.'

Reina blinked in surprise. The blood drained from her head, leaving her dizzy. She knew just what Alicia was going through because she had endured the same tumultuous emotions herself. And not just for a day, but for the last three years. Since Ulysses came home from law school, to be exact!

'Is something wrong, Reina? You're as pale as a ghost.'

'Wrong?' Everything was wrong. Why hadn't she realized it before? She was in love with Ulysses Pride – a man who thought less of her than the dirt beneath his feet.

Now she understood why she had clung to her virtue with such fierce determination, why she had shunned all masculine attention. She had been saving herself for Ulysses.

The knowledge sickened her. Her stomach spasmed and bile rose up her throat. How Ulysses would laugh if he knew. His teasing and tormenting would be endless.

Had she ever done anything to make him suspect the truth? She pressed her hands against her abdomen, grimacing at the thought.

'You really do look sick,' Alicia said, leaning closer and touching Reina's brow. 'Maybe we'd better go back to your house and get you into bed.'

Reina had no desire to be alone with her thoughts. 'You wanted to talk.'

'We can talk another time, when you're feeling better.'

'I'm fine. Honestly.'

Thank heaven Alicia was too caught up in her own dilemma to be aware of Reina's. 'May I ask you something personal?' Alicia said.

'Certainly. I have no secrets,' Reina blurted out.

'Have you ever had a man kiss you, or kissed one back?'

Reina had been wrong about not having secrets. She had been kissed twice. The first time had been hell. The second had been heaven. She could only tell Alicia about the first, though. 'One of the hands cornered me in the stable a couple of years ago and kissed me so hard, he bruised my lips.'

Alicia's eyes widened. 'How did you make him stop?'

'I kneed him in the privates. He let me go fast enough after that.'

Alicia gazed at her with something akin to reverence. 'How did you know that would work?'

'My mother told me what to do if a man tried to force himself on me.'

'My mother hasn't told me much of anything about – about—'

'About sex?' Reina prompted, knowing how difficult it would be for Alicia to say the word.

Alicia nodded. 'She says we'll have a long talk after I get engaged. Here I am, twenty-two years old, and I don't know what men and women do when they're alone. I overheard one of our maids saying her mother told her to lie back and think of England on her wedding night. I asked my mother about it and she got so flustered. Your mother is so liberated by comparison.'

'I guess you know she was a whore?'

'My mother told me that Velvet used to make a living by comforting lonely men.'

Reina could hardly believe Alicia's naiveté. 'That's one way to put it.'

'Would you tell me what you know about sex?'

'Now that Terrell has come into your life, I reckon somebody better – not that he isn't a gentleman. But he's a man too. A lonely man who has a man's needs.'

'What needs? What has all the backstairs whispering and giggling been about all these years? Please, Reina, you've got to help me. My body does the most peculiar things when I think about Terrell.'

'What things?'

Alicia blushed, then gestured at her breasts. 'I get

all tingly and swollen hard up here, and warm and wet down below.'

Reina swallowed. Alicia was in a bad way. She had to be told the facts of life for her own protection. The question was, where to start?

The frigid air in the line shack warmed as Reina explained – in the simple anatomical terms her mother had used – how a man's body differs from a woman's, and how they can be used for mutual pleasure as well as procreation. It never occurred to Reina that what she told Alicia was both revelatory and revolutionary.

Alicia punctuated Reina's explanation with gasps and sighs. Her complexion grew rosier with every disclosure. By the time Reina finished, Alicia looked as red as the rubies her mother had given her for Christmas.

'I don't know if I could ever . . . do that. It sounds so – so – so disgusting.'

'My mother told me that being with a man you love, having him inside you, can be the most wonderful thing in the world.'

Alicia lowered her voice, although they couldn't have been more alone. 'Have you ever seen a man's privates?'

It was Reina's turn to blush. 'I saw Ulysses' penis when he was seven and I was four. We were skinny-dipping. I can't say his male parts impressed me. Mother told me they get bigger with age. Seeing how little and shriveled Ulysses' were, I sure hope so.'

Alicia chuckled. 'Now I know what men hide in their trousers, I'm afraid I won't be able to stop myself from staring.'

Reina laughed out aloud. 'I've ruined you.'

'No, you haven't. You've helped me. But I really

didn't intend to ask you about sex today. I wanted to talk about Terrell.'

'If you really are in love with him, the two go hand in hand.'

'How long have you known him?'

'All my life. Terrell's parents were farmers – not very successful ones. They died of a fever when he was fourteen. He was alone in the world so my father asked Mr Pride to give Terrell a job. My daddy wasn't married then and he took Terrell under his wing. They've been close ever since. When I was growing up, Terrell treated me like his little sister.'

'When did Terrell join the rangers?'

'He was twenty-three, and itching for adventure. He's taken part in just about every major action the rangers have been involved in.'

Alicia's eyes flashed. 'Please tell me about them.'

'You'd do better to hear it from Terrell, but I'll do my best.'

While the fire burned down, Reina held Alicia in thrall with thumbnail sketches of Terrell Meeks's exploits.

'I knew Terrell would be the perfect subject for my first book,' Alicia exclaimed when Reina finished.

'What in the world do you know about writing books?'

'Almost as much as you do about ranching,' Alicia replied with quiet confidence. 'Being a writer has been my goal for as long as I can remember.'

Alicia was certainly full of surprises today. 'Isn't that a man's line of work?'

'Yes – except for a few women like the Brontë sisters and Mary Shelley. I intend to join their ranks.'

'Does your mother know what you want to do?'

'No. And you must promise not to tell her.'

AN INDECENT LADY 179

'I want to be the foreman of the Pride ranch one day just like my daddy,' Reina blurted out.

'Isn't that a man's line of work?' Alicia mimicked.

Reina let go a sour laugh. 'I suppose that's why they called *foremen.*'

Alicia erupted from her chair and paced the line shack, her riding habit sweeping the dusty floor. 'Don't you ever laugh at your dreams, Reina.'

'I won't have to. Everyone else will do it for me.'

Alicia came to a stop directly in front of Reina. 'I believe we're on the brink of a new age – an age when women will be able to take their lives in their own hands and control their destinies, the way men do. When we first met, I said to myself, there's a woman who dares to be different. I admired you so. You've been a true inspiration to me.'

Reina managed a smile. 'Most folks don't approve of the way I act or dress.'

'Are you talking about Ulysses?'

'Among others.'

'Methinks he doth protest too much.'

'What does that mean?'

'It means that some people say and do the exact opposite of what they think and feel. I may not know the things you know but I do know a lot about people. A writer has to observe people to understand their motives. Ulysses doesn't take his eyes off you when you're together.'

Reina thought about what Alicia had just said, then quickly squelched the ember of hope the words ignited. Alicia didn't know Ulysses the way Reina did. He only looked at her to look down on her.

'With an imagination like that, you're bound to be a success,' Reina said. 'What kind of books do you plan to write?'

Alicia looked as though she wanted to say more about Ulysses, but thought better of it. 'I've heard there's a lot of money to be made in dime westerns. Unfortunately, we didn't have any in our library at Glenhaven.'

'I have lots of them. One of my favorites is *Jack Long, or Shot in the Eye, a True Story of Texas Border Life*. Then there's *Maleaeska, the Indian Wife of the White Hunter*. But I especially like the ones about Calamity Jane. She could do everything a man could do — except pee standing up.'

Alicia giggled. 'Reina DeVargas, you are scandalous.'

'I'd be happy to lend those books to you if you think it will help.'

'Help? It will be a gift from heaven.' Alicia squared her shoulders. Her lower jaw jutted with determination. 'Once I've had a chance to analyze their style and contents, I'm going to write one based on Terrell's exploits.'

Weeks ago, Reina had been sure she and Alicia had nothing in common. After the afternoon's mutual confessions, she thought of them as sisters under the skin. 'If you like, I'll read your chapters to make sure you get the Texas stuff right — the geography, the guns, the horses, that sort of thing.'

'That's wonderful,' Alicia exclaimed. 'Now all I need is some time alone with Terrell to hear his stories first hand.'

Reina grinned. 'I suspect that isn't the only reason you want to be alone with him. If you promise not to do any of the things we talked about, I'll try to arrange it.'

Alicia sighed. 'How? My mother watches me like a hawk.'

Reina got up and spread the embers so they would

burn out completely. 'When the four of us have supper at my house next week, I'll suggest we go skating afterwards. Elke taught us years ago. We've got lots of extra blades, and one of the stock ponds is frozen hard.'

'I don't see how that will help.'

'It will get the four of us out of the house.'

'I don't know how to skate,' Alicia objected.

'That's even better. Just make sure you don't admit it until we reach the pond. You can ask Terrell to take you for a walk instead.'

'Oh, Reina, you're a genius,' Alicia replied gleefully, 'to say nothing of being the best friend I ever had. I don't know how to thank you.'

Guilt reddened Reina's face. Had she come up with the idea for a skating party because Alicia wanted to be alone with Terrell – or because she wanted to be alone with Ulysses?

She'd be a fool to think a few moments with him would change anything.

Thirteen

It was damn foolishness, Ulysses thought. Four adults had no business going skating in the middle of the day – even on a Sunday. Certainly he had better things to do at home, a brief to complete, legislation to study before the coming session in Austin.

For the life of him, he couldn't imagine how he'd permitted himself to be talked into this outing – or why a sensible man like Terrell Meeks had agreed so eagerly. But for Terrell's enthusiastic response, Ulysses would have insisted on taking Alicia back to Pride's Passion right after supper at the DeVargases'.

He had no idea what had gotten into the ranger. Terrell's mustache had spent the afternoon twitching from one smile to another like a caterpillar on a vine.

Ulysses had always thought Terrell to be a taciturn, thoughtful, eminently sensible man – a hard one, too. However, the Terrell he'd dined with today seemed to have blurred around the edges, as if something had softened him on the inside and it had gentled his features.

This new Terrell laughed a lot, and even held his own in a conversation. He acted more like a youth at his first adult social than a man with a deadly reputation.

AN INDECENT LADY

Now, here the four of them were, strolling toward the stock pond with skating blades in hand when any rational right-minded adult would have the good sense to stay indoors.

'Remember how Miss Elke taught us all to skate?' Terrell asked of no one in particular. 'I thought I'd break an ankle, or some other unmentionable part of my anatomy, before I got the hang of it.'

Ulysses couldn't help smiling at the memories Terrell's remark invoked. Elke had been as graceful on the ice as the rest of them had been clumsy. She had learned to skate during her childhood in Germany, and insisted on teaching them the skater's waltz when they could barely keep their feet. The echo of her voice counting a one-two-three waltz cadence echoed in his mind and he increased his pace, as if Elke might still be waiting for him at the pond.

'I wish I'd had the chance to know Elke,' Alicia said breathlessly, hurrying to keep up.

'You would have loved her,' Ulysses replied past the lump in his throat.

'We all did,' Reina said.

'Amen to that,' Terrell seconded.

The frozen grass crunched under their feet. The smell of wood smoke drifted on the quiet air. The sun hung in the afternoon sky like a newly minted penny. Puffs of clouds drifted like balls of cotton escaping the harvest. Overhead, a few black vultures spiraled ever upward as though in search of heaven's gate.

Ulysses recalled learning to skate on just such a day. Caught up in memory, the thought of spending an hour on the ice seemed less repugnant. Besides, he hadn't spent much time with Alicia since Christmas – and she'd clearly been hurt by it.

Although she clung to his arm now, she'd spent

the supper hour hanging on Terrell's every word. He grinned to himself. If she had hoped to make him jealous, she had failed.

Alicia would never be able to rouse his deepest emotions – and he thanked God for it. He'd seen too many men set adrift by passion, had watched promising careers roasting in the flames of an ill-conceived attachment.

He had neither the time nor the inclination for such juvenile behavior – not if he hoped to accomplish his goals. He wanted a peaceful marriage, a serene home, a gracious hostess to govern it, and well-mannered children. Who better than Alicia to fulfill those needs?

Just then, she slipped on an icy patch and he tightened his grip on her arm. He gazed down at her, noting that she looked especially radiant today. How pleasant it was to be able to enjoy her beauty, without feeling a soul-deep ache because of it.

'I'm so glad you didn't insist on going home after supper,' she enthused. 'It's a fine afternoon to be outdoors.'

Sure it is, he mused, *if you're fond of freezing your balls off.* His own certainly were approaching the icicle stage.

Why had Reina insisted on this fool's expedition when a warm fire burned at home – and why had Terrell and Alicia agreed?

'Are you warm enough?' he asked.

'I'm just fine,' Alicia trilled merrily, although her hand trembled in the crook of his arm.

Reina gestured past a grove of oaks. 'The stock pond's just ahead. Why don't we gather some wood so we can have a fire after we skate?'

As far as Ulysses was concerned, that was the first sensible thing she had said all day. He let go of Alicia and began to gather dead-falls, bundling the branches in his arms. By the time the four of them reached the pond, he and Terrell were carrying enough wood to build quite a bonfire. They piled the branches for later use, then carried a fallen log to the edge of the pond so they'd have a place to sit while they attached the skating blades to their boots.

'Are you sure the pond is frozen hard?' he asked Reina.

She gave him a look that clearly said she thought he was an over-cautious fuddy-duddy. 'I was out here a couple of days ago and it's solid.'

'Did you skate on it?'

'I didn't have to. I have eyes!' she declared, sharpening her tongue on him as usual.

She had tucked her hair up inside her hat. As she bent to attach the skating blades to her boots, the nape of her neck looked as graceful as a swan's.

Although he'd been nursing a grudge against her since Christmas – husbanding his ill will like a miser hoarding coins – he had an almost irrepressible urge to press his lips against her vulnerable flesh.

Instead, he turned his attention to Alicia. She was looking at the skating blades, turning them end over end as if she'd never seen a pair before.

'Where did you learn to skate?' he asked.

'I didn't,' she responded with an insouciant lift of her shoulders.

'Then why in the world did you make such a fuss when I suggested we go home?'

'It would have been rude to leave so quickly. Besides, I'm tired of sitting at home. Don't you ever need to have fun, Ulysses?' She gazed up at him as though he were one card short of a full deck when, in fact, her behavior was in question.

'I enjoy a good time as much as anyone,' he

demurred. 'It just so happens that I enjoy my work, too.'

'You know what they say about all work and no play making Jack a dull boy,' Alicia replied.

Ulysses was on the brink of asking Alicia if she considered him dull. Before he could though, she turned to Terrell, extended her feet toward the ranger and said, 'Would you put the blades on for me?'

'Be happy to, Miss Alicia,' Terrell replied, his ginger-colored mustache twitching in yet another mindless grin. He dropped to his knees, grasped a dainty foot in one hand and a skating blade in the other.

'It really isn't hard,' he said solemnly.

For some unknown reason, Terrell's remark unleashed a gale of unseemly laughter on the part of Reina and Alicia. Every time Ulysses thought they'd gotten control of themselves, they looked at one another and the laughter began all over again. Ulysses didn't expect anything better of Reina – but what had gotten into Alicia?

'I'm so sorry,' she said, not to him but to Terrell, as though Terrell alone merited an apology.

'I like a joke as much as the next fellow,' Terrell replied. 'I just wish I knew what was so funny.'

Alicia giggled again. 'Someday, I promise I'll tell you. Now, please show me what to do with the blades.'

What the hell had gotten into her? What had gotten into Terrell for that matter? Ulysses turned away and concentrated on fixing the blades to his own boots. By the time he finished and looked up, Reina was already on the ice.

'I feel as free as a bird,' she called out, effortlessly skimming across the frozen surface. She was every bit

AN INDECENT LADY

as graceful as Elke had been. Floating over the ice in her dark pants and jacket, she reminded Ulysses of a bird. A crow, he decided uncharitably.

He finished with his own blades and stood up, feeling his ankles wobble a little. Unlike Reina, he'd never been an accomplished skater, and it had been years since a pond had frozen hard enough to practice.

'Do you need any help?' he asked Alicia although, truth to tell, he wasn't in shape to give her any.

'I'm sure Terrell and I can manage,' she replied, dismissing Ulysses with a careless wave.

'See you on the ice, then,' he said.

Alicia waited until Ulysses committed himself to the frozen pond before hiking her skirt a little higher, affording Terrell a long look at her legs under the guise of giving him easier access to her high-buttoned shoes.

She felt positively giddy at her own temerity. The flush on Terrell's cheeks told her he wasn't entirely immune to her charms. *So far so good*, she thought, glancing toward the pond where Reina and Ulysses studiously ignored each other as they skated back and forth.

'That's all there is to it,' Terrell said, finishing with the blades and getting to his feet. 'Why don't you try standing up.'

Alicia glanced down at her feet. The skating blades gleamed like rapiers. They seemed far too narrow to support her. 'I'm not sure I can.'

'Let me help you.' He moved so close that she caught his scent – an intoxicating blend of soap, spicy shaving lotion, and something musky that she intuitively identified as pure male.

He put his hands on either side of her waist and lifted her to her feet. She felt more unsteady than she had anticipated – and not just because she was having trouble balancing on the skates. Being so close to Terrell turned her legs to mush.

Her ankles gave way and she fell against his chest. When he caught her in his arms, she thought she would swoon from the thrill of it.

'Oh, dear,' she gasped, her face pressed against his neck, 'I don't think I'm going to be able to do this. My ankles are too weak.'

'They did look awfully dainty,' he remarked.

Although layers of clothing prevented her from intimate contact with his body, she had never experienced anything as seductive as the caress of his breath on her cheek. The points of her breasts hardened. A fire seemed to start deep in her abdomen, radiating outward to warm her from the top of her head to the tips of her toes.

'I reckon Ulysses won't mind if we cut this party short,' Terrell said. 'He didn't seem all that happy about skating in the first place.'

Pretending to be unable to stand without his support, Alicia continued to cling to him. She could have listened to him talk all day as long as he held her close. She would sooner have died than give up what might be her only chance to be alone with him. Besides, she'd be damned if all the scheming she and Reina had done would be for nought.

'I would hate to spoil Reina's fun,' she said. 'If we go back now, I have no doubt she'll spend the rest of the afternoon riding fences or mucking out stalls. She deserves an afternoon off.'

'So where does that leave us? It's much too cold to sit here like bumps on a log.'

Cold? Who was cold? Certainly not Alicia. She felt warm enough to take off her clothes and dance barefoot on the frosty grass. 'We could

AN INDECENT LADY

take a walk. I have been most anxious to talk to you.'

'Suits me.' He lowered her back down, handling her as carefully as though she were made of porcelain rather than flesh and blood. Knowing his fierce reputation, his gentleness touched her.

'I'll just take those blades off for you,' he said.

Terrell grit his teeth and struggled to subdue the heat pooling in his groin as Alicia extended her legs and lifted her skirts halfway to the knee. She was wearing silky stockings that clung to her limbs like a second skin.

He had gone one on one – mano a mano – with some of the worst desperadoes in Texas and never so much as blinked. But his hands trembled as he removed the skating blades. Good God almighty, Miss Alicia had the prettiest legs he'd ever seen.

Feeling his erection pressing against his trousers, he thanked heaven for the concealment afforded by his long coat. A lady of Miss Alicia's caliber would probably swoon dead away if she realized she'd given him a boner. And what a boner it was. He felt as hard as a fence post.

A man with his history had no business being alone with a lady like Miss Alicia. And yet, he silently thanked whatever gods other men believed in for the chance.

He'd come to supper, planning to pay court to Reina. But he hadn't been able to keep his eyes off Alicia – and if he ever got the chance, he feared his hands would follow where his eyes had been.

Considering his state of arousal, getting her off alone was every bit as dangerous as chasing rustlers across the Mexican border. She was much too innocent to know the effect all that touching and holding and looking had had on him.

'That's better,' Alicia said, jumping to her feet as soon as he freed them from the blades. 'You really must excuse me for holding on to you like that, Mr Meeks. I felt certain I would lose my balance and twist an ankle.' Alicia glanced over at the pond where Reina was leading Ulysses on a merry chase across the ice. 'I can't imagine how Reina does it.'

'Reina's fearless. But then, she's skated since she was three or four,' Terrell replied. 'You don't fear falling when you're that close to the ground. Anyway, her ankles aren't as slender as yours.'

Alicia lifted one delicate brow. 'How would you know what Reina's ankles look like, Mr Meeks?'

'I don't,' Terrell quickly said.

Alicia gave him a sideways glance with those beautiful eyes. 'Then you weren't making an informed comparison?'

'I don't know how Reina's ankles look anymore – but I used to. I even changed her diapers a time or two,' Terrell admitted, before he realized Alicia had been teasing him.

It had been so long since a woman had dallied with him that he didn't know how to react. *Hell*, he decided. He might as well go along for the ride.

'Shall we walk, Mr Meeks?' Alicia asked, offering him her hand.

He tucked it in the crook of his elbow. The contact sent a tingle up his arm. If her gloved hand could do that, what would happen if he ever touched her bare skin? Most likely, he'd explode into flame like a lightning-struck tree.

'Shouldn't I tell Ulysses we're going?' he asked.

'I doubt he'll even notice,' Alicia replied. 'Besides, we won't be gone long.'

She sure did have answers for everything, Terrell mused. It was probably just as well since his own brain didn't seem to be functioning too well, seeing as how so much blood had pooled at his crotch.

'Isn't it a beautiful day?' Alicia said, as they strolled back toward the grove of oaks.

'Prettiest day I ever did see,' he replied, gazing down at her.

They walked in companionable silence until Alicia broke the spell woven by their solitude. 'Reina told me you were involved in something called the Flores Affair. She said you singlehandedly put an end to rustlers coming into Texas from Mexico.'

Terrell had an irresistible urge to boast a little. However, years of being close-mouthed tempered his words. 'I may have chased the Flores bunch into Mexico by myself. Thank heaven the cavalry and a contingent of rangers caught up with me, or I'd have been a goner for sure.'

Alicia's grip tightened. 'You went after a group of rustlers all by yourself! That's the bravest thing I've ever heard.'

'There were only thirty men in the Flores gang. It shouldn't take more than one Texas ranger to handle a sorry bunch like that.'

Reina couldn't have been happier as she saw Terrell and Alicia stroll off arm in arm. They certainly made a handsome couple – far handsomer than Alicia and Ulysses, she decided. The truth was, she wouldn't have liked seeing Ulysses paired up with anyone.

She glanced back to see how he was doing.

'Hold up, Queenie,' he called out.

She spun around, cutting deep into the ice with her blades as she skated backwards, a feat Ulysses had never mastered.

'What's the matter, Useless? Am I going too fast for you?'

'Don't you think you ought to look where you're going?' he questioned with typical caution.

'I know this pond as well as I know my own room.' She flashed an impudent grin as she increased her speed.

Every rancher put in stock ponds to insure a supply of water during the long, hot summers. This particular pond had been created by building an earthen dam at the end of a wash that ran fierce and strong every time it rained.

Reina had helped her father choose the site five years before. She had watched the pond fill – had fished in it every summer since. But it had never been cold enough to freeze over before. She wished she dared look back over her shoulder to check for thin ice. However, she wouldn't give Ulysses the satisfaction.

Although he skated with a will, scowling all the while, he couldn't catch her. Thirty feet separated them when she heard a loud crack, like the sound of rifle fire. From then on, time seemed to slow down.

Ulysses shouted a warning.

She looked down.

A spider web of cracks laced the ice beneath her.

The frozen surface heaved, then gave way beneath her.

Ulysses' horrified expression was the last thing she saw before she plunged into the water.

Ulysses' heart spasmed so hard that, for a moment, he couldn't breathe. He had a sense of unreality as he saw Reina disappear in the pond's frigid depths. Her hat bobbed to the surface as merrily as a child's toy in a bathtub.

For a couple of eternities, there was no sign

of Reina. He skated forward warily. 'Reina,' he shouted in a rasping voice that seemed to emerge from someone else's throat, 'Reina, for the love of God, where are you?'

Twenty feet away, she popped through the break in the ice like Venus emerging from the waves – only this Venus wore clothes and her lips had turned blue.

Thank God, he silently breathed. She had been a thorn in his side as long as he could remember – but he couldn't imagine life without her.

'I'll be fine as soon as you can get me out of here,' she said with considerable fortitude under the circumstances.

But then, Reina had always been long on grit. She tried to heave herself onto the ice and failed – then tried again. The effort weakened her visibly.

'Ulysses,' she called out, her voice already thinning as the frigid water took its toll. 'What the hell are you waiting for? Come get me.'

Instinct urged him to rush across the ice. Logic commanded him to stay put long enough to determine a course of action. 'Hang on, Reina,' was the best he could manage as his racing brain sought for a way to rescue her.

He wasn't a good enough skater to do her any good while the blades were attached to his boots. Besides, the ice would never hold them both. He stroked the few feet to the shore and ripped the blades from his boots, not even noticing that he sliced his palms in the process.

If only they had ridden to the pond the way he'd suggested, he'd have a rope to toss her. How could he ever save her without one?

'Don't leave me,' Reina begged as he raced for the nearby trees. 'I'll die if you leave me.'

'I'll be right back. Hang on, Queenie,' he shouted, using the hated nickname to rouse her fighting spirit.

He forced himself to ignore the fear in her voice – to quell the fear rising inside him at the thought of what she must be enduring.

He forced himself to outrun his hammering heart, to move faster than his thick clothes should have allowed.

His gaze raced ahead, searching for a sapling. He saw one at the edge of the wood and attacked it with savage fury, sawing at the trunk with his pocket knife.

The blade had been made for gentler tasks. It snapped close to the handle.

Driven by an urgency that gave him a madman's strength, he grasped the tree with both hands, bent it over his knee and snapped the trunk near its base, then raced back to the pond.

Relief almost unmanned him as he saw Reina still clinging to the edge of the ice. If he managed to pull her free, he wouldn't say anything cruel to her again – no matter how she provoked him, he thought, making a silent bargain with God.

When he reached the edge of the ice, he fell to his hands and knees, then belly-crawled onto it, his stomach heaving with dread. He'd always been a cerebral man rather than a man of action. Men like his father and Terrell were far better suited to heroic deeds.

'I can't come get you,' he called out. 'The ice won't hold me. You'll have to grab hold of the tree.'

He extended the sapling toward Reina. It didn't quite reach and he had to move further out onto the ice. It moved beneath him and his stomach moved with it. The delicious meal he'd had at the DeVargases' rose in his throat.

He crept forward an inch at a time, not daring to move faster. Please God, let him get to Reina in time – and let her still have the strength to hold onto the tree.

At last, the trunk extended over the break in the ice.

'I'm afraid I'll go under if I reach for it,' Reina wailed.

'No, you won't,' he reassured her in his best lawyer's voice – the one he used when he was trying to convince a guilty client there was nothing to fear from the wrath of the law. 'The pond can't be that deep. Just latch on and I'll pull you out. Come on, Queenie. You wouldn't be in this fix if you'd been looking where you were going, so don't expect me to do all the work.'

As he had hoped, an ember of anger flared on Reina's frozen face. With agonizing slowness, she wrapped first one hand and then the other around the sapling. Ulysses rolled onto his back. Digging his heels into the ice, he struggled back toward the edge of the pond, fighting for every inch, his muscles straining with effort.

The ice continued to crack, trembling beneath him with every movement – or was it only his body trembling with fear?

Remembering how Reina had assured him it was perfectly safe, he longed to throttle her. First, though, he had to save her. He was determined to do just that – at the cost of his own life, if that's what it took.

Time seemed to inch along even slower than he did before he felt solid ground under his body. With a convulsive heave, he rolled onto his knees.

'Just a few more feet and I'll have you out of there,'

he encouraged Reina. God alone knew how she had found the strength to hang on to the sapling.

At last, the ice stopped breaking and she was able to lay flat on top of it. He pulled harder, not caring that his bleeding palms spotted the edge of the ice with crimson droplets. When Reina finally came within his grasp, he snatched her up, holding her against his chest, unaware of the tears that streaked his face.

Cold and fear had slowed his agile mind. At first, he thought she was fighting his embrace. Then he realized the tremors running through her body were caused by the cold – a cold that could kill if he didn't act quickly. Still holding her tight, willing his warmth into her, he ran for the pile of branches he and Terrell had collected.

Hating to let Reina go for even a second, he set her down on her feet, then removed his daily ration of three cigars from his coat pocket and crumbled them into tinder.

'Take off your clothes,' he commanded, while he struck a match on his boot and held it to the tiny heap of tobacco and cellophane.

'Are you out of your mind? I'm cold as it is,' Reina said.

'You're going to get even colder if you don't get out of those wet clothes.' He added branches to the smoldering tinder until a blaze sent smoke curling upward.

Reina still stood where he'd set her down, trembling like an aspen in a gale.

'Damn it, Reina, this isn't the time for false modesty. You'll catch pneumonia if you don't get out of those wet clothes.'

'I can't make my hands move.'

'I'll do it for you, then.'

'Don't you dare!' she sputtered.

Thank God she still had some fight left. She was going to need it before he got her safely home. One of these days, her spunk was going to get her in even worse trouble than she was in right now.

He closed the distance between them. Her trembling increased. Was it caused by the cold – or by the thought of revealing herself to him?

'Promise you won't look,' she said past teeth that clattered like castanets.

He didn't answer.

She was wearing a sheepskin-lined jacket much like his own. He undid the toggles that held it shut, then pulled it from her shoulders. She stood as motionless as a sculpture – except for the tremors racking her body.

Dropping the jacket at her feet, he unwound a sodden scarf from her neck. Ice water rained down from her flannel shirt. His fingers felt stiff as he undid the buttons, then tugged the shirt from her trousers. For once, he was grateful she had worn them. Yards of woolen skirt might have pulled her under for good.

Pushing her closer to the island of warmth created by the fire, he tugged the shirt away from her body and cast it aside. He bent down and tugged her boots off, skating blades and all, then undid her belt and stripped off her Levi's. His fingers shook as he undid the tiny pearl buttons that ran down the front of her underwear.

A swift tug and Reina's body emerged from the last of its sodden cocoon.

Thank heaven he hadn't promised not to look. He prided himself on keeping his promises – and a saint wouldn't have been able to keep that particular one.

In the few seconds it took him to strip off his own coat, he looked his fill.

Any other woman would have reacted to his plundering gaze by attempting to shield her sex.

Reina's hands hung limp at her sides. Either the icy plunge had stripped away her modesty – or she was too brassy and bold to care where his gaze lingered.

The cold had metamorphosed her body into marble. Her skin was so white that it seemed translucent. Her breasts jutted from her ribcage, tipped by rigid nipples as blue as her lips. Her torso narrowed to an impossibly tiny waist before flaring again at her hips.

A drop of moisture oozed from her navel. He nearly flung himself down in front of her to lap it away. The thick black curls between her thighs were dripping wet, too – and even more inviting.

He saw all that and more in the seconds it took him to wrap her in his own dry coat – and those seconds would forever be engraved in his soul. Although he hadn't time to give words to the thought, he knew that from then on he would judge feminine beauty by Reina's standard – and that all other women would come up short.

He stepped closer and began rubbing her skin, his hands almost harsh in his desperate effort to get her blood circulating again. He tried to close his mind to the knowledge that her naked body was his to plunder, that she was too weak to fight him.

He was, he reminded himself, a gentleman on a life-saving mission of mercy – not a hungry man who had been without a woman too long, and who had now been offered a feast.

Fourteen

To Ulysses' amazement, Reina offered no resistance as his hands worked down her naked back. At first, he only meant to bring her frozen flesh back to life. By the time his hands reached her buttocks, though, he'd lost track of his original intention.

Brisk rubbing became sensual caresses as he immersed himself in forbidden pleasures. The geography of Reina's body was his to explore and plunder. He'd never wandered over such sweet hillocks, or traversed such a fascinating valley.

With a start, he realized what he was doing and quickly moved his hands to the front of her body. Despite his best efforts to comport himself like a gentleman, even greater temptations waited for him there. The curve of her belly pushed against one palm – the weight of a breast filled another. He lowered a hand to the sodden curls between her legs, and cupped the heart of her femininity.

Heat surged in his groin like a blast furnace. His cock pressed against his trousers. His testicles felt heavy with need.

Although she wore his jacket, he was oblivious to the cold. Desire overwhelmed his brain, obliterating all other sensations. Minutes earlier, he had prayed Terrell and Alicia would return. Now, he prayed they wouldn't.

Only a monster would dream of making love to a woman who had been through so dreadful an ordeal.

Such a monster lived in him.

He wanted Reina – here – now – in this frozen place . . . and she seemed to want him, too. Why else would she permit him to take such liberties?

He pushed the coat aside, the better to expose her lush body – and she sagged in his arms. Only then did he realize that fierce, bold, indomitable Reina was beyond fighting.

Although her eyes were open, a glaze sheened them. She seemed to be looking off to a place only she could see. If he didn't do something quickly, she just might slip away to that place and never come back.

Cursing himself for a cad, a bounder – and yes, even a bastard – he gathered her up in his arms and clutched her to his chest so tightly that the sinews in his arms and neck ached.

The shadows of the trees had lengthened. The sky had grayed. A storm was on its way. He had to get Reina safely home before it hit. With her lolling in his arms like a discarded rag doll, he raced the cold and the clock back to the DeVargases' home.

He had never hated himself more than he did now. How in the name of all that was holy could he have put Reina's life at risk while he took his own pleasure?

Terrell couldn't remember the last time he had talked so much. Perhaps he never had. The way Alicia hung on his every word had made his tongue feel as agile as a bushy-tailed squirrel racing up a tree. He'd spouted words like a traveling salesman

… hawking snake oil. Feeling uneasy at his unaccustomed verbosity, he brought the story of the Flores affair to a hasty conclusion.

'In the years following the Civil War, Texas ranchers lost thousands of cattle to rustlers who came over the Mexican border. I convinced the Flores bunch to give some of those cattle back. Someone had to stop what was happening. I just happened to be in the right place at the right time.'

Alicia let go a long sigh. 'I've never heard a more thrilling story. You're so modest. How you found the courage to face that gang all alone, and demand the return of the cattle—'

Her voice trailed off. Her hold on his arm tightened. Considering how dainty she looked, she had one hell of a grip.

'Was there a woman involved in the incident – perhaps a fallen angel with a heart of gold?'

'Of course not!' he declared with a flare of temper. 'What kind of man do you think I am? I would never endanger a woman like that.'

They had been strolling at a leisurely pace. Now, Alicia tugged him to a stop. She had the damndest look in her eyes, as if she had fallen into some sort of trance. 'I'll just have to make one up then,' she murmured, gazing off into space.

Bemused, confused, he said, 'You'll what?'

Her trance ended as abruptly as it started. 'I just mean that heroes are supposed to have heroines.'

What nonsense was she talking now? He wasn't a hero. He'd only done his job, the same as every other man who wore a ranger's badge over his heart. He stared into her eyes, wondering if he would ever know what was going on behind them.

She stared right back. 'May I be your heroine?'

The cathedral-like quiet of their surroundings

seemed to add a profound weight to her question. For a moment, Terrell had the bizarre idea that Alicia was asking him to marry her.

Talk about wishful thinking! Hell, he must be delusional. She was just passing the time in idle flirtation. Speaking of which, what time was it?

He looked up at the sky, noting the clouds bunching on the horizon like Longhorns at a river crossing, then pulled his pocket watch from under his coat. Good Lord, they'd been walking and talking for half an hour.

'We had better get back to the pond,' he said, taking a firm hold of Alicia's arm.

'There's something I have to do first.'

'What?'

'I have to kiss you,' she replied, as though he had no say in the matter.

'I don't think – that is – you—' His spluttered objections ground to a halt like a calliope running out of steam.

'In my country, it's customary to kiss someone to thank them. I want to thank you for telling me about the Flores affair. My feelings will be dreadfully hurt if you don't let me.'

Terrell had known her father just well enough to remember that the English had some very weird customs – like drinking tea instead of coffee, calling a plain old biscuit a crumpet, and saying *bloody this* and *bloody that* as if the world were even gorier than he knew it to be. He supposed this kissing business to be just another of their peculiar traditions.

'I wouldn't dream of hurting your feelings,' he said in a strangled voice.

'I'm glad you see it my way.' She opened her arms, closed her eyes, and tilted her face up to his. 'You may kiss me now.'

AN INDECENT LADY

He leaned down, only meaning to graze her lips. But she tasted so sweet that he deepened the contact. At least he wouldn't put his arms around her, he promised himself.

When her arms circled his back, his seemed to rise of their own volition to pull her close.

His lips tingled. The tingle spread, racing down his spine and curling his toes.

The thank you lasted a long time – too long for Terrell's composure, and not long enough for his pleasure. Coming to his senses, he finally broke free. His heart pounding, he drew in a ragged gasp of frigid air.

'Are you sure that's how your countrymen say thank you?' he asked.

'That's how I always say it,' Alicia replied sweetly, a butter-wouldn't-melt-in-her-mouth smile on her delicious lips.

'For God's sake, this isn't England. A beautiful woman like you could get in a world of trouble in Texas, thanking men like that.' A terrible thought knifed into his vitals. 'Have you ever thanked Ulysses that way?'

'He's never done me so great a favor.'

The spasm in Terrell's gut relaxed a little. 'All I did was tell you about the Flores affair.'

Alicia's laughing blue eyes turned suddenly solemn. 'Someday, I hope to tell you why it meant so much to me.' She paused, and the laughter returned. 'Didn't you like my thank you?'

Like it? The kiss had damn near lifted him out of his boots.

'It wasn't bad,' he admitted grudgingly. To be honest, he wouldn't mind having her thank him that way every day for the rest of his life. Only that wasn't likely to happen, and the realization made him feel a hundred years old. 'We'd better be getting back.'

'Not until you promise to come out to the ranch soon and tell me more about your experiences.'

Terrell nodded his agreement. He had an anxious feeling, a peculiar flutter in his gut that he would have attributed to the kiss – if the feeling hadn't intensified after he let go of Alicia.

Intuition had served him well in the past. He'd been gifted with a sixth sense that warned him of trouble before it smacked him in the face. Now, that sixth sense sent a chill through him that had nothing to do with the cold. He turned a full circle, as if he expected someone or something to come out of the woods, his eyes narrowing to sharpen their focus, his right hand easing down to the gun at his hip.

'Is something wrong?' Alicia asked, picking up on his disquiet.

'Reina or Ulysses should have missed us by now.'

Hurrying Alicia along, he led the way back to the pond. What he saw there stiffened the hair on his neck and drove the breath from his lungs.

The ice had been broken. A hat floated on the black still water. A pile of sodden clothes lay scattered by the remnants of a fire.

Hell and damnation. While he'd been jawing, showing off like a damn fool, Reina or Ulysses had fallen through the ice. Letting go of Alicia, he ran to read the signs on the ground.

Alicia raced after him. 'Those are Reina's things,' she called out with an unerring female eye for apparel. 'Where is she? What happened?'

Studying the tracks that led from the pond to the fire, and then towards the trees, he said, 'Reina fell through the ice. It looks like Ulysses is carrying her back to the house.'

Alicia leapt forward like a jack rabbit with a coyote on its tail. 'Velvet will never let the four of us go out again if she find out I left Reina alone. We're supposed to be chaperoning each other. We've got to catch up to them.'

By the time Alicia finished what she had to say, she was in a flat-out gallop. Terrell raced after her, amazed at how quickly she could run in her long skirts.

Reina stood in a sun-dappled meadow with Ulysses by her side. The longing she saw on his face stirred a response deep in her womb.

'God, I had no idea you were so beautiful,' he breathed. 'You're the most beautiful thing I've ever seen.'

She stared into his eyes, looking for falsehood in their depths – and saw only truth. Then she gazed down at her own body and realized she was naked. Instead of feeling ashamed, she experienced a fierce pride at knowing Ulysses took pleasure from seeing her that way. And it *was* pleasure she saw on his face – and longing, and hunger, and need.

Suddenly, without quite knowing how she got there, she was in Ulysses' arms, molding her body to his, reveling in the throaty groan that poured from his throat as his hands caressed her.

She had dreamed of this moment night after lonely night – and shut her waking mind to the dream.

Now, she gave herself up to it.

Ulysses' explorations left trails of fire on her skin. She flamed with need, incandescing with the pleasure he gave her yearning flesh. He touched her breast and she felt it swell into the curve of his palm.

Then, inexplicably, they weren't in the sun-dappled meadow any more. She felt the wind rushing past her face the way she did when she rode Starfire at a gallop.

'No,' she moaned, wanting to return to the heaven she had just left.

'It's all right. You're going to be all right,' came Ulysses' voice.

Where in God's name were they? What had happened? She struggled to pierce the veil of unreality that sheathed her mind.

Prying her eyes apart, she saw Ulysses' face just inches from hers and realized he was holding her in his arms.

Questions ratcheted through her mind like broken spokes on a wheel. Why was he carrying her when she was perfectly capable of walking? Why was she so cold? Where were Alicia and Terrell?

Damn and double damn, Ulysses thought. A man who had spent his life in sedentary pursuits had no business pitting himself against the grim reaper in a winner-take-all foot race, while carrying a woman in his arms.

His legs felt like mush. His heart labored like a steam engine pulling a load up a hill. The pond couldn't be more than a mile from the DeVargas house, but every step was taking its toll.

He had always counted on his brain to see him through any situation. Aside from playing intramural sports at Harvard – and not very well at that – he had spent his adult life behind a desk. Now, he mentally cursed himself for not being in better shape.

He stumbled and barely managed to keep his balance. Out of breath, out of strength, he ran on sheer willpower. As long as Reina was still alive, he'd keep right on running until his heart burst.

Intent on his mission, he never heard Terrell and Alicia approach. 'You look played out,' Terrell called out, reaching for Reina. 'Let me take her.'

Ulysses had seen horses run to death. He'd never thought it would happen to him. He stumbled to a stop and fell to his knees so abruptly that Reina would have hit the ground if Terrell hadn't managed to catch her.

'Is she alive?' Alicia asked.

Ulysses barely had the strength to nod. He wheezed and gasped. His whole body trembled.

'Catch up when you get your breath,' Terrell said, moving off at once.

'No, no,' Alicia cried out, her body rigid with alarm. 'Don't leave yet. The two of you have to promise not to tell a soul that we weren't together when Reina fell through the ice.'

Ulysses was too winded to argue, and too exhausted to wonder why it seemed so important to Alicia.

'I don't lie – and I don't have time to debate you either,' Terrell replied, setting off at a trot.

Alicia trotted right along beside him. 'Please, Terrell. You won't have to lie. Just let me tell Velvet what happened,' she said, as they ran out of earshot.

Velvet was alone in the kitchen, setting a bowl of sour dough to rise, when the door burst open and Terrell came in carrying Reina in his arms.

'Oh my God, what happened to my little girl?' Velvet cried out as Terrell unceremoniously swept the bowl of dough crashing to the floor and laid Reina out on the table. She looked as white as a corpse.

'The four of us were skating, and Reina fell through the ice,' Alicia explained, the words tumbling out so quickly that Velvet wasn't sure she got the sense of them.

There'd be time for questions later. And Velvet would have lots of them – like why Reina was mother-naked under that coat, and why there were streaks of blood on her body, and where the hell was that low-account bastard, Ulysses?

This, however, was the time for action. 'Alicia, get the covers off Reina's bed and bring them here. Terrell, build up the fire, then get the brandy from the sideboard in the dining room.'

Having marshalled her troops like a general, Velvet took her daughter in her arms. Reina's skin was deathly cold, but a pulse beat in her throat. She was alive and she'd damn well stay that way if Velvet had anything to say about it.

She spent the next thirty minutes fighting for her daughter's life the way she had fought for Elke's so many years ago, wrapping Reina in blankets, setting heated bricks at her feet, rubbing her arms and legs to get the blood circulating again, trickling brandy down her throat a drop at a time – and talking to her, calling her back from the dark place where her spirit had gone.

Alicia stuck by Velvet's side like a tick on a dog, telling Velvet what had happened without being asked.

Reina was a much better skater than the rest of them. She'd gone off into the middle of the pond by herself and fallen through. Ulysses and Terrell had pulled her out. Fearing she would freeze in her sodden garments, Alicia had undressed her while the men built a fire. They tried to warm Reina, and then Ulysses and Terrell had carried her home.

While Alicia talked, Terrell built up the fire until

the kitchen felt as hot as a Comanche sweat lodge. Sometime during the proceedings, Ulysses showed up looking almost as bad as Reina.

Rio arrived shortly afterwards, took one look at Reina, and went as white as a sheet. Alicia repeated the story all over again for his benefit. Thank God, Reina was showing signs of life when Alicia finished or Rio might have taken out his shock and fear on Terrell and Ulysses.

Seeing Reina recover turned Rio talkative. He thanked Terrell and Ulysses for saving Reina's life so many times that it was all Velvet could do not to tell him to shut up.

Deep down, she had the feeling that there was more to the afternoon's mishap than anyone had revealed. She wouldn't sleep easy until she learned the truth.

Fifteen

Reina did everything in her power to return to the sun-dappled meadow, and the warmth of Ulysses' embrace.

She abandoned her body and soul to the dark, hoping it would lead her back to him. She ignored her mother's distant voice, disregarded the hands kneading her frozen flesh, closed her mind to the heated bricks that sent painful prickles of warmth shooting up her legs.

But she couldn't dismiss the brandy trickling down her thoat. *Stop it*, she silently implored, *let me go back to Ulysses*. The relentless trickle continued. Either she choked – or she swallowed.

She gulped convulsively, gasping as the liquor flamed past her gullet.

'Wake up, Reina,' her mother said, 'please wake up. Come on, sugar, you can do it.'

Confused, and hurting – halfway to heaven and eager to go the rest of the way – Reina couldn't ignore the love and concern in her mother's voice. It pulled her up from the shadowy pit, an inch at a time. Ever so slowly, she became aware of the hard surface she lay on, of the smothering quilts covering her from head to toe, of the residual smell of their supper.

The kitchen. She was in the kitchen. The last thing she remembered was the meadow where

Ulysses had made love to her. How did she get here?

Her eyes fluttered open. Four anxious faces — Velvet's, Rio's, Terrell's and Alicia's — hovered over hers.

Where was Ulysses? Had his lovemaking been a dream? She tried to call his name — and only managed a wordless croak. Needles of pain shot up from her feet and hands as her heart pumped blood to her half-frozen extremities. God. She felt so weak.

'Don't try to talk,' Velvet said. 'There will be plenty of time to talk later. You need to save your strength.'

'Damn right, you do, baby girl,' Rio declared, sweeping her up in his arms, covers and all. 'It's time we got you into your own bed.'

Tears flooded Alicia's eyes as she watched Rio carry Reina from the kitchen. She had come so close to losing the best friend she'd ever had. Dear Lord, if Reina had died, she would have spent the rest of her life on her knees asking forgiveness. Why, she might even have joined a nunnery in penance.

She never should have coaxed Terrell away from the pond, never have left Reina alone with Ulysses — not that he would ever have done her any harm. He slumped against one of the kitchen walls, as if his legs didn't have the strength to keep him upright. With his white face, bloodshot eyes, and disheveled hair, he looked like a man who has had a glimpse into hell.

Leaving Reina and Ulysses to the unknown perils of the frozen pond had been utterly selfish. However, Alicia knew she'd do it all over again if she had the chance. The minutes alone with Terrell had been the most memorable, thrilling, exhilarating minutes in her life – and she wanted more of them.

Why did the right things have to happen at the wrong times? Why couldn't she have met someone like Terrell in England instead of falling in love halfway around the world from her home? Why couldn't she have given her heart to someone her mother would have accepted without question or complaint?

Talk about star-crossed lovers, she thought, her misery deepening, knowing Romeo's and Juliet's problems weren't any worse than the ones she and Terrell faced. The knowledge that he cared for her only deepened her concern.

A frisson lifted the fine hair on Alicia's neck as she contemplated the future. If she got caught in the lie now, there would be hell to pay.

At the very least, she would get a memorable lecture. At the worst, Charlotte might book passage on the next ship to England. Either way, she would never be alone with Terrell again.

The prospect generated a low moan that rose up her throat to reverberate through the sudden quiet.

'Don't fret, Miss Alicia,' Terrell said, giving her a sympathetic smile, completely misunderstanding the cause of her misery. 'Reina's going to do just fine.'

His words comforted her – but she would have felt ever so much better if he'd come and put his arms around her. Instead, he walked over to Ulysses and clapped him on the shoulder.

'You did a hell of a job, getting Reina out of the pond. She owes you her life.'

'You'd have done better. It took me a long time—' Ulysses' voice cracked. 'Thank God you caught up to us when you did. I don't think I could have carried Reina another step.'

AN INDECENT LADY

Alicia ignored the stricken look on Ulysses' face. What if the DeVargases heard him? What if Rio or Velvet walked into the room this very minute? Her stomach heaved at the thought.

'Hush, you two.' She reinforced the command by putting a finger to her lips.

Terrell glared at her.

'Sorry,' Ulysses mumbled.

She had no time to waste on either of them. Her mind was on Reina – and what Reina might say to her parents. The thought galvanized Alicia into action.

'You promised not to say anything,' she whispered urgently. 'I'm holding the both of you to that promise.'

Ulysses nodded his head, yes.

Terrell's gaze intensified. 'I didn't promise any such thing.'

She glared right back. 'You didn't say no, and now it's too late.' She'd deal with him later. Right now, she had more urgent business.

'If you two will excuse me,' she said, 'I want to sit with Reina.' To Ulysses, she added, 'Please tell my mother not to worry if I spend the night here.'

Giving Terrell one last warning glance, she gathered her skirts and hastened after the DeVargases.

The door to Reina's bedroom was wide open. Rio sat in a chair by the window, holding Reina in his arms. Her eyes were closed. She seemed to be asleep. Useful lay at their feet, his great head held erect, his reproachful gaze riveted on Reina as if to say, 'You shouldn't have left me behind.'

Velvet was making the bed up with fresh linens. Alicia hastened to help her. 'If you don't mind,' she said, 'I'd like to stay with Reina until she wakes up.'

'That might be quite a while,' Velvet replied, her voice shaking now that the crisis seemed to be over.

'I don't care if it takes all night,' Alicia replied fervently. 'I told Ulysses to tell my mother not to worry if she didn't see me until morning.'

'That really won't be necessary.' Velvet smoothed a quilt over the blankets. 'I'm perfectly capable of looking after my daughter.'

Alicia's voice – and her courage – broke simultaneously. 'I want to be with Reina,' she sobbed. 'I'll sleep on the floor if I have to. I feel as if what happened was my fault.'

Velvet looked up from her task. Her dark eyes probed Alicia's blue ones. 'Was it?'

'I'd sooner die than do anything to hurt Reina. She's my best friend. She's like a sister to me.'

Her heartfelt response seemed to banish Velvet's hostility. Velvet came around the side of the bed and enveloped Alicia in a hug. 'Don't take on so. That was just my nerves talking. I didn't mean anything by what I said. I know how you feel about my little girl. She feels the same way about you.'

Rio's voice interrupted the spontaneous outpouring of female solicitude. 'If you two will quit hugging each other, I'd like to get our girl to bed.'

When Ulysses returned to Pride's Passion, Patrick and Charlotte were sitting in the parlor playing chess, looking as at ease with one another as an old married couple. They seemed unaware of Ulysses' presence.

'I'm going to beat you one of these days,' Charlotte declared with a laugh, as Patrick captured her queen.

'One of these days, I just might let you,' Patrick replied, taking a contented puff on his pipe.

AN INDECENT LADY

Ulysses cleared his throat, as much to announce his presence as to rid himself of the choking lump that had lodged over his Adam's apple when Rio carried Reina from the kitchen – and out of Ulysses' sight.

Charlotte looked his way and, with a mother's innate instinct for trouble, bolted to her feet. 'Where's Alicia?' she demanded.

'There's been an accident.' The words no sooner left Ulysses' mouth than he realized he'd made an unfortunate choice of them.

'Oh my God,' Charlotte cried out, pressing a hand to her bosom as if to contain her anxiety. 'What kind of accident? Was Alicia hurt?'

'Don't worry,' Ulysses answered quickly. 'Alicia's fine.'

'Are you sure?'

'I swear it.'

'Thank God.' Her complexion chalky, Charlotte subsided back into her chair even faster than she had risen from it.

With instant solicitude, Patrick went to her side to put a steadying hand on her shoulder, then glared at Ulysses. 'Couldn't you have broken the news easier? You've scared Charlotte half to death.'

'It's all right, Patrick,' Charlotte said, looking up at him before turning back to Ulysses. 'What kind of an accident was it?'

Balling his hands into fists in an effort not to lash out at his father, Ulysses managed to keep his tone level. 'I'm sorry, Charlotte. I didn't mean to frighten you. As I said, Alicia is fine. Reina insisted on a skating party after supper. Terrell and Alicia agreed, so I went along with the idea although, frankly, I thought the three of them had lost their minds. Unfortunately events proved me right. Reina fell through the ice.'

'How awful,' Charlotte gasped.

'I imagine Terrell made quick work of getting her out,' Patrick said without a moment's hesitation, as though he couldn't imagine any other possibility.

Ulysses' mind thundered out a denial.

His mouth stayed firmly closed.

He should have known Patrick would assign the hero's role to Terrell. For a second, he considered revealing the truth. But then he remembered the anxiety on Alicia's face when she asked for his silence.

Her request made sense. The DeVargases were none too fond of him as it was. If they knew he'd been alone with Reina when she fell through the ice, they might not take it too well. Considering Rio's hot temper, it was best to let sleeping dogs lie.

What the hell did it matter anyway? One heroic act wasn't likely to change his father's opinion of him. Besides, he could hardly boast about being a hero when he'd been terrified every second he spent out on the ice. What he'd done had nothing to do with true heroism – and everything to do with necessity.

'Why didn't Alicia come back with you?' Charlotte asked, anxiety vibrating in her voice.

'She wanted to sit up with Reina.'

'How like Alicia,' Charlotte quavered, still shaken by Ulysses' news. 'She's always so considerate of others.'

Patrick's hand continued to rest on Charlotte's shoulder in a mute gesture of comfort and support. For a moment, Ulysses flashed back to another afternoon and another woman.

'Alicia's a daughter to be proud of,' Patrick said. 'Reina, too. They're both fine girls.'

The look he shot at Ulysses seemed to hold a

hint of accusation, as if he blamed Ulysses for the accident. 'Are you sure Reina's going to recover?'

'Do you really think I'd have left if she was in any danger? She's too ornery to let a little thing like an ice-cold swim slow her down for long.'

Patrick let go a low chuckle. His love for Reina lent a sparkle to his eyes. 'You're right about that. She's a real fighter. If I know her, she'll be up and about tomorrow, chomping at the bit to continue Starfire's training.'

As if it were an afterthought, he added, 'How about you, son? You look like you've got an axle dragging. I guess all the excitement wore you out.'

'I am a little tired.' Ulysses shoved the words past his clenched jaws. 'If you'll both excuse me, I think I'll go to bed.'

He spun on his heels and hurried from the room before he said something he would regret. He and his father had patched over their quarrels. But the patch was fragile at best. Angry words could easily shred it into so many pieces that all the good will in the world couldn't put it back. And God knew, Ulysses felt angry – at his father, at Reina, and most of all, at himself.

He opened his bedroom door, then shut it so hard that it shivered in the frame. His bed had been turned down and a kerosene lamp burned on the nightstand – no doubt at Charlotte's behest. She certainly put a fine point to the niceties of running a home. In his fury, he even resented her thoughtfulness.

What he wouldn't give to be able to go back in time just one year. Nothing in his life had made sense since his mother's death.

He stripped off his clothes, extinguished the light, and stared into the darkness. His weary body begged for the release of sleep. However, his cut palms stung him into wakefulness. And his traitorous mind kept on replaying the afternoon's events.

His heart gave a wild leap as he remembered seeing Reina disappear under the ice.

His limbs trembled as he recalled crawling out on it to save her.

Moisture pooled in his eyes as he thought about what a close call she'd had.

His errant cock tented the bedclothes as he relived what had happened afterward.

Longing for Reina created an aching void that only her physical presence could satiate. What he wouldn't give to have her here in his arms and his bed just once, and forget who they both were for a single night.

He had never wanted anything more. Desire became an almost physical pain. His body shook with the thought of what he would surrender to have such a night. Money, reputation, status? Was any woman worth all that?

Reina had come near death at the pond. Living in a world without her would be like living in a world without sunshine – or like eating greens without vinegar, he mused, coming up with a more appropriate simile.

Reina was – and always had been – a consummate pain in the ass. He'd be an idiot to romanticize her irascible nature just because he lusted for her body.

He had blamed her for their first kiss. In view of her half unconscious state, he couldn't blame her for what had happened today. Although each moment had been etched in his brain with crystalline clarity, he prayed she wouldn't remember any of it.

How could he ever look her straight in the eyes again if she did?

He wished he had someone to confide in. But

he'd never been a man to share his deepest feelings. Strangely enough, he thought Charlotte would understand his dilemma. But he could hardly tell her how he felt about Reina while he was courting her daughter.

Damn Reina for causing his emotional impasse, *damn her to hell*, he thought.

Yet, as sleep finally numbed his troubled mind, he thanked God for giving him the strength to save her.

Terrell rode back to the boarding house without once giving a thought to the cold wind blowing at his back. Memories of Alicia's kiss warmed him through and through.

It was damn uncomfortable, sitting on a saddle with a boner between his legs. But every time he recalled the way Alicia's lips had opened under his – the feel of her breasts through her coat – or the sight of her legs in those silky stockings – his manhood stood at attention again.

No doubt about it. Alicia Hawthorne had her hooks into him so deep they might never come out.

He had been wounded five times in the course of his career, once by a Comanche arrow and four times by bullets. However, he never thought he'd fall victim to Cupid's arrow. He felt its sweet ache clear through his body.

Those other wounds had scarred his mortal flesh. This one threatened to transform his soul.

He had always valued law, order, and honesty above all things. He believed that a man's word should be his bond and couldn't remember the last time he had so much as shaded the truth. Yet, given all that, he had lied for Alicia today.

The memory of what he'd done – and what he'd

failed to do — brought a stinging flush to his face. According to the good book, sins of omission were as bad as sins of commission. And he had committed both today.

First, he had taken unforgivable advantage of Alicia's innocence, kissing her the way a man kissed a woman before he took her to bed. If that wasn't bad enough, he'd let his oldest and dearest friends believe a lie.

If he had any sense, he'd ask to be reassigned to another county. If he had any sense, he would never see Alicia Hawthorne again.

He laughed out loud. Who was he kidding? The man who had gone after the Flores bunch by himself didn't have any sense.

He'd spent his life doing the right thing — living up to other people's expectations — and where had it gotten him? To this lonely place on this lonely road, with nothing to look forward to but a lonely boarding house bed.

Then and there, he made up his mind to play out the hand he'd been dealt, and give what he felt for Alicia a chance. Hell. As long as he was alone with only his thoughts for company, why not call a spade a spade? He would give *love* a chance.

It would be, he realized, the bravest thing he'd even done. Although he'd risked his life before, he'd never risked his heart.

Reina woke in the small hours of the morning. Her hands and feet still ached from exposure to the cold. Her heart ached even more.

Ulysses had come so close to making love to her — and it might never happen again. She'd happily have risked pneumonia to have spent a few more

AN INDECENT LADY 221

moments in his arms – to have had the strength to return his caresses.

She'd seen so much in his eyes as he crawled out on the ice to save her – fear, determination, and something more. Something she had only seen in her father's eyes when he looked at her mother.

Damn Ulysses – damn him to hell for letting her see it in his eyes, for letting her hope when the situation was hopeless. He wanted her. He might even love her if he let himself.

But she knew his pride would never give in to his heart. His social position, his career would always weigh too heavily in the balance. His feelings for her would forever remain unspoken. He would never admit he loved a whore's daughter.

Filled with the need to escape an inescapable truth, Reina sat up in the dark and swung her legs over the side of the bed. She felt something warm and yielding on the floor. The something emitted a startled yelp.

'Reina, is that you?' Alicia asked in a sleep-sodden voice.

A match flared. A disembodied hand reached up from the floor and lit the kerosene lamp. Its flickering light played over Alicia's face as she rose from a pallet on the floor. Useful was crumpled up beside her. He opened his eyes, thumped his tail once, then fell back asleep like a sensible dog.

'What are you doing down there with Useful?' Reina asked.

'I was worried about you.' Alicia brushed a wisp of dog hair from the corner of her mouth. She wore a nightgown Reina recognized as one of her own. 'How are you feeling?'

'Fine . . . I think.' Reina stretched, testing her body for aches and pains.

'Thank God.' Alicia let go a sigh. 'If you're up to it, we need to talk.'

'What about?' Reina bit her lip. What had been so important that Alicia stayed the night to discuss it? Did she know what happened after Ulysses pulled Reina from the pond? Dear Lord! Did Velvet and Rio know, too? Reina steeled herself to hear the worst.

'I told your mother and father the four of us were together when you fell through the ice. I hope you won't hate me for it, but I hinted that you were showing off a little.' Alicia sat on the edge of the bed and took one of Reina's hands in both her own. 'I don't tell lies normally – in fact, I hated doing it – but surely you see I didn't have any choice.'

Reina let go her pent-up breath. 'You did exactly the right thing.'

'I'm so glad you feel that way. I made Terrell and Ulysses promise not to let anyone know what really happened.'

'What really happened?' Reina probed at Alicia's knowledge. Did she know more than she had admitted?

'I didn't want anyone – and most especially not my mother – to know Terrell and I went off alone. He kissed me,' Alicia whispered. 'Oh Reina, it was the most wonderful feeling – like eating the most delicious meal, like having the most wonderful dream and then waking up to find it was true, like all birthdays and Christmases happening on the same day,' Alicia gushed, giving free rein to her talent for hyperbole. 'But I feel so guilty for leaving you and Ulysses. I know you would have been rescued a lot quicker if Terrell and I had been there to help. By the time we caught up with Ulysses, he'd carried you three-quarters of the way home.'

AN INDECENT LADY 223

So Alicia and Terrell didn't know what had happened in the meadow. Only Ulysses did. Was he thinking about her tonight the way she had been thinking about him?

Not a chance, Reina thought bitterly. If she knew Ulysses, he wouldn't lose a minute's sleep over her.

The sound of Alicia's voice brought her back to the present. 'I spent the night to make sure we all told the same story.'

Seeing the anxiety on Alicia's face, Reina repeated her previous reassurance. 'You did the right thing – and I'm glad you had a chance to be alone with Terrell. Do you think he cares for you?'

'He's much too shy to declare himself – at least not yet, although I know he'll say the words someday.' Alicia broke into a smug smile. 'He said he'd come out to the ranch to see me next week.'

Reina repressed a twinge of jealousy. 'I'm very happy for you.'

'That isn't all. I've started my book.'

'Your book?'

'You were the one who suggested I write one of those dime westerns. Terrell gave me the most wonderful idea – not that he knows it. I'm going to base my novel on the Flores affair. I can't use Terrell's name either, so I'm calling the hero Duke Bastrop. It has a nice sort of Texas ring, don't you think?'

'It sounds like you have it all thought out.'

'Not just thought out. I asked your mother for writing materials earlier tonight. I finished a rough draft of the first chapter. I know it's the middle of the night – but would you like to hear it?'

'I'd love to.' Anything would be better than thinking about Ulysses.

Alicia hopped off the bed, walked to the dresser

and retrieved a sheaf of papers. She turned the kerosene lamp up, then plopped down beside Reina. '*The Ranger's Revenge — A True Story of Life on the Texas Border* by Al Devereux,' she began in a melodramatic voice.

Reina couldn't help giggling. 'Who is Al Devereux?'

'It's my pen name. I abbreviated my first name, and used my mother's maiden name. Just hush up and listen — and promise you won't interrupt or laugh in the wrong places, even if it's the worst thing you ever heard. I haven't had a chance to polish it yet.'

Reina nodded, then sagged back against her pillows.

'*The X bar A hands never knew what hit them,*' Alicia began. '*One minute they were riding night herd, nodding in their saddles with only the silent stars and the restless Longhorns for company — and the next, they were caught up in a maelstrom of thundering hooves, lethal horns, and maddened beasts. The cattle exploded into motion, urged by gunfire and shouting masked men.*

'"*Stampede,*" *one of the cowboys called out. They would be the last words he spoke on earth.*'

Sixteen

The storm was born in the land of the walrus and the white bear. Wind was its father – and cold its mother. It nursed at the polar cap's icy breast, gathering strength and size with every hour, then toddled south onto the tundra.

There were no mountains to slow its growth, or to slow its passage on their jagged peaks, and only a few Native Americans – Innuits, Assinboin, and Cree – to mark its journey as it roiled through the Canadian Provinces.

It drank from Lake Winnipeg, sucking up moisture until its tumescent clouds soared beyond the reach of any bird. Mature now and filled with the potential for harm, it ripped through the Dakotas and tore into Nebraska with high winds and record cold.

Kansas, and then Oklahoma, fell victim to its mindless fury. The Texas Hill Country lay but a few hundred miles to the south.

The wind woke Patrick before dawn – a wind like no other he had ever heard. It shrieked at the eaves and battered the windows.

The huge limestone house fought to repel the intruder, its roof timbers groaning under the assault. Patrick had built the house himself and knew its strength as he knew his own. His home had withstood tornadoes and could survive the worst winter storm. His cattle might not be as lucky.

He bolted from his bed and raced to the window to part the heavy velvet curtains and gaze out. The snow fell so thick and fast that he couldn't distinguish land from sky. Hell, he couldn't even see the porch roof.

The cold seeping around the window frame raised goose bumps on his skin. Wind rattled the pane as a wall of white hurled itself against the glass. The curtains fell from his hands as his mind sped ahead, anticipating a fierce battle with nature and enumerating the forces at his disposal.

Two dozen men slept in the bunkhouse. Half a dozen more had been riding night watch – if they hadn't already frozen in the saddle. If Rio had heard the storm, he would already be on his way. And, of course, there was Ulysses.

Would that be enough?

It had to be.

He dressed hurriedly, putting on two pairs of long underwear and two pairs of socks. They made a snug fit of his flannel shirt and woolen trousers. The layers of clothing restricted his movement as he made his way into the hall and knocked on Ulysses' door.

To his surprise, the door swung wide to reveal Ulysses, fully dressed, too. 'You're up early,' Patrick said.

'I've had a lot on my mind lately. Once it started blowing, I couldn't get back to sleep. What's happening out there?'

'It looks and sounds like the mother of all northers. The cattle won't be able to graze. We've got to get hay to them.'

Ulysses joined Patrick in the hall. 'What can I do to help?'

Patrick reached for his son's upper arm and squeezed it in a rare gesture of fatherly affection. His son may have grown up on the ranch but he had never worked with cattle, and didn't know much about handling them. However, Patrick was going to need every able-bodied man. And there was no doubt that his six-foot-three-inch son was able-bodied.

'I'm on my way to the bunkhouse to roust the hands and tell them to dress for a long, cold day. I suspect it's cold enough outside to freeze a brass monkey's balls. You'd better put on an extra set of longjohns. When you're done, wake the women and the servants and have them make breakfast for all the hands. The bunkhouse cook is going to work cattle for the duration. And coffee, we'll need lots of coffee to keep going. It's going to be a bitch outside.'

Patrick's words proved prophetic. That first day, he drove his men to the limits of their stamina – and drove himself beyond the limits of his own. Like a man possessed, he led his small army into battle against the elements in a desperate effort to save the cattle.

From sunrise to sunset, they filled wagons with bales of hay, fighting their way through a world of white to deliver it to the hungry Longhorns.

Patrick woke on the second day to find the blizzard still clawing at the house. He hadn't dared ask anyone to ride night herd. Unattended, the cattle would have sought protection from the wind in gullies and washes. There, they might founder and die.

Snow was rare in the Hill Country – a break in the routine that sent men, women and children outdoors to exclaim in wonder. When it fell, it was almost always gone the next day.

This snow showed no sign of ending. Everything

he had built with the sweat of his brow and the toil of his back was at risk. If he lost the cattle, he might as well abandon the land, too.

He would have to divide the hands into two groups. The first, under Rio's command, would continue taking hay out to the pastures. He would lead the second group himself, and man it with the youngest, most vigorous of his men. Driving cattle out of gullies and washes wasn't going to be a Sunday in the park.

The second day came and went and still the wind blew and snow fell. Men and women returned to their beds, too weary to eat, too tired to dream, praying the storm would end before it took lives they valued a great deal more than they valued the Longhorns.

Wind woke Charlotte on the third day and she shuddered as she realized the storm still held Pride's Passion in its implacable grip. She blinked in the darkness, wishing she could pull the covers over her head and hide from trouble the way she had in her youth.

The knowledge that Patrick depended on her brought her to her feet. She had devoted a great deal of thought, time, and energy to coaxing him back to life − and had succeeded brilliantly. His gaunt frame had filled out, bringing him back to the glorious manhood she remembered. He had even begun to laugh again.

The storm put him at risk. She couldn't bear the thought of anything happening to him.

During their brief marriage, she had perceived Patrick as a stick-in-the-mud who had no concept of fun. Nigel, with his devil-may-care personality, had been Patrick's antithesis. What a blind fool she had been. Patrick had more worth in his little finger than Nigel had had in his entire body.

Three days ago, seeing Patrick go out into the teeth of the storm, and waiting what seemed an eternity for his return, she'd been so anxious, so fraught with worry that she realized what she felt for him had passed beyond friendship – beyond gratitude – beyond affection.

When Patrick finally came through the front door, shaking snow from his coat like a grizzly bear, it had been all she could do not to throw herself in his arms and cover his face with kisses.

She had come to Pride's Passion planning to trick him – and fate had turned the tables. Falling in love with Patrick all over again – and knowing she was even less worthy of him now than she had been the first time – was the cruelest trick of all.

As she dressed, Charlotte thrust aside her unhappiness. She would face her problems later – head on – just as she had faced all the other problems life had put in her path. Right now, she needed all the energy and fortitude she could muster for the coming day.

The house's other female occupants were already assembled in the kitchen when she joined them. Alicia stood at the counter, beating a batch of biscuits. The maids were making sandwiches with last night's ham. Maria presided at the stove, stirring a huge pot of porridge, while Conchita sat hunched at the table, her obsidian eyes downcast as she drank a cup of coffee.

'Good morning,' the younger women said in unison.

'Madre de Dios. There isn't anything good about it,' Conchita muttered.

Alicia finished beating the biscuits and put the

bowl aside. 'I wish the storm would end. I don't know how much more the men can take.'

'They're Texans, honey, and Texans are a tough breed,' Charlotte replied with more confidence than she felt.

Just then, wind blasted down the chimney, sending smoke into the room and sparks flying from the hearth. Alicia and the maids jumped for the broom to sweep the stray sparks back into the fireplace.

In their haste, they bumped into one another, laughing at their own awkwardness. The girlish sound broke the tension. Charlotte helped herself to coffee from the huge enamel pot on the stove, then joined Conchita at the table.

'How are you today?' she asked.

The elderly woman stared at her with hooded eyes. 'Someone is going to die before the storm ends,' she said, crossing her ancient breast. 'I feel it in my bones.'

'What you feel in your bones,' Charlotte snapped, 'is arthritis – nothing more and nothing less.' The women were already jumpy. They didn't need Conchita's superstitious nonsense to fray what remained of their nerves.

Conchita straightened her spine as best she could considering its curvature, and stared into Charlotte's eyes. Obsidian met amber in a battle of wills that had begun the day Charlotte came to Pride's Passion as a bride.

'It's well known that death comes in threes, *senora*,' Conchita intoned like a doomsday bell. 'You lost your husband – and *Senor* Patrick lost his wife. That makes only two.'

On the fourth night, while weary men and women slept too deeply to mark its departure, the storm moved south. Weakened by its epic battle with the Hill Country, it barely managed to kiss Houston with a coat of ice before it drifted to old age and death in the Gulf of Mexico.

Patrick woke to silence and sunshine. A profound sense of relief swept over him. The blizzard was over.

He reached for the pocket watch he'd left on the night-table. It was after seven. He'd set one hell of an example for his men sleeping so late, he thought as he crawled from his bed.

He'd been too weary to bathe since the storm began and the musky scent of his own body made his nostrils twitch. It would feel good to soak in a hot tub tonight.

His muscles ached and his joints throbbed. He was getting too damn old to spend fourteen hours a day in the saddle. But he'd spend fourteen more today. Tomorrow and the day after, too, if that's what it took.

He dressed with even greater haste than was his custom, and took the stairs two at a time, his aches and pains forgotten as he contemplated having breakfast with Charlotte.

She had done such a good job, anticipating all of his needs, that he half expected her to be waiting for him in the dining room. Not finding her there, he headed for the kitchen.

But for Velvet DeVargas, the room was empty.

'What are you doing here?'

'Now, Patrick, that's not very hospitable.'

He grinned and took the cup of coffee she held out. 'I didn't mean it that way. You're the last person I expected to see, though. I don't imagine getting here was easy.'

Velvet poured coffee for herself and joined him at

the table. 'Actually, it felt good to get out. The way the sun is shining, the snow won't last long. Reina insisted on coming. She's been anxious about her father. So have I.'

'He's been worrying about the two of you. But he was too tired to head for home at night. Did you manage all right without him?'

'He told Reina what to do before he left, and she told the hands. I think she loved being the boss.'

'Did she have any trouble getting them to listen to her?'

Velvet let go one of the deep laughs that always made Patrick laugh, too. 'Are you serious? Half of them want to sleep with her. The other half are scared to death of her. Either way, they jump if she says jump.'

'Too bad she's a girl. She'd make one hell of a foreman someday.'

Velvet frowned. 'She'll make an even better wife and mother.'

If anyone ever plucks up the courage to marry her, Patrick thought. 'Where is everyone?'

'Charlotte gave the servants a couple of hours off, now that the worst is over. I believe she's taking a bath. Reina is up in Alicia's room.'

'Why didn't anyone wake me?'

Velvet grinned at him. 'Aren't you full of questions this morning. Charlotte said you needed your rest.'

Half an hour later, Patrick walked out to the barn, his stomach full of eggs, biscuits and bacon, a sense of well-being flowing through his body. He felt rested, well fed, and ready for whatever the day held.

He turned and looked back at the house. Snow softened its angular curves, lending it a sort of cozy charm despite its size. Charlotte stood at her bedroom window, gazing down at him.

Seeing her there lifted his spirits even higher. He gave her a jaunty wave, then walked into the barn. The stalls were filled with weary animals, Longhorns who were too young or too weak to survive outdoors, and played-out horses. The odor of urine, manure, and dander mingled with the sweet scent of the hay stored in the loft.

He walked down the rows of stalls, seeking a mount for the day. He had already ridden the best of his string. He finally saddled an ancient roan with a slight sway in its back. He had loved the horse once, and hoped it still had its fighting heart.

As man and horse went outside, they both blinked. The sun reflected off the snow with a brilliance that hurt their eyes. Squinting, Patrick tipped his broad-brimmed hat low on his forehead, then headed for a creek bottom his crew hadn't yet had time to explore.

Most likely, he'd find a few half-starved cows there. With any luck, they'd be strong enough to drive to one of the feeding stations.

Ulysses returned to the house at sunset, feeling rather proud of himself. A week ago, he'd been in such poor physical condition that he'd had trouble carrying Reina in his arms.

Four days spent loading hay, and manhandling wagons through the snow, had given him a new awareness of his own strength. He had worked his way through all the aches and pains to arrive at a new sense of his own manhood.

He turned his horse over to one of the men in the barn, then made his way to the house on a path someone had shoveled. He stopped on the porch, kicked his boots free of snow, and opened the front door.

During the blizzard the house had been noisy with the comings and goings of hungry men arriving at all hours to grab a meal. Now, silence reigned – a strangely ominous silence.

'Hello? Is anyone home?' he called out, feeling a little foolish at the way his heart was jumping.

Charlotte appeared in the entry hall before the last word left his mouth. 'Is Patrick with you?' she asked anxiously.

Ulysses shook his head. 'I've been working with the hay crews. Dad and his men have been rounding up strays.'

'He didn't go with his crew today. I let him sleep in.' Charlotte's lower lip trembled as if she were on the brink of tears. 'I thought I was doing him a favor. But he rode off by himself and now he's alone out there.'

Ulysses put his arm around her shoulder. He'd grown fond of her over the last few months. 'I'm sure he'll walk through the door any minute.'

She pulled away from the comfort he offered. 'His crew got back an hour ago. They hadn't seen him all day.'

No wonder she looked so worried. Still, he tried to reassure her. 'Don't worry about Dad. He knows how to handle himself in any situation. He probably found a big bunch of cattle and is trying to drive them to one of the feeding stations by himself. He'll show up.'

'I'm sure you're right,' Charlotte said. But worry still clouded her eyes. 'Would you mind eating in the kitchen tonight? We're all waiting for your father there.'

'Whatever is easy for you works for me,' Ulysses replied.

AN INDECENT LADY 235

To his surprise, Rio, Velvet, and Reina were in the kitchen along with one of the wagon crews. Their greetings were subdued. They looked beat.

Rio coughed. Then young Luke Teague sneezed and blew his nose in his neckerchief. All they needed was an epidemic of influenza, Ulysses thought as Reina handed him a plate of stew.

He hadn't seen her since her near drowning, and wondered just how much she remembered. Not much, he decided, or she would have thrown the plate at him.

Rio coughed again, much harder this time, doubling over with the force of it and gasping for breath when the spell passed.

'You sound terrible, Dad,' Reina said, her eyes so dark with worry that they looked almost black.

'I feel terrible, too,' Rio admitted, 'like a horse kicked me in the chest.'

Velvet had been sitting at the kitchen table next to her husband. She rose and tugged him to his feet, her expression grim. 'We had better go home and get you to bed.'

'I'm not going anywhere until Patrick shows up,' Rio declared, red-faced with the effort to suppress his cough.

Ulysses studied the foreman. Rio looked his age and then some. 'Velvet's right. You sound like hell. To tell you the truth, I'm not anxious to get whatever you've got. Go on home. I'll handle things here. If Dad isn't back in the next thirty minutes, I'll send out a search party.'

Ulysses expected Rio to put up a fight. Instead, the foreman nodded his agreement, then opened his mouth to say something but coughed hard instead.

'Do you feel up to riding home?' Ulysses asked.

'It beats the hell out of walking.' Rio looked more like himself after the coughing fit passed.

'If you don't mind,' Reina said, 'I'll stay until Patrick gets here.'

Despite their constant clash, Ulysses was glad she wanted to stay on – but not for himself, never for himself. Reina was resourceful – and she knew Pride's Passion better than he did. He would value her advice in the event Patrick didn't show up.

'I'm sure Alicia and Charlotte will be happy to have your company,' he said.

He sent a hand to saddle the DeVargases' horses, accompanied them to the front door and saw them on their way before returning to the kitchen. The wagon crew was finishing supper as he walked in.

'You said you'd only wait a half hour,' Charlotte said as Ulysses helped himself to coffee. 'It's been thirty minutes since you got home.'

Ulysses hated the thought of sending weary men and horses out into the cold again – but he hated the thought of his father being alone out there even more.

'It's time we sent out a search party,' he agreed, putting the coffee aside.

Several of the men shifted in their chairs. 'I sure don't feel like looking for any damn cows tonight, Mr Pride,' one of them said.

'You'll be looking for my father.'

The man jumped to his feet so abruptly that his chair fell backward. 'Why didn't you say so?'

'I thought he'd be back by now.' Ulysses looked the men over one by one. 'I wish I could tell you all to go to the bunkhouse and get a good night's sleep. I know how badly you need it after what you've been through. But my father is outside somewhere, and he may be in trouble.'

AN INDECENT LADY

Luke Teague was the first to head for the door. 'There isn't one of us willing to sit in a warm bunkhouse while Mr Pride is freezing his ass off, begging the ladies' pardon. Tell us what to do and we'll do it.'

'Come on, boys,' another said, pushing away from the table. 'It's time to saddle up.'

The room filled with the jangling of spurs, as to a man the rest of the hands headed for the door, then bunched there, waiting for Ulysses' orders.

'I'll be with you in a minute. Meanwhile I'd be grateful if you asked the men who got back earlier to join us.'

The mantle of command slipped onto his shoulders with ease. He heard the cadence of his father's voice in his own speech. Perhaps they weren't so different after all, he mused.

'I want to go, too,' Reina said, untying her apron.

'Forget it. I'm worried enough about my father. I'll not be worried about you, too.'

'I can take care of myself.'

'The way you did at the stock pond?'

'You're going to need me. I know the ranch better than you do.'

Her lower lip jutted out in what would be a pout on any other woman's face. On Reina's, however, it was a sign of steely determination. It was also quite kissable – but he couldn't let himself think about that now.

'You're right about knowing the ranch better than I do. But I'm in charge in my father's absence, and I will not let you risk your life. I would value your advice, though. Do you have any idea where my father would have gone?'

She took a moment to consider his question.

'Patrick will have spent the day looking for strays, and he won't have covered territory he's covered before. Once you know where he and his men have been, you'll have an idea where to look. It's a simple matter of elimination.'

Without thinking, Ulysses bent down and kissed her forehead. To his surprise, she didn't pull away.

'Thanks for the tip,' he said – and wanted to say so much more.

'If you won't take me, at least take Starfire. You're going to need a fresh horse.'

Her words were matter-of-fact. But her eyes – dear God, what were her eyes saying? Had she offered Starfire out of concern for him?

'You're more than generous.'

'Just bring your father home.'

So the offer had been made out of concern for Patrick. He should have known that was the case. So why did it hurt him?

He turned to Charlotte. 'We're going to need every kerosene lamp you can spare. Make sure they're full of fuel and the wicks are trimmed. They won't do us any good if they go out. Leave them in the entry hall.'

He left the women to their work, and headed for the library. He picked up a couple of brandy bottles for the men's canteens, then went on to the entry and got back into his cold weather gear.

By the time he finished, Charlotte had joined him. She set the kerosene lamps she was carrying down on the floor. 'We've got sixteen more. The ladies are getting them ready.'

'I'd better get on over to the bunkhouse. I'll come back for them, though,' he said, taking her hand. 'And Charlotte, thank you for everything.'

She looked as white and drawn as she had the

day he told her of Elke's death. 'I don't need your thanks – I need your father. Bring him home.'

'I will,' he promised, then opened the door and stepped outside. The cold hit him like a fist.

He didn't know who faced the more difficult task – the men who would join him in the search, or the women they left behind.

Seventeen

Patrick's teeth chattered uncontrollably, sending staccato bursts of sound into the air. Although he clamped his jaws tighter, the chattering continued. Spasms of shivering racked him as his body attempted to generate a little heat.

He'd heard that freezing to death was an easy way to die. The damn fool who had passed on that particular piece of information didn't know what the hell he was talking about. Patrick had never felt worse.

He leaned against the tree – at least he thought it was a tree – trying to get more comfortable. Was it day or night? Night, he suspected. If only he could see. He would have liked to gaze up at the stars one last time before he joined Elke.

He missed her so terribly – and had dishonored her memory so badly. He should have handled her death like a man. Instead he had behaved like a sniveling coward, embracing misery as fervently as he had once embraced his living wife. If Charlotte hadn't appeared on his doorstep, to set an example of courage in the face of loss, he might have spent the rest of his days in a permanent retreat from life.

He regretted the way he had treated Ulysses most of all. Now it seemed he would never have a chance to hold out a hand in love to his son. How in God's name could he explain that failure to Elke when he saw her?

Pride. That had always been his greatest sin, as if he'd been born to define his name. He'd never been able to admit he was wrong – and had come close to losing Elke because of it years ago. Instead, he had lost his son.

He cringed, thinking of the way he had called Ulysses a bastard even though he'd known nothing could have been more hurtful. The only bastard in the dining room that day had been him.

If only Ulysses had chosen another line of work, he might have forgiven his lack of interest in the ranch. But how could a father be proud of a son who had chosen to be both a lawyer and a politician?

Damn! A dying man shouldn't lie – not even to himself. His problems with Ulysses went much further back – right to Ulysses' birth. He would need a lifetime to make up for the way he had treated the boy. And his life was running out. He could almost feel it oozing into the snow-covered ground like molasses trickling from a jar.

He chuckled mirthlessly. The cold must have affected his mind. *Boy?* Ulysses was a man – a fine strong man with good instincts, a brilliant mind, and a noble heart. He should have been proud of his son. He *was* proud of his son. Only he'd never have a chance to tell him.

Pride. Foolish pride. He'd had so much of it. Now he was going to pay the price for all that hubris.

He'd told the hands not to ride out alone until the snow was gone. He knew the dangers, and yet he hadn't heeded his own mandate. He'd been so sure of himself and his ability.

So damn proud . . .

So damn stupid . . .

So damn cold . . .

Take me, Lord – take this foolish old man into your kingdom – take me to Elke. He had never begged for anything in his life but he would gladly have gotten to his knees if it would have speeded the process of dying. However, his frozen limbs refused to cooperate.

He waited impatiently, hoping to hear trumpets or a choir of angels – and heard only the sound of the wind moving through the trees. It was the son-of-a-bitch wind that had done him in.

He'd lost his hat to an unexpected gust that seemed to spring up out of nowhere – and his spavined mount had been too old to chase the hat down. No big loss, he had thought at the time, not even considering the way the battered old stetson had shaded his eyes from the sun. It had been the first of several miscalculations that had brought him to this sorry end.

He'd lost the horse two hours later when it stepped into a prairie dog hole hidden beneath the snow. Most horses struggled to get up when they broke a leg. This one just lay there, whinnying as if to say, *help me.* He'd fired a bullet through that big skull and put the creature out of its misery – and still he hadn't had the sense to worry.

It had been a beautiful day – typical of the days that followed a norther. The sun had been shining in a sky so blue that it seemed God had just reinvented the color. Hell, shining didn't do justice to the light the sun gave off. Reflected by the snow, it burned into his retinas like a fiery brand. He even saw it with his eyes closed.

He still hadn't been smart enough to be concerned, though. The unrelenting glare had seemed no more than an annoyance. After all, he knew the way back to the ranch as well as he knew the way from his bedroom to the bathroom. He could get there with his eyes shut, he told himself.

Sometime later, his eyes began to water. Thinking he'd gotten something in them, he'd rubbed them hard. Another mistake. Tears flowed from his aching orbs. He blinked repeatedly, glad no one was there to see how owlish he must look.

He had struggled on, using a hand to shield his eyes from the unrelenting light. Despite his best efforts, his vision became so blurred that he could no longer read his watch. Knowing the ranch couldn't be more than a couple of miles away, he felt certain he still had a chance to arrive safely.

And that had been the biggest conceit of all. By the time he admitted he was in serious trouble, he was damn near blind – and completely lost.

Even now, with his eyes shut, he felt them burning. But he'd long since run out of tears to ease the hurt. He gathered snow in both hands and pressed it to his face. The burning sensation let up. Perhaps he could die in comfort after all.

First though, he'd have to stop shivering. Recalling how he'd read that Eskimos built houses from blocks of snow, he reached out, piling snow closer to his body. If he lay down, he could cover himself completely.

Only he didn't want anyone to find him that way. He wanted people to know Patrick Pride met his death sitting ramrod straight. And if that was another example of overweening pride, so be it.

In any case, he'd be flat on his back soon enough. He'd sleep his last long sleep next to Elke. The thought comforted him ... and suddenly, she was there. That comforted him even more. She was decked out in a flowing white gown with the prettiest pair of wings sprouting from her shoulders.

He'd always thought folks exaggerated when they said something took their breath away. Now he knew they had spoken the truth. The sight of Elke blasted the breath right out of him.

'I knew you'd be the most beautiful angel the good Lord ever saw!' he exclaimed, breaking into a smile.

She didn't smile back. Her wings fluttered in agitation. 'Oh Patrick, you're not supposed to be here!'

'That's ridiculous. I want to be here. I'm damn happy to be here. I want to be with you.'

Her wings fluttered even harder. 'Don't swear,' she admonished as she had so many times before.

He didn't care what she said. Seeing her made him so happy that he felt as if his heart would burst with joy.

'Is this heaven?' he asked, wondering why there weren't any puffy white clouds to sit on.

'Not quite.'

'It can't be hell – or you wouldn't be here.' Dread took hold of him as he studied the featureless void surrounding them. 'Is this purgatory?'

'Of course not!' Elke declared with considerable vehemence. She had a feisty look in her eyes that told him more clearly than words that he had better watch what he said.

'Then why can't I stay with you? I'd fancy a pair of those wings for myself. Can you really fly with them?'

Elke gazed at him as if he were a recalcitrant child instead of a full-grown man. 'Don't change the subject. I told you, it's not your time. If you hadn't gone off by yourself today, you wouldn't be in such dire straits. But then, you've done lots of things you shouldn't have since I died. You need a full-time guardian angel. I volunteered for the job.'

AN INDECENT LADY

'Are you angry because I asked Charlotte to stay at the ranch?'

'Don't be silly. The two of you have been very good for each other.' When she smiled, Elke's eyes crinkled just the way he remembered. Unfortunately her smile quickly faded. 'I heard what you said to Ulysses the day I died. How could you have been so cruel?'

'I feel real bad about that – real bad, honey. But it's too late to do anything about it now that I'm dead.'

'You're not dead, my love.'

How he wished she would touch him instead of keeping her distance. He longed to hold the woman he had loved so long and so well. 'What do you mean – not dead? How come I'm talking to an angel, then? I'm stiff as a board from the cold, I'm lost, and if that isn't bad enough, I'm blind.'

That wasn't accurate though. He could see her – and that sweet vision eased his eyes so much that he forgot all about the pain in them. Desperate to touch her, he stretched out a trembling hand.

Her wings beat so powerfully that he felt a rush of air as she moved further away. When she finally spoke, her voice seemed to come from a great distance.

'Patrick, dearest, you've going to have a second chance. This time, I know you'll correct all your mistakes. I'll be watching over you, dearest heart.' She gave him one last loving glance and then vanished into the void.

'Elke,' he called out with all the strength he could muster, 'Elke, come back!'

It took Ulysses and the hands half an hour to plan the search, collect the lamps, saddle up, and pair off. He found himself riding with Luke Teague, the acne-faced cowboy who had made such a messy job of blowing his nose during supper.

'I sure hope we're the ones to find Mr Pride,' Luke said, then sneezed explosively. 'It would be something to tell my kids about.'

'I didn't realize you had children.' Ulysses had never gotten to know the men who lived in the bunkhouse – had only put names to faces while working with them during the blizzard.

'I don't, sir. I'm only nineteen. I'm not married yet. But I do have a girl in Kerrville.'

'Is she fond of you?'

'Reckon so.'

'How can you tell?' Ulysses felt like a damn fool, asking a nineteen-year-old such a question – but he didn't have anyone else to ask.

'Well, sir, she let me kiss her a time or two.'

Ulysses had difficulty imagining the female who would relish Luke's kisses. It reinforced his belief that there was no accounting for the female mind.

'She's a decent girl, sir,' Luke continued, 'from a church-going family. She wouldn't let just any man kiss her.'

A decent girl from a church-going family. The words reverberated through Ulysses' mind. How he wished Reina and her mother fit that description. He might as well wish the world would tilt on its axis and turn this winter night into a summer day.

Settling in for a long hard ride, he turned to his companion. 'Would you do me a favor, Luke?'

'If I can, sir.'

'Call me Ulysses.'

'Sure thing, Ulysses, sir,' the boy said, then lapsed into silence.

Was he thinking about his girl – and wanting her

AN INDECENT LADY

the way Ulysses wanted Reina? A grimace narrowed Ulysses' mouth. He wouldn't wish such a fate on any man.

As they rode, the moon shone so brightly that they didn't need the lamp. Surely his father could see well enough on a night like this to find his way home. Where the hell was he, and what had happened to him?

Ulysses called out his father's name in the vain hope that Patrick would be near enough to hear. In the distance, he heard other search teams 'hallooing' too, the sound mingling in eerie harmony with the sibilant whisper of the wind. From then on, he and Luke took turns calling.

The further they rode, the more Luke sneezed. By midnight, the sneezing had been replaced by a dry hacking cough and the young cowboy slumped in the saddle. Clearly, he wasn't going to be much help in his present condition. If his health continued to deteriorate, he'd be a real hindrance.

'Let's stop a minute,' Ulysses said, reining in Starfire. He took a box of matches from his pocket and lit the kerosene lamp.

'What's that for, Ulysses, sir?' Luke rasped. 'I can see fine without it.'

'I want to get a good look at you.' Ulysses adjusted the lamp and held it high.

Just as he'd feared, Luke was whey-faced but for the bright spots of acne on his cheeks. A gloss of sweat slicked his skin. Ulysses stripped off a glove, leaned toward Luke, and touched his forehead.

Affronted manhood made Luke sit up a little straighter. 'Aw, sir, you didn't need to do that. I'm just fine.'

'You're not fine. You're running a fever. I'm no doctor, but I know a sick man when I see one. I sent

Rio home earlier and now it's your turn. I want you to go back to the bunkhouse and get into bed.'

'But sir—'

'Those are my orders, Luke.' Ulysses wished he could think of a way to salve the boy's pride. He didn't dare take the time. 'Are you sure you can make it back on your own?'

'I'm sure, sir.' Reproach swam in Luke's eyes as he turned his horse back the way they had come. The sound of his coughing kept Ulysses company long after he disappeared into the cold and the dark.

Ulysses turned off the lamp, waited a moment until his eyes reaccustomed themselves to the moonlight, then nudged his heels against Starfire's flanks. The horse responded with a steady lope he could maintain for hours.

Ulysses prayed he wouldn't have to ask that much of the stallion. He called his father's name out every few minutes and, not getting a response, rode on, his heart aching with premonitory grief, his agile mind leaping ahead to imagine every possible contingency – and settling on the worst one. He didn't want to be stuck with the ranch, forced to live his father's dreams instead of his own.

'Damn you, old man, where are you?' he shouted, giving voice to his frustration and anxiety.

There had been times – too many of them – when rage and hurt drove him to wish his father dead. Surely God knew he had never meant it. No matter how great their differences or how fierce their quarrels – he loved his father.

He couldn't really fault Patrick for being disappointed in him. Ulysses had done nothing to earn his father's love, and damn little to win his respect.

Patrick had wanted a son fashioned in his own stalwart mode, a son who would love the ranch as he did. Patrick had made it crystal clear that he wanted Ulysses to stay home and learn to run the ranch instead of going off to Harvard. That hadn't stopped Ulysses from packing his bags and taking the next train back east.

Patrick had always been vocal in his opinion of lawyers, describing them as blood-sucking leeches, but that hadn't stopped Ulysses from becoming a lawyer. Patrick held politicians in low regard, too, but Ulysses had run for the legislature just the same.

He had never meant to hurt his father, and he suspected Patrick had never meant to hurt him.

'Patrick,' he called again.

His heart leapt as he heard a male voice cry out, 'Elke, come back!'

There could be no doubt it was his father's voice. A frisson rippled down Ulysses' spine and lifted the hair on his nape at the lunacy of Patrick's words. Peering in the direction from which the sound had come, he spied a lone tree silhouetted against the moon, a tree with an unnaturally broad base.

Suddenly, the tree sprouted two new branches. Ulysses barely had time to register the fact that the branches were his father's arms when instinct drove him from the saddle. He hit the ground running, his long limbs churning through the snow.

'Dad, are you all right?' he asked, dropping to his knees at Patrick's side.

It was a ridiculous question. Snow obscured the lower half of Patrick's body and frosted his hair and eyebrows. With his white skin, he looked more like a figure carved in ice than a living man.

'Ulysses, did you see your mother? She was just here.'

Ulysses' gut knotted in the face of his father's mania. Had he found him in time to save his body but too late to save his mind? 'Mom's been dead for months, Dad,' he said, gentling his tone as he brushed snow from his father's legs.

'What the hell are you doing out in the middle of the night, son? You'll get sick again, and your mother's mad at me as it is,' Patrick mumbled.

Fighting to maintain his equanimity, Ulysses took his brandy-filled canteen from his coat pocket and poured a little down Patrick's throat, then gave him a shake, hoping to rouse him from his demented stupor. 'Come on, Dad, I'm taking you home.'

His father didn't move.

It took all Ulysses' newly honed strength to tug Patrick to his feet. He might manage to carry him over to Starfire, but he'd have one hell of a time hoisting his dead weight up into the saddle.

'Damn it, Dad. You've got to help a little.'

'I'm too tired. I just want to sleep a while.'

'If you sleep, you'll die.'

'I am dead.'

'No, you're not. You're just tired and half frozen. I've already lost my mother. I'm not about to lose you, too. For God's sake, help me.'

Something in Ulysses' voice must have reached Patrick's befuddled brain. Although he swayed on his feet, he stood a little straighter. 'How far is it to your horse?'

Dismayed by this new evidence of Patrick's dementia, Ulysses pointed to Starfire. 'You can see for yourself.'

'No. I can't see a damn thing. I'm blind,' Patrick replied in a matter-of-fact tone. He let go a weak chuckle. 'You don't think I'd be sitting out here if I could have found my way home?'

Ulysses choked back an instinctive groan of sympathy. Right now, Patrick needed a strong helping hand a lot more than he needed a display of emotion.

'Starfire is just a few feet away,' Ulysses replied in the same matter-of-fact manner. Taking most of Patrick's weight, he helped his father to the waiting horse.

He guided Patrick's right foot into the stirrup, heaved him into the saddle, then mounted behind him. Ulysses hated subjecting Starfire to so much weight, but he didn't have any choice. Patrick would never manage to stay upright by himself on the ride home.

Supporting Patrick with his left arm, he slid his revolver from the holster on his right hip and fired off several shots in a prearranged signal that the search was over. Patrick gave no sign he had heard.

Ulysses held his father close, willing his life and warmth into him. He stopped from time to time to pour more brandy down Patrick's throat. The spillage made them smell as if they had spent the night in a saloon.

When they reached the ranch house a couple of hours later, their ride had been transformed into a triumphal procession. A dozen cowboys rode with them, whooping in jubilation and firing off their guns to tell the other search teams of Patrick's rescue. They were so happy that Ulysses couldn't bring himself to voice his fears about his father's well-being.

Charlotte was waiting for them on the porch steps, her diminutive form wrapped in a blanket. Caught between a smile and a crying jag, her lips trembled. Her eyes widened with delight, even as tears slid down her cheeks.

'Is he alive?' she asked in a breathy quaver as two men removed Patrick's supine body from the saddle.

'He sure is,' one of them replied with a grin.

'Bring him inside,' she said, turning to lead the way.

Ulysses swung from Starfire's back, and dismissed the remaining hands with instructions to sleep as late as they liked in the morning.

Ulysses hurried up the porch steps and into the house. He hated being the bearer of bad news, but he didn't want Patrick's condition to take Charlotte by surprise when Patrick came to.

Two cowboys were supporting Patrick while Charlotte struggled to remove his heavy coat.

'I'm so glad you found your father,' she said.

Ulysses hastened to help her. 'So am I. I don't think he could have lasted much longer. He wasn't in his right mind when I found him. He can't see, either.'

'Are you saying he's blind?' Charlotte let go her breath with the audible whoosh of a deflating balloon. 'I think he'd rather die than spend the rest of his life that way.'

Seeing the devastation on her face, Ulysses hastened to reassure her. 'Unless I miss my guess, he's snow-blind. He should get his sight back in a few days.'

Charlotte's shoulders squared. She looked as though she'd grown an inch. 'Oh, I do hope so.'

At that moment, Patrick lifted his head, opened his mouth and began to sing a bawdy song that Ulysses hadn't heard in years – and certainly never in the presence of a lady.

It didn't appear to faze Charlotte, though. Perhaps she had already been through too much to respond to any but the strongest emotional stimuli.

'There is something else I forgot to tell you,' Ulysses said. 'I wanted to warm Dad and get his circulation going, and brandy seemed the best way under the circumstances. He's drunk.'

The take-charge gleam in Charlotte's eyes wasn't diminished by the hint of laughter sparkling in them. Ignoring Patrick's caterwauling, she said to the cowboys, 'Carry Mr Pride up to the bathroom and take off his clothes.'

Ulysses had grown terribly fond of Charlotte, but not fond enough to subject his father to further risk. A bath was the last thing Patrick needed after almost freezing to death. Although, come to think of it now his coat was off, he certainly did smell ripe.

'Can't cleanliness wait until tomorrow?' Ulysses asked, raising his voice to be heard over Patrick's singing.

'I want him to come out of this with all his fingers and toes intact. The best way is to raise his temperature gradually. We'll put him in a cool tub and add hot water a little at a time. If you're concerned about propriety, remember I've seen your father naked before.'

Ulysses laughed out loud. Propriety had been the last thing on his mind. 'I'm sure you're right on all counts. I'll be up to help you in a few minutes. Right now, I could use a drink myself.'

Charlotte nodded. 'What are you waiting for?' she said to the waiting men.

It had been the longest day of his life, Ulysses thought as he removed his cold weather gear and put it away in the closet under the stairs. Weariness mated with relief to weaken his knees. The hero business was harder on a man than he had imagined. He didn't know how Terrell kept it up year after year.

He needed a few moments to sort through his feelings, to rein in the triumph and worry, to find his way back to the bookish man he had been a week ago. He headed for the library where Patrick kept a fine French brandy in a decanter on a sideboard.

A fire burned low on the hearth. Flickering shadows danced on the walls. He looked for the lamp that usually sat on the big partners' desk, then remembered it must be with the lamps Charlotte had sent with the hands.

He made his way to the sideboard, picked up the decanter and realized it was empty. The brandy was either inside the men's canteens – or inside their stomachs. Somehow, it seemed a fitting end to the day.

As he made his way from the dark room, he saw something – or someone – huddled on the tufted leather sofa in front of the fireplace.

Moving closer, he recognized Reina. She was curled up like a kitten, her knees tight to her chest, her head cradled in the crook of one arm. Strands of midnight black hair fell over her cheek.

He reached out to wake her – or to touch her, he wasn't sure which – then thought better of it. If she knew Patrick had been found and brought back, she'd probably insist on going home to tend to her own ailing father.

She looked so childlike and vulnerable that an instinctive male need to protect her ballooned in his chest. He couldn't send her home alone, and he was far too weary to go with her.

Don't be a fool, he told himself. Reina had never needed his protection. If anything, it had been the other way around. He had never forgotten that long ago day in the bakery when she had launched herself at their tormentors without a thought for her own safety.

As if she sensed his presence, she mumbled his

name. God in heaven, did he live in her dreams the way she lived in his?

It didn't matter, he reminded himself. He could never put aside the moral principles that had ruled his life. Reina was a whore's daughter. She was as inaccessible as if the length of Texas separated them.

Eighteen

Patrick slept through the night and on into the middle of the day. He woke to myriad aches and pains. His muscles felt stiff, his joints creaked when he moved, and he was suffering from what could only be a killer hangover.

He hadn't drunk to excess since his youth. What the hell had made him do so yesterday?

Memories of the last week bled into one another like clothes in a dye vat, until he finally arrived at the very last memory he possessed. He saw himself riding alone into a winter-white world, saw his hat fly from his head, saw himself shooting his crippled horse, and then . . . then what?

He had no recollection of returning to the ranch, yet here he was safe and sound in his own bed. Knowing hangovers and daylight made miserable companions, he opened his eyes slowly – and saw nothing but blurred shapes. Panic sent his heart up his throat. Why the hell couldn't he see? What had happened to him?

'Patrick, I've been waiting for you to wake up.'

He knew that breathy voice as well as he knew his own. 'Charlotte, what's wrong with my eyes?' he asked.

She took hold of one of his hands and gave it a reassuring squeeze. 'You were out all day yesterday

AN INDECENT LADY

with nothing to protect your eyes from the glare. You're snow-blind.'

'Is the condition permanent?'

'Ulysses says it isn't.' He heard the scrape of chair legs and the rustle of her gown. 'Can you see me?'

He blinked to lubricate his eyes. 'I can just make out your silhouette – and perhaps a bit of color. You aren't wearing black today, are you?'

'No. I'm wearing green. Can you really see it?'

'Sort of. You always looked wonderful in green.'

'I thought it was time I got out of mourning. Besides, I wanted to celebrate your safe return. I know your eyes hurt, but how does the rest of you feel?'

'Like an old man.'

'You're not an old man. I can attest to that,' she replied with a throaty giggle.

The intimacy of her laugh mystified him almost as much as what she had said. How could she possibly testify to his not being an old man? Had he been idiot enough to try and seduce her while he was inebriated? He'd been feeling the need of a woman lately. He sure wished he could remember.

She leaned over and wrapped her arms around his shoulders. Her cheek touched his and he felt her tears. His hands seemed to rise of their own volition and he hugged her back. God, she felt good – warm and alive, soft in all the right places.

He never thought to hold a woman again – and certainly not Charlotte. Now though, he didn't want to let her go.

'I was so worried when you didn't come home for supper last night,' she murmured against his chest. 'Ulysses did a wonderful job of organizing the search party.'

'Then it wasn't Rio?' he asked to her perfumed neck.

'Rio went home sick. Ulysses did it all. In fact, it was Ulysses who found you.' She gently extricated herself from his embrace. 'He brought you back to the ranch about two in the morning. He saved your life, Patrick.'

Those simple words restored the missing piece of his memory, setting it in place like a keystone in an arch. He could almost hear Ulysses saying, *I've already lost my mother. I'm not about to lose you, too.*

'I want to see my son,' Patrick said.

'You just woke up. It's been a long time since your last meal. Don't you want to eat something first?'

The mention of food brought his empty stomach to life with an audible growl. He ignored the hollow feeling in his middle. 'Food can wait. I came close to dying out there. The good Lord saw fit to give me a second chance. This time, I intend to do it right.'

'Do what right?'

'Everything, my dear Charlotte, starting with being a father – a real father. You see, a very special guardian angel is watching over me. I wouldn't want to disappoint her. I owe Ulysses my life – and so much more. It's time I started paying on the debt.'

Until yesterday, he'd had no intimations of his own mortality – not even when Elke died. Her passing had seemed like a hideous prank played by a cruel God, rather than a normal and inevitable part of life's cycle.

No one thinks they are going to die, he mused. If they did, soldiers would never charge across a battlefield, and women would never risk childbirth. People thought death was something that happened to someone else.

No, it wasn't his brush with the grim reaper

that urged him to be a better father. He longed to become the man that, in his pride, he always thought he was.

Charlotte read the need for a reconciliation with Ulysses on Patrick's face. She knew the look because she had seen it on her own many times in the early years of her marriage, when she still thought she and Nigel could work out all their problems.

Nigel had never responded to her overtures, but something told her Ulysses would rejoice at Patrick's.

A terrible realization streaked across her mind like heat lightning across a summer sky. If Patrick reconciled with his son, he wouldn't need her companionship any more.

The day she learned of Elke's death, Charlotte had set sail in a fragile ship of contrivances and half truths. The slightest shift in the wind could send her ship spinning off course.

A reconciliation would blow away the stale air of misunderstanding that had hung like a pall over Pride's Passion. It could as easily blow away her plans and hopes, too.

Despite her misgivings, she wanted what was best for Patrick. His happiness mattered to her more than her own. And that, she admitted, was the true measure of love.

'I'll fetch Ulysses at once,' she said.

She moved to the door, closed it behind her, and weak-kneed, sagged against it. Nigel had been the *wrong man* at the *right time*. Thanks to the web of deception she had woven, Patrick was the *right man* at the *wrong time*.

She could almost hear herself telling Velvet that propinquity would lead Ulysses and Alicia to friendship – and ultimately to love. She had never imagined she would fall into her own carefully set trap.

Damn propinquity.

She hadn't expected to feel anything – other than the need to make him well – when she bathed Patrick last night. Now, just thinking about Patrick's rugged male body made her heart flutter against her rib cage like a bird trying to escape a cage.

The last time she had seen a nude man, it had been her husband – dead of a heart attack in his latest mistress's bed. The sight of his white skin, his flaccid penis, and his round stomach had filled her with revulsion.

Patrick's body was as different from Nigel's as good rich soil is from swamp mud. Patrick's musculature offered silent testimony to the virtue of hard work. Nigel's flab had spoken of a wasted, dissolute life.

She would give almost anything if she could walk back into Patrick's room this very minute and make a clean breast of everything, from her ruined finances to her newly awakened love for him. However, Patrick had never been a man to suffer fools or liars gladly. And she had been both.

No, she thought, as she straightened and headed for the stairs, she didn't have any choice, Alicia still had a chance to win Ulysses' heart. She couldn't and wouldn't do anything to ruin things for her daughter.

Ulysses sat at the partners' desk in the library, trying to polish a speech he planned to give when the legislature went back into session. But his eyes kept on straying to the sofa where he had left Reina asleep last night.

He would have liked to see the way she looked first thing in the morning. He would have liked to

AN INDECENT LADY

see the expression on her face when she learned he had found Patrick. He would have liked to thank her for letting him ride Starfire. And then he would have liked to escort her safely home.

Fate, in the enchanting form of Alicia Hawthorne, had denied him all those things. Alicia had risen early, found Reina on the sofa, and told her of Patrick's rescue. Reina had been gone by the time Ulysses returned to the library – gone but for her scent still lingering in the air. And even that was fading.

It was just as well, he told himself. He needed no reminders of her existence. In fact, he'd be better off if he found a way to wipe her from the slate of his mind. Thank God the legislature would return to session in a couple of weeks. Perhaps distance would accomplish what his will could not.

A knock interrupted his musing. 'Come in,' he called out.

The massive mahogany doors swung inward to reveal Charlotte, looking exceptionally attractive in an emerald dress. He barely had time to note that she had given up her mourning when she said, 'Your father's awake. He wants to see you.'

Ulysses' pulse accelerated. 'How is he?'

'A little muddled. He said something about having a guardian angel.'

'And his eyes?'

'He can see – not clearly yet – but he can see.'

The jubilation in her voice eased the tightness in his chest. 'Thank God for that.'

'Go on up. He's waiting for you. I'll bring the two of you some coffee in a bit.'

With a flash of emerald, Charlotte left as suddenly as she had arrived. It wasn't like her to be so abrupt. She wasn't one to overstay her welcome or talk a man to death, but she did enjoy a bit of conversation.

Although she seemed happy about Patrick, Ulysses had the feeling that something was bothering her. Could Patrick have said something to upset her? Knowing his father, it seemed the most likely explanation for her behavior.

When Ulysses walked into the bedroom, Patrick was propped up on the pillows, looking surprisingly hale and hearty for a man who had come within hours of freezing to death.

He patted the bed and said, 'Sit down by me, son.'

'I don't want to disturb you.'

'You won't.'

Ulysses gingerly took possession of the bed's edge.

Patrick let go a huge sigh, then groped for Ulysses' hand. The unaccustomed touch startled Ulysses — and he almost pulled away.

'Now you're here, I find I don't have the words to thank you for saving my life.'

'You don't have to thank me. You're my father. Besides, all the men were involved in the search. Any one of them could have found you.'

'*Any one* of them didn't. *You did*. I wouldn't have blamed you if you left me out there.'

'Now Dad, there's no need to—'

'There is a need. I've been a rotten father. And yet, you saved me.'

Last night, Ulysses had wondered if Patrick had lost his grip on reality. Now he wondered if he had. Could he really be hearing the things his father was saying, or were they some sort of bizarre wish-fulfillment? Patrick's powerful grip, the rough feel of his work-hardened hand, told Ulysses this was real.

AN INDECENT LADY 263

During the long hours of the search, Ulysses had gone through an epiphany concerning his relationship with his father. Had Patrick gone through a similar experience concerning him?

'You haven't been that bad,' Ulysses said, happily granting Patrick absolution.

'You're more generous than I would be in your place. Last night when I thought I was dying I saw my mistakes so clearly—'

'You don't need to explain anything.'

Patrick didn't seem to hear him. 'I want you to know why I've acted the way I have all these years. You see, I was jealous.'

'Jealous? Of me?' Ulysses burst out. 'Whatever for?'

'I was jealous of all the time your mother spent with you. When we first met, she was married to Otto. I never thought I'd have her for my own. By the time I did, you were on the way. After you were born – it's a terrible thing to admit – but I resented you.'

Ulysses had forgotten to breath. Feeling lightheaded, he filled his lungs to capacity. He'd never had such an intimate discussion with another man before – had never discussed emotions and the behavior that flowed from them. His father's revelations were painful, embarrassing – and yet healing.

'I couldn't talk about it to anyone,' Patrick continued, 'especially not your mother. Sometimes, hearing you gasp and fight for breath in the middle of the night, I wanted to go to you. But every time I did, your mother was already there. Later, when you outgrew all the sickness and went off to Harvard, I told Elke you had disappointed me by not staying on the ranch. The truth is, I disappointed you every day of your life by not being a better father.'

Ulysses blinked back the moisture in his own eyes. 'You never disappointed me. When I was little, I used to look up to you and dream of being like you. Somewhere between boyhood and manhood, I finally realized I couldn't – and it damn near broke my heart. Mom helped me to understand the importance of being myself.'

'I'm glad she did. I wouldn't want you to be like me considering the botch I've made of things. I may never change my opinion about lawyers and politicians – but I sure as hell am proud of you. I'd like to come watch you give a speech to the legislature sometime.'

The fist-sized knot in Ulysses' throat threatened to make speech impossible. 'I've waited a long time to hear you say that,' he croaked.

'Then it isn't too late?'

'Hell no. I'd say your timing was perfect.' He paused, then plunged ahead. 'The truth is I never needed a father's advice more.'

His eyes shining, a huge grin on his face, Patrick enveloped Ulysses in a bear hug that damn near cracked both their rib cages.

'I'll try to help in any way I can.'

'I think I'm falling in love,' Ulysses blurted out.

'That's wonderful news.' Patrick gave him a thump on the back that would have felled a tree.

It took Ulysses a second to catch his breath. 'The trouble is – I'm not sure. Perhaps if you told me how you felt about Mother when you first met . . .'

His voice trailed off. Last night, he'd asked Luke Teague – a boy he hardly knew – a personal question. Now, he had asked an even more personal one of his father. What the hell had come over him?

Patrick didn't seem to find anything odd in his request. 'I'm sure you know your mother was the world to me. Before we married, I used to think about her day and night – but especially night. Lord, the dreams I had! It was all I could do to keep my hands off her when she was married to Otto, even though he was my best friend. I was a real stiff-necked ass in those days, and I hated being out of control like that.'

'What did you do?'

'I couldn't keep away from her – just couldn't do it.' Patrick chuckled. 'I used to ride to Fredericksburg once or twice a month – a two-day round trip – just to see her. I told her I had a real craving for Otto's baked goods. I think she knew I had a real craving for Otto's wife. We used to argue all the time, about everything and anything. There were enough sparks between us to ignite a prairie fire.'

'I know what you mean,' Ulysses replied. Did he ever. He felt the same way about Reina.

'I knew it, son – I just knew you were in love with Alicia!' Patrick declared with profound satisfaction. 'You couldn't have made a better choice. If you don't mind taking some advice, don't wait too long before you pop the question. Women get real impatient with a man who shilly-shallies.'

Shit. Ulysses had been on the brink of confessing how he felt about Reina.

'I'm not ready,' Ulysses said, stalling for time, and wondering how to set matters straight.

'No man is ever ready,' Patrick's voice vibrated with sympathy. 'We're all cowards when it comes to getting down on our knees in front of a woman.'

Excuses flew from Ulysses' mouth like a sinner's prayers. 'Alicia's only been here a short time. We don't know each other that well. She doesn't seem to have any romantic interest in me. I don't think Charlotte will stay long enough for me to get to know Alicia. They have an exciting life in England. I'm sure they're anxious to get back to it.'

Ulysses finally sputtered to a stop like a train engine running out of steam. Charlotte's departure would put an end to this ridiculous *contretemps*. Although he'd grown fond of her, he found himself wondering if he could come up with a way to speed it up.

A beatific smile blossomed on Patrick's face. 'I know just how you feel. It took me a long time to admit Elke was the only woman for me. But I think I have the perfect solution to your dilemma.'

'I'm not following you.' Nor did Ulysses want to. It had been a very strange conversation. Now, it threatened to get even stranger.

'I've been wondering how much longer we could convince our lovely guests to stay on – and I've come up with the perfect reason. There isn't a woman born – with the exception of your mother – who can resist a shopping spree.'

'I don't see what that has to do with Charlotte and Alicia.'

'Your mother never got around to decorating the new wing. I used to chide her about it. I guess she didn't have the strength, and didn't want me to know. But it is a damn shame to let all that space go to waste – and it would be a perfect place for you and your bride to live.'

'I still don't understand.'

'I'll ask Charlotte to decorate the new wing – with Alicia's help, of course. It should keep her here for months.'

Despair clutched at Ulysses' innards. And yet, Patrick's scheme was so perfect that he couldn't help laughing. 'I had no idea you had such a devious mind,

Dad. I know you won't be flattered, but you would have made one hell of a politician.'

Terrell Meeks had never known such a winter. Last year had been so bad that folks still talked about it – and this one promised to be even worse. The blizzard had dumped more snow than any old timer could recall.

He felt like a damn fool, riding out to Pride's Passion on such a cold day just to make sure Alicia hadn't come to any harm during the storm. Patrick Pride would have seen to her safety. Most likely, she hadn't set foot outdoors in days. By now, her biggest problem would be a bad case of cabin fever.

Still, he had to see her for himself. He had even worked out an excuse for showing up at the ranch – one Patrick would undoubtedly swallow without question.

Terrell wasn't as sure about Miss Charlotte. She had a way of looking at a man as if she could see right through to his heart. And if she ever once got a good look at what was going on inside of his, she'd take her daughter away from Pride's Passion faster than a scalded cat left a kitchen.

He came to the lane that led to the DeVargas ranch and reluctantly turned his horse onto it. His conscience wouldn't let him drop by the Prides' until he checked on Rio and Velvet.

Cresting a gentle rise, he saw their house cradled in the saucer-shaped valley below and paused to admire the view. Smoke rose from the chimneys, promising a warm haven.

A few minutes later, he jumped from the saddle and tied the reins to a hitching post by the front door. Velvet answered his knock. Although less than two weeks had passed since his last visit, she looked more careworn than he remembered. However, her hospitality hadn't changed a bit.

'Come on in and get out of the cold,' she said, taking his hand and tugging him into the entry. 'Lord, it's good to see you.'

'It's good to see you, too,' he replied. He took off his hat and coat and hung them on the hall tree. 'I've been worried about you.'

'About Rio and me – or about Reina?' Velvet gave him one of those inscrutable female looks that hinted at secret knowledge no mere man could ever fathom.

'I've been worried about all of you – and the Prides, too,' he explained, rubbing his hands. 'It sure was cold out. I wouldn't mind a cup of coffee.'

'There's a fresh pot on the stove,' Velvet replied, leading the way to the kitchen. Although the corners of her mouth twitched in a smile, her eyes had a speculative expression, as if she were measuring him for a new suit.

'As long as you've ridden such a long way, you might as well stay for lunch. Reina will be home soon to check on Rio. You wouldn't believe what a help she's been since he took sick. That girl can run a ranch as well as any man.'

It took Terrell a moment to process everything Velvet had said. 'What's wrong with Rio?'

'He came down with the influenza right after the blizzard. He's still in bed, but I don't know how much longer I can keep him there. Maybe you can talk some sense into him.' She poured coffee into an enamel mug and held it out. 'You know the way to our room. Take the coffee with you.'

Although Terrell was anxious to see Alicia, he couldn't think of any way to refuse Velvet's request. 'Are you sure lunch isn't too much trouble?'

Velvet let go one of her trademark throaty laughs. 'A good-looking man is never trouble, sugar.'

Rio's appearance shocked Terrell. He looked as white as the sheets he lay on, and he seemed to have shrunk. *Lord, he's an old man*, Terrell realized with a start, trying to remember Rio's age. He'd been forty-five when Terrell went to work for the Prides. That made him seventy.

Rio's smile erased a few of those years as he greeted Terrell. Then he coughed and the years reappeared – plus a few more. 'What brings you this way?' he asked when he finally caught his breath.

Terrell managed to return Rio's smile, although he ached at seeing Rio so sick. 'I heard you were giving Velvet a hard time about staying in bed, and I rode on out to read you the riot act.'

'Son, it would take more man than you'll ever be to keep me flat on my back,' Rio boasted, sounding more like his old self.

'I left cuffs and leg irons in my saddle bags just in case.' Terrell paused. 'Seriously, old hoss, how are you feeling?'

'I'll do,' Rio replied succinctly. 'Now, what brings you out here? Don't tell me you're plumb out of criminals to chase.'

'They do tend to stay indoors when the weather turns ugly – which shows they have more sense than you or me. I'm here because I wanted to see how you and the Prides came through the storm, and to give you news of your neighbors.'

Terrell talked easily for the next thirty minutes, filling Rio in on local and state-wide conditions, making sure that Rio didn't talk too much in return.

It was Reina who came to tell him lunch was ready. She gave him an exuberant hug, then made a typically female fuss over Rio, plumping his pillows, smoothing his covers, and feeling his brow. Rio just grinned through it all.

Reina wore her habitual Levi's and a heavy sweater over a man's work shirt. The layers of clothing failed to conceal her lush curves. Terrell gave one last thought to what a fine wife she would have made him, if his heart hadn't strayed in another direction.

Then he gently and permanently shut the door on such useless speculation. Reina deserved to be loved for her own self – not because it seemed like a sensible thing to do.

He followed her to the kitchen where two places had been set at the table. 'Aren't you eating with us?' he asked Velvet.

'I take my meals with Rio,' she replied, 'but I'm sure you and Reina will find something to talk about.'

'I'm sure we will,' Reina replied, emphasizing each word as if they meant more than what they seemed.

The look in her eyes mirrored the look that Terrell had seen in Velvet's earlier. *Women*, he thought with a shrug as he sat down to lunch.

Reina waited until the sound of Velvet's footsteps had faded, then turned to him. 'You might have fooled my parents, and you will probably fool the Prides, too – but I know you didn't ride all the way out here to visit us. You want to see Alicia, don't you?'

Terrell had been lifting a spoon to his mouth. His hand shook and a tiny waterfall of chicken soup splattered onto the table. Muttering apologies, he hurried to blot it up.

'Terrell, look at me,' Reina commanded.

AN INDECENT LADY 271

As obedient as an old hound, he lifted his eyes. 'What makes you think I want to see Alicia?'

'You and I go way back, Terrell. In all the years we've been friends, I've never known you to tell a lie – or even to shade the truth to make a story more interesting. And yet, you lied for Alicia.'

'How do you know I wasn't lying to protect you?'

'Because I wasn't alone with you in the woods. You didn't kiss me, buster.'

Damn. He should have realized Alicia would have told Reina the truth. Women opened up to each other in a way men never did. 'Is she furious with me for taking advantage of her?'

Reina burst out laughing. 'You think you were taking advantage? I'd say it was mutual.'

'Mutual. Does that mean – ?' He had stared down more gun barrels than he could remember, but he didn't have the courage to finish the question.

Reina gave him a conspiratorial smile, leaned across the table, and lowered her voice. 'It means she wouldn't mind if you kissed her again. In fact, I think she'll be very upset if you don't.' She gave Terrell time to think about what she said before adding, 'I have very good news. Alicia will be staying at Pride's Passion for the foreseeable future.'

He blinked in surprise. 'How did that come about?'

'You can thank Patrick. It seems he asked Charlotte to decorate the new wing. She told Alicia it will take months.'

Months, Terrell thought happily. He smiled so broadly that it hurt his face. He'd been living in dread of the day Alicia returned to England. But she wasn't going back for a long time. Even better, she shared his feelings.

His jubilant heart rushed heavenward. His more logical rear end remained firmly attached to the chair. He may have won a battle. He sure as hell hadn't won the war.

'That is good news,' he replied. 'But I don't think Miss Charlotte would approve of me courting her daughter no matter how long they stay. To be honest, I don't blame her. I'm too old for Alicia and, God knows, I don't have any money or any prospects.'

'Alicia doesn't like men her age. She says they all look as bland as boiled eggs. She sure doesn't care about money, either. And she has some pretty exciting prospects of her own. But you're right about Miss Charlotte. That's where I come in.'

'Prospects? Do you mean money she inherited from her father? I could never take money from a woman.'

'Alicia hasn't mentioned an inheritance. As far as she knows, her mother got everything. As for her prospects, I'm sure she'll tell you all about it one day soon.'

Terrell needed a moment to regroup. Experience had taught him that there was a time in the ebb and flow of events when a prudent man pulled back – thereby saving his ass, as well as other appendages he didn't want to live without.

This was one of those times. He already knew Reina and Alicia were conspirators. If he joined them, he might win his heart's desire. But he would never again be the man he had been.

A line he had read somewhere popped into his mind. *I could not love thee dear so much loved I not honor more.*

He had memorized it because he admired the sentiment. It was the sort of thing men said before they went into battle.

He shook his head, as if to rid himself of notions like honor. He had lived honorably all his life and it had never filled his heart the way Alicia had. He wanted her badly enough to risk anything and everything.

'What do you mean about that's where you come in?' he asked Reina, plunging ahead with even less caution than the Light Brigade on their ill-fated charge.

'Charlotte thinks Ulysses is courting Alicia. If my mother thinks you're courting me, the four of us will be able to spend a lot of time together.'

Terrell had never worried about having a rival. The thought sent an icy chill through his innards. 'Is Ulysses courting Alicia?'

'She swears he isn't – and she ought to know.'

'Do you really think your plan will work?'

'It worked the day we went skating.'

Terrell's heart gave a bump. 'The two of you planned it?'

Reina nodded. 'Everything but my swim. That was an accident.'

He pushed his soup bowl away. Conspiracy had its virtues, he thought with boyish glee. 'You've been a real friend, Reina. Could I prevail on you for another favor?'

'What do you have in mind?'

'Would you mind riding over to Pride's Passion with me today? If you help me find a way to be alone with Alicia – I'll help out with the chores after we get back.'

Reina gave him a cryptic smile. 'How can I refuse?'

Nineteen

Alicia had immersed herself in the world of dime novels for weeks, first as a reader and then as a fledgling author. Only the blizzard had interrupted her progress. Now, as she sat in a chair by her bedroom window, writing in her well-schooled Spencerian hand, emotions played across her face and her lips formed silent words.

She had read that Alexandre Dumas laughed with his characters, cried with them, cheered their successes and bemoaned their failures, and she had been thrilled to discover herself doing the same thing. It strengthened her belief that she had been born to write.

She rose before dawn and spent a couple of hours writing before breakfast every morning, filling up page after page with a rough draft, then making excuses to retire early at night to continue her work.

After a careful editing, she typed each chapter on a Remington she had borrowed from Ulysses. Although she had prepared an elaborate excuse for needing a typewriter, he hadn't questioned her motives. His attention was firmly fixed elsewhere.

The four hours she stole from other activities were never enough. As she went about her daily chores, lines and paragraphs kept popping into her head. She

AN INDECENT LADY 275

had taken to carrying a small notebook and writing them down when she was sure no one was looking. This afternoon, pleading a headache, she had come up to her room to write some more.

Thank heaven her mother had been too preoccupied to comment on Alicia's sudden need for solitude. When Patrick was home, Charlotte spent all her time fussing over him. When he wasn't, she spent hours in the new wing, armed with a tape measure and note pad.

She told Alicia she was getting the feel of the rooms, and planning how to furnish them. However, if she had been seventeen instead of forty-seven, Alicia would have been certain she was daydreaming about some man. Alicia didn't dare try to ferret out the truth, though – not while she had so many secrets of her own.

Writing a book had come to her as naturally as eating and sleeping. She loved playing God, creating the world and peopling it with an intriguing cast of characters – although the effort would take her considerably more than the six days mentioned in the Bible. She would need two months at the very least!

While researching dime novels and compiling a list of publishing houses, she learned the public seemed to have an insatiable appetite for such books. Despite their popularity, some preachers regarded them as a threat to morality because of the way they portrayed women as resourceful and independent, subject only to the men they loved.

Many of the successful dime novelists wrote about real men like Kit Carson, Wild Bill Hickock, George Armstrong Custer, and Buffalo Bill Cody as if they were on a first-name basis with them when in fact they had never met.

At least her book would have a ring of authenticity. She might be a novice when it came to balancing narrative, dialogue and description, but the time she had spent on the ranch had given her a feel for the setting and the people. When she made mistakes, Reina pointed them out and corrected them.

All Alicia had to do was get the story down. And darling Terrell had supplied her with the perfect one. Her plot, based on the Flores incident, contained the requisite scenes of derring-do.

Her hero, Duke Bastrop, was daring, courageous, and honorable. Her heroine, Serena St Cloud, was both beautiful and virtuous – despite being forced into prostitution by the dastardly Juan Torres.

This afternoon, Alicia had reached the chapter in which Duke followed the infamous Torres bunch across the Mexican border – only to learn Serena was hot on his trail.

Serena appeared out of the night, Alicia wrote, *slipping between the trees like a beautiful wraith garbed in ghostly white. Her flimsy night clothes barely concealed her womanly curves. A zephyr parted her negligee to reveal a breast as pure as alabaster.*

'I've found you at last,' Serena cried out. 'Oh Duke, I shall perish if you ever leave me again.'

Alicia's heart pounded with the passion coursing through Serena's veins. Her pencil poised in mid-air, she gazed down at the page, wondering if she could come up with a more sensual way to convey how Serena looked in Duke's eyes without getting censored in Boston or some such puritanical place.

People were certainly weird about sex, she mused, chewing on the end of her pencil. Everyone did it – but no one talked about it. If it hadn't been for Reina, she still wouldn't know how a man and a woman fit their differing sexual parts together. Now, she could hardly wait to experience it for herself.

She chuckled deep in her throat. Months ago, she would never have entertained such a bawdy thought. Today, she could contemplate the possibility with considerable *sang froid*. No, make that *sang chaud*, she decided, automatically editing her own thoughts. There wasn't anything cold about her blood when she imagined what it would be like to make love to Terrell.

Did he have coppery freckles and red hair in other places? The question was so titillating that it pushed her to the brink of sexual arousal – and beyond. Before her talk with Reina, she wouldn't have known why her nipples firmed and her womb tightened. Now, she delighted in her response.

Eons ago, a particularly odious nanny had told Alicia that her brain would decay and her teeth would fall out if she touched her female parts. It had been utter rot – the sort of dangerous drivel that had kept generations of virgins from enjoying the marriage bed.

Armed with information, Alicia had examined her naked body in the mirror over her dresser – first with her eyes and then with her hands, all the while muttering words like vagina, breasts, penis and testicles, until she felt at ease saying them.

The experience had been so liberating – so incredibly thrilling, physically and mentally – that she had repeated it several times since. When she finally disrobed in Terrell's presence – as she knew she would someday – she would do so with joy rather than shame. Visions of their entwined bodies played across her mind. It took a determined effort to return to her book.

* * *

'You shouldn't have followed me. You're in mortal danger,' Duke exclaimed, his gaze riveted by Serena's near nudity. 'The villainous Torres bunch is close by. I cannot bring myself to speak the words, but we both know what they will do if they find you here.'

He could see Serena's heart beating beneath her breast like the fluttering of a dove's wings. Her luminous eyes filled with tears. 'I don't fear Juan Torres. He has already done his worst to me.'

'An evil deed he shall pay for in the coin of blood,' Duke declared. 'I swear it on my honor. You shall be avenged. But you must leave while you can.'

Serena threw herself into his arms. 'I would sooner die than leave you. Oh Duke, you know the secrets of my body. It's time you knew the secrets of my heart. I love you more than life itself.'

A tear trickled down Alicia's cheek as she imagined herself saying those very words to Terrell. She started when a knock at the door broke the spell she had woven with words.

Reina marched into the bedroom, bringing a hint of frosty outdoor air with her.

'I wasn't expecting you,' Alicia said. 'Is something wrong?'

Reina glanced at the tablet on Alicia's lap. 'I can see you're busy writing – but I think you'll be glad for this interruption. Terrell is downstairs, waiting to see you.'

The tablet fell to the floor as Alicia bolted to her feet. 'Oh, dear. I'm not dressed properly. My hair isn't done. I must look a mess.'

'You look fine to me. Besides, Terrell won't care.'

'How can you be sure he didn't come to visit the Prides?'

AN INDECENT LADY

'Because he told me.' Reina took Alicia's arm and tugged her toward the door. 'You're wasting time.'

Alicia planted her feet like a balky mule. 'Reina DeVargas, I'm not going anywhere until you tell me if Terrell said anything else.'

Laughter danced in Reina's eyes. 'Are you asking me to break his confidence?'

'I most certainly am!'

'He's in love with you.'

Alicia's heart stuttered to a stop. Her mouth gaped open. Her eyes widened. Suddenly the world – or at least the part she occupied – seemed to have been repainted in vivid hues. 'Oh Reina, you don't know what this means to me.'

'You're wrong,' Reina replied. Her eyes stopped dancing and filled with pain instead. 'I know. But I don't expect it will ever happen to me.'

The easy creak of saddle leather, the bell-like chink of metal on metal, and the muffled sound of hooves on packed snow added to Ulysses' feeling of peace as he and Patrick rode back to the house. Working together this last week had cemented their newly forged bond.

His father was a truly remarkable man, he thought, giving him a sideways glance. He sat his horse with a style and ease that Ulysses couldn't match if he spent the rest of his life on a saddle. The only indication of Patrick's recent ordeal was the red that still rimmed his eyes.

'We got off easy,' Patrick was saying. 'The cattle we lost would have died of age or infirmity this year or the next. If our supply of hay holds out until the grass comes in, we should make it through the rest of the winter without losing more of the herd.'

'You weren't lucky, Dad. You were smart. If

you hadn't moved the animals closer to the ranch before the storm hit, your losses would have been much worse.'

'I wonder how other ranchers fared. It could have a drastic effect on the price of cattle.'

'I hadn't thought about that.' Ulysses had always seen ranching as purely physical work. He was just beginning to realize how much thought and planning went into a successful operation.

'I don't like getting richer at my neighbor's expense, but I won't turn away from a fair profit,' Patrick declared, then turned to Ulysses. 'Speaking of profit, you've done a fine job with the books. Your mother would be proud of you – and so am I. I'm going to miss your help when the legislature goes back into session.' He cleared his throat. 'The truth is, I can do the books myself. It's not your accounting skills I'll miss. It's you, son.'

Patrick's declaration fell on Ulysses like rain on a long-parched desert. 'I've been thinking how much I'll miss you, too. Would you consider coming to Austin for a visit? You could sit in the public gallery at the state house and watch me in action.'

Patrick's grin widened. 'I saw you in action the night you saved my life.'

Ulysses chuckled. 'As I recall, you couldn't see a damn thing.'

'I'm not much on city life.'

'Charlotte and Alicia would certainly enjoy themselves,' Ulysses said, dangling bait he knew his father couldn't refuse. 'They've been housebound for quite a while.'

A smile carved deep grooves on both sides of Patrick's mouth, and a twinkle appeared in his gray eyes. 'Now I get it. You want to show Alicia a good time. And by God, you're right. She and her mother have been stuck on the ranch all winter. It's time they had a change of scene. And Charlotte does need to do some serious shopping.'

Ulysses could only shrug. Patrick had an absolute genius for misunderstanding his motives when it came to Alicia. He had yet to find the right time to tell his father the truth. But then, the truth seemed as difficult to grasp as quicksilver.

His feelings for Reina shifted from week to week like wind-driven sand. He hadn't seen her since the night he found Patrick – and he had sworn to avoid seeing her in the future. It had been an uncomfortable decision at first, like having an itch he couldn't scratch. Even now, despite his best intentions, sensual images of the intimacy they had shared swirled through his mind like an erotic kaleidoscope.

'Is something wrong?' Patrick asked.

'No.'

'You don't need to hide your feelings from me anymore, son. I reckon you're anxious about leaving Alicia behind. It will certainly put a crimp in your courtship. If having her come to Austin is that important to you, I'll see she gets there.'

'Thanks, Dad,' Ulysses replied automatically.

He hadn't given Alicia much time or attention of late – and even less thought. Perhaps away from the ranch, in a sophisticated social setting where she was bound to shine, he'd be able to school his heart and mind to appreciate her virtues – and forget all about Reina and her lack of them.

Ulysses and Patrick had approached the house from the back. Now, as they rode around to the front, Ulysses saw two horses – and his stomach knotted. The big chestnut belonged to Terrell. The other was Starfire.

'We've got company,' Patrick said cheerfully.

Ulysses needed a moment to collect his thoughts and paste the proper expression on his face before he saw Reina. 'Go on in,' he said. 'I'll stable our horses.'

When Ulysses walked into the parlor fifteen minutes later, Patrick and Terrell were deep in conversation. Charlotte, Alicia, and Reina were listening to them with varying degrees of interest.

Alicia stared at Terrell with single-minded intensity, as if he'd just come down from the Mount with God's word inscribed on stone tablets. Charlotte's gaze kept flitting from Patrick to Terrell to Alicia, as if something had unsettled her. Only Reina seemed aware of Ulysses' arrival. Their eyes met briefly, and he couldn't say who looked away faster.

'The telegraphers have been working overtime since the blizzard,' Terrell was saying, 'and the news is all bad. This is the second hard winter we've had. The loss of cattle is said to run as high as eighty-five percent in Montana and the Dakotas.' He finally looked up, saw Ulysses, and acknowledged his arrival with a nod.

'I suspected it would be bad. But I had no idea—' Patrick seemed to run out of words. His horrified expression said it all.

'Barbed wire killed as many Longhorns as the weather did,' Terrell continued. 'The poor beasts ate all the grass they could get to, then, held in by fences, starved to death.' He gazed at Patrick. 'I wish everyone was as judicious about stringing wire as you have been. I've settled more than one dispute between ranchers when one of them fenced the other's herd off from water. Damn! I've seen nesters fence off roads to protect their grain fields.

I've seen ranchers cut off schools. The XIT alone has run six thousand miles of wire. It's a hell of a mess.'

Terrell was so caught up in the emotion of the moment that he seemed unaware that he had cursed in front of the ladies. To their credit, they didn't draw it to his attention.

Terrell turned his steely gaze on Ulysses. The implacable look in his eyes gave a glimpse of the Terrell who had gunned down so many criminals. 'The legislature ought to do more about regulating the use of barbed wire.'

Ulysses locked eyes with Terrell's. 'The legislature will,' he replied, making a promise of those simple words.

The tension in Terrell's body eased. 'Things are so bad that folks are calling this winter *the great die-off*. Some of them think ranching as we know it is finished.'

'That's ridiculous,' Reina declared, shaking her head for emphasis. 'From what I've read in the newspaper, the flow of immigrants is bigger than ever. Those people need meat and lots of it to work twelve-hour days in factories back east.'

'You don't understand. No business can sustain losses of that magnitude,' Patrick explained patiently. 'After this, banks won't be eager to lend more money to ranchers.'

'There's talk up north of raising sheep rather than cattle,' Terrell added.

'I know some ranchers will be forced to sell out – and I'm sick about it. It's a sad example of survival of the fittest,' Reina said, surprising Ulysses with her reference to Darwin's theory. When had she read Darwin? She certainly had everyone's attention – and most especially his.

'This isn't about money,' she continued with a zealot's ardor. 'It's about change – leaving the old ways behind – modernizing the way we raise beef – getting ready to meet the demands of a twentieth-century market. We all know Longhorns produce tough meat. Restaurants have been asking for beef with more fat and marbling for years. Some of them import beef from France and England because we haven't given them what they want. It doesn't make sense to surrender a lucrative part of our market to foreigners. We can do anything Europeans can do – and we can do it better.'

'What do you suggest?' Ulysses asked, giving Reina enough rope to hang herself.

'There's going to be a shortage of cattle this year. The price will go up. Your father and mine ought to use some of that windfall to buy prize bulls like the Herefords Miss Charlotte told us she bred on her estate.'

Ulysses was taken aback by Reina's acumen. He had forgotten all about the Glenhaven Herefords. Although he was an admitted novice when it came to ranching, he knew enough to realize they would make a marvelous addition to his father's stock. 'Have you talked to Rio about your ideas – or are they *his* ideas?'

Reina shot him a scathing look. 'I have talked to him – and they are *my* ideas. He happens to agree with them.'

'And so do I,' Patrick said, getting to his feet to pace the floor and talking all the while. 'I've stayed with Longhorns because they're what I know best. Other ranchers have started cross-breeding programs – with limited success. There are so many potential problems. The calves may be so big that their mothers die birthing them. Then there's the problem of climate and weather. It takes a sturdy, rugged animal to survive on the range.'

'Have you heard of hybrid vigor?' Reina asked. 'According to Mendel's theory, cross-breeding produces plants and animals that are stronger than either parent.'

Good God, now she was quoting Mendel. What would she come up with next? He'd been so sure he knew everything there was to know about her. Now he realized he didn't know her at all.

'You've made some very valid points,' Patrick said. 'But I won't buy a pig in a poke. I'd like to be sure I'm getting what I've paid for.'

Charlotte sat forward. To Ulysses, she looked anxious – even a little nervous. 'This couldn't have happened at a more auspicious time. I've been thinking about putting Glenhaven Hall on the market – along with all its goods and chattels. That includes the Herefords.'

She sounds like a lawyer, Ulysses thought – or like she's been talking to a lawyer.

Alicia tore her gaze from Terrell and stared, wide-eyed, at her mother. 'You're thinking about selling Glenhaven?' she said with obvious bewilderment.

Although Ulysses was startled by the direction the conversation had taken, he kept his own counsel. The undercurrents of emotion, the sudden change in Charlotte's plans, mystified him. For the time being, he put the paradoxes aside and turned his attention back to the conversation.

'I'm sorry. I should have told you sooner, darling. Will you mind so very much?' Charlotte asked, leaning forward to soothe Alicia with a touch.

'I haven't had a chance to think about it.'

Charlotte seemed to be fighting to maintain her composure – and losing. She didn't meet her daughter's perplexed gaze. 'I know it must seem sudden but I've been thinking about it since your father's death. I can't go back and face all those memories.'

'What about the London townhouse?' Alicia asked.

'Darling, this isn't the time or the place to discuss our personal business.' Charlotte turned back to Patrick. The smile on her face was so brittle that Ulysses feared the wrong word would shatter her. 'If you're interested in the Glenhaven Herefords, and most particularly in the Grand Champion Glenhaven's Nabob, I'd be happy to have my manager send papers and pictures. I'm sure we can come to an agreement on price if you like what you see.'

'I couldn't take advantage of you that way,' Patrick replied. 'Whoever buys Glenhaven is bound to want the bulls, too.'

'You would be doing me a great favor. Nabob is generally regarded as the finest of his breed in all England. I wouldn't have any trouble selling him, but I couldn't bear to let him go to just anyone. You see, he was hand-raised. He's terribly spoiled. Knowing he was in your care would make parting with him easier.'

Charlotte went on to describe Nabob's lineage, his conformation and the achievements of his offspring, while Patrick listened with increasing interest.

'If he's all you say he is, there really isn't any need for pictures or pedigrees. I trust you implicitly, Charlotte,' Patrick said.

Charlotte paled. For a moment, Ulysses wondered if she was going to faint. Either she had something in her eyes – or something was truly amiss, Ulysses decided, as she blinked back tears.

AN INDECENT LADY 287

An echo of his previous suspicions of her came flooding back. But he quickly dismissed them when he realized that selling such an animal – even to an old friend – was bound to be an emotional undertaking.

'There's no need to worry about Nabob,' Patrick said, his voice brimming with sympathy. 'I promise to treat him like a member of the family. In fact, you can decorate one of the rooms in the new wing for him if it will make you feel better.'

Patrick's sally produced the desired response. Charlotte smiled. 'Pardon me for being so sentimental. Nabob is yours, if you want him.'

'That is good news,' Patrick replied, returning to the sofa, sitting down beside her and taking her hand. 'Now I have some good news for you and Alicia, Ulysses has asked the three of us to Austin for a visit. I thought we'd go in mid-April. It's a beautiful time of year to travel. I know you'll find the stores there to your liking.'

'I'll be there myself,' Terrell interjected, 'testifying at a trial.'

'That sounds wonderful,' Alicia said with unbridled enthusiasm. She certainly was an emotional chameleon. Ulysses thought. Seconds before, she had clearly been disturbed by the impending sale of her ancestral home. Now, she looked absolutely gleeful.

She turned her winning smile on Patrick. 'Would you mind if Reina came with us? Mother will undoubtedly spend most of her time shopping for furniture, and I would like to have someone to see the sights with.'

Damn all interfering females, Ulysses thought. 'I'm sure Reina has other things to do.' His voice sounded harsher than he had intended, but it was too late to do anything about it.

A tiny shudder ran through Reina. Was the thought of spending time with her that loathsome?

'It's kind of you to want to include me,' she said to Alicia, 'but I couldn't leave my father.'

Patrick gave both girls a benevolent smile. 'Rio will be fine long before then. I won't take no for an answer, Reina. You're coming with us as my personal guest.'

'But— ' Reina sputtered.

'I won't listen to any buts. I'll talk to your parents about the trip myself,' Patrick said.

'There's no need. I'll do it.'

Reina's eyes met Ulysses' and the anger he saw in them took his breath away. Good God, she must remember what had happened at the stock pond — and despise him for it.

Reina spent the ride home marshalling arguments against the proposed trip to Austin. She could never tell her mother the real reason she didn't want to go — that she couldn't bear to be with Ulysses because it hurt so much.

She found Velvet in the parlor, enjoying a rare moment of leisure.

'How's Dad?' she asked, taking a seat across from Velvet.

'He's sleeping. Where's Terrell? I thought he might ride back with you.'

'The Prides asked him to stay to supper.'

Velvet frowned. 'Didn't they ask you?'

'They did, but I was anxious to get home to you and Dad. That wasn't their only invitation, though.'

Reina wasted no time telling Velvet about the trip to Austin. As she had feared, Velvet was instantly enthusiastic. 'This calls for a brandy,' she said, hurrying to the sideboard. 'It's the best news I've had in a long time.'

'I'm not going,' Reina declared.

'As long as you live in my house, you'll do as I say. And I say you are going,' Velvet replied with equal intensity. 'I hope you thanked Patrick for the invitation.'

'I wasn't feeling very thankful. Besides, Dad needs me here.'

Velvet carried a brandy-filled glass back to the sofa, and stood over Reina. 'Your father will be up and about in a few more days. By the middle of April, he'll be fit as a fiddle.'

'Mother, you don't understand. Patrick said there will be all sorts of parties. I don't have the right clothes.'

Useful sat between them, looking as miserable – with his ears laid back and his tail tucked between his haunches – as a dog can look. He wasn't used to hearing them argue, Reina thought, and neither was she.

Velvet held her brandy glass so tight that her hand shook. 'You're the one who insists on wearing Levi's. Your father and I can afford to dress you properly – and there's lots of time to have new frocks made.'

'It's more than the clothes, Mother. I won't know how to act or what to say. I've never been to a big city like Austin.'

'There's nothing wrong with your manners, young lady – and it's high time you went somewhere other than the outhouse.'

Reina grimaced. 'Mother, will you please sit down and listen to me? You can dress me up all you want, but you can't make a silk purse out of a sow's ear. All the fancy clothes in the world won't make society people accept me. Put a diamond tiara on my head and I'll still be Reina DeVargas.'

'No one will dare say anything unkind while you're with Patrick and the countess. Besides, you told me Terrell will be there. I suspect nothing could please him more than having you there, too.'

Reina choked down a quick retort. She could hardly tell her mother Terrell and Alicia were head over heels in love. 'I'm not interested in Terrell that way,' she said, telling as much of the truth as she dared.

'Wait until he waltzes you around a dance floor a time or two. Being in a man's arms has a way of changing the way a woman feels.'

No, it doesn't, Reina thought, feeling as if a vise was tightening around her chest. Ulysses had held her in his arms more than once, and it hadn't changed a thing – except to make him think even less of her, if such a thing were possible.

She planted her hands on her hips. This was one argument she had to win. No way was she willing to risk being humiliated by Ulysses – or anyone else – ever again.

'If you had been at the Prides' today, you would know that Alicia invited me – not Patrick. She put him in a terrible position.'

'I'm sure he would have extended the invitation in due time.'

Reina fired one last desperate salvo. 'Ulysses doesn't want me in Austin. And I don't go where I'm not wanted.'

'Since when do you care what he thinks?' Velvet fired back.

Since forever, Reina answered silently.

'I don't like fighting with you,' Velvet said, 'and if we keep it up, we'll wake your father. But I'm not about to let you pass up the opportunity of a lifetime. You're going to Austin and that's that. I'll ask one of the hands' wives to sit with Rio tomorrow so we can go to town and get started on your new wardrobe.'

Reina took a deep breath, then let it out in a sigh. 'All right, I'll go if you insist. But I have the feeling I'm going to regret it.'

Twenty

Reina prepared for the trip to Austin like Hannibal getting ready to cross the Alps. She wouldn't permit her lack of social graces to be on display ever again.

She enlisted Charlotte's help in planning a wardrobe fit for a queen, and then went to Kerrville's finest dressmaker to see those plans carried out. Knowing it would be expensive, she insisted on paying for the clothes herself with the money she had earned working at Pride's Passion.

Over the years, she had felt funny accepting money for what she would happily have done for free. However, as the costs of her new wardrobe mounted, she was grateful she had.

In addition to dresses for different times of day, the dressmaker fitted her for a traveling suit, a riding habit, and a ball gown. Reina also purchased the accoutrements to go with them, including corsets, corset covers, camisoles, pantalettes, bustle cages, petticoats, gloves to hide her work-worn hands, and an astonishing array of hats, parasols, and reticules.

Wearing that paraphernalia proved to be torture. The corset compressed her hips, inhibited her breathing, and lifted her breasts so that they seemed to be riding a wave. The stylishly narrow skirts hobbled her as thoroughly as she had ever hobbled any horse. And the fourteen or more yards of material that went into every outfit weighed her down like a pack mule.

But the first time she saw herself in the ball gown, she had to admit the results were worth it!

She spent hours with her mother, learning to fix her hair a dozen different ways, from cascading curls that framed her face to the high upsweep that looked good under a hat and added inches to her height.

Alicia volunteered to tutor her in etiquette and ballroom dancing. By the time the lessons came to an end, Reina could preside at tea like the lady of the manor, partake in an eight-course meal without worrying which utensil to use, and dazzle dancing partners with her footwork.

Alicia also taught her the subtle language of the fan – how to convey interest or displeasure or boredom by the way she spread it open or snapped it shut.

Lastly, Alicia insisted Reina have her own calling cards printed, and that she separate the parts of her last name on them. 'De Vargas,' she had explained, 'is very different from DeVargas. It implies money, nobility, and social standing.'

Now, with the journey underway, Reina hoped she would remember everything she had learned. The scenery unfurled outside the train window like a flag opening in the breeze. The sensation of speed took her breath away. Her pulse pounded even faster than the train's wheels.

Assaulted by a barrage of new experiences and strange sensations, she comforted herself by concentrating on the familiar. Nature had strewn the spring landscape with a rainbow of wild flowers. She could name every one, from the indigo of Bluebonnets and the scarlet of Indian Paintbrush to the deep mauve of Wine Cups.

She would have loved to open the window to breathe in their subtle perfume, but suspected that doing so would label her a rube who had never traveled by train before. Instead, she pretended a nonchalance she was far from feeling.

The parlor car, with its maroon velvet upholstery, gold tasseled drapes, and crystal light fixtures looked as luxurious as a drawing room in a palace. Only this drawing room hurtled along at fifty miles an hour. The well-dressed occupants filled the car with a boisterous cacophony that almost drowned out the drumming of the wheels.

It seemed all of them knew Patrick, and stopped by to chat. When introductions were followed by approving smiles as they gazed at Reina, her confidence grew. Her masquerade would never be detected, she reassured herself.

An over-dressed woman was the last person to make her way to the Prides' seats. Although her greeting sounded as cordial as all the others', Reina saw something disturbingly cold in her eyes.

'Isobel Singleton, I'd like you to meet Countess Hawthorne and her daughter, Lady Alicia,' Patrick said, 'and our dear friend, Reina DeVargas.'

'It's a pleasure to meet you,' the woman replied without a hint of warmth. She had a surprisingly thin voice, in view of her girth. Her gaze fixed on Charlotte a moment before she looked at Reina. 'DeVargas,' she said, rolling each syllable as if she had a mouth full of marbles. 'Are you related to the New Orleans DeVargases by any chance? They're such lovely people – and their home in the Garden District is too enchanting.'

'My parents never mentioned them,' Reina replied, wondering if she was about to be unmasked.

'It's such a unique name,' the woman continued.

'If you'll give me your card, I'll be happy to pass it on to them.'

Thinking that she wanted the woman gone, Reina produced a thick vellum card from her reticule and handed it over.

'Who is that odious creature?' Charlotte asked Patrick after the encounter ended.

'Isobel Singleton is married to the president of this railroad,' Patrick replied. 'Elke used to say Isobel regarded the parlor cars as her personal kingdom. She's a harmless busybody.'

Reina hoped he was right. But there had been something about Isobel Singleton that frightened her.

She had never cared how she looked in the past. Now, she knew why other women did. Her fashionable traveling outfit had armored her against Isobel Singleton's unfriendly stare.

When Ulysses had returned to Austin in February, he made a determined effort to forget his personal problems and concentrate on the public's interests. Fortunately the crowded legislative calendar gave him lots to think about.

Although he had been born to power and privilege, he had run for public office to champion the working man. Their aspirations and goals had never seemed in more jeopardy.

An ever-widening chasm divided the rich from the poor. Unless laws helped to close that gap, Ulysses feared that America's democracy would exist in name only, and that an old-world social structure based on an aristocracy of money and lineage would control the nation's destiny.

Texas had an enormous asset, an abundance of land, that set it apart from the eastern states. Ulysses wanted to see that land used for the common good rather than the profit of a few.

He spent March and April fighting to pass legislation insuring that the vast acres given to Texas school systems could no longer be sold to powerful outside investors – and that the lands deeded to the railroads for their right of way would be taxed at their fair market value rather than the current pittance. He also backed the Farmer Alliance's battle to place legal controls on the banks, cotton gins, and merchants who reaped the profit from the farmers' work.

Along the way, Ulysses earned some powerful enemies. The last time he gave a speech, a group of ruffians in the visitors' gallery had booed so loudly that the sergeant at arms had been forced to remove them. Ulysses had even received a few threatening letters. Unsigned, of course.

Now, as he parked his brand new surrey in front of the railroad station, he hoped his enemies didn't do anything to ruin his father's visit.

He walked over to the line of waiting cabs, hired one to transport luggage, and instructed the driver to wait until he reappeared with his party. It took a few more minutes to find a trainman with an empty luggage cart. A liberal tip guaranteed he would wait on the platform with Ulysses until the train came in.

Having done everything he could to insure the transfer from the train to the hotel went smoothly, Ulysses lit up a cheroot and stared off into space, taking a few contemplative puffs.

He could hardly wait to see his father again. Their new relationship gave him an almost visceral satisfaction. He looked forward to seeing Charlotte as well, and to squiring Alicia to the busy schedule of social functions he had planned.

However, he dreaded seeing Reina – for her sake as much as his. She was bound to look as out of place in Austin as a cabbage in a rose garden. He could only hope she had the sense not to wear Levi's – or to bring that damned dog. Hill Country people might accept her eccentricities. Austin society wasn't likely to be so tolerant.

He was so deep in thought that he didn't realize the train had pulled into the station until the metallic squeal of brakes drew attention to its arrival. Ulysses ground out his cheroot, told the baggage handler to stay put, and walked toward the parlor cars, scanning the exits for familiar faces.

Patrick disembarked first, looking very much the country gentleman in a grey tweed suit. He helped Charlotte and Alicia onto the platform. Then he offered his hand to a stunning woman who might have stepped straight out of the pages of *Godey's Ladies Book*. There was something very familiar about—

Ulysses never got to finish the thought. As the woman paused on the top step, looking about as though she were searching for someone, the man next to him whistled under his breath and said, 'I sure hope she's going to be in town for a while. I don't know who she is, but I certainly hope to find out.'

Ulysses was about to say that he shared the stranger's sentiments when he realized he did know the woman. It was Reina.

He couldn't tear his gaze from her. For one spellbound moment, their eyes met and the noise and confusion of the crowded station faded away. Everything they had ever said to each other – all the hurt and the passion – seemed to blaze between them. Numb with shock, and afraid he might reveal the impact she was having on him, Ulysses broke the contact.

'It's good to see you, son,' Patrick said, sweeping him into a bone-crushing hug.

'I'm awfully glad you're here,' Ulysses said, pounding his father's back.

After Elke's death, Patrick had seemed to shrink in on himself, as if the particles of his being were eaten up by grief. Now, despite the gray at his temples and the lines around his eyes and mouth, he looked in the full flower of his manhood. Patrick seemed to be living through his own Indian summer.

Charlotte and Alicia claimed Ulysses' attention in turn, greeting him with smiles and hugs. Then Reina acknowledged his presence, holding out her hand like a duchess, as if she expected it to be kissed.

'I've been looking forward to seeing you in your natural habitat,' she said with an almost supercilious lift of her brow.

Her manner was so elegant, her gaze so cool, that it was all he could do not to click his heels like some damn idiot in the foreign service.

Even her voice sounded different. If her behavior was an act, it sure as hell was a good one, he mused, his agile brain grappling with the conundrum she presented.

Was the real Reina the tomboy who could rope and ride better then most men?

Was she the well-read rancher who could discuss Darwin and Mendel?

Was she the seductress who had returned his kisses so passionately?

Was she the sophisticated lady who stood before him now?

Or was she an amalgam of all those women – and others he had yet to meet?

And last, but far from least, did he have the courage to learn the answer?

AN INDECENT LADY

Mercifully, the next few minutes were occupied with rounding up the luggage – a seeming mountain that included a trunk full of Reina's clothes – and transporting it to the waiting cab. Reina chatted with Alicia the entire time. She seemed oblivious to either Ulysses' interest – or his discomfort.

He told the cabby to deliver the trunks to the Driskill Hotel and turn them over to the bell captain. When he walked back to the surrey, Charlotte had already taken her place on the back seat and Patrick was helping Alicia aboard.

It fell to Ulysses to aid Reina. She gathered her skirts, exposing a shapely ankle as Ulysses grasped her elbow. He was surprised to feel her trembling. So she wasn't as cool and confident as she pretended.

Her insecurity touched him in a way her seeming confidence never could. He wished he could reassure her, even tell her he approved of her gallant masquerade.

He climbed up into the front seat beside Patrick and took the reins. The matched bay geldings pricked up their ears, waiting for his command.

'Would you like a quick tour of downtown Austin before we go to the hotel?' he asked, looking over his shoulder. He hoped his practiced social smile concealed the turbulent surge of his emotions.

'I'd love to see a little of the city first, if it wouldn't be too much trouble,' Charlotte answered for them all.

Ulysses set the horses in motion with a snap of the reins, then turned to his father, raising his voice so that his other passengers could hear him above the din of passing carriages and mule-drawn street cars.

'Invitations poured in as soon as people heard you were coming to town. I took the liberty of accepting some of them. Governor and Mrs Ireland are hosting a reception in your honor tomorrow evening. Major Littlefield's giving a tea the next day. The Bremonds and the Houghtons are holding dinners later in the week, and the Butlers are planning a barbecue in the country on the weekend. They've engaged Banton's excursion cars to transport their guests. I purchased tickets for a theatrical presentation at the Millett Opera House, too. And J. L. Driskill is giving a ball at the hotel before you leave.' Tension made Ulysses talk too much. He didn't stop until he felt Patrick's hand on his arm.

'You don't need to entertain us the entire time we're here, son. I know you're a busy man.'

'I just want you to have a good time.' Despite Patrick's reassurance, Ulysses' tension didn't abate. Knowing Reina was in the back seat kept his innards in an uproar.

'Maybe *you* don't want to be entertained, Patrick,' Charlotte said with a breathy chuckle, 'but I assure you the girls and I are looking forward to every single event.'

Ulysses cut a glance at her. 'I hope you don't mind my asking Terrell to join us for dinner at the hotel tonight.'

'Of course we don't mind!' Alicia burst out with surprising vehemence.

Ulysses had invited Terrell in the hope that Reina's rough edges wouldn't be so obvious in Terrell's company – and because an extra woman at the table always presented a seating problem.

He'd also hinted that Reina and Terrell were as good as engaged when he accepted all those invitations, and he had no doubt that all their hosts and hostesses would feel obliged to invite the ranger, too. Terrell would show up everywhere they did.

AN INDECENT LADY

Now, thinking of the stunning woman in the back seat, he could have strangled himself for his own thoughtfulness. He'd be damned if he would be able to enjoy the next two weeks with Terrell paying Reina court.

For the next half hour, Ulysses played tour guide as he drove the surrey up Congress Avenue at a stately pace. He pointed out the better stores, the post office and federal building, the Travis County Courthouse and the temporary State House before stopping at the southern edge of the capitol grounds. A massive dome circled by scaffolding crowned the pink granite structure.

'We're hoping to move in some time next year,' he said. 'I hope you'll return for the celebration.'

'I've never seen a building that big,' Reina exclaimed, her awe making a lie of her previous sophistication.

'It's two hundred yards long and a hundred yards across,' Ulysses explained. 'There are eight acres of floor space. The dome is higher than the one on the Capitol building in Washington.'

'I hate to think what it cost the taxpayers,' Patrick grumbled.

Urging the horses forward again, Ulysses drove past the capitol grounds and turned right on Brazos. The ladies oohed and aahed their approval as he pulled up in front of the rococo splendor of the Driskill Hotel.

'I hadn't expected anything quite this grand,' Charlotte said approvingly as they walked into the high-ceilinged splendor of the main lobby.

'Why don't you look around while I register?' Ulysses suggested. 'If the trip tired you out, there's a ladies' reception parlor where you can rest.' To

Patrick, he added, 'The bartender makes the finest mint juleps this side of Kentucky.'

While Ulysses waited at the registration desk, Patrick and the ladies went their separate ways. Patrick headed for the bar, Charlotte to the ladies' parlor, and the girls went off to explore their new surroundings.

'Did you see the way Ulysses looked at you when we arrived?' Alicia asked as she led the way up a broad stairway to the grand hall on the second floor.

'If you're talking about his sour expression, I could hardly miss it. But it's nothing new. He always looks that way when he sees me,' Reina replied.

Although she tried to match Alicia's nonchalance as they strolled along the pillared space, she was dumbfounded by the elegance of the decor. She had never seen so much gold leaf and marble – to say nothing of the rugs that miraculously fit the floors from end to end and side to side.

'He didn't look sour to me,' Alicia declared. 'He looked love sick.'

Her words reclaimed Reina's attention. 'You couldn't be more wrong. Ulysses doesn't want me here. He's afraid people will think less of him if they see us together.'

'Why would they? You're young and beautiful.'

'I'm also a whore's daughter,' Reina replied, after looking around to make sure no one could hear what she said.

'That's ancient history. I'm sure no one knows or cares about your mother's past.' Alicia walked over to a couple of gilt chairs, sat down in one and motioned Reina to take the other. 'You're wrong about Ulysses. He's madly in love with you.'

'Since when are you an expert on men and love?'

Alicia lifted her brow. 'My dear Reina, I've spent my life watching and listening to people. I can tell as much by the way they gesture and move as I can by what they say.'

'And you really think Ulysses cares for me?' Reina still couldn't bring herself to use the word *love*.

'I don't think it. I know it. Haven't you noticed the yearning way he leans toward you, as though you were a magnet?'

Although the cavernously high ceiling kept the room almost chilly, Reina broke out in a sweat. She had never voiced her feelings for Ulysses out loud – had hardly dared admit them to herself.

'Assuming you're right – and I'm far from agreeing with you – what do you think I should do about it?'

'To start with, you could stop holding him at arm's length. And don't call him *Useless* anymore either.'

'I only do it in self-defense. In case you haven't noticed, he doesn't treat me very well.'

Alicia took Reina's hands in her own. 'This isn't a game where you keep score. This is your life.'

'Don't you think I know that?'

'The next few weeks, you have a golden opportunity to show Ulysses how you really feel about him.'

Reina shook her head so ferociously that her feathered bonnet threatened to fall off. 'I couldn't do that.'

'Why not? I firmly believe there's nothing more irresistible than love.'

Reina tried to make her lips move – and failed. The mere thought of confessing her love to Ulysses made her feel as if a bottomless chasm gaped at her feet. One misstep and she knew she would fall into it.

Sympathy warmed Alicia's cultured voice. 'You're afraid, aren't you?'

'I'm not afraid of Ulysses Pride!'

'You're afraid he'll reject you.'

'I don't care what he does one way or another.'

Alicia's grip tightened. 'Don't lie to me – and more importantly, don't lie to yourself. I know you're as much in love with Ulysses as I am with Terrell. All the money you spent on clothes – the hours you worked on etiquette – you did it all for him, didn't you?'

Denial rose up in Reina's throat. The need to verbalize the truth crowded it out. 'You're right. I am in love with him,' she said hoarsely.

'Then you must find a way to let him know.'

'I can't. I just can't,' Reina whispered.

'Reina, honey, think about it. What's the worst thing that can happen?'

'He'll laugh in my face.'

Alicia shook her head. A knowledge beyond her years or her experience burned in her eyes. 'You're wrong. The worst thing would be to go through the rest of your life wondering what might have been.'

Twenty-one

Ulysses kept a suite of rooms at the Millet Mansion while the legislature was in session, stayed at hotels in Kerrville and Fredericksburg when he was practicing law, and returned to Pride's Passion in the time that remained. But a man who was contemplating taking a wife ought to have a home to take her to.

A wife. Good Lord – had his thinking really progressed that far?

Damn right it had, a resounding inner voice replied – and high time.

He threaded the last jet stud through the placket of his starched dress shirt, then checked his appearance in the mirror over the dresser. His reflection grinned back at him. For a serious man, he'd certainly smiled a lot lately. With good reason. Dreams he hadn't even acknowledged were coming true.

He was in love. Gloriously. Madly. Head over heels. All the words he'd ever heard people apply to the condition suddenly applied to him.

Had Cupid's arrow found its mark at Governor Ireland's reception when Reina dazzled him with her unexpected *savoir faire*? Had it happened while he watched her pouring tea for Major Littlefield's guests? Had it been at the Butlers' barbecue when she enchanted all the children by teaching them how to twirl a rope just like a real cowboy – without ever once acting less than a lady? Or had it been all those moments and a thousand others, stretching back into his childhood?

The last ten days had given him the opportunity to see Reina in a new light. She had moved from one social triumph to another with a sureness and grace that first astonished – then thrilled – and ultimately overcame all his reservations.

His peers had welcomed her in their midst with open arms. If any of them knew about her mother's lurid past, they didn't mention it. In fact, they had treated Reina as if she were every bit as good as Charlotte or Alicia. And, of course, she was.

Reina's new wardrobe was an expression of an inner refinement he hadn't known she possessed. Her manners would have done credit to a member of New York's four hundred. Her warmth and sweetness had charmed all the women – her beauty had intrigued every single man.

He grinned again, anticipating the feel of her in his arms the first time they danced at the ball tonight. He had held her at a time of personal sorrow – and later by the pond, in the white heat of lust. But he had never held her with tenderness or pride. Tonight, he intended to do both.

He wanted all Austin to see him claim her for his own. If he had his way, he'd write his name on every line of her dance card – although doing so would be as difficult as getting the railroad tax bill passed, considering the swath she had cut through the local male population.

Humming a waltz, he straightened his white pique tie, then buttoned his vest. A black tailcoat, black patent leather slippers, and hat and gloves completed his outfit. A last glance in the mirror told him he was ready for what he expected to be a memorable night.

* * *

Charlotte finished dressing for the ball half an hour before she and the girls were due to meet Patrick and Ulysses in the hotel lobby. She walked over to the window and gazed out on the April evening.

Her pulse fluttered as she contemplated standing in a receiving line with Patrick tonight. In the last week, a dozen people had told her what a handsome couple they made.

Did Patrick realize his size and rugged masculinity were the perfect foil for her feminine charms? Did he even know she had feminine charms – or did he think of her only as a friend?

Leaving the window, she stared into space as her thoughts turned to another party years ago. She had stood in a receiving line with Patrick then – as his wife. Her dress had been the same amber shade as the one she had put on tonight. She had worn her topaz necklace and earrings then, too.

She reached up and touched the heavy gems at her throat. Would Patrick remember them? Did he ever think about the months they had been married, and wonder what might have been if Nigel and Elke hadn't been on the scene?

Damn. She was too old, too experienced, too buffeted by a lifetime of unpleasant realities, to indulge in ill-advised speculation or wishful thinking. She had done enough of that during her marriage to Nigel, sowing hopes and dreams and reaping heartache.

She could no more rewrite the past than she seemed to be able to control the present. Patrick would never have married her if she hadn't tricked him into it – just as she was tricking him now. He wouldn't have asked her to stay at Pride's Passion if he hadn't been half-mad with grief.

She couldn't make Patrick love her. She had tried it years ago – and failed miserably. He had always belonged to Elke. Not even death could change that.

Charlotte swallowed the lump in her throat and dabbed away the moisture in her eyes. She ought to be thinking good thoughts – happy thoughts. It had been a wonderful week. She had enjoyed the hours she and Patrick spent shopping for the new wing.

Patrick had admired her carefully detailed plans. They had established a level of intimacy and mutual respect they hadn't achieved during their brief marriage. Their new relationship was a source of deep satisfaction – and increasing anguish.

When she permitted herself to contemplate the lies she had told, she felt sick. Patrick and Ulysses would never forgive her if they learned the truth. Alicia would never trust her again, either.

She shuddered at her precarious situation. It was getting as hard to contemplate the future as it was to remember the past.

Alicia knocked on Reina's bedroom door, then let herself in. Reina sat at her dressing table, her hair spilling around her shoulders in a cascade of ebony curls. Her ivory lace ball gown set off her dusky coloring to perfection. Her decolletage revealed a tantalizing glimpse of cleavage.

She looked beautiful, Alicia mused, then automatically edited herself. Reina wasn't beautiful in the traditional sense. She had an indefinable quality that drew every eye.

Glamour. Yes, that was the right word. Reina had glamour – a dangerous trait for someone who had gone through most of her life trying not to attract attention.

There was no doubt that Reina was going to attract a great deal tonight, Alicia mused as a frisson of apprehension did a dance along her spine.

'Can I help you put your hair up?' she asked.

'I've just about decided to wear it down,' Reina replied. 'What do you think?'

With her hair down, Reina looked incredibly seductive, as though she had just gotten out of bed and would happily return to it with the right man.

Alicia couldn't think of a man who wouldn't want to try out for the part. While women were painfully aware of their physical defects, most men seemed to think they looked just fine, whether they were fat or thin, balding or gray, even-featured or gnarly-faced. She giggled as a vision of Reina being besieged by a panting horde popped into her mind.

Reina was entitled to look as gorgeous as she possibly could, no matter how it affected the male population. Besides, Ulysses wouldn't let her come to any harm. His feelings couldn't have been more obvious if he'd had *I love Reina* tattooed on his forehead.

'Leave it down,' she said.

'I'm a little nervous about tonight.'

'You shouldn't be. You look positively smashing.'

'I've never been to a ball. What if I make a complete fool of myself? I do so want to make a good impression on Ulysses.'

'You already have.'

Reina finally turned from the mirror and looked at Alicia. 'I'm sorry for running on about myself. You look like a princess in a fairy tale.'

'A fairy tale with a happy ending, I hope,' Alicia said, preening a little in the blue watered taffeta that matched the color of her eyes.

'You deserve one. You've been a wonderful friend.

If you hadn't given me all those lessons, this trip would have been a disaster.'

'It has turned out rather well,' Alicia replied smugly. 'I've had almost as much time with Terrell as I could want – and Ulysses has certainly been attentive to you.'

'Have you told Terrell about your writing yet?'

'I don't plan to tell anyone until the book is sold. Mailing the manuscript was just the first step.'

'It's a wonderful story. I know Mr Beadle will buy it.'

Alicia lifted a single brow, pretending disinterest. 'Erastus Beadle is the most successful publisher of dime novels in New York. I'm sure he gets dozens of manuscripts a week.'

'But none as good as yours,' Reina insisted.

While working on the manuscript, Alicia had been able to bury all her doubts and fears. After she mailed it last week at Austin's main post office, they had come crowding back. Now, she clasped her hands together to keep from wringing them.

'I don't know what I'll do if the book doesn't sell. I'll never be free to lead my own life otherwise. But I'm well aware of the odds – and they aren't in my favor. I'm a twenty-two-year-old woman with no training as a writer, and no experience of life. Without Terrell, I wouldn't have had a story. I stole a piece of his life.'

'I honestly don't think he's going to mind,' Reina said.

Alicia managed to smile at Reina – but that damn frisson continued to dance up and down her spine.

Ulysses had never looked more handsome, Reina thought as he led her away from the dance floor for the fifth time that evening. His black evening clothes accented his golden coloring. The cut of his jacket emphasized the breadth of his shoulders while the tails framed his narrow hips. She loved leaving the floor on his arm, knowing other women envied her his company.

'Have I told you how lovely you look tonight?' he murmured, bending low so that his breath caressed her cheek.

'About half a dozen times,' she replied with a saucy grin. 'I wouldn't complain if you told me again.'

Over the years, she had been subjected to so many of his jibes that she couldn't seem to get enough of his compliments. She kept on expecting to wake up to the reality of his disdain.

'You're the most beautiful woman here.'

'It's the clothes. If I had known what an effect they would have, I'd have spent a fortune on my wardrobe long ago.'

'It's not the clothes. It's you.' His eyes darkened. 'As I recall, you look even better without them.'

She stared up at him, not knowing what to say.

'I don't mean to overstep the bounds of propriety,' he murmured throatily, 'but I've never forgotten that day by the pond – and I never will. I'll spend the rest of my life thanking God for giving me the strength to pull you out of the water.'

Did he really mean it? If only she could be sure. Her knees went weak. She would have stumbled if he hadn't tightened his grip on her arm. She had no reason to hide her true feelings from him anymore, and yet caution tempered her answer. 'You've been very kind to me this last week. I've appreciated it more than you can possibly know.'

'It hasn't been kindness, Reina: I'm just beginning to realize how much you mean to me – and I feel like a fool for not realizing it sooner.'

He yearned to pull her into his arms, to kiss her long and hard and deep. Surrounded by merrymakers, all he dared do was take her gloved hand in his own. Words of love trembled on his lips. However, he didn't think Reina would believe them. Not yet. Not until she'd had the chance to test his love – a test he expected to pass with flying colors.

They had all the time in the world, he thought with a surge of happiness. The legislative session would soon draw to a close. He would return to Pride's Passion and ask Velvet and Rio for permission to court Reina properly. It was the least he could do in view of his past behavior.

He didn't want to see disbelief in Reina's eyes when he finally got down on his knees and presented her with an engagement ring.

The chime of the dinner gong interrupted his happy musing. The buffet had been set up in the grand dining salon.

A forty-foot table held a cornucopia of gourmet delights, including roast suckling pig, beef Wellington, quail, and venison. Gilt-edged platters were piled high with aspics, pâtés, raw oysters and gulf shrimp. An array of vegetables and fruits, many of them out of season, added splashes of color.

'I've never seen so much food,' Reina exclaimed, her eyes as wide as a child's on Christmas morning. 'It must have cost a fortune.'

Ulysses chuckled at her practicality. Not a bad trait in a future wife, he thought cheerfully. 'J. L. Driskill has a fortune to spend.'

He helped Reina fill her plate, then guided her across the room to a secluded corner table. On the way, they passed Isobel Singleton sitting with a woman he didn't know.

'Good evening, Mrs Singleton,' he said dutifully.

AN INDECENT LADY

'I fail to see anything good about it,' she replied.

'Mrs Singleton doesn't seem to like you,' Reina commented in a low voice as they sat down at their own table.

'The feeling is mutual,' he replied.

Ulysses beckoned to a waiter carrying a champagne-laden silver tray, helped himself to two glasses, and offered one to Reina.

He was about to toast her when the sound of Isobel Singleton's voice stopped him. 'The nerve of some people!' she said to her middle-aged female companion.

Either Isobel was deaf – or she wanted to be overheard.

'What woman?' her companion said.

'The one with Congressman Pride.'

The toast forgotten, Ulysses lowered his glass. He wished to hell he had chosen another table. It was too late now. He and Reina would just have to ride out whatever storm Isobel Singleton conjured up.

'I haven't met her, but she looks like a lovely girl.'

'That lovely girl shouldn't be permitted in the same room with decent women. She's a disgrace to her sex. Her mother was the most notorious whore in all Texas.'

Ulysses felt himself pale. Isobel was a gossip – but he had never expected her to be so cruel. She deserved a good horse-whipping. Although he didn't believe in hitting women, at that moment he would have liked being the one to administer it.

'Surely, you're mistaken. I can't imagine a gentleman like Ulysses Pride bringing someone like that to J. L. Driskill's ball,' the other woman said.

'How much do you know about the congressman?'

'I know he's a fine legislator from a good family.'

'A good family? The Prides are trash. Always have been. The senator's mother was his father's housekeeper. Patrick Pride didn't marry the woman until the boy was three. Ulysses is a bastard, and the De Vargas woman is a whore. They deserve each other. I'm sure he and that slut are sleeping together.' The last words were said in a ringing voice that bounded off the room's high ceilings, echoing and re-echoing until Ulysses couldn't hear anything else.

Reina sat still as stone, but for the tears spurting in her eyes. She knuckled them away angrily. She wouldn't cry – not here and not now. She refused to give Isobel Singleton the satisfaction.

How could Ulysses just sit there? Why didn't he do something? Anything? Reina had seen him defend the rights of the poor and downtrodden in a speech in the legislature. Why didn't he defend her? Was she less worthy of his concern? He was a magnificent orator who could easily shrivel Isobel Singleton with a few well-chosen words.

Her heart pounded. Her hands fisted. She gazed at him over their untouched plates of food. He sagged in his chair. His shoulders slumped. His eyes had an unfocused glaze, as though he were trying to pretend he was someplace else.

Damn him for a coward. Damn him for keeping silent. Damn him for not loving her enough – or even at all. Damn him for not hearing her heart breaking. She had been right about him all those years ago. He was *useless* after all.

Maybe he could sit there and pretend nothing had happened – but she was made of sterner stuff. Picking up her champagne glass, she gathered her skirts, got to her feet and stalked over to Isobel Singleton's table.

Isobel ignored Reina's presence. She continued eating.

'Look at me,' Reina demanded, picking up Isobel's plate and dropping it on the floor. The resulting crash made them the cynosure of all eyes.

Reina's gaze swept the room, then returned to her adversary. 'It's true. I am a whore's daughter,' she said in a ringing voice, wanting everyone to hear, 'but my mother raised me a lot better than yours did. At least I'm not a bitch like you.'

Reina hadn't realized she was still clutching the champagne glass Ulysses had given her just moments before. Seeing it in her hand, she held it up to the light for a moment as if to judge its clarity. Then, ever so slowly, she emptied the contents over Isobel Singleton's hennaed curls.

Gathering what remained of her dignity, Reina stalked from the ballroom. She didn't hear the smattering of applause or the murmur of admiration that accompanied her departure. The death knell of her own dreams drowned out everything else.

Once she was sure no one could see her, she gathered her skirts and, with a sob, raced to the service stairway. It took all her strength to open the fire door. It shut behind her with a dull thud, sealing her off from the world.

A sob tore up her throat. She choked on it, pushed it back down, and pounded up the three stories to the safety of her room. Only then did she give in to her emotions.

Her throat burned with the force of the sobs that wracked her. She had been such a fool, thinking Ulysses and his stuck-up friends really accepted her. They must have been laughing behind her back all the time, waiting for her to make a mistake. And she hadn't disappointed them.

To think she had actually allowed herself to believe Ulysses cared for her. He could no more become a sensitive, caring human being than leopards could change their spots. She could just picture him with his cronies, enjoying a belly laugh at her expense this very minute.

The painful vision had one benefit. It brought her tears to an abrupt halt. She'd never cry over Useless again, she vowed, catching a glimpse of her red-eyed face in the mirror. He wasn't worth it.

Suddenly, she felt as though she were suffocating. She couldn't go on breathing the same air that Ulysses breathed. She didn't want to stay in Austin another minute, she thought, tearing her beautiful gown in her haste to be free of it.

She left clothes scattered across the floor as she changed into her traveling suit. When she finished she wrote a note asking Alicia to pack up her new wardrobe and give it to charity. God knew, Reina couldn't bear the thought of wearing any of it – not when each dress carried memories of Ulysses.

Never again would she try to make a good impression – not on him or anyone else. If people didn't like her as she was, to hell with them. Her parents had gotten by without friends and she could too, she told herself – forgetting her parents had each other.

She picked up her reticule, checked to insure she had enough money for the trip home, and then cracked the hall door open. Not seeing anyone, she headed back to the service stairs. She planned to go to the train station and wait for the next train to Kerrville, even if she had to wait all night.

As she descended past the second floor ballroom, the sound of music and merriment grated in her ears.

At that moment, she felt certain she didn't have a friend in the world.

She was even angry with Alicia. If Alicia hadn't insisted on her going to Austin, Reina would never have met Isobel Singleton. She wouldn't have permitted herself to think Ulysses was in love with her, either.

She made it halfway through the lobby when the desk clerk called out her name. 'Miss De Vargas, I just got a telegram for you,' he said, hastening to her side. He thrust a piece of paper into her hands, adding, 'I hope it's not bad news,' before he hurried back to his post.

The fact that he wouldn't look at her aroused Reina's suspicion. He must have heard about what happened at the ball.

She hid behind one of the pillars that marched down the lobby in serried ranks and tore the tissue-thin telegram open.

COME HOME AT ONCE. YOUR FATHER IS SICK, the message read.

Ulysses closed his eyes, as if doing so would shut out the memory of Isobel Singleton's words. He felt as though he had been pulled back in time to the Dietz Bakery, stripped of his maturity, his accomplishments – reduced to child-like impotence.

Shame froze him in place as the scrape of Reina's chair told him she had left the table. Then he heard her clear, strong voice rising above the sounds of the party. 'It's true. I am a whore's daughter,' she said, 'but my mother raised me a lot better than yours did. At least I'm not a bitch like you.'

Although he longed to applaud her bravery, he couldn't overcome the sense of hopelessness that filled his gut like an insidious cancer. By the time he finally staggered to his feet — as punch drunk as a boxer who had been beaten in the ring — Reina was gone and Isobel Singleton's enraged wail filled the dining salon like a siren.

'Did you see what your whore did to me?' she screeched.

Ulysses' head finally cleared. 'Have you ever heard of defamation of character?' he asked through clenched teeth.

'My husband is going to hear all about you and your whore. You'll be impeached by the time he's finished with you.'

He wanted to strangle her. However, words were the only weapon he would ever use against one of her sex. 'Tell him what you like. While you're at it, be sure to tell him that defamation of character is punishable by a fine and a stay in prison. Unless you long to wear a convict's stripes, I suggest you keep your thoughts about me, my family, and — most especially — about Reina De Vargas to yourself.' Then, knowing nothing would deflate her overweening sense of importance faster than the derision of her peers, he added, 'Miss De Vargas was absolutely right, though. You are a bitch.'

Isobel's companion let go a nervous titter. 'Oh, dear, you do have a point, Congressman Pride,' she said, getting to her feet. 'I'm afraid I shall have to be more careful of the company I keep in the future.'

At that moment, Ulysses could have kissed the unknown woman. However, he had far more important things to do. He had almost reached the ballroom's exit when Alicia and Terrell appeared at his side.

'We heard what happened,' Alicia said. 'It's all my fault. I should never have insisted on Reina coming to Austin.'

AN INDECENT LADY

'It's not your fault. It's mine. I should have taken better care of her,' Ulysses replied.

'If you two will stop blaming each other, I think we should find Reina. She needs our support right now. Where is she?' Terrell asked.

Ulysses felt his face heat up. He hated telling Terrell he'd let Reina leave without him. How could he ever have imagined he was some kind of a hero? A hero wouldn't have failed the woman he loved. Certainly Terrell wouldn't.

'I don't know where she is.'

'Perhaps she went up to her room,' Alicia said, giving Ulysses a less than friendly look.

The three of them took an elevator to the fourth floor. When it stopped, Ulysses left it at a run. He could hear Alicia and Terrell pounding along behind him. He knocked on Reina's door and called her name. Getting no response, he knocked even louder.

A door across the hall opened and an elderly man peered out. 'If you're looking for the girl who was staying in that room, she left about half an hour ago. She was crying so loud before she left that it woke me up.'

Guilt swelled in Ulysses' chest at the thought of Reina's tears. 'You wouldn't happen to know where she went?' he asked, knowing the futility of the question even as he voiced it.

'I'm not one to mind other people's business. I went back to bed and I'd still be there if the three of you hadn't been knocking loud enough to wake the dead,' the man said, withdrawing back into his room like a turtle retreating into a shell.

Ulysses turned to Alicia. 'Could Reina be with your mother?'

'Mother went up to her room early. She said she

had a sick headache. I don't think Reina would wake her. She's much too considerate. Perhaps she just went for a walk. I know I would have wanted to get away if I were her.'

'The doorman would know,' Terrell said.

By the time the three of them returned to the lobby, the ball had ended. Ulysses cut through the crowd, ignoring the well-wishers who tried to congratulate him on cutting Isobel Singleton down to size. What he'd done had been too little, too late.

His worst fears were confirmed when the doorman told him Reina had gone to the train station. 'She must still be there, though,' the man said. 'There aren't any passenger trains until morning.'

'I'm going to the station,' he told Alicia and Terrell. 'I'd appreciate it if the two of you would stay here in case she shows up. If she does, tell her I need to talk to her – and don't let her go to bed until I get back.'

His surrey was several blocks away at the livery stable. It would take longer to walk there and hitch up the horses than it would to get to the station – if he ran all the way.

Reina refused to cry as the cabby drove her to the station. She had already cried enough over the things Isobel Singleton had said at the ball. Her troubles faded into insignificance when she thought about her father.

She had left him when he needed her the most. She had played at being a lady, had convinced herself that Ulysses cared for her, and all the while Rio had been getting sicker and sicker. Perhaps he could forgive her. She could never forgive herself. She would never again permit herself to be seduced away from her duty.

AN INDECENT LADY 321

She jumped down from the buggy's seat the moment the cabby reined the horse to a stop, handed a dollar up to him and ran into the station without waiting for change.

An elderly-looking man snoozed behind the ticket counter. She reached through the bars, shook him awake, and said, 'When's the next train to Kerrville?'

'Ten tomorrow morning, miss,' he replied, blinking the sleep from his eyes.

She waved the telegram under his nose as if to reinforce what she said. 'I can't wait that long. My father's very sick. I've got to get home.'

He shook his head. 'I'm sorry for your troubles, miss, but the next passenger train doesn't leave until ten.'

She sagged against the counter. Despite her intentions, tears spurted in her eyes. 'Please, can't you help me? I've got to get there.'

He studied her carefully. Sympathy slowly warmed his eyes. 'This may cost me my job, miss. Still, I'm a father. I can't stand seeing a pretty little girl like you in trouble. There is a freight train in the yard. Follow me and I'll talk to the engineer. If he lets you ride with him, you'll be back in Kerrville by seven.'

Ulysses' heart pounded and his lungs felt like an overworked bellows as he ran into the train station. Along the way he'd stripped off his tailcoat, his vest and his tie, not caring where the costly garments fell.

Nothing mattered except his need to see Reina, to explain what had happened to him in the ballroom – and to get down on his knees and beg her forgiveness.

Sweat plastered his shirt to his chest and ran down

his face in rivulets as he raced over to the ticket cage. To his surprise, the man behind it took one look at him, drew a gun from under the counter and pointed it at Ulysses.

'I'm not looking for any trouble,' the man said, 'but I can dish it out if I have to.'

The man must think he was a lunatic. God knew, he probably looked like one, Ulysses realized, glancing down at his half bare chest.

'I don't intend to give you any trouble,' he gasped, fighting for breath. 'I'm looking for a lady.'

'What lady would have anything to do with the likes of you?'

A damn good question. 'We had an argument.'

'I'll just bet you did.'

'I need to tell her I'm sorry. I think she might have taken the train back home. She shouldn't be traveling by herself.'

'She didn't tell me about no fight. She said her father was sick,' the ticket master blurted out, then covered his mouth with a hand as he realized what he'd revealed.

'I really do care for her,' he said, with a catch in his voice. 'Did she catch a train?'

Something in the man's gaze shifted. He looked less hostile. 'Seein' as how you're so concerned, I guess I can tell you the truth. Besides, it's too late for you to do anything about it. Your lady friend seemed so desperate to see her father, I just had to help. I got her a ride on a freight train.' He looked down at his watch. 'She'll be home in a couple of hours.'

Although the man continued talking, Ulysses no longer heard him. The details didn't matter. He was too late.

Reina had gone, taking his broken heart and his shattered manhood with her.

Twenty-two

Patrick dreamed of making love, and woke up with a hard-on. A fifty-eight-year-old widower had no business doing either one, he brooded as he stared at the tented covers.

He thought he had buried that part of his life along with his beloved Elke. Much to his embarrassment, that part of him had come roaring back to life.

He had seen the hurt in Charlotte's eyes when he excused himself and went to bed early last night. But he'd had no choice. A man his age could hardly waltz with a lady when he had a full-blown erection in his drawers.

He felt disloyal to Elke's memory, to the life they had shared. He tried to wish his erection away, and found he had no more control of it now than he'd had in his youth. Perhaps he'd just been away from the ranch too long.

The land had rooted him, sheltered him, occupied him. He felt lost without it. He closed his eyes and pictured himself riding over Pride's Passion, and instantly envisioned a disaster happening in his absence – a plague of blow flies, a bout of hoof-and-mouth or some other disease. At least it rid him of his erection.

Common sense told him not to borrow trouble. The future had never looked rosier. The winter die-off had raised the price of cattle. He would make a huge profit when he sent his to market. The new wing had the makings of a showplace. And Ulysses – who had the dazed look of a man in love – would undoubtedly ask for Alicia's hand soon.

He had no cause for complaint, Patrick thought. He sat up, swung his long legs over the side of the bed, and saw a telegram on the floor. His heart bucked and his stomach contracted. He didn't need to borrow trouble. Someone had slipped it under the door.

He picked the telegram up and scanned the message. Dear God, Rio was dying. While he had imagined other disasters, fate had delivered a sucker punch.

While he dressed, Patrick made a mental list of things to be done. He would wake Reina later, he decided. This might be the last good night of sleep she'd have for a long time. First, he needed to talk to Ulysses. He took the elevator to the lobby and asked the doorman for directions to the Millett Mansion.

To Patrick's surprise, Ulysses was slouched on a porch rocker, smoking a cheroot, his long legs stretched out before him. He still wore his dress shirt, black trousers, and dancing slippers. They looked worse for wear – and so did he. Ulysses reminded Patrick of a horse who has been ridden hard and put up wet.

'You must have had one hell of a time last night,' Patrick said with an indulgent smile.

Ulysses didn't smile back. 'I guess you could say that. It was a hell of a time. Did something bring you here at this hour? Or are you just out for a walk?'

'I've got bad news. Rio is sick. I've got to get back home, and I'm going to need your help.'

Ulysses bolted to his feet so quickly that the rocker

AN INDECENT LADY 325

fell over. 'Sick? I thought Reina just used that as an excuse to leave town.'

The last time Patrick had seen Reina, she had been very much the belle of the ball. 'Are you saying Reina's gone? I thought we'd travel together.'

'Reina left last night – on a freight train.'

'She should have asked me to go with her. Hell, son. You should have gone with her.'

'Believe me, Dad, I wish I could have.'

'It's not too late. You can go with me this morning. I plan to take the first train to Kerrville.'

The misery in Ulysses' eyes deepened. 'I'm afraid I can't.'

'Can't? Rio is more than our foreman. He's family. What could be more important?'

'The railroad bill is in committee. It's coming up for a vote. If I'm not here, it may not pass. Besides, I doubt the DeVargases would want me at Rio's bedside.'

Patrick studied his son's haggard face and saw so much regret written on it that he didn't press him. 'Do what you have to do.'

'Tell Rio I wish him a speedy recovery. And tell Reina—' Ulysses' voice cracked. He chewed on his lower lip the way he used to do when he was very young and very upset. 'Oh hell, just tell her I'm sorry – about everything.'

Now what did he mean by everything? Patrick had the distinct feeling that Ulysses was holding something back – something important. But he couldn't take the time to ferret it out.

'I'm going to leave Charlotte and Alicia here. They'd never get packed in time, and Charlotte still has some shopping to do for the new wing. I'd appreciate it if you were with me at breakfast when I explain things to them.'

Ulysses nodded. 'I need to change. I'll be at the hotel in half an hour.'

He headed for the front door, then turned back. 'Dad, I want you to promise me something.'

'If I can, son.'

'Take care of Reina. Watch over her. If anything happens to Rio, she's going to need you.'

'That will be easy, son. I love that girl.'

'So do I,' Ulysses said under his breath before disappearing inside the Millet Mansion.

For the next couple of hours, Patrick was too busy to think about Ulysses' last words. However, as the train pulled out of the station, they resurfaced in Patrick's mind.

What sort of love had his son been talking about? The love a man felt for a girl he'd known all his life – or the love he felt for a woman he wanted as his wife? And where did Alicia fit into the picture?

Reina arrived in Kerrville at dawn and hitched a ride home with an obliging drover. He left her at the end of the driveway. The house looked so normal, with smoke rising from the chimneys and spring flowers nodding in the breeze, that she allowed herself to believe nothing could be seriously wrong.

As she entered the kitchen a few minutes later, the scent of perking coffee reinforced her sense of normalcy. Rio always made coffee first thing in the morning. She half expected him to appear and offer to pour her a cup.

'Daddy,' she called softly.

'Reina, is that you?' her mother answered from the hallway.

Velvet's disheveled appearance quickly dispelled Reina's hopes. Velvet's shoulders were slumped, her hair and dress in disarray. Dark shadows underscored her eyes.

'I wasn't expecting you yet,' Velvet said, sweeping Reina into her arms. 'How did you get here?'

'It's a long story.'

Velvet stepped back and looked Reina up and down. 'I'm so glad you're home, honey.'

'I came as soon as I got your telegram.'

Velvet peered over Reina's shoulder. 'Where's Patrick? Didn't he come with you? I sent him a telegram, too.'

Reina barely reined in her anxiety. 'I don't know anything about Patrick. What's wrong with Dad?'

'He's got pneumonia, honey.'

Relief swept through Reina. She'd been afraid Rio's heart had given out. 'Dad's strong as an ox. He'll get over it.'

Velvet's eyes sheened. 'I wish I could tell you different – but I don't want you holding out any false hopes. Your daddy is dying.'

Reina's knees buckled. She grabbed the back of a chair for support. Her mother wasn't one to exaggerate. 'I don't understand. He was fine when I left ten days ago. He can't be dying.'

'Doc Vosbein said the flu weakened your father's lungs. When the pneumonia came – well, he didn't have anything to fight it with.'

'Was Daddy sick when I left?'

'We both thought he had a cold – nothing more.'

Guilt coiled in Reina's stomach like a serpent as she thought about her frivolous pursuit of pleasure in Austin. 'You should have told me. I would have stayed.'

'Honey, your daddy and I talked it over. By then, you'd spent so much money on those fancy clothes.

You've worked so hard all your life – we just wanted you to have some fun. And you did, didn't you? That postcard you sent – the one with the picture of the Driskill Hotel – sounded so happy.'

Reina realized she could never tell her parents what really happened. They were entitled to keep a few illusions about Ulysses – even if she had been stripped of all of hers.

'I had a wonderful time. Still, I would rather have been here when you needed me.'

'You're here now – and that's what counts.'

'Can I see Daddy?'

'Of course,' Velvet answered, leading the way to the master bedroom.

Reina paused on the threshold, almost choking on the sour effluvium of stale air and sickness. Her father's rasping breath was the only sound in the room. He seemed to be sleeping.

She tiptoed across the floor and gazed down at Rio. His inhalations were so shallow that she could barely discern the rise and fall of his chest. His weathered bronze skin had a greenish patina. The lines of his face seemed so much deeper than she remembered. When had he gotten so timeworn?

Just then, Rio opened his eyes. They had the rheumy look that Reina had seen in very old animals. He coughed, and the force of it shook the bed.

'I'm glad you're here, honey,' he said when the spell passed. 'Your mother is going to need you after I'm gone.'

Reina wanted to throw herself across her father's body and shelter in his arms. His obvious frailty nailed her in place, though. 'We both need you, Daddy. You're not going anywhere without us.'

'Yes I am, sweetheart.' He gave her a wry smile. 'This is one trip everyone makes by themselves.'

'Don't talk, Daddy. You need your strength.'

'This may be our last chance.'

'Don't say that. Don't even think it. You've got to fight, for our sake.' Reina looked at her mother for support. Surely Velvet couldn't accept Rio's death as inevitable.

'Let your Daddy say his piece,' Velvet said.

Rio patted the bed, indicating that Reina should sit beside him. 'I need to tell you what's in my will.'

'No – no, you don't.'

He didn't seem to hear her. 'I left the ranch to you, Reina – and the house to your mother. There's some money too – enough to get you past a hard patch.' He panted after every couple of words, as if he were running in place. 'I know you've dreamed of running the place since you were knee-high to a grasshopper.'

She had – but not this way. She moaned, remembering how she had boasted of her ambition to Alicia that day in the line shack. 'I'll never be the rancher you are.'

'You'll be better.' Pride shone so bright in Rio's eyes that for a moment, he looked almost well. 'Don't be too stiff-necked to ask Patrick for help if you need it. He loves you almost as much as I do.'

Reina felt tears sliding down her cheeks. They seemed to come from her breaking heart rather than her eyes. This couldn't be happening.

'Don't cry, honey. You're my fearless girl.'

But she wasn't fearless. Terror pierced her innards like a cruelly twisted knife. The lump in her throat was so huge that it threatened to cut off her breath. She couldn't imagine the future without her father – she didn't want to try.

Any courage she possessed came from knowing he was always there to back her up. She stared down, trying to equate what she saw with the vital man who had dominated her life.

'He's asleep,' Velvet whispered, taking Reina's hand and leading her back to the kitchen.

She poured two cups of coffee, set one down on the table in front of Reina and took a sip from her own. 'Would you like something to eat?' she asked.

'How can you even think about food at a time like this?' Reina said. 'We ought to be in there with Daddy, doing everything we can to . . .' Her voice trailed off. She had no idea what they could do. But someone ought to do something. They couldn't just sip on coffee while her father lay dying.

'You've got to be brave enough to let your father go,' Velvet said as if she had read Reina's mind. 'He'll try to hang on for your sake – and he's suffered enough.'

'Dad's never been a quitter.'

'And he isn't now. He's a seventy-year-old man and he doesn't have any fight left. He knows you don't want him to die. He doesn't have any choice – and I'd like him to go as peacefully as possible. The next time he wakes up, I want you to say goodbye instead of urging him to hang on for your sake.'

The words sank into Reina's mind like boulders falling to earth. She felt the impact of each one.

Her head drooped and her back bowed under the burden. 'I don't mean to be selfish. It's just that I'm going to miss Daddy so much.'

'I know, sugar – Lord, do I know.' Velvet came around the table and kissed Reina's cheek. 'You're stronger than you think. You'll do the right thing.'

She pulled Reina to her feet and gave a little shove in the direction of the master bedroom. 'Go sit with your father a spell while I fix us a proper breakfast

– and take your coffee with you. It's going to be a long day.'

The next time Rio woke, Reina did as her mother asked. She told him she loved him and that she would always miss him, but that she and Velvet would do just fine. To her credit, she did it with a smile.

Patrick arrived at noon and joined Reina's and Velvet's vigil. Rio woke one last time in the middle of the afternoon, but he was too weak to speak. He smiled at the three of them, then drifted back to sleep. Doctor Vosbein came and went, offering consolation rather than hope.

As the cruel day dragged itself into night, Rio's breathing grew more stertorous. Ignoring the knowing glances Patrick and Velvet exchanged, Reina clung to her father's hand, willing her strength into him. But all the will in the world couldn't keep Rio from taking his last journey. He died on the cusp of the new day.

They buried him at sunset. In accordance with his last wishes, Patrick spoke a few words, his rumbling baritone husky with unshed tears.

No one sang Rio to his final rest as the hands lowered his coffin into the ground – at least no human voice. Useful had watched the proceedings from a distance. Suddenly, he lifted his great shaggy muzzle and bayed. As if they had been waiting for a signal, a chorus of coyotes took up the mournful howl.

It was, Reina decided, as fitting a requiem as any mass sung by a church choir. She wished she could lift her head and howl, too.

In the next few weeks, she spent the first cruel coin of her grief on hard work. The calves needed to be weaned, castrated and branded before being moved onto fresh pasture away from their mothers. They bawled their outrage and heartbreak and it was all Reina could do not to bawl out loud with them.

She was eternally grateful that the hands pretended not to notice when her eyes swam with tears. She drove them hard – and drove herself harder. Back-breaking labor numbed her mind and body – and Reina counted herself lucky to have it.

She worried about Velvet until Charlotte came home. Charlotte kept Velvet company as much as she could – and several women from Kerrville paid condolence calls, bringing gifts of food which Reina refused to eat. As far as she was concerned, their interest came far too late.

Alicia kept on sending messages, asking to see Reina, but she never replied except to say she was busy. She didn't want anything or anyone to remind her of the foolish hopes she had entertained in Austin.

She had made up her mind to forget all about Ulysses – and for a while, she almost succeeded.

His letter came two weeks after the funeral. It was waiting for her when she came home from a day spent clearing cedar. Of all the jobs on a Hill Country ranch, it was the most brutal. Every time Reina succeeded in hacking a cedar to bits and pulling it out of the ground, she felt a sense of release.

Rio had waged war on the tree-sized shrub because it could invade a pasture and destroy all the grass. Reina waged war on the cedar because she couldn't wage war on humanity. Her muscles ached from the battle as she walked into the kitchen at the end of the day.

'You look like you could use a brandy,' Velvet said, hurrying off to fetch some.

AN INDECENT LADY

'I could use a new body, too,' Reina called after her. *And a new heart*, she silently added. Hers ached so much that she swore she could feel the broken pieces grinding together.

Velvet returned quickly and handed Reina a brimming shot glass. Reina drank the contents greedily. The brandy felt like new life going down.

'Feeling better?' Velvet asked when she finished.

'Much. Thanks, Mom.'

'There's a letter for you,' Velvet said, pulling an envelope from her apron pocket.

Reina recognized Ulysses' writing. Her breath shortened and a nerve jumped to life under one eye.

'Aren't you going to read it?' Velvet asked as Reina stuffed the envelope into the pocket of her Levi's.

'I don't want anything to spoil my appetite,' Reina replied.

Velvet filled two plates while Reina washed up at the sink. 'I thought you and Ulysses called a truce in Austin.'

'What gave you that idea?'

'Charlotte told me Ulysses did a complete about-face where you're concerned. In fact, if she hadn't known he was courting Alicia, she would have thought he was courting you in Austin.'

Reina let go a brittle laugh. 'Courting me? That's a joke. He was rude and horrible – the way he always is. Frankly, I'll go through the rest of my life content if I never see him again.'

'That's not very likely, considering we're neighbors. Did something happen I should know about?'

Reina had no intention of telling Velvet the truth. It would shame them both too much. 'Mom, it's been a long day and I'm exhausted. Can't we talk about something more pleasant?'

Velvet shrugged, then began discussing her vegetable garden. Reina couldn't concentrate on the merits of head versus leaf lettuce, though. She felt the letter's presence all through supper, like a brand burning through her Levi's.

At nine, yawning prodigiously, Velvet excused herself and went to bed. Reina waited until she heard her mother's door close, then pulled the now-wrinkled envelope from her pocket. *Oh, well*, she rationalized, she might as well see what Useless had to say.

Dearest Reina, he began.

Seeing the salutation, Reina's hand shook so hard that she almost dropped the letter. How dare Useless call her *dearest*? How dare he write her after what had happened? She hated him – didn't she?

Who cared if he had finally found the gumption to compose some mealy-mouthed, half-assed apology for his shameful behavior – as if he gave a damn for her feelings or what she had been through.

Although she loved books, and reading was her only entertainment, she would sooner never read anything again as read what he had written. And yet, her hands picked the letter up as if of their own volition, and spread it open.

Dearest Reina, I am so sorry about your father. He was a truly wonderful man. I know how lost, how empty you must be feeling. I wish I could be there to comfort you as you comforted me after my mother's death. I have never forgotten your generosity of spirit the morning I came to your parents' home with the news.

Who the hell did he think he was kidding? She had let him kiss her that morning – and would have let him do even more if he hadn't stopped. If he wanted to call mutual lust generosity of spirit, that was his business.

AN INDECENT LADY 335

For the life of her, she didn't know why he was the only man ever to spark her into flame. Velvet had told her that such a flame could sustain a woman instead of devouring her. But it had come near to killing Reina.

Even now, after everything that had happened, the memory of Ulysses' body – his scent, his masculine power – made her stomach clench and her nipples harden. She hated her traitorous body for acting that way, almost as much as she hated him. She would sooner spend the rest of her days in spinsterhood than succumb to her feelings for Ulysses, she thought, before reading on.

My father wrote that Rio is buried very near my mother. It pleases me to think they are as close now as they were in life. Their presence ennobles the ground where they rest.

He certainly had a way with words, the silver-tongued snake.

Although I hate to remind you of the unpleasant incident at the ball, I am enclosing a newspaper clipping in the hope that it will give you some satisfaction.

The only thing that would give her any satisfaction would be decimating the source of his potent masculinity with a well-aimed kick.

You were an innocent bystander in a very nasty business. Isobel Singleton's husband is my enemy. She attacked you to get at me. I authored a bill that will force the railroads to pay their fair share of taxes. Singleton and other railroad barons did their level best to keep the bill from passing. I even received death threats before the ball.

I went to the Singletons' home for a talk the day you left Austin. The enclosed article is a result of my visit. I know it can never make up for the embarrassment you suffered at the ball. It was, however, the only thing I could think to do.

He had enclosed the first page of the *Austin Republican* – dated a few days earlier – and circled a small article on the bottom left-hand corner. It took but a moment to read.

Mrs Howard Singleton takes this opportunity to express her abject apology for the things she said about Miss Reina De Vargas at the ball hosted by J. L. Driskill at his hotel on April 12, 1886. Mrs Singleton admits that her remarks were both unkind and unjust. As a token of her deep regret, Mrs Singleton is pleased to donate one thousand dollars to the Austin Sanatorium for diseases of the lung, in memory of Mr Rio De Vargas.

Reina crumpled the paper in her fist. If Ulysses thought apologies – his or Isobel Singleton's – meant a damn thing, he was very much mistaken. And if he or that bitch thought her family's good name and peace of mind were for sale for a measly one thousand dollars, they could both think again.

A letter and a scrap of newsprint couldn't change what had happened. She had trusted Ulysses. She had even permitted herself to think they had a future.

Fool me once, shame on you, she thought. *Fool me twice, shame on me.*

At least the patients at the sanatorium had benefited from her misery. She opened her fist and methodically shredded the letter and the newspaper into pieces no bigger than the end of her thumb. Then, she made her way to her room, undressed and went to bed.

Her weary body demanded sleep, but her eyes refused to close. Had Ulysses really received death threats? Was he in any danger? Or was it a ploy for sympathy?

What the hell did she care? she reminded herself. She didn't need a man – and certainly not a golden-haired excuse for one like Useless.

Hope had shriveled inside her the night of the ball.

She had buried her youth with her father. She had one goal left, one dream that gave her life meaning – to build the DeVargas ranch into a showplace, a fitting tribute to her father's memory.

And heaven help anyone who got in her way.

Twenty-three

As the train traveled the last few miles to Kerrville, anxiety vibrated through Ulysses like tension on a high wire. Had Reina gotten his letter? Had it made a difference? Would she ever forgive him for not defending her honor at the ball? The questions circled his mind with every revolution of the train's wheels – his mood swinging from elation to darkest despair depending on the answers.

The day he learned of Rio's death, he had hurried to the train station to buy a round-trip ticket home. By the time he'd paid for it, though, he knew he would never use it. He had walked up Congress Avenue to the legislature's temporary quarters, feeling like a man on the way to his own hanging.

He longed to be with Reina when her father was buried – to offer his love and support, to do anything and everything to ease her loss. But he weighed the good he could do for her against the good he could do for Texas if the railroad tax bill passed – and the greater good won.

Damn his conscience. Damn Texas for demanding so much of him.

Deep in thought, he didn't realize the train had pulled into the station until the conductor tapped him on the shoulder. 'This is your stop, Congressman.'

Ulysses nodded his thanks and got to his feet. Luke

AN INDECENT LADY 339

Teague was waiting on the platform. 'It's good to see you, sir.'

Ulysses managed a bleak smile. 'I thought I told you to call me by my first name.'

The young cowboy had filled out since the blizzard, and his acne had faded. He had a new air of confidence, too. Between the two of them, they made quick work of transferring Ulysses' luggage to one of the ranch's wagons.

'Ulysses, sir, would you like me to drive?' Luke asked when they were done.

'Suits me,' Ulysses replied. Considering his state of mind, he might run the wagon off the road.

'How are things at home?' he asked, as Luke urged the horses to a trot.

'Fine, as far as I know.' Luke gave Ulysses a sly grin. 'Your father doesn't exactly confide in me. But I do have some news of my own. Me and my Nellie Sue are going to get married next month. I sure would appreciate it iffen you would stand up for me.'

'I'm honored,' Ulysses said, although he didn't know if he could get through the ceremony without his envy showing. The only marriage he wanted to attend was his and Reina's. 'But I don't understand why you'd want me. You must have closer friends.'

'I told my Nellie Sue I would have died if you hadn't sent me back to the bunkhouse the night we went after your father. I was so set on proving myself, I didn't have any sense. Another couple of hours in the cold would have done me in for sure. I reckon I owe you my life. Besides – ' the sly grin returned. ' – my other friends don't own suits.'

Ulysses laughed for the first time in weeks. 'In that case, I'll be there. Just let me know where and when.'

'I knew I could count on you, Ulysses, sir. You're a good man, just like your father.'

The balm of Luke's approval erased some of the calumny the railroad barons had heaped on Ulysses. During the fight to pass the railroad tax bill, his bastard birth had been brought up so many times that he had almost gotten used to having it thrown in his face.

However, nothing anyone said could be worse than the opprobrium he heaped on himself. He had let Reina down so many times – in so many ways. He had imagined himself a gentleman, and behaved like a scoundrel. How could he ever convince her he had changed?

As the wagon approached the cut-off to the DeVargas ranch, he realized he couldn't wait another minute to see her.

'Before I go home, I'd like to call on the DeVargases,' he told Luke.

'It sure is sad about Rio,' Luke replied with an eloquent shrug. 'Ain't no one ever goin' to take his place.'

'Has my father hired a new foreman?'

'Not that I know.' Luke turned the wagon down the DeVargases' drive. Their ranch looked as prosperous as ever, Ulysses noted. The spring grass was knee high and emerald green. They would be cutting hay soon.

'Who is running the DeVargas spread?' Ulysses asked.

'Miss Reina. I hear she's a crackerjack boss.'

'How do the hands feel about working for a woman?'

'I ain't heard no complaints. Half of them are in love with her, and the rest treat her like a daughter. Either way, she can't lose.'

AN INDECENT LADY   341

'Is she seeing anyone?'

'I don't take your meaning, Ulysses, sir.

'Is anyone courting her?'

Luke chortled. 'She won't let any man get that close.'

Thank God, Ulysses thought.

Luke reined the wagon to a stop and Ulysses jumped down from the front seat. 'I won't be long,' he said, wondering if he would even be allowed in the front door.

'Don't hurry on my account.' Luke gave Ulysses a wink, sat back, then tilted his broad-brimmed hat over his eyes. 'It ain't often I get a chance to sit and dream about bein' a married man.'

Velvet answered Ulysses' knock. Her somber black dress made her look older than he remembered. 'I wasn't expecting you,' she said frostily. Useful stood beside her. His growl reinforced the coldness of her greeting.

'May I come in?' Ulysses asked, counting on Velvet's inbred hospitality.

For a moment, he read refusal in her gaze. She looked him up and down, as if measuring him against some standard. Then, with a shake of her head, she said, 'I suppose it can't do any harm. I just made a pot of fresh coffee and I sure don't like drinking it by myself.'

She stood aside to let him in, then led the way to the kitchen. Useful followed so closely that Ulysses could feel the dog's hot breath on his legs.

'Is Reina here?'

'She's riding fences today. And it's a good thing for you that she is. She would never have let you in.'

Instead of getting out the china she kept for company, Velvet poured coffee into two chipped enamel mugs. If she intended to send him a message, he certainly got it. He was in her home on sufferance. One misstep and he'd be out on his ear.

'Sugar or cream?'

'I take it black,' he replied, striving to sound calm although his worst fears had been confirmed.

Velvet handed him one of the mugs, then pulled out a chair and settled in it.

Ulysses took a chair opposite hers. Useful lay down at his feet and glared up at him.

'You don't have much of a way with animals,' Velvet remarked with a sour grin. 'Some folks say they're a better judge of character than we humans.'

'They might be right.' God knew, Ulysses didn't think very much of himself these days.

Velvet's expression softened. 'I want to thank you for the flowers you sent to the funeral. Rio always did have a special liking for lilacs.'

'I can't tell you how saddened I felt when I heard about his passing. He was a fine man.'

Velvet looked him straight in the eye for the first time. 'Did you just figure that out?'

Ulysses met her stern gaze without flinching. 'I just figured a lot of things out, Velvet. I've been so many kinds of a fool that I don't know where to start apologizing.'

Her eyes narrowed. 'Start any place.'

He didn't blame her for wanting her pound of flesh. She had no reason to go easy on him. 'I've been a stiff-necked, self-righteous, judgemental prig where you and your family are concerned. I let my own doubts and fears control my actions. I just wish I'd come to my senses sooner so I could have apologized to Rio.'

Ulysses was horrified to find himself looking at Velvet through a sheen of tears.

AN INDECENT LADY 343

She pulled a handkerchief from a pocket and handed it over. 'I thought nothing you could say or do would surprise me. But you have surprised me this day. I don't know what to say.'

'You don't need to say anything. I think that's my department. You and your husband were – are – two of the finest people I've ever known. And you raised a wonderful daughter.' His voice cracked the way it used to in his teens. The turbulent emotions that plagued him then tormented him now.

'What's all this about, Ulysses? Why are you really here?'

Suddenly, he knew he had to tell her the truth – all of it. If he ever hoped to win the daughter, he had better have her mother on his side.

He related what had happened in Austin, from his realization that he loved Reina to the scene at the ball, to the letter. 'I'm here to ask permission to court Reina,' he concluded lamely.

Velvet started like a deer at gunshot. 'You what?'

'I want your permission to court Reina.'

'After all that's happened? Besides, I thought you were courting Alicia.'

'I'm very fond of her. However, I never said or did anything to make her think we were more than friends.'

Velvet sat up straighter. 'Be that as it may, Terrell is courting my daughter.'

Denial rose up Ulysses' throat. He could picture his lips shaping the words, telling Velvet that Alicia and Terrell were head over heels in love. It wasn't his place, though.

'I can't speak for Terrell. I can only speak for myself. I'm in love with your daughter, so in love that I know I'll never feel this way about anyone else. I'm deeply ashamed of the way I treated her in the past. I think you know the reasons – but they don't excuse my behavior. I'd like to spend the rest of my life making it up to Reina – and to you, too.'

'Is this your idea of a joke,' Velvet burst out, 'or have you been drinking?'

'The answer to both those questions is no.'

'Then what's this all about?'

'It's about love, Velvet – the kind of love you and Rio shared. It's about needing someone so much that you don't care what anyone else thinks or says. It's about wanting to spend the rest of your life with one woman, having children with her, growing old together, sharing the good times and the bad, being there for each other. It's about putting all your dreams – everything you are and hope to be – in someone else's hands. It's about trust and friendship – and passion, too – but I imagine you'd rather not hear that part.'

Velvet knew her mouth was hanging open. She couldn't summon the presence of mind to shut it, though. She had never heard a finer speech from any man. Only this was so much more than a speech, she realized, looking into Ulysses' eyes. His feelings shone in them like a light to guide a loved one home. The boy had finally become a man, she thought with a sigh – and what a man. If she were younger . . .

She let the thought drift away and turned her mind to other possibilities – to the merger of two families, and to the grandchildren she would someday dandle on her knees. She could hardly wait.

'You're Elke's son after all,' she said past the lump in her throat.

Ulysses produced a weak grin. 'I used to think of you as a second mother. I'd like to think of you that way again.'

'Don't you mean mother-in-law?'

AN INDECENT LADY

A spark of hope flamed in his eyes. 'That, too.'

'Is there anything I could do or say to keep you from courting my daughter?'

'Not a damn thing – short of shooting me and putting me out of my misery. I'd walk through fire to be with Reina.'

That was certainly the right answer, she mused with considerable satisfaction. 'You may have to. Reina isn't in a very forgiving mood.'

'And you, Velvet – are you in a forgiving mood? I'm going to need your help.'

'Maybe I'm just a sentimental, romantic old woman. You've won me over. My daughter won't be as easy. She's got a stubborn streak a mile wide.'

'I wonder where she got it?' Ulysses asked with a soft chuckle.

Lord, he was a pretty man when his heart was in his eyes. 'If you want my permission to court Reina, you have it.'

'It wouldn't hurt if you put in a good word for me. I imagine you've done as much for Terrell.'

'You sure know how to drive a bargain, son.' Velvet finished her coffee and put her cup in the sink. She had been feeling half dead since she buried Rio. And Reina had been in even worse spirits. The two of them had been going through the motions, putting one foot in front of the other without thinking where the path would lead.

Now, Velvet saw their destination. All Ulysses had to do was convince Reina they were all heading for the same place.

Ulysses left the DeVargas home in a considerably better frame of mind than he had been in when he arrived. Velvet's brandy warmed his stomach. Her friendship warmed his soul. Like her daughter, she was a remarkable woman.

Patrick, Charlotte and Alicia were waiting on the porch when Luke reined the team to a stop. The three of them looked so right together that Ulysses felt a momentary twinge of regret, thinking they would never be a real family.

He hoped for time alone with Patrick to confide what he had already told Velvet. However, Charlotte's plans precluded a father–son talk. She had champagne on ice in the living room.

After toasting the passage of the railroad bill, Charlotte and Alicia settled in the parlor for a long visit. Alicia wanted to know if Ulysses had seen Terrell lately, then asked polite questions about the friends she had made in Austin.

Charlotte gave him a detailed account of her purchases for the new wing, dwelling at great length on the master bedroom as though she expected him to move in as soon as it was finished.

Patrick detailed the plans for shipping Nabob. A Glenhaven stockman would travel with the bull by sea from London to New York, and would look after him during the quarantine period. Nabob and the stockman, one Ian McTavish, would arrive in Indianola on the Gulf Coast in mid-August.

The conversation continued while the golden day slowly drowned in evening's dark embrace. Charlotte and Alicia excused themselves after the meal and retired for the night.

'I think I'll go on up, too,' Patrick said, getting to his feet and stretching. 'I've been doing double-duty without a foreman.'

'I stopped by to talk to Velvet on my way home,' Ulysses said.

'She's a brave woman. I imagine you conveyed your condolences.'

'That's not all I conveyed, Dad. Would you mind staying up a little longer? There's something I need to tell you.'

Patrick returned to his place on the sofa. 'That sounds a little ominous. Are you in trouble? Reina told Alicia about the death threats – and Alicia told me.'

So Reina had read his letter. 'I am in trouble – but not the kind you think. I'm in love.'

'That's no secret. When are you going to propose to Alicia?'

'I'm not. I'm in love with Reina.' Lord, it felt good to finally speak the truth. He could only hope his father wasn't too disappointed.

A frown knit Patrick's brow. 'I thought you were in love with Alicia. Did you have a change of heart?'

'You assumed I was in love with Alicia. You seemed so happy about it that I couldn't bring myself to tell you the truth.'

'I am very fond of Alicia. But I'm even fonder of Reina. There was a time when Rio, Velvet, your mother and I hoped the two of you would marry.'

'I never knew that.'

'We talked about it after Reina was born. And we kept right on talking – wishing and hoping – until that day in the bakery. I didn't have to remind you how things changed afterward. I thought we'd lost you for all time. But you're back – all the way back,' he declared, giving Ulysses another of his bone-cracking hugs. 'Have you told Velvet yet?'

Ulysses spent a few minutes detailing his meeting with Velvet, and then went on to describe the disaster at the ball. 'So you see,' he concluded, 'it's possible that nothing I say or do will matter to Reina.'

'There was a time when I thought the same thing about your mother. She didn't want anything to do with me.'

'How did you get her to change her mind?'

'You know about the gunfight with the Detweilers. I went after them because of what they had done to your mother. After I took a bullet, she finally figured I meant it when I said I loved her.' Patrick smiled. 'And then – I seduced her.'

'Are you suggesting I seduce Reina?'

Although they were alone, Patrick lowered his voice. 'Most men can say more with their bodies than they can with words. Hell, son. I'll leave the details to you. Just remember, all's fair in love and war. When it comes to you and Reina, I suspect it's a little of both.'

Ulysses would have given all he possessed – his worldly wealth, his good name – to follow his father's advice. However, he didn't think Reina would ever let him get that close. 'I've spent my adult life acting as though I thought I was better than Reina. I didn't want to be in love with her. Considering Velvet's past, I don't think Reina was worthy of being a politician's wife. I told myself the way she dressed and acted were an embarrassment. When she came to Austin with a trunk full of fancy clothes and my friends accepted her, I gave myself permission to accept her, too. *Accept her*. Can you believe my gall?'

'Hell, son. Most men like to think they're better than their woman – smarter, stronger, more capable. It's easier than facing the truth.'

'And what's that?'

'It's women who civilize us, who potty-train us and teach us our manners. It's women who show us the meaning of words like beauty, tenderness and loyalty. Of course, they're better than us,' Patrick said with considerable force. Then he chuckled. 'Let me give you one last piece of advice. If all else fails where Reina is concerned, you might try groveling. There's nothing like the sight of a repentant male on his knees to make a female take notice.'

'So you advise seduction and groveling. In that order.'

Patrick winked. 'I know which you'd prefer. However, I suspect you'll get further with Reina by groveling. Speaking of groveling, I had better tell Charlotte the lay of the land.'

'I'd appreciate it. I know how much you wanted her back in the family.'

'Son,' Patrick said, giving Ulysses such a hard clap on the back that it would have broken a lesser man's bones, 'there's more than one way to skin a cat.'

Ulysses took a moment to ponder his father's cryptic remark. 'Are you thinking about asking Charlotte to marry you?'

Patrick looked as guilty as a schoolboy caught licking icing from a cake. 'How the hell did you know?'

'It was just a lucky guess.'

Patrick's steely eyes probed his. 'Do you mind? It's only six months since your mother passed on. I love her and I always will – but I don't want to spend the rest of my life with nothing but memories.'

A few months ago, Patrick's admission would have infuriated Ulysses. Now, he knew a man couldn't always govern his heart.

Velvet wasn't the only romantic, he thought as he grasped his father's hand. 'If you want my blessings, you have them. I suspect Mother would approve, too. Did you ever stop to think she may have been playing the matchmaker, insisting that Charlotte visit even though Mother knew she might not live to see her arrive?'

Patrick continued to hold Ulysses' hand. 'I'd appreciate it if you didn't say anything to Charlotte. We married too quickly the first time. It's not a mistake I want to repeat.'

Charlotte often lulled herself to sleep with a book. Tonight though, the words seemed meaningless. When she read the same paragraph for the third time, she marked her page and closed *Princess Casamante*.

Henry James' novel dealt with the social and sexual ferment underlying London society's placid surface. She grimaced, thinking she could have told the author a thing or two.

She had just reached up to turn out the light when someone knocked on her bedroom door. *Who could it be?* she wondered, getting out of bed. Alicia never emerged from her room once she'd excused herself for the night.

'Who is it?' Charlotte called out.

'Patrick. I'd like to talk to you for a few minutes – unless you're ready for bed.'

Charlotte's heart fluttered – then pounded like a blacksmith's hammer. Why did he feel the need to talk to her when they had just spent the afternoon together?

Dear God, was he on to her? She jumped out of bed, smoothed the covers, then put on her best dressing gown – the one with the maribou-feather trim. She spent a minute fluffing her hair and pinching color into her cheeks. A quick look in the mirror told her nothing could disguise the worry in her eyes, though.

'I don't want to disturb you,' Patrick said, his

gaze taking in her dishabille when she let him in.

'You aren't disturbing me.'

She led the way to the easy chairs by the window. Although dread gnawed at her innards, being married to Nigel had taught her to mask her feelings. 'What did you want to discuss?' she asked, settling in one of the chairs.

Patrick took the opposite chair, crossed his long legs and took one of her hands. He wouldn't touch her if he were angry, she thought.

'We need to talk about our children,' he said.

She almost laughed out loud as hope swept her anxiety away. She had heard Patrick and Ulysses talking when she went to her room. Ulysses must have said something to Patrick about Alicia. 'Nothing could make me happier.'

Patrick's expression sobered. 'I hope you still feel that way after I'm done. Ulysses has asked Velvet for permission to court Reina. I know – that is I thought – you might have harbored hopes for a match between my son and your daughter. I wanted you to hear the truth from me.'

Charlotte felt the blood drain from her head. Her vision narrowed. *Don't faint*, she commanded herself, willing the darkness away.

'I'm very glad you told me,' she said with all the dignity she could muster. 'I wish them both every happiness.'

'Then you aren't upset?'

Thank God men are so blind, she thought. Upset? Hell, no. She was half out of her mind with worry. She and her daughter had no place to go now – no home, no money, and no future.

'Of course I'm not upset. It's true, I did hope Ulysses and Alicia would form an attachment. But

I would have hated leaving my daughter behind in Texas when I returned to England.'

'Then you do plan to return?'

'As soon as the new wing is finished. Surely you didn't think I'd stay away from Glenhaven Hall forever?'

She managed to exchange a few more pleasantries, and was relieved when Patrick seemed as anxious to go as she was to be alone. After he'd gone, she collapsed on her bed and muffled her sobs in a pillow.

She had sown deceit and reaped the bitterest of harvests.

Twenty-four

Alicia rode down the long drive to the Prides' mailbox, grateful to escape the cheerless miasma that had enveloped the household since Ulysses announced his intention to court Reina.

Instead of being a cause for celebration, it had resulted in a palpable atmosphere of gloom and doom. Why was her mother going around in a blue funk, getting teary-eyed every time she thought no one could see her? Why did she care who Ulysses wanted to marry? And why did Patrick get the saddest expression on his face whenever Charlotte wasn't looking?

Ulysses' behavior had changed most of all — undoubtedly as a result of his difficulties with Reina. The few times he took meals with the family, he had a distracted air that precluded any sort of conversation.

Not that she'd been acting lighthearted, either, she reminded herself. She had even been short with Terrell the last time he came calling. She couldn't tell him the cause of her bad temper, though. She couldn't tell anyone.

She lifted her forearm and wiped the moisture from her brow. Ladies were supposed to glow rather than perspire, but the June heat and humidity had her as lathered as the mare she rode.

Or was it just her nerves?

Two months had passed since she mailed her manuscript to New York with a heart full of hope. Now, she didn't have much hope left. Keeping up a carefree facade was getting more difficult with every passing day.

Could it really take weeks and weeks for an editor to read her book? Didn't anyone care enough about all the work that had gone into it to respond? Honor didn't permit her to send her book to another publisher until she had heard back from Erastus Beadle or one of his minions.

Her imagination immediately conjured up a cubby hole of an office filled with tenebrous shadows. An editor sat at a desk piled high with manuscripts. Hers topped the pile.

A cigarette dangled from the editor's lips. His features reflected boredom as he systematically folded page after page of her novel into paper airplanes that he sent sailing out an open window. *What a rotter*, she thought, consigning the imaginary editor, and all his ilk, to eternal hellfire.

She arrived at the mailbox and jerked it open so forcefully that the contents spilled to the ground. 'Great, just great,' she muttered seeing them land in a puddle left by last night's rain.

Riding sidesaddle made it difficult to dismount unaided. As she slid to the ground, her skirt caught on a stirrup. Just then, her mare sidestepped and Alicia fell, face first, into the mud.

'Bloody hell,' she cursed, relishing the feel of the epithet on her lips.

She was about to get up when an envelope bearing a New York postmark and the letterhead of the Beadle publishing company riveted her in place. *Don't get excited*, she told herself, feeling her breath shorten. It was probably a rejection.

She picked the envelope up along with the rest of the mail and got to her feet. Why was the envelope so thick? Would it really take several pages to say no?

Her mare stood a few feet away, placidly munching on grass. 'Thanks a lot. You've been a great help,' Alicia said, walking over and depositing the rest of the mail in one of the saddlebags.

She wiped off the envelope she'd kept and tore it open, ignoring the dirty smear the mud left on her skirt.

Dear Mr Devereux, the letter began.

Her heart stopped. Who in the world was Mr Devereux? she fretted, too flustered to remember she had used that particular pseudonym. *I am pleased to let you know I have accepted your book for immediate publication.*

Lucky Mr Devereux, she thought sourly. Then, it hit her like a thunderbolt. *She* was Mr Devereux!

She read the first page through a shimmer of tears. Words like *excitement, authenticity, emotional depth*, and *page turner*, leapt up at her like tossed bouquets.

Erastus Beadle wanted to buy her book. He loved it. He thought she had a great future as a writer. He wanted to sign her to an exclusive five-book deal. When she saw the amount of money he was offering, she almost fainted. She was rich!

The last paragraph read, *Please sign the enclosed contract and return it at your earliest convenience. I am going to be in New Orleans at the end of July, and will travel on by ship to the port of Indianola if you can join me there on or about August 10th.*

He wanted to meet her in person to discuss his plans for her career, including a possible lecture tour. She immediately saw herself on a stage, giving a reading to thunderous applause, the gaslights adding an aura of mystery and sophistication to her appearance.

There was something terribly wrong with the picture though, because Mr Beadle's letter referred to *her* as *he*. He was expecting to meet a man.

Reina hadn't objected when Ulysses offered to help probate her father's will. She didn't say a word when he volunteered to bring the ranch's books up to date, either.

She wasn't foolish enough to refuse legitimate help, no matter the source. But she would never forgive him for making friends with Useful. He had to be sneaking food to the Wolfhound behind her back, she mused as she headed back home at the end of a long day. Useful was far too intelligent to have anything to do with Ulysses unless he was being bribed.

Most of all, Reina resented the way Ulysses had wormed his way into Velvet's good graces. She sang his praises as though he was some sort of paragon, when Reina knew him to be an unmitigated scoundrel and a coward to boot. He had bribed the dog with tidbits. What in the world had he promised her mother?

If Velvet hadn't been so lonely, Reina would gladly have driven Ulysses off the ranch with the business end of her father's shotgun. Tarring and feathering him had even more appeal, although she wasn't sure he merited the sacrifice of a chicken's life.

His constant presence had forced her into exile. The more time he spent with Velvet, the more she stayed away.

Just yesterday, she had ridden up to the barn long after the dinner hour, her empty stomach grumbling for food. She had intended to give Starfire a quick rubdown and an extra ration of oats before having her own supper. When she led the stallion inside the barn, she saw Ulysses mucking out stalls as if he did it every day.

'What in the name of heaven are you up to now?' she demanded.

'Isn't it obvious?' he replied with a devilish grin.

Her stomach spasmed and her mouth dried as she took in his naked torso. How did a deskbound man develop such glorious muscles?

Her hand inched out, eager to feel all those masculine curves. Her fingertips were mere inches from his sweat-glistened skin when she finally realized what she was doing and jerked her hand back, imprisoning it in one of her Levi's pockets.

She glared at Ulysses as resentment and desire fought for supremacy over her emotions. 'I want to know why you're really here. What can you possibly expect to gain from spending so much time on my ranch when you have one of your own?'

He lifted a hand to wipe the dampness from his brow. Her gaze caught on the golden tuft in the pit of his arm. Her nose caught the pungent aroma of masculine sweat. She breathed deeper, inhaling him greedily.

The lantern light glowed behind him, turning his body hair into a golden nimbus. Did that golden pelt extend inside his trousers?

Her body ached for his touch.

Her mouth longed for his kisses.

Her mind screamed to beware. She had been down this path before and had the scars to show for it.

He was studying her as intently as she had been

studying him. 'You don't understand, do you?' he said.

His voice – as potently masculine as everything else about him – seemed to travel from her ears straight to her blood. It bubbled through her like champagne, leaving her light-headed. She steeled herself against the effect.

'I understand that you're a manipulative, mealy-mouthed, no good—'

He closed the distance between them in one oiled stride and silenced her with a kiss. His lips were warm – so warm that heat pooled low in her groin and liquefied her most private place. She felt as if her very boncs were melting.

Before she could stop herself, her mouth opened to admit his tongue. Her breasts swelled and her nipples crested against his chest. He felt and tasted like her own personal heaven.

'I may be all those things and worse,' he murmured against her mouth. 'I'm also the man who loves you. That's why I'm here every day, Reina. You refused to let me court you properly – but you can't stop me from helping you.'

'You didn't help me in Austin when it would have mattered. I don't want your damn help now,' she cried out, pulling free of his embrace.

She ran from the barn as though a pack of fiends snapped at her heels, not even caring that she had left Starfire saddled and unfed. Let Ulysses put the stallion up for the night since he was so set on being helpful.

Now, riding home in the twilight, she clenched her jaws as she saw one of the Prides' horses tied up to the hitching post by the front door. She was so upset that she didn't stop to think that Alicia – not Ulysses – usually rode that particular mare.

AN INDECENT LADY

Not again, she thought. She didn't have the energy for another confrontation. Ulysses couldn't be serious about courting her. He didn't love her, didn't want to marry her – and the feeling was mutual. He was just hanging around because he took pleasure in upsetting her.

Instead of stabling Starfire, she tied him to the post next to the mare. The stallion could wait. Ulysses couldn't. She intended to tell him exactly what she thought of him. When she finished, he wouldn't dare talk about courting – let alone think about kissing. He'd be too busy licking his wounds.

She slammed the kitchen door and glared around, feeling like a cornered catamount preparing to unsheath its claws. To her surprise, Alicia and Velvet were seated at the table – and Ulysses was nowhere in sight.

'You sure work late. I thought you'd never get home,' Alicia said, jumping to her feet.

'I just do what needs doing,' Reina replied, wondering why Alicia looked as though she'd taken a mud bath. 'What happened to you? Did you have an accident on your way over?'

'I fell off my horse,' Alicia replied with a grin, as though she couldn't imagine a more exciting or fulfilling experience. She tugged a grimy envelope from the jacket of her riding habit. 'Reina, I have the most wonderful news.'

'You didn't get hurt, then?' Reina walked over to the sink to scrub the grime from her own hands.

'That's not my news. I finally heard from Erastus Beadle. He wants to buy my book! In fact, he wants to buy four more, too. He says I'm going to be famous.'

'Book? What's this about a book?' Velvet asked.

Panic widened Alicia's blue eyes until the whites

showed all around. She looked like a startled raccoon. 'Oh, dear, I forgot you were here, Mrs DeVargas.'

'Why wouldn't I be here? This is my kitchen.'

'You're absolutely right.' In a display of nerves, Alicia busied herself picking bits of mud from her skirt and dropping them on Velvet's pristine floor. 'I don't know what to do except throw myself on your mercy, and beg you not to repeat a word I've said. I don't want Mother to know about this letter – or my book – until I'm certain what's going to happen.'

Velvet looked none too happy. 'No good ever comes of keeping secrets.'

'Please, say you will keep mine for awhile.'

Velvet tilted her head the way she always did when she couldn't quite make up her mind, then abruptly said, 'As long as you aren't doing anything illegal or immoral, I suppose I can. Now, if you'll stop fiddling with your skirt, I'll get a dust pan and sweep up the mess you've made.'

Alicia managed to look properly chastised. However, after Velvet went to fetch a dust pan and broom, Alicia almost elevated off the floor with sheer happiness.

'Isn't it wonderful?' she exclaimed, waving the letter under Reina's nose.

'I won't know how wonderful it is until you let me read it.'

Reina's unwillingness to trust any man kept her from joining Alicia's celebration. She sat at the table, turned up the kerosene lamp, and read the letter and then the contract, word for word. Although the contract was couched in legal folderol, the letter couldn't have been more clear.

'I told you it was a good book,' she said when she was done, 'but how could you have told Mr

AN INDECENT LADY

Beadle you were really a man? Of all the silly, stupid things—'

Alicia's glow faded. 'I wanted to establish my credentials. I never dreamed Mr Beadle would want to meet me. Instead of wearing a badge on my chest, all I have to show him are two breasts! What in the world am I going to do?'

Ulysses and Patrick stood on the porch, watching the daylight fade.

'How are things at the DeVargases?' Patrick asked.

'Reina's doing a fine job of running their ranch,' Ulysses replied.

'Come on, son – that's not what I mean. How are things going between you and Reina?'

'Going, going, gone,' Ulysses answered glumly. 'I've tried everything I can think of from apologizing to mucking out their barn yesterday. I've groveled. I've played the seducer. Nothing works. Reina can't – or won't – let herself forget the past.'

'A shared history is what binds most couples together,' Patrick said. 'Unfortunately, it's keeping you and Reina apart.'

'I haven't given up hope yet. But I'm fresh out of ideas. I guess, you wouldn't happen to have any magic up your sleeve.'

Ulysses tossed his half-finished cheroot onto the drive. It arced through the air, trailing a plume of pungent smoke. He used to enjoy an occasional Havana. Not anymore, though. Nothing gave him that sort of easy pleasure anymore. His failure with Reina had washed all the joy from his life.

'Perhaps I do,' Patrick answered with a grin. 'Remember my telling you how getting wounded in a gunfight finally won your mother over?'

Wondering where his father was headed, Ulysses nodded.

'It didn't happen here,' Patrick explained. 'It happened in Llano.'

'I don't see what that has to do with my situation.'

'I think our being out of town made all the difference. It gave us both a chance to take a second look. No one knew us. We were pretty much alone.'

'If you're suggesting I get Reina out of town, it's a grand idea. However, I don't think she'd agree. She wouldn't even let me take her to dinner in Kerrville.'

'That's the trouble with your generation,' Patrick said with a fond chuckle. 'You give up too damn easy.'

Ulysses ignored the jibe. He'd heard similar complaints from other men his father's age. He supposed passing the torch was never easy. 'It's obvious you have something in mind. How about filling me in?'

'I was going to ask you to go to Indianola to take delivery on Nabob.'

'I assumed that you were going. I know how anxious you are to see that bull.'

'It's true. I am anxious. However, I'm even more anxious to stay here during Charlotte's last days on the ranch.'

'Do you really think she'll go back to England?'

'So she says.'

'Aren't you going to try and stop her?'

'I am indeed. That's why I want you to go to Indianola. I'll have time alone with Charlotte – and you'll have time alone with Reina. You can create a few new memories to replace some of the old ones. Think of it, son. Nabob will need a few days' rest to get over the sea journey. You'll have time to dine out in the best restaurants, attend the theater, take star-lit walks along the shore.'

Ulysses salivated at the thought of doing those things with Reina. 'It sounds like the perfect recipe for romance. How in the hell am I going to get Reina to go along with it?'

'Not you, son. Me. I'm going to tell her I don't trust you to bring the bull back safely.' Patrick chortled. 'Come to think of it, that's not too far from the truth.'

A few months back, Ulysses might have taken umbrage at Patrick's humor. Now, though, he laughed right along with him. The plan might just work. 'Reina has been anxious to breed Nabob to her best cows. If you offer her a few free stud services in exchange for her time and effort, I don't see how she can refuse.'

Alicia opened the door to Terrell's office and peaked inside. Pictures of wanted men glared from the walls. The setting left a great deal to be desired. It couldn't have looked less like a confessional. However, she had chosen this time and place to admit everything, from using the Flores incident, to borrowing Terrell's story – to falling hopelessly in love with him.

It's now or never, she encouraged herself, trying to take a deep breath despite her whalebone corset.

'You never mentioned a thing about coming to town today,' Terrell said, looking up from his work as she shut the street door.

His voice held a hint of reproach. If he was upset over a little thing like a surprise visit, how would he react to all the other things she had done?

'I just made up my mind to come last night,'

she said bravely. Then, her voice faltering, she added, 'I wanted to show you a letter that came in yesterday's mail.'

She held out the creased envelope.

He rose and came around from behind his desk, studied the envelope a second, then looked at her. 'It's from a publishing house – and it's not addressed to you. Are you sure you want me to read it?'

Her hands shook as she handed it over. 'I know who it's from and who it's for – and yes, I want you to read it.'

'I can't figure you.' He scratched his head. 'The last time I saw you, you were downright short-tempered. Now, you want me to read another man's mail. What's going on?'

'I'll explain everything after you've read the letter. Please, Terrell, do this one thing for me.'

He opened the letter carefully, as if he expected it to blow up in his hands.

She watched as curiosity, surprise, agitation and ultimately anger took turns rearranging the expression on his face.

When he finished, he dropped the letter on his desk. 'Who the hell is this Devereux fellow? What makes him think he has the right to use my name? Is he a beau from home? Is this your way of telling me you're going back to England to get married? If it is, I don't want to hear it. In fact, you had better forget all about going home!' The last was said in a roar that would have intimidated the fiercest criminal whose picture hung on the walls.

However, it didn't intimidate Alicia. In fact, it was music to her ears. 'What makes you think you have the right to tell me what to do?'

'Seeing as how I don't, I can only ask.' His tone softened. 'Please don't go back to England.'

AN INDECENT LADY

'Would it make that much difference to you?'

He had never declared his feelings in so many words. Now, she seized the opportunity to make him do so in precise English.

'It would make all the difference in the world.'

'Why?'

'You're going to make me say it, aren't you?'

Her lower jaw jutting with determination, she nodded *yes*.

He groaned. 'All right, have it your way. I'm in love with you. So in love that I can almost forget I'm the wrong man for you.'

'You couldn't be more mistaken,' she burst out.

'I wish I was. We're from totally different worlds. We don't have anything in common. You're used to the best of everything, and I've had a hard-scrabble sort of life. You're a blueblood. I'm a killer. I'm too old for you, too uneducated – too damn Texas.'

'Those are the very reasons I fell in love with you, Terrell Meeks,' she declared.

Not waiting to be asked, she walked into his arms, pulled him so close that his badge dug into her left breast, and planted a kiss squarely on his mouth – and not a demure kiss, either, but an open-mouthed, knee-jellying, soul-touching kiss.

Terrell wasn't a ranger for nothing. He knew when and how to take the initiative, she noted with relief as he deepened the exchange, drawing her tongue into his mouth and pressing her body so close that she became aware of his burgeoning manhood.

So that's what a penis feels like, she mused with a tinge of awe. It reminded her of a flower unfolding. No, she automatically edited herself – it reminded her of the proverbial bean stalk because it got big so fast.

By the time they finally ended the sexually charged contact, her face felt beet red and every one of

Terrell's freckles stood out against his blanched skin. He looked like a man who has had either a terrible fright, a fearful pleasure – or both.

'Where did you learn to kiss like that? Was it from the Devereux fellow?' he growled.

'I love it when you're jealous,' she replied, giving him a butter-wouldn't-melt-in-her-mouth grin. 'And there isn't an – as you put it – Devereux fellow. It was my mother's maiden name. I used it because I didn't think Erastus Beadle would buy a western written by a woman.'

A slight widening of Terrell's eyes was the only indication of his surprise. 'You wrote the book?'

'Guilty as charged.'

'And this Mr Beadle actually wants to pay you all the money for it? Are you sure that's all he wants from you? What the hell do you really know about the man?'

'I assure you, it isn't a hoax.' She loved it when he sounded so protective. 'Can we talk later? I'd like to get back to the kissing part.'

He lifted his right arm to fend her off. 'Don't you dare come a step closer. If I kiss you again, I'll never get around to asking the questions I need to ask. Why did you tell Beadle you were a Texas ranger named Terrell Meeks?'

'I wanted to give him the impression that I knew what I was writing about.'

'And what were you writing about?'

'I based my book on the Flores incident.'

He clapped his hand to his brow. 'Oh my God, I'll be a laughingstock.'

'Mr Beadle didn't laugh. He thought the book was fabulous. Furthermore, I was going to suggest that you leave the rangers anyway.'

'What?'

AN INDECENT LADY

'You have those four other books to think about. Being a ranger would interfere with your writing.'

Poor Terrell couldn't have looked more baffled. 'Alicia, you're running me up a tree here. You're the writer – not me.'

'I know that, and you know that. But Erastus Beadle can't ever know that. I came to town today to ask you – to beg you – to meet him in Indianola and pretend to be me.'

'That's crazy. I don't know anything about writing. I haven't even read my book.'

'It's *my* book,' she replied tartly. 'You have lots of time to read it between now and then. You don't have to know about writing. Wear your uniform. Talk to him about your exploits in the rangers. Show him your badge and your gun. That's what he wants to see.'

Terrell shook his head. 'I will not go down to Indianola and try to pass myself off as an author. Your Mr Beadle will see through me in no time flat. Besides, I can't just take time off when it suits me.'

The more he argued, the more she knew he was considering the idea. 'I meant what I said about you leaving the rangers. I'm going to make more than enough money for the both of us.'

Terrell stiffened. 'I don't want you to support me. I'm not one of those big city gigolos.'

'I know you aren't, darling.' It was the first time she had used the endearment. She watched while it registered in his eyes. 'I've had lots of time to think about this. I couldn't have written my book without you – and now Mr Beadle wants me to write four more. I've already started the second one and it's based on your experiences, too.'

'So?' The skeptical look in his eyes told her she hadn't convinced him yet.

'Don't you see? You're my inspiration. I always dreamed of being a novelist but I didn't start until we met.'

'You're really serious, aren't you?'

'Deadly serious. I don't want to spend the rest of my life writing dime westerns, either. I want to travel the world and base books on my experiences. I can't do it alone, though. It's too dangerous. I need you along to protect me.' Passion infused her words. 'Think about it, my love. Wouldn't you like to see the pyramids along the Nile, or hunt tigers from an elephant's back?'

To her immense relief, the tension in Terrell's body eased. 'I'd be lying if I said I wouldn't like to do those things. To be perfectly honest, I have given some thought to leaving the rangers as well. But there are still a lot of obstacles to overcome before you write "happily ever after".'

'Name one.'

'Your mother.'

'I'll handle my mother. Name another.'

'Your publisher. I'll never convince him I'm a writer – at least not until I've had some time to learn a little about what you do. And we don't have time.'

'Then I'll just have to go to Indianola with you.' The minute she suggested it, she knew she'd come up with the prefect solution. 'You can introduce me to Mr Beadle as your scribe.'

'My what?'

'Scribe. Secretary. Typewriter. The terms are interchangeable. If Mr Beadle asks questions about writing, I could answer them.'

'I suppose that would work.'

Pressing her advantage, she held out her hand. 'Is it a deal?'

He took her hand, turned it over, and kissed her palm. The erotic contact sent a burst of energy up her arm. She could have danced all night, climbed a mountain, and still felt fresh enough to write a bestseller.

'It's crazy,' he muttered. 'I have the feeling that I'm going to make a fool of myself – but it's a deal. There is another problem, though.'

'I'm listening.' How many more objections could he possibly come up with?

'If we go off together, I won't be responsible for my actions.'

The threat sent a delicious shiver across her skin. 'In what way?'

'Don't play games, Alicia. You damn well know what I'm talking about. I'm old-fashioned enough to think we ought to get married first.'

'So am I.' She blinked back tears. Things had worked out better than she could possibly have hoped.

'That brings us back to the kissing part,' she said huskily.

Terrell didn't have to be told twice.

Twenty-five

Reina thrust clothes into the suitcase with abandon, not caring that they would be wrinkled when she unpacked. She didn't give a damn how she would look in Indianola.

Nabob was the only one she wanted to impress, and the champion bull wouldn't notice what she wore. Appearances, genealogy, social standing, and bulging bank accounts didn't impress animals. Gentleness, affection, and empathy did.

How in the world had she ever permitted herself to be talked into this trip? she fretted as she forced the suitcase shut. One minute she and Patrick had been discussing the problems of shipping a valuable bull thousands of miles, and the next she had agreed to be there when Nabob's ship docked at Indianola.

'Ulysses will go with you,' Patrick had said without any warning.

'Ulysses?' she stuttered. 'He doesn't know a thing about cattle. Doesn't care to know, either.'

Patrick gave her a smile of beatific innocence. 'My son has changed. He is aware of his deficits – all of them – and he is bound and determined to correct them. He couldn't have a better teacher than you.'

'I have no doubt Ulysses needs all the help he can get,' she replied, feeling her gorge rise, 'but he won't get it from me. I'd do anything for *you* – but

I will not be tricked, maneuvered, or coerced into spending time with your son.'

Patrick drilled her with a gimlet gaze. 'I can't believe my ears! Are you going back on your word? Your Daddy – God rest his soul – wouldn't approve. He taught you better.'

'My father wouldn't approve of my going off unchaperoned with Ulysses, either,' she fired back, hoping she had scored a winning hit.

Patrick looked positively wounded. 'I wouldn't do anything to harm your reputation. I planned to ask Alicia to accompany you.' He paused, as if he expected her to thank him for his thoughtfulness. 'I don't want you to be unhappy, though, so I'll sweeten the deal. In return for Nabob's safe delivery to Pride's Passion, you can use him at stud a couple of times at no charge.'

She had dreamed of infusing her stock with Nabob's impeccable blood lines. Knowing a bull could only service so many cows during a season, she hadn't dared broach the subject.

Her steely resolve melted. She could almost feel it puddling at her feet. The incentive was too great to resist. 'How soon do you want me to leave?'

'Nabob's ship comes in on the tenth. He's going to need a few days' rest before taking the train to Kerrville. I'd like you to get to Indianola a day early so you can check on the accommodation at the livery stable. At most, you'll be gone a week.'

'What about my ranch?'

'I'll send a top hand to keep an eye on things.'

'You certainly have thought of everything.'

'I try.' Patrick looked as sly as a fox hunting a way into a henhouse. 'I do need one more favor.'

'And what might that be?'

He took one of her hands and gave it an

affectionate squeeze. 'You know how I feel about you.'

She nodded.

'Won't you give Ulysses one last chance to prove he deserves your love? Now your father's gone, I'd sure like you and your mother to be part of my family.'

'I'll go to Indianola with him. But that's as far as I'll go.'

She would have happily taken a journey with Mary Shelley's Frankenstein monster if it meant adding Nabob's superior blood lines to DeVargas stock. At least Ulysses was no monster, she thought as she picked up her suitcase. She was so deep in thought that she collided with Velvet in the hall.

'I just saw Alicia and Ulysses pull up in the buggy.' Disapproval flashed in Velvet's eyes as she took in Reina's attire. 'Why are you wearing Levi's when you have a lovely traveling suit?'

'I'm comfortable this way. Besides, I'm finished pretending to be something I'm not.'

'What pretending? You're a beautiful young woman. You ought to dress like one.' Velvet's eyes went to the suitcase. 'Have you packed any of your new outfits?'

'A few,' Reina grudgingly admitted.

'I'll go let Alicia and Ulysses in while you change into something more suitable.' Before Reina could object, Velvet added, 'You wouldn't want anyone to think your father left us so destitute that you can't afford to dress properly.'

Reina dropped the suitcase with a thud and stomped back to her room. She tore her clothes off and donned new ones with jerky motions that betrayed her anger. Her mother had used the only argument that had the power to sway her.

* * *

AN INDECENT LADY

Ulysses hadn't expected to see Terrell Meeks at the Kerrville train station. The renowned ranger had an expectant look on his face, as though he was waiting for someone. Considering the shine on his boots and the press of his trousers, he wasn't there to meet a felon.

Terrell hurried over to the buggy, helped the ladies down, then, without being asked, unloaded their luggage. 'I hear you're going to Indianola to pick up a bull,' he said. 'Since I'm going there, too, why don't we travel together?'

'I'd be obliged to have your company,' Ulysses answered. Privately, though, he couldn't help thinking there was something downright peculiar about the way Terrell had showed up.

Ulysses hoped the ranger wouldn't get in the way of his plans. He intended to wine and dine Reina, to atone in a small way for Austin. This time, if anyone dared say anything about her or her parents, he vowed to draw and quarter them on the spot.

He'd done all the mucking out of stalls he planned to do. Shoveling manure wasn't the way to Reina's heart. Neither was keeping books or giving free legal advice. From here on, he was going to court her properly – whether she liked it or not.

Considering the scornful looks and cold words she heaped on him at every opportunity, it was going to take an act of God to win her over.

Terrell volunteered to stay with Alicia and Reina while Ulysses left the buggy at the livery stable. On the way back, he stopped at the freight office to confirm plans to ship Nabob back to Kerrville in a private livestock car.

As Ulysses rejoined Reina, Alicia, and Terrell, their lively discussion came to an abrupt end. They had the look of conspirators caught in the act. But what act?

What could the three of them possibly be planning? he mused as the train arrived in a cloud of steam and a shower of cinders.

As if by prior agreement, Reina and Alicia chose side-by-side seats in the half empty parlor car, leaving Ulysses to sit with Terrell.

'Are you going to Indianola to testify at a trial?' he asked, as the train started with a series of ponderous jolts.

'Not exactly. I do have business with a judge though.'

Terrell's face had a pinched, anxious look, as though he were afraid of something – although Ulysses couldn't imagine what. He'd never known a braver man.

'Ranger business?' Ulysses asked, unbuttoning his coat and settling in for the long ride.

'Personal business.'

Ulysses had seen similar expressions on the faces of would-be clients. 'Do you need a lawyer? Rest assured, I'll hold what you say in confidence.'

Terrell leaned closer. 'I wouldn't want this to get around.'

'It sounds serious.'

'It is.' Terrell cleared his throat. It didn't help, though. When he spoke, he sounded as if he had swallowed gravel. 'I'm getting married in Indianola – and I'd like you to be my best man.'

Ulysses couldn't have been more surprised. No wonder Terrell looked like he'd seen a ghost. As much as Ulysses dreamed of marrying Reina, he knew he'd be shaking in his boots when the time came.

'Who is the lucky lady?'

'Alicia,' Terrell replied.

'That's the best news I've had in a long time.'

Ulysses had been concerned that Reina might be the magnet that had drawn the ranger into their orbit. Relief washed over him as he reached out to pump the ranger's hand.

Misery constricted Charlotte's chest as she watched the buggy carry Alicia away. She stood on the porch and continued waving long after it disappeared from sight. The trip to Indianola might be her daughter's last chance to have a good time. How sad to think Alicia had been asked to go along as Reina's companion and chaperone.

With the new wing nearing completion, she had run out of reasons to delay their departure. And she still didn't know where they would go. Glenhaven Hall and the London townhouse had been auctioned off last week. Nigel's solicitor was pressing her to return her jewels, too. *To hell with him,* she thought. *To hell with England.*

She reached up and brushed a tear away. Beneath her smooth skin, she sensed the bitter lines that would define her face in old age.

'Are you going to stand out here all morning?' Patrick called from the doorway.

The lump in her throat prevented a response.

She heard his footsteps and then felt his warmth as he stood beside her. 'Why the tears? Don't tell me you miss your daughter already?'

'Of course not. I have something in my eye.'

He put his hands on her shoulders and turned her so that she faced him. 'You've been so melancholy the last few weeks. Have I said or done something to offend you?'

She shook her head in vehement denial. 'You're the kindest man I've ever known.'

'You flatter me.'

'It's not flattery.'

'Surely Nigel was kinder?'

The facade she had maintained since her arrival cracked. She felt as if little bits and pieces of her soul were open to Patrick's sympathetic gaze. 'Nigel was many things. Kind wasn't one of them.'

Patrick's grip on her shoulders tightened. 'You don't mean that. I knew Nigel.'

'You didn't know him at all. As it turned out, neither did I.'

She had hoped to take Patrick's good opinion away with her when she left Pride's Passion. Now, nothing mattered except telling him the truth — even if he hated her afterward. 'I never wanted you to know the truth about my husband and me, but I think I'll go mad if I keep the secret much longer.'

'We can talk inside,' he said.

Charlotte followed him into the parlor on leaden feet and collapsed on the sofa.

Patrick hovered over her. 'I know it's early, but you look as though you could use a brandy.'

'I'd love one. Six would be even better. But I want to have a clear head when I tell you the truth.' She laced her fingers to keep her hands from shaking. 'No matter how angry or upset you get, I want your promise that you won't interrupt or ask any questions until I finish.'

'You have my word — however, I can't imagine getting angry at you after everything you've done for me.'

Charlotte scanned his face and saw only concern written there. At that moment — knowing she was about to lose him — she loved him more than she ever had as his bride. She had been infatuated by his good looks and heroic reputation then. Now, she truly cared for the man.

'I came here under false pretenses. I'm not a wealthy widow. I'm not a grieving one, either. I'm not any of the things you think — and neither was my husband.'

It took all Patrick's considerable will power not to break his word then and there. How could she not be a wealthy widow? Had Nigel left his fortune to someone else?

Patrick listened with mounting fury as Charlotte told him about a man who had lost control of his actions, his emotions, and his finances — a man who had squandered his patrimony and thrown his wife's love away — a man whose final perfidious act was to die in his mistress's bed.

'The day Nigel's solicitor read the will, I learned my husband had left me a mountain of debts, a heart filled with bitterness — and nothing else.' Charlotte's tone said more about despair than her words. 'He managed to stay one step ahead of his creditors by robbing Peter to pay Paul. If he hadn't died, he would have been forced into bankruptcy. Instead, it's happened to me and my daughter.' Her voice finally faltered. 'I think I'll have that brandy after all.'

'I'll just be a minute,' he replied, grateful for the respite. Her story had shaken him. He hurried to the library, poured two generous tots, drank down the contents of one glass and refilled it. Charlotte was standing at a window, looking out when he rejoined her.

'Are you all right?' he asked. 'If this is too hard on you—' His voice trailed off. What could he possibly say to erase the pain in her eyes? Would she ever be able to trust another man? Wordless, he held out a snifter.

'I haven't told you everything. Alicia doesn't know our true circumstances. I hope and pray she never will. That's one reason we left England.'

'She's a strong girl – and a sensible one. You should be honest with her.'

'That's not the only reason I brought her here. Elke wrote me a great deal about Ulysses. I knew he wanted a wife who could forward his political ambitions. I didn't think he would be able to resist a well-bred girl with a title. I brought Alicia to Pride's Passion in the expectation that she would rule over it one day. So you see, in my own way, I'm no better than Nigel. I lied to you – about everything. My only excuse is that I did it for my daughter.' She drank her brandy down in a long gulp that left her gasping. 'Now that you know the truth, I'll leave as soon as Alicia returns.'

'Leave? You just told me you don't have any place to go.'

She choked back a sob. 'Either you hate me – or you pity me. I couldn't endure either one.'

He reached out and touched her cheek. 'Sweet girl, nothing could be further from the truth. I have always admired your gallantry.'

'I'm not gallant. And I was never a sweet girl – we both know that. I'm the same Charlotte who tricked you into marriage all those years ago. Only this time, I tried to trick your son.'

'You didn't trick anyone. You just put two attractive young people together and hoped for the best. To tell you the truth, I was hoping right along with you. I thought you might stay on if our children married.' Caution tempered Patrick's words. He wanted to say a great deal more – and didn't quite dare while the

AN INDECENT LADY

specter of Nigel's perfidy hung between them. 'Have you ever thought your coming here when I needed you wasn't pure coincidence?'

'I just told you it wasn't.'

'What you said is only part of the truth. Elke invited you, didn't she?'

Charlotte nodded. The brandy had given her a little color. 'I took advantage of her kind nature.'

'Elke was kind to a fault – but she didn't let anyone take advantage of her. She knew she was dying. She knew Nigel had passed on. She knew we loved each other once. I think she wanted us to be together.'

Just then, a breeze brushed Patrick's cheek, as if something had stirred the air.

'Did you feel that?'

'Feel what?'

The air stirred again. The room seemed to fill with a lambent light. Suddenly, Elke appeared, so close that he could have touched her. Her gossamer wings fluttered softly. *There will never be a better time,* she said from somewhere inside Patrick's head. *Charlotte belongs here with you. Ask her to marry you.*

'Do you mean it?'

Elke nodded. Her encouraging smile fell on him like a benison.

'Mean what?' Charlotte asked.

Be happy, my love, Elke said.

His eyes full of tears, Patrick nodded.

Charlotte seemed unaware of Elke's presence. 'Are you all right?' she asked anxiously.

She took his hand and rubbed it the way she had the night he almost froze.

Her touch banished all the ghosts – the good and the bad. With a last loving smile, Elke faded away. Nigel's misdeeds seemed to go with her.

Patrick turned his full attention back to Charlotte.

'I was well on my way to becoming a recluse when you showed up. I didn't care if I lived or died. You brought me — you brought Pride's Passion — back to life. We've shared so many bad times. I'd like to think we were finally going to share some good ones.'

'So would I.'

'Then you accept?'

'Accept what? Your continuing hospitality?' Her wonderful amber eyes blinked in confusion.

Damn. Why were women so dense? He thought he'd made his intentions perfectly clear. 'My marriage proposal,' he explained impatiently. 'Would you do me the honor of being my wife?'

'You dear, crazy man. Wasn't once enough?'

'When it comes to you, Charlotte Devereux, once is never enough.'

Indianola had its beginnings in 1844 when German settlers landed on the shores of Matagorda Bay on their way to the Texas Hill Country. The town's early years were plagued by epidemics of yellow fever, malaria and dysentery, as well as by Comanche raids.

The deep water port, a natural gateway to the west, assured the city's survival. The citizens lived through the epidemics, the attacks, a Civil War blockade, and a series of hurricanes. The population grew in fits and starts — and then leaps and bounds when settlers poured into Texas after the war.

As Ulysses and Alicia headed down Main Street to the Morgan long wharf, Indianola exuded prosperity. The stores lining the busy avenue surpassed those in Austin for variety and opulence.

Windows displayed luxury items — jewelry, china, the latest washing machines, and even Steinway

AN INDECENT LADY

pianos. Groceries offered such out-of-season delicacies as peaches, bananas, and grapes shipped from the tropics. Two photography studios stood ready to commemorate any occasion. Four hotels, a multitude of fine restaurants, and even an ice cream parlor vied for customers.

The Calhoun County courthouse anchored one end of the bustling thoroughfare. A distant lighthouse anchored the other. In between, a series of wharves stretched like fingers into the bay. The smokestacks of half a dozen steamships pointed skyward imperiously.

'I can't wait to see Nabob,' Reina said, as they reached the Morgan pier where the newly docked *I. C. Harris* rocked in its berth.

She hurried up the gangplank – heedless of the hungry leers of sailors and longshoremen – and asked directions to the bull's quarters.

Ulysses didn't share her oblivion. *They can look – but they had damn well better not touch*, he thought as he followed Reina down into the belly of the ship.

The bull had a huge stall amidships. Ian McTavish, the stockman who had accompanied Nabob, was waiting for them. Reina could hardly keep her eyes on McTavish's face as they introduced themselves.

The amenities attended to, she wasted no time climbing onto the lower rung of Nabob's stall to get a better look at him.

Her lips parted. Her eyes sparkled. 'He's magnificent,' she said reverently.

Ulysses wished she would look at him that way just once. Lord, he had sunk low, envying a bull.

'That he is, lass,' McTavish said, 'although he is a bit peckish right now. We had a rough go a few days back.'

'Can I get in the stall with him?'

'Ay. He's been hand-raised. You treat old Nabob right, and he's as gentle as a lamb.'

Considering the animal's bulk, the power implicit in his muscled shoulders and haunches, Ulysses didn't think that was an apt comparison. He repeated Reina's question.

'Are you sure it's safe, Mr McTavish?'

'Why don't you see for yourself?' Reina challenged, letting herself into the stall.

Heart hammering, Ulysses followed at her heels.

Just then, a dog emerged from behind the great bull. Not just any dog, either, Ulysses thought with relief. He'd paid a fine price for this one.

For a moment, Reina looked like a child on Christmas morning, unable to decide which present to open. The dog solved her dilemma by demanding her attention.

'What have we here?' she asked as it licked her hands.

'This is Glenhaven's Brianna, as fine a thoroughbred Wolfhound bitch as you're likely to see,' McTavish explained.

'I can see what she is – but what is she doing here?'

'Miss Charlotte sent instructions for her to make the journey with Nabob. Your friend,' he gestured at Ulysses, 'bought her.'

Reina couldn't believe her ears. Ulysses had no use for dogs. He'd only recently made friends with Useful. Why would he want a bitch?

'Do you like her?' Ulysses asked over her shoulder.

She stroked the dog's head. 'Of course I like her. She's beautiful.'

'I'm glad. She's yours.'

'Mine? You bought her for me?'

AN INDECENT LADY 383

Someday, he vowed to kiss away the line that appeared between her eyes when she was perplexed. 'I didn't buy her for you. I bought her for Useful.'

'Why? There was a time when you didn't even like him.'

'Let's just say I've come to appreciate Useful's sterling character.' Ulysses gave her a sheepish grin. 'I didn't want him to be lonely the rest of his life. He needed someone to love. We all do, Reina.'

Hearing his plaintive tone, and seeing the longing in his eyes, Reina felt as though a log jam had given way inside her. Her carefully constructed defenses broke apart and drifted away. She couldn't go on ignoring the thoughtful things Ulysses had done.

She couldn't ignore her own feelings either. She made up her mind to give him one last chance to prove himself.

Could she trust him – or would he fail her again?

When Alicia conjured up Erastus Beadle, she had imagined a man of heroic proportions who would bear a striking resemblance to Michelangelo's sculpture of Moses.

The dapper man who walked into the lobby of Indianola's Enterprise Hotel late in the afternoon – carrying a copy of the *New York Times* for identification – was modest in every aspect. His only remarkable feature was his eyes. A lively curiosity showed in their hazel depths.

'Here we go, ready or not,' Alicia whispered, clutching Terrell's arm and stepping forward to intercept the publisher.

'Mr Beadle, I believe you're looking for us,' Terrell said.

'I'd have known you anywhere, Captain Meeks. And this must be your wife.'

Terrell turned as red a sunset. 'Permit me to introduce Alicia Hawthorne, Lady Glenhaven.'

'We're such newlyweds,' Alicia interjected, 'that my husband forgets I'm Mrs Meeks.'

Beadle's gaze locked with hers. 'Do you really have a title, Mrs Meeks?'

'My mother is the Countess of Glenhaven,' she replied with a touch of hauteur, then softened it with a smile. 'But you may call me Alicia.'

Beadle framed Alicia and Terrell with his hands, then drew imaginary letters in the air with a showman's flamboyance. 'You two will make headlines when you come to New York. I can see it now. *The Lawman and the Lady*. It has a ring. What a book title!'

'I'll be happy to write it – that is, my husband will be happy to write it for you.'

She would have to be more careful, she thought, as Terrell escorted Beadle to the registration desk. She'd been afraid Terrell wouldn't be able to carry off their charade. Now, she realized how difficult it would be to let someone else – even the man she loved – take credit for her work.

They ate at Barrate's, a restaurant the desk clerk recommended for its fine French cuisine. The meal was neither French nor fine, but Alicia was too interested in what Erastus Beadle said to do justice to the food if it had been ambrosial.

Beadle held her spellbound as he recounted, between mouthfuls, how he came to be a successful publisher. 'My brother and I put out a magazine in Cooperstown, New York, before we moved to Manhattan. It was small potatoes compared to our current operation. Our very first book, *Malewska The Indian Wife of the Indian Hunter*, sold hundreds of thousands of copies. Yours will sell millions.'

Alicia gasped. 'I knew dime westerns were popular, but I had no idea they were *that* popular.'

'Not all of them are,' Beadle replied with smug satisfaction. 'Our success has a great deal to do with our packaging. We use bright salmon covers to attract buyers, and we advertise more than other publishers. I like to think we draw the best writers because we pay advances and royalties the minute they are due.' He reached into his jacket and with a flourish produced a bank draft. 'It gives me great pleasure to deliver this, the first of many advances, in person, Captain.'

Terrell handed the draft over to Alicia.

'Your book impressed me,' Beadle continued, 'however, you impress me even more. I can only imagine how busy you've been, fulfilling your duties as a ranger. How and when did you take up writing?'

'It was an accident.' Bless Terrell for keeping a straight face. 'One minute, I had no thought of writing and the next, I had a book in my hands.'

'You're far too modest. I know how much work goes into a manuscript.' Beadle leaned closer and lowered his voice. 'Some of the people who write dime westerns have never been west of Hoboken. You, Captain, are the real thing. If we play our cards right, you're going to be as famous as Wild Bill Hickock.'

'I'm overwhelmed, sir.' Terrell's eyes had a dangerous glint. 'I was wondering – if someone else had written my book – say, a woman – would you have been as enthusiastic?'

Damn him. He hadn't believed her.

Beadle let go a brittle laugh. 'I can't imagine any woman writing a rousing adventure like yours. They are, after all, the weaker sex.'

Weaker sex indeed, she thought.

'However, Captain, I dare say you will have many devoted female readers. You have such a sensibility when it comes to portraying women.'

'I do have a way with them, if I do say so myself,' Terrell responded.

She kicked him under the table.

'You've heard a bit about my business,' Beadle continued. 'I'd love to hear a little about yours. Is it true that rangers always get their man?'

Alicia relaxed as Terrell began talking about his experiences. Every time he showed signs of stopping, she prodded and encouraged with another question.

An hour later, the publisher checked his watch, then got to his feet. 'I could listen to you all night, Captain, but I am a bit weary. It's been a long day.'

'Are you sure we can't convince you to stay on for a few more?' Alicia asked.

'My ship departs in the morning. Frankly, I won't be unhappy to leave. We came through a storm yesterday. It looked quite threatening. I don't want to be here when it hits land.'

'We Texans are quite used to bad weather,' Terrell said, helping Alicia to her feet. 'You should be here during a blue norther.'

'A blue norther,' Beadle repeated, leading the way out to the street. 'That sounds like another marvelous title.'

To Alicia's dismay, Beadle didn't say good night in the lobby. He followed them to Terrell's second-floor room. 'I'm just next door,' he said. 'Give me a knock in the morning and we'll have breakfast together.'

'I'll look forward to it,' Terrell replied, opening the door and tugging Alicia inside.

She looked around, her heart pounding. Terrell had warned her what would happen if they were ever alone. It was too soon. They weren't getting married for a few more days.

'What do we do now?' she whispered. 'If I leave and go to my room, Beadle's certain to hear. I don't want him asking any awkward questions tomorrow. I don't want anything to ruin the good impression you made.'

'Oh, I made a good impression, all right. I'm turning out to be a first-class actor – and an even better liar.'

Alicia quivered before the fire in Terrell's eyes. She had never seen him so upset. 'You know it's all been necessary.'

He took hold of her upper arms and drew her so close that her breasts brushed his chest. He shook with emotion – undoubtedly anger. 'Alicia Hawthorne, you have turned my life upside down. You have changed me in so many ways that I don't know myself anymore. But I'm still a ranger – and you know what that means.'

'What – what does it mean?'

'You heard what I told Beadle about how rangers always get their man.'

'I remember.'

'Since it seems you will have to stay the night, I'm going to have my way with you, my dear. Rangers don't just get their man. If they're very lucky, they get their woman, too.'

His sudden smile banished her fears. He wasn't shaking because he was angry. He was shaking with repressed laughter.

His first kiss sent tingles racing from the top of her

head to the tips of her toes. A deeper kiss awakened her desire. If she was writing this scene, this was where she'd pen *The End*.

No, she mused, editing herself for the last time that night. This wasn't the end. It was the beginning.

Twenty-six

How could Alicia sleep so soundly on her wedding day? Reina wondered, gazing across the dark hotel room at the motionless form in the other bed. In Alicia's place, she would be tossing and turning. If nerves hadn't wakened her, the wind certainly would.

Yesterday, a bold breeze had sent tourists to the beach to watch combers crashing onto the shore. Now, in the predawn, the wind tore at the Enterprise Hotel like a demon seeking entrance. Were Nabob and Brianna all right in their shared stall?

Reina had just decided to dress and check on them when she heard a knock at the door. She fumbled for her robe, found it at the foot of the bed, and belted it securely at her waist.

'Who is it?'

'Ulysses.'

They had grown close the last few days – but not close enough to warrant such an intrusion. What in the world could he possibly want at such an ungodly hour?

She cracked the door open. The hall lamp cast his handsome features in almost eerie relief. He wore trousers, boots, and a half-buttoned shirt.

'Is Alicia awake?'

Reina kept her voice low. 'Not yet. What's the matter?'

'I think a hurricane is headed to shore.'

A premonitory chill raised goose bumps on her skin. 'Surely the weather service, or the Coast Guard, would have warned us.'

'They should have. When it's too late to do any good, someone will figure out why they didn't. Ian McTavish mentioned a storm at sea. So did Erastus Beadle. He even warned Terrell about being in town when the storm hit. You saw the waves yesterday. You can hear the wind. What more warning do you need?'

Before she could answer, he pulled her into his arms and crushed her against the broad expanse of his chest. Her cheek touched his bare skin. He smelled of bed linens, sleep – and pure male.

Their hearts beat in unison. His unshaven beard felt scratchy as he lowered his head to hers. She expected a kiss.

Instead, he said, 'I promised myself I wouldn't let anything bad happen to you ever again. Come hell or high water, I'm going to keep that promise.'

The talk of a hurricane had aroused a primal fear that made her cling to him and burrow into his maleness. She had been almost arrogantly proud of her independence. For the first time, she felt the need of a man's protection – but not just any man. *This man.*

She had denied her feelings so long that it had become a habit. The realization melted the last of her resistance. She loved Ulysses – and he loved her.

He was so big, so strong, so utterly masculine, that she could happily have stayed in his arms while nature's fury washed over them both. However, Rio

AN INDECENT LADY 391

hadn't raised her to hide from anything – not even a hurricane.

'Alicia is going to be heartbroken. She counted on getting married today. Can't we stay long enough for the wedding?'

'We're at sea level here, and the gulf is rising.'

Reluctantly, she left his arms. The hoped-for kiss would have to wait. 'Are you sure?'

'I woke Terrell half an hour ago. We went down to the lobby to check things out. We could see waves breaking on buildings a block away, and a couple of inches of water were running across Main Street.'

'Dear God.' Reina crossed herself reflexively. 'What do you want me to do?'

At that moment – with that question – she surrendered her heart and her life into Ulysses' care.

'Wake Alicia, get dressed, and bundle up a change of clothes. Wear your Levi's and, if you have an extra pair, give them to Alicia.'

'Where's Terrell?'

'At the livery stable, trying to get us some horses.'

Her courage faltered at the thought of making a ride under these conditions. 'I saw a train in the station last night. Surely the engineer will move it inland. Can't we go with him?'

'That train isn't going anywhere. The engineer drained the boiler last night. We're going to have to leave on horseback.'

The depth of their danger hit Reina full force. 'Where will we go?'

'Victoria. It's forty miles inland. We should be safe there.'

She couldn't stay her tears – but they weren't for herself. She wept for the animals in her care. 'Poor Nabob. He's been cooped up for months. I'm not sure he'll make it – let alone Brianna.'

'They'll make it if I have to carry them both,' Ulysses vowed grimly. 'We haven't time to waste. Do what I asked and meet me in the lobby.'

She hated to let him go. 'What will you be doing?'

He flashed a piratical grin. 'Raiding the hotel kitchen for supplies.'

Fifteen minutes later, Reina and Alicia met Ulysses downstairs. A few other people were already there in the lobby, their faces white with fright.

'You're crazy to go out in this weather,' one of them warned as Ulysses shepherded Reina and Alicia to the entrance. 'You'd be wise to sit the storm out right here.'

Although the man continued talking, the wind swept his words away. It tore the hat from Reina's head and sent it scuttling into the darkness. She and Alicia clung to Ulysses for support as they stepped off the wooden sidewalk into a maelstrom.

It couldn't have been an hour since Ulysses had checked the water's depth. Now, though, at least four inches foamed over the street. The current threatened to push them off their feet.

Seeming to read her mind, Ulysses said, 'It's not as bad as you think. The current will be running with us, pushing us along when we head inland.'

By the time they walked the three blocks to the livery stable, they were wet through. A single kerosene lamp swung to and fro in time with the gusting wind. Horses whickered anxiously as if they sensed their imminent doom.

Terrell stepped from the shadows and swept Alicia into his arms. Their kiss was so passionate that Reina would have known they were lovers without Alicia telling her. Lucky Alicia, Reina thought, wondering

AN INDECENT LADY

if she would die without ever knowing the joys of physical love.

Terrell let Alicia go and turned to Ulysses. 'Has the water risen much?'

'A couple of inches. It will be in the stable soon. Were you able to buy horses?'

'Four, complete with saddles, bridles, saddle bags, extra blankets and oilskins. The owner was here checking on the stock when I arrived. He was only too happy to sell his best animals. He thought it might be their only chance for survival.'

Reina struggled to master her agitation. 'If he thinks it's going to get that bad, why isn't he going with us?'

'He has a family. He went home to be with them.'

Her throat constricted at the thought of the helpless women and children in Indianola. God help them all.

'We'd better get out of here,' Ulysses said. 'Terrell, you go first. Reina and Alicia will follow, and I'll bring up the rear.'

She was surprised at how naturally he assumed command. She had supposed Terrell would take on that responsibility. 'What about Nabob and Brianna?'

'I put them on long leads,' Terrell explained. 'Alicia can take the Wolfhound, and you can take Nabob. He's so fond of you already, I don't think he'll give you any trouble. Here, put these on.' He handed out the oilskins. Their bright yellow color seemed incongruously cheerful in view of the circumstances.

The two men led the horses outside, helped Reina and Alicia up into their saddles, then mounted, too. All four horses danced nervously when the rushing water hit their legs. Brianna woofed a couple of times, then took up a position at Nabob's side, as if she sensed the bull's bulk would protect her from the wind.

In the years to come, Reina would tell her grandchildren of the journey's endless terror – the malevolent mustard-gray sky, the wind that increased in fury with every passing hour, the lashing rain, the rising water that made progress a supreme effort.

The order of their march never changed. Terrell rode ahead, warning of unseen sloughs that forced their horses to swim. Ulysses stayed at the rear, his gun at the ready should they encounter alligators or poisonous snakes. To conserve strength, they only spoke out of need – and then they had to shout to be heard.

Late that day, Brianna could walk no more. True to his word, Ulysses bent from the saddle and picked her up as easily as though she were a spaniel rather than a hundred-fifty-pound Wolfhound.

Vomiting water, the exhausted dog lay draped over his lap. The faltering horses were in desperate need of rest, too.

The water ran inland, extending Matagorda Bay as far as the eye could see. Weeks later, Reina would learn that the wind-driven tide had transgressed twenty miles north over the flat, featureless prairie.

Bad as their situation was, she couldn't help thinking about the people trapped in Indianola. Debris – timber from buildings, some of it brightly decorated with wallpaper, pieces of furniture, dead livestock – drifted by with increasing frequency. The smell of death mingled with the salt air.

'How far do you think we've come?' she asked Ulysses as the hideous sky dimmed with the onset of evening.

AN INDECENT LADY 395

'No more than fifteen miles,' he replied.

'Are you sure we're going in the right direction?'

He managed a weak grin that didn't quite reach his eyes. 'I'm not sure. That's why I put Terrell in the lead.'

Fear clutched at Reina. She had a horrible vision of them struggling in endless circles. 'How does he know which direction to take?'

Alicia had been silent most of the afternoon, her gaze riveted on Terrell's back. 'He'll tell you it's pure skill. The truth is, he has a pocket compass.'

The night advanced with such cruel swiftness that Reina feared they would never find a haven from the deepening water. As the last menacing light dissolved into an even more menacing dark, Terrell pointed ahead.

'I can see trees on a small rise.' He altered his course, and the rest of them followed like magnets attracted by the polar star.

Other creatures had preceded them to the refuge, Reina discovered as she urged her weary horse onto dry land. A small deer herd clustered under a stand of scrub oaks. Armadillo, raccoon, rabbit and opossum peered out from the high prairie grass. A catamount lay on a log, heedless of the prey animals nearby as it tongued away a coat of mud.

'It's a Noah's ark,' Reina exclaimed, taking comfort in the small sign that life would go on.

'I just hope there's aren't any snakes,' Alicia remarked with considerably less enthusiasm.

Reina looked around, taking note of the tenuous nature of their refuge. The wind and rain had stopped, and an eerie stillness had fallen over the land. 'I think we should eat, rest the horses, and then go on,' she said. 'If the water continues to rise, we could drown in our sleep.'

'The water isn't going to rise,' Ulysses replied, dropping Brianna to the ground with an agonized groan that told her what an effort it had been to carry the dog. 'We're in the eye of the storm. When it passes, the tide will turn and all that water will go out into the bay a hell of a lot faster than it came in. If we're caught in it, we'll die for certain.'

Although she had never been in a hurricane before, instinct told her he was right. How could she have questioned his ability to handle trouble? He had been magnificent from the time he knocked on her hotel room door.

'In that case, we had better make camp. I'll look after the animals,' she volunteered.

'I'll see what I can do about supper,' Alicia chimed in.

The two men exchanged what could only be described as a meaningful look, then without a word, began setting up brush shelters at opposite ends of the island. Reina and Alicia exchanged a meaningful look of their own, then went about their business.

Rio had taught Reina that a good stockman looks to his animals' comfort before he looks to his own. There wasn't much she could do for the horses except hobbling them so they were free to graze. She tethered Nabob in the shelter of the trees, pulled bunches of grass and piled them within his reach. Brianna decided to use the grass as a bed and stretched out on it, leaving Nabob to munch wearily at the edges.

By the time Reina joined Ulysses he had finished their shelter. An oilskin tied to low hanging branches would keep out the worst of the weather.

A single pallet made from the extra blankets would serve as their bed. Ulysses sat on it, finishing a can of beans. He held another out to her as she sat down beside him.

'I'm too tired to eat.'

He put the can in her hand. 'You'll need your strength tomorrow. Eat up.'

She did as she was told, downing half the beans. Then she carried the remainder to Brianna.

When Reina rejoined Ulysses, he lay so still under the blanket that she thought he must be sleeping. She lifted the cover to join him and her hand touched bare skin.

A week ago, she would have jerked her hand away.

A week ago, she had been a blind fool.

Her eager hand traced the solid strength of his shoulders, then trailed down his spine.

'You had better get undressed, too,' he said in a languid voice. 'You'll be warmer without your wet clothes.'

'Where have I heard that before?' she teased, remembering the pond.

The nearness of death had been an aphrodisiac that day. It was now as well. She could hardly wait to lie in his arms and feel the full-length of his body against hers.

She stripped off her sopping shirt, Levi's and stephins, draping them across the nearest bush.

'Make love to me, Ulysses,' she murmured throatily as she lay down beside him.

A soft snore was his only answer.

Ulysses woke to the roar of the outgoing tide. A few days ago, he had been sure it would take an act of God to win Reina over. The hurricane had done the job, he thought, feeling her body spooned against his back. He was instantly and powerfully erect.

Her breasts pressed into his shoulder blades. Her arm draped around his waist. Her fingertips brushed his groin.

A gentleman would let her sleep.

He had never been a gentleman where she was concerned.

He rolled over.

She came into his waiting arms like a dream come true. He kissed her softly – then kissed her hard when she began to respond. Her lips parted to his questing tongue. She tasted of beans. Beans had never tasted so good.

She smelled of wind and wet – and Reina. He ran his hands through her hair, reveling at its damp silk, then caressed her bare back. He knew he should take his time – but he couldn't school his hands to patience.

They found her breasts and teased her nipples into hard buds. His mouth followed where they led. No man had ever feasted so well.

'I love you,' he murmured, 'God, how I love you.'

Reina had heard him say those words before. But she had been unwilling to believe them. Now, they seeped inside her very soul.

'I love you, too,' she replied, making it a promise, a vow, an eternal bond. It took no church, no man of God, to make a wedding. It took only two loving people. This was her wedding night.

Her need for Ulysses burned so bright that she thought he might see the glow. She had never made love before, but her hands and her body seemed to know what to do. Velvet had told her that making love to a man could be a sublime experience.

Velvet had been right.

Ulysses' touch flamed through Reina, chasing

away the damp and the cold. He suckled at her breasts again while his hands trailed down her stomach and parted her legs. His fingers found her center, and entered gently. Her insides melted. She wanted more than his mouth and his hands. She wanted all of him.

'Is this your first time?' he asked.

Would he stop making love to her if she confessed her virginity? She could hardly conceal the truth. 'Yes,' she whispered. 'I'm so glad you're my first.' He would be her one and only, she silently added.

He let go a throaty chuckle. 'I'm glad, too.'

His fingers continued moving inside her. The exploration made her moan with pleasure.

'I don't want to hurt you.'

'Waiting is hurting me. Make me a woman, Ulysses. Do it now.'

'Are you sure? I didn't save your life to ruin it.'

'I'm sure.'

He positioned himself over her, then rested on his elbows and looked deep into her eyes. 'I wanted you the day you were born. My parents brought me to see you, and I cried because your mother and father wouldn't let me take you home. It's taken me twenty-seven years to get my wish. Will you marry me, Reina DeVargas?'

Did he mean it – or had passion prompted the question? 'You don't need to say that. I know I'm not the sort of wife you need. I'm a rancher, not a lady.'

He silenced her with a kiss. 'You're all the woman I'll ever want. Just promise you'll take time out from ranching to have my children.'

She smiled into the darkness. 'Would you like to try and start a baby now?'

* * *

Three days after the hurricane swept over Indianola, word of the disaster reached the rest of Texas. Patrick learned about it from a cowboy who got the news from a cousin who worked at the telegraph office in Kerrville.

It's just gossip, Patrick told himself, one of those wild stories people dream up in the dog days of summer. Unwilling to alarm Charlotte unnecessarily, he sent word that he wouldn't be home for lunch, and rode into Kerrville. A visit to the newspaper office confirmed his worst fears.

A reporter told him that Captain Lewis, commander of one of the Morgan steamships, had sailed into Galveston late yesterday flying a distress signal. He brought a message from Indianola.

Reprinted on the front page, the message read, *We are destitute. The town is gone. One tenth of the population are gone. Dead bodies are strewn for twenty miles along the bay. Nine tenths of the houses are destroyed. Send us help, for God's sake.*

His eyes swimming, Patrick read on. The hurricane had hit three days before Ulysses' scheduled departure. The hotel he had been staying in had washed into the sea, along with the wharves, stores, restaurants, and even the courthouse. The railroad track and rolling stock between Indianola and Victoria were so severely damaged that they were useless to a relief party.

Patrick could read no more. The newspaper dropped from his hands. His legs gave way. The reporter caught him before he fell, and helped him to a chair.

'Did you have family in Indianola, Mr Pride?'

Unashamed of his tears, Patrick replied, 'My son was there on business.'

When he regained control of his emotions and his

AN INDECENT LADY

limbs, Patrick thanked the young man for his help, put the newspaper into a pocket, and headed for home. He told himself that Ulysses was a resourceful man who could handle any emergency. But he kept on picturing a frail boy who had been afraid of his own shadow.

If he didn't believe in Ulysses' courage and resourcefulness, how could he convince Charlotte that all would yet be well? Just yesterday, they had been planning their wedding – and wondering how to tell their children. Would any of them ever have reason to rejoice again?

Four hours later, Patrick, Charlotte and Velvet were on their knees in the parlor, praying for the safety of their children. Useful sat close by, his ears laid back as if he knew what had happened.

Velvet's joints ached. Her legs felt like stone. She wouldn't give up praying, though. God had to hear them.

She tried to concentrate, but her mind kept on wandering to happier times. She had shared so much with the Pride family. The echo of all those comings and goings reverberated in her ears. It seemed so real that she swore she could hear a buggy coming up the drive.

It wasn't her imagination, she realized, bolting to her feet. Useful reached the window first. He barked, then jumped over the sill to the porch.

Velvet looked out to see Reina, Ulysses, Alicia and Terrell getting out of a buggy. A huge bull was tied to the tailgate. A Wolfhound stood by the bull.

'God heard our prayers. They're back,' Velvet cried out, expecting to see Patrick and Charlotte where she had left them.

They were already running for the door. Forgetting all about her aches and pains, Velvet picked up her skirts and ran, too. Parents and children met in a melee of tears, kisses and hugs.

'I knew you'd make it,' Patrick said, pounding Ulysses on the back.

'This calls for champagne,' Charlotte declared.

'I could use a touch of brandy myself,' Velvet chimed in. She was the first to notice Terrell. 'What are you doing here, son?'

'It's a long story,' he said.

For the next hour, over champagne and brandy, Velvet, Patrick, and Charlotte listened while their offspring took turns telling that long story. *Dear Lord*, Velvet thought, when they were finally finished, the propinquity Charlotte had spoken of all those months ago had worked its magic. Only there were going to be three weddings — not one.

'Are you angry with me?' Alicia asked Charlotte.

'How could I be angry? I thought I'd lost you, darling,' Charlotte answered.

'Then you don't mind my marrying Terrell?'

'You're a grown woman, and from what you've told us, a very talented one. If Terrell makes you happy, I'm happy.'

Reina left Ulysses and came over to Velvet. 'How about you, Mom? Do you wish me well?'

Damn it, Velvet refused to cry. She wasn't one of those spineless females who bawled at every opportunity. 'I knew you were in love with Ulysses before you did, sugar. I'm so happy for the two of you — for all of you.'

Her damp gaze touched the six of them, one by one. They were the dearest people in the world — and the luckiest. 'Have you given any thought to a triple wedding?'

Just then, Useful marched into the parlor with Brianna by his side. It had obviously been a case of love at first sight.

'Make that a quadruple wedding,' Velvet said, laughing through her tears.

TO SPEAK OF TRIUMPH

ALEXANDRA THORNE

A scorching, poignant and unputdownable story of passion, ambition, betrayal and love.

Glory Girard has everything any girl could want – love, admiration and fabulous wealth.

But Glory's dream is to become an artist.
And she determines to pursue her deepest desires – whatever the cost . . .

As she journeys from San Francisco's glittering society to a seedy boarding house and on to the competitive world of New York's galleries, she is influenced by three powerful men:

Noble Girard, the millionaire father who plans to use Glory to polish his image

Dimitri Konstantine, the sensual Greek sculptor whose passion for Glory is only exceeded by jealousy of her talent

Lawrence Wyant, the genteel New York art dealer who sacrifices his love for Glory on the altar of loyalty to an invalid wife.

HODDER AND STOUGHTON PAPERBACKS

THE ULTIMATE SIN

ALEXANDRA THORNE

Young, vulnerable and unaware of her beauty, Elke has given her hand to the elderly man who rescued her from poverty, and offered her his heart as well as his home. It's a vow that determined Elke has promised to keep.

But when she meets her husband's best friend, Patrick Pride, Elke is horrified to find him so attractive. With each visit comes the pain and pleasure of feelings to which neither dare admit, bound as they are in their respect for the same man.

Then Patrick announces his engagement to a social belle and it seems that neither will be ever free to love . . .

The Ultimate Sin is a heart-melting love story from the author of *Sophisticated Savages*
('good, raunchy stuff' – Publishing News), *Past Forgetting, Creative Urges* and, most recently, *To Speak of Triumph*, all of which are available from Coronet.

HODDER AND STOUGHTON PAPERBACKS